the
rebel
king

the
rebel
king

GINA L.
NEW YORK TIMES BESTSELLING AUTHOR
MAXWELL

Entangled Publishing, LLC
644 Shrewsbury Commons Ave., STE 181
Shrewsbury, PA 17361
rights@entangledpublishing.com

Amara is an imprint of Entangled Publishing, LLC.

Visit our website at www.entangledpublishing.com.

Edited by Stacy Abrams
Cover design by Elizabeth Turner Stokes
Cover images by funnyangel/Shutterstock,
Paitoon Pornsuksomboon/Shutterstock
Interior design by Toni Kerr

ISBN 978-1-64937-348-9
Ebook ISBN 978-1-64937-349-6

Manufactured in the United States of America

First Edition July 2023

10 9 8 7 6 5 4 3 2 1

ALSO BY GINA L MAXWELL

THE DEVIANT KINGS

The Dark King
The Rebel King

FIGHTING FOR LOVE

Seducing Cinderella
Rules of Entanglement
Fighting for Irish
Sweet Victory

PLAYBOYS IN LOVE

Shameless
Ruthless
Merciless

STAND-ALONE ROMANCES

Hot For the Fireman

To Alyssa Rose.
My first child, my only daughter, and my very best friend.
Thank you for the most amazing mother-daughter
relationship I could've ever asked for. Not a day goes by
I don't thank the Universe and all the Stars
for you and your love.
"For as long as I'm living, my baby you'll be…"

At Entangled, we want our readers to be well-informed. If you would like to know if this book contains any elements that might be of concern for you, please check the back of the book for details.

CHAPTER ONE

TIERNAN

Power is as ruinous as it is advantageous.

To reap the rewards, you need to be willing to risk the dangers. And that's only one of the many reasons why I never desired to have more power than I was born with, not the least of which is the ancient adage made famous by Spider-Man's wise uncle. I'd like to pass on all that "great responsibility" shit, thank you very much.

And yet, barring a very unlikely miracle, I'm going to be the next ruler of the Dark Fae—the fucking Night Court *king*—whether I want it or not.

I was given six months before C-Day—what I've taken to calling my impending coronation—and already half of it is gone. Three months, that's all I have left. I've never been so acutely aware of time passing. It's like there's a clock in the back of my skull, ticking away the seconds, each one pushing me closer to the day I'll be thrust into a position I've never wanted and was never meant to have.

My brother Caiden was born to the role, quite literally as he's the eldest. But it was never merely a sense of duty for him. Caiden aspired to follow in our father's footsteps; he was often referred to as "the king's shadow," always taking his training seriously and learning everything he could on how to be a good ruler when it was his time.

When our father died, Caiden was only a hundred and fifty-two years old—the youngest to rule in the history of the fae by several centuries. But all that dedication and diligence paid off, because Caiden made a *great* king.

Finnian, my younger brother, would no doubt rise to the occasion, too, even though they'd never consider him viable at only a hundred and sixteen years old. But he's fiercely loyal and immeasurably brave. If he were needed to step up, he wouldn't hesitate. He'd rule with confidence, trusting in his deep-seated love for our people and the guidance of the crown's advisors, and he would succeed in that the same as he does with everything else.

But then there's me.

The one the people dubbed "the Rebel Prince" before I was two decades old. I'm cut from a different cloth entirely. No matter what you call it—an aversion to responsibility, middle child syndrome, a defiant nature, or a perpetual party boy nature—the fact remains that I'm the Verran brother *least* suited to wear the king's crown.

Figuratively speaking, of course. Literally speaking, I'd fucking smash that look, no question.

"Checkmate."

Yanked back from my distracted thoughts, I refocus on the blue and black checkered board sitting in the middle of the cherrywood dining table. Sure enough, my opponent's queen made of frosted glass is standing victoriously in the first row.

I glance up at the old man sitting across from me and give him a smile I hope isn't as half-assed as it feels. "Good game, my friend."

Robert scoffs, causing his silver beard to twitch where it rests on his chest. "That was a shit game and you know it. My great-granddaughter could've beaten you."

Since Robert brags about her only *every* time I visit, I know that nine-year-old Hailey is already a regional chess champion at her school. Grinning, I start to swap the pieces we'd collected during the game. "Not much of an insult, old timer. Hailey's a great player."

He leans in, arching a bushy gray brow. "I meant *Alexa*."

My grin dies. Alexa is only two years old and a bit of a terror from what I hear. If you handed her a chess piece, she'd probably giggle and chuck it at your head. I clutch at my chest dramatically. "Now that's just hurtful."

He grunts in response while scrutinizing me. You'd think he had laser vision for as hard as he's staring. But he's right—a novice could kick my ass today for as shitty as I'm playing. I haven't lost consecutively this many times since *my* novice days, when Robert started teaching me shortly after we met. It was frustrating as hell in the beginning—I'm a self-admitted sore loser, and he never went easy on me—but it wasn't long before I fell in love with the game.

I've never been known for the kind of precision focus my brothers have. It's a trait they've used to become grossly successful in business (Caiden) and a master of every fighting style known to man- *and* fae-kind (Finnian). I, on the other hand, find it hard to stay interested in any one thing for too long, my mind constantly bouncing among a dozen different thoughts at warp speed.

But this game has a way of shutting everything else out, allowing me to think clearly and concentrate on my strategies and the thousands of possible moves. Chess is only one of two things that quiet my mind. Since I can't indulge in the other thanks to our frustrating victims-of-circumstance situation, these weekly matches with my friend have been a welcome distraction.

Until recently, anyway. Once I passed the halfway mark

of my six-month reprieve, reality hauled off and bitch slapped me in the face, and I've thought of little else since.

I could have avoided Robert's shrewd scrutiny if I'd just canceled. But I've never missed a Sunday afternoon match in the fifty-six years we've been friends. Everything else in my life has been flipped on its head—I'll be damned if this simple pleasure gets taken away from me, too.

Robert reaches over to where a white teapot dotted with rooster heads (or *cock* heads, if you ask him, and if you do, he'll laugh at his own joke for a good five minutes) sits on an electric warmer. He pours himself another mug of the Longjing green tea I bring back for him whenever I take the company jet for a weekend of partying in Hong Kong. Then he switches out the teapot for the bottle of Devil's Keep whiskey I "borrowed" from Caiden, but brought for myself, thank you very much.

I arch an admonishing brow. "Didn't the doctor tell you to cut out alcohol?"

"Maybe," he says gruffly, adding a generous shot to his tea. "But my hearing isn't what it used to be. He could've said cut *down*, which I have, so zip it."

Lifting my own glass, I pin him with a dubious look over the rim as I take a drink. "Fine. But when you start putting shots of tea in your whiskey, I'm calling Wanda." His daughter lives on the East Coast, but she's a pro when it comes to nagging her father about his health.

"Instead of being a snitch, how about you tell me why you're playing like you don't know your queen from your bare ass?"

Rolling my eyes, I start to set up the next game. "I can't be exceptional at everything all the time, you know. What is it you're fond of saying? I'm only human."

Robert snorts. "I wish you were. Then I wouldn't be the only one of us wrinkly as a raisin."

I chuckle at that. He's always been sour about my eternal

youth. Using a glamour—a magical ability all fae have to disguise themselves—I make myself appear as an old man, with weathered skin and balding white hair. "That better?" I ask in my normal voice.

He draws back with a disgusted expression. "Christ, no, you look like shit. Now I feel bad that that's what *you* have to stare at every week."

Dropping the glamour, I huff out a laugh as I place the opaque pawns on each of the squares in his second row. "Don't pretend you don't still have game at eighty. How many girlfriends do you have at the senior center now?"

"Never mind how many," he says, pointing an arthritic finger at me. "And you know damn well I'm not eighty, so don't be a smart-ass."

Lining up the clear glass pawns on my own second row, I do a quick mental count of the weeks until Spring Equinox, which is also his birthday. "March twentieth is only ten weeks away. I'd say it's safe to round up."

"Ha! At my age, it wouldn't be safe to round up if it was only one week away."

My heart lurches in my chest. He meant it as a joke, but it's hard for me to find any amusement in it. Robert's the only human I've allowed myself to get close to for obvious reasons. They're breakable, prone to sickness or disease, and even if they live to be a hundred, their lifespans are a mere fraction of what ours are in this world.

For five years, I kept up the ruse with Robert that I was human. He became my closest friend during that time, which is why I made the decision to reveal who I really am. I didn't want to pretend with him anymore. Surprisingly, he was more excited and awed than anything else, but it didn't take long before things between us went back to normal.

Sometimes, in my more selfish moments, I wish I wouldn't have asked for those chess lessons all those years ago. You can't lose someone if you never had them to begin with. But I can't regret having Robert Blackburn as my friend, even knowing our time together will be short.

As is my habit, I stuff my emotions deep down where they belong and deflect with humor as I place the final pieces on the board. "You're too stubborn to kick the bucket. You're gonna live forever just to spite your doctors."

His brown eyes challenge me over the rim of his mug as he takes a sip of his doctored tea. "I *could* if you gave me the magical mushrooms." Since he knows I can't lie, he occasionally takes a wild guess at what the fae might have that could grant a human eternal life. And since I've neither confirmed nor denied that such a thing exists, he insists one does. For the record, there's no such thing, but it's fun to see what he'll come up with next.

I grin wide, flashing my fangs, and wink. "Nice try, old man. There are no magical, immortal-making mushrooms. Your move."

He opens with pawn E4, staking a claim on the center of the board. "Don't think I didn't notice you changing the subject earlier. I'm still waiting for you to tell me what's rattling around in that head of yours."

I counter with pawn C5, the Sicilian defense, and battle for the center on my terms. "Other than wiping the board with you this game? Nothing at all."

He responds by bringing his knight to F3, preparing to push the D pawn to D4 on his next move. Scoffing, he says, "I've known you half a century, Tiernan. Try again. Or should I be calling you *Your Majesty* now?"

Pausing, my eyes snap up to his and narrow. "No, *Bob*, you shouldn't," I say, retaliating with the nickname he hates. "Because I'm not the king." He raises an eyebrow at me. "Yet," I amend.

And thank the gods for that. I don't dare utter that part

out loud, though, because I'm never alone. Not anymore. I'm constantly shadowed by members of the Night Watch, the personal security to the royal crown.

Two are posted outside, and with our preternatural hearing, they could easily pick up our conversations in a quiet neighborhood like this one. And despite them being close friends, I can't risk them knowing my true feelings.

Rebel or not, I'm still a Verran, and I have a legacy to uphold. If it gets out that I don't want to be king or I give them any reason to find me incompetent, they'll say our royal line is no longer fit to rule, and steps can be taken to replace us. I can't let that happen. I *won't*. The only reason Caiden's abdication was supported by the people is because being king had become a life-threatening situation, for both him and his mate.

No, the only ones who know about my reservations are Seamus and my brothers, and that's how it needs to stay. Besides, I'm still secretly hoping for that miracle—the one that involves finding a way to break a centuries-old curse— that will allow Caiden to be back where he belongs and me squarely back at Party Central.

Stranger things have happened. Probably.

I lift my glass of Keep and toss it back in one go, enjoying the trail of smooth fire that snakes down my throat. Robert lifts the bottle and pours me another three fingers, his tone more sober than before. "Look, Tiernan, I get there's a lot you can't talk about. But you don't have to put on airs with me. I would never judge you, you know that. And if there's anywhere you can simply be yourself, it's here. That hasn't changed."

He's right. His is the only place I've ever been able to shed my royal persona and just be *me*. Offering him a wan smile, I say, "Everything changes eventually, old friend." I nod at the board. "It's your turn."

Stroking his beard in thought, he studies me and tries

to see several moves ahead. Not in the game, but in life. It's something I learned early on that he does, trying different conversations or actions in his head to see which might have the most favorable result. I wait him out patiently, as I always do, wondering what he'll decide.

After a bit, he sits back in his chair and waves a hand over the board. "I've had enough of beating you for one day. Any more losses and your enormous ego will be in danger of bruising."

Lighthearted humor. Gods bless him. I smile—a real one this time—and place a hand over my heart. "My enormous ego is grateful for your mercy."

Robert snorts a laugh and takes a drink of his tea. Lowering the mug, he frowns at the contents and reaches for more whiskey, but I'm faster. I grab the bottle and set it well out of his reach. He gives me his best grouch face but doesn't bother arguing. "If you're going to ruin my tea, the least you can do is let me live vicariously through your stories. Tell me about the wild nights you've had recently."

"Nothing to tell, I'm afraid. All work and no play makes Tiernan a very dull boy."

Robert sighs. "Guess I'll watch the news then. Maybe *they'll* have something interesting to say." He picks up the remote and aims it at the TV that's always on but muted during our games, then turns his attention to the local news.

What has my life come to when the news channel is more interesting than what I've been up to? I used to regale Robert every week with stories about wild parties I attended with A-list celebrities, or a new prank I pulled on one of my way-more-serious brothers.

But parties and pranks feel like they happened a lifetime ago.

As soon as the change in rule was announced, Seamus Woulfe, the senior advisor to the throne, told me I wouldn't be able to continue my *extensive extracurricular habits*. And yes, that's what he called them. But even with the power he temporarily holds as the king regent, he can't stop me from doing what I want.

However, he does hold a different kind of power over me: *guilt trips*. As my father's closest friend, Seamus is like an uncle to me and my brothers. His twin sons, Connor and Conall, are not only *our* closest friends of well over a century, but they're also co-leaders of the Night Watch. Seamus knows we'd rather chew glass than disappoint him, and he wields it well.

Using our familial bond to get me to rein in my "wild side" is his idea of playing fair. I say it's cruel and unusual punishment. Regardless, I tried hitting up the occasional party or club for a while, if only to prove a point to myself. But it's not nearly as fun when you have a conspicuous-as-hell security detail tagging along.

Then again, ever since this godsforsaken noose was looped around my neck three months ago, I haven't enjoyed much of anything. So there's that.

Part of me resents Caiden for abdicating and forcing this on me as the next in the Verran royal line. But most of me understands he had no choice.

Last year, my strait-laced older brother did the most impulsive, Vegas thing ever and woke up married to a human woman named Bryn. Neither of them had any memory of it happening. Under normal circumstances, it wouldn't be a big deal. A quickie annulment and it'd be over before it even began.

Except it turned out that Bryn isn't human; she's the only hybrid fae, or Darklight, in existence, and because the wedding was actually a fae marriage rite, they ended up bonded as true mates. A situation that could've meant certain death for Caiden due to the One True Queen's blood curse on the royal lines of both Celestial Courts of Faerie, the magical realm parallel to this one where all fae live.

At least it *was*. About four hundred-ish years ago, the Day and Night Court royals pissed the OTQ off bad enough that she exiled them and all the members of their courts to the human world. But Aine didn't stop there. Along with the perma-ban, she placed several curses on us, like stripping us of our wings and respective court-born powers.

But the *blood* curse was specific to only the royal bloodlines. Essentially how it works is that when a king is separated from his mate, the curse begins to ravage his body, slowly and painfully from the inside out, causing his imminent death. And since there's another curse that prevents either king from killing the other, whether "by their hand or their command," there's only one way to do it.

Kill the queen...kill the king. Checkmate.

But back to the exile. Adding insult to injury, Aine sent us through the veil into what's known today as Joshua Tree in the western part of the United States, where the harsh and barren desert is so unlike the lush beauty of our homeland. After playing the blame game and warring with each other for a hundred years or so, the Treaty of Two Courts was forged, and we agreed to go our separate ways.

Under my father's rule, the Dark Fae adapted and thrived, and eventually we built a new empire in the middle of the Mojave Desert we called Vegas: the city where deviance and nightlife reign supreme and half its residents are secretly magical beings.

The Light Fae established Phoenix. We win.

At any rate, since the treaty, we've lived in a tenuous peace. Both courts stuck to their own territory with Joshua Tree being neutral ground, and all was well.

Until the fucking Light Prince, Talek Edevane, ascended as their new king and decided he wanted to pursue expansion by way of hostile takeover. In order to usurp our throne, he devised a plan to assassinate Caiden by activating the blood curse.

For years, he made moves against Caiden in a game of real-life chess that my brother wasn't aware he was playing, using Bryn as the queen piece until he had everything lined up the way he wanted. It wasn't long after Caiden and Bryn said their drunken "I dos," bonding them as true mates, that several attempts were made on her life.

We tried taking Edevane down, but the slippery bastard managed to escape. With the threat still out there, abdicating was the only way Caiden could keep his mate safe and protect our people from the devastation of losing their king and the power vacuum that would make them vulnerable. Since Caiden is no longer king, Edevane has no reason to go after him through Bryn. A fact I'm glad of because I wholly adore Brynnie-Bear.

However, putting *me* on the throne has its own problems. For starters, I have no idea how to rule. I never had to learn all the diplomatic shit Caiden did while our father was still alive. In our world it's unheard of for anyone other than the firstborn to be crowned.

Which is why no one saw it coming when Caiden announced that he was stepping down at the Ivy Moon Celebration last October. Not even me, since I'd skipped the meeting about it earlier that day to play chess with Robert. Hell, I almost missed the *actual* announcement, since I'd found something better to do. Or more specifically, some*one*. Just before, I'd been nine inches deep inside my favorite smart-mouthed redhead in a janitorial closet down the hall.

My stolen minutes with Fiona Jewel—my SWB, or subject-with-benefits—are the only carefree times I've had since that fateful night. But it wasn't long before they were impossible to come by, and that sure as fuck hasn't helped my mood any.

"Tiernan…look."

Robert's earnest tone makes the tips of my ears tingle. I turn to face the TV and see a professional headshot in the corner of the screen of an attractive male. A male I recognize as one of our employees and a Dark Fae, despite his human appearance in the photo.

I motion to the remote in his hand. "Turn it up."

He raises the volume until the female news anchor's voice fills the living room. "…police say Myrddin Kelly was badly beaten, however, the cause of death appears to be a fatal stab wound to the chest. The victim's body was found early this morning in the alley behind the upscale gentlemen's club he managed, Deviant Desires, which is owned by Onyx Inc, a Fortune 500 company comprised of the real estate magnates and brothers commonly referred to as the Verran Kings of Vegas. CEO Caiden Verran could not be reached for comment at this time. If you have any information concerning this crime, please call…"

Robert lowers the volume again, his somber gaze meeting mine. Like everywhere else, there are plenty of murders that happen in Vegas every year. But none of the victims have ever been fae. We're not that easy to kill.

Back in Faerie, our people are practically immortal, living for thousands of years before moving on to the Otherworld known as Mag Mell. But here in the human realm, our lifespans are severely shortened to an approximate five hundred years, give or take, courtesy of Aine.

It's the reason my father died when we were so young. He'd already been six hundred when our courts were exiled. He lived another three centuries before his body could no longer sustain its Faerie magic, and he passed on peacefully with his sons at his side. That's the *natural* way we die in this world.

The only way to kill us before that is to use a weapon made from the one element we're severely allergic to, something you won't find in your average human arsenal.

"Jesus, Mary, and Joseph," Robert mutters as he makes a hasty sign of the cross.

My cell vibrates in my pocket just as Connor enters the house, leveling me with a look that tells me it's time to go before he retreats outside to wait with his brother. Doing my best to ignore the sick feeling in the pit of my stomach, I push to my feet and check my phone, hoping for more information. But it's only a link for the newscast I just watched, and the accompanying text from Seamus is brief.

Emergency mtg @ manor in 30. Return ASAP.

I apologize to Robert for the short visit as we say a quick goodbye. Like always, he walks me to the door. Before I can leave, he stops me, concern swimming in his kind eyes. "What do you suppose the odds are that the knife just happened to be made of pure iron?"

I wish I had the ability to lie, even to myself. But I'm fae, so I have no choice but to tell him the truth. "Slim to fucking none."

CHAPTER TWO

TIERNAN

The drive from Robert's home to Midnight Manor—the residence of the Night Court king—usually takes twenty minutes. With Conall behind the wheel of the Range Rover, we pull onto our street in less than ten.

"Great, now I need a shower before the meeting," I say from the back. "I've sweat through my shirt thanks to your obnoxious driving."

Conall snorts. "This coming from the guy with a decal that says 'I drive like a Cullen' on his 8-series Beamer."

"But I—much like the Cullens—am a fast *and* excellent driver. You, my friend, are shit at it."

"He's got you there, bro," Connor says with a chuckle. Conall answers with a middle finger as we turn into the gated drive that automatically opens for us from a sensor.

As soon as we're parked safely on the far side of the ten-car garage, I watch the Woulfe brothers exit the vehicle and wait impatiently for them to let me out. Ever since I bailed out of the car at a red light to try and shake them for fun, the assholes engaged the child lock system on all the security vehicles.

If I'd known they were gonna get so butt-hurt over it, I

wouldn't have bothered. Maybe. It's not like I thought it would work. The twins come from a long line of fae wolf shifters. They could track a house fly across the entire state of Nevada to the scene of its demise on the front grill of a semi if they needed to. There was zero chance of me losing them. But it was worth it to see the looks of aggravation on their faces when they finally caught up to me.

Usually, Connor takes his sweet time in opening my door, waiting until I start making ungentlemanly threats to his manhood. But today he lets me out right away, underscoring the urgency of the situation despite our attempts at keeping things light. If there's one thing I can depend on the twins for, it's cracking jokes with me at inappropriate times. Immature coping mechanisms? Check.

"Thanks, Jeeves One and Jeeves Two," I say to my friends as I walk away. "See that you give her a thorough detailing before our next outing, will you?"

The guys fall into step with me as we cross the large expanse of the garage. Connor flashes his fangs at me. "How 'bout my fist details your face, smart-ass?"

"Nice of you to offer, but the only one I trust to detail this perfection is my aesthetician, Dante."

Conall snaps a hair tie off his wrist and pulls his shoulder length reddish-brown hair into a man-bun as we near the door that leads into the manor. "My favorite thing about you, T, is how down to earth you are."

"I totally get that," I say, feigning all seriousness. "*My* favorite thing about me is my enormous di—"

The door whips open, cutting off my snarky—and mostly honest—retort. Seamus stands in the doorway, greeting us with a sober expression that effectively reminds us of why we raced back to the manor in the first place.

At four hundred and fifty years old, Seamus looks as young as an attractive human male in his fifties. His hair and beard are silver, and his amber-colored eyes—the color all Dark Fae possess—are framed by distinguished lines. But his six-foot frame is still strong and agile, even though Finnian and I enjoy ribbing him about being slow and ancient.

Braden Verran was a good king, but he was only ever a good father to Caiden, his heir. It was his best friend and advisor who gave me and Finn the attention and guidance we craved when we were young. For as shallow as I pretend to be, I don't place much value on material things or attach feelings to them, and that includes the handful of places I've lived in my hundred and sixty-four years. So, aside from when I'm with my mother, the only time I feel I'm truly *home* is when I see Seamus Woulfe.

"Boys," he says with a solemn nod, then leads us down the long hall, past the theater room, to the main living space.

The entire back wall of the house is made up of floor-to-ceiling glass panels that slide open with the push of a button in each room, creating a fluid transition to the multiple outdoor areas and pool. As it's the beginning of January, we're not in danger of melting, so we often leave them open during the day, giving us a multimillion-dollar view of the distant skyline of The Strip.

Stopping near the huge sectional couch, Seamus addresses his sons. "Do a perimeter run and then call a meeting for the Night Watch. I want security on level orange. Make sure everyone understands the new protocols."

Both men nod, then stride past their father. Once they cross the threshold, they break into a run across the expansive veranda. Just as they reach the end, they leap off the edge and magically shift into their wolf forms the size of small horses with rust-red fur. As soon as their paws touch the ground, they take off in different directions, their giant strides and inhuman speed eating up the distance so fast, they're almost a blur. Gotta hand it to 'em—it's fucking cool.

I used to be jealous of their ability. The Verrans may be royals, but our only special power was the one unique to the Night Court—stripping away a person's inhibitions and sense of morality until they're consumed by their darkest desires— which we were divested of at the time of our exile, centuries before I was even born. When I was young, it hardly seemed fair. Now I'm content just glamouring my appearance to blend in with the humans I enjoy being around.

Seamus checks his watch. "Finnian is already in the study, and Caiden and Bryn will arrive shortly."

"I'm grabbing a quick shower. I'll meet you there in ten."

Not wasting any more time, I take the stairs to the second level and shed my clothes as soon as I enter the main suite. This massive room used to be Caiden's. Sometimes it still feels strange to be in it, but the posh digs are the only upside of this whole situation.

When the Dark Council—a group of geriatric males who make decisions on behalf of our people in the rare absence of an official ruler—allotted me the six months to learn everything I'll need to know about being king, Seamus suggested I move into the manor right away to begin the transition and make it more convenient for him to teach me.

I agreed because the twelve-thousand-square-foot mansion with its resort-style amenities is a lot nicer than my penthouse apartment. An apartment I still own in case the gods feel like blessing me with that miracle I'm holding out for. *Mental note: start making regular trips to the temple and get right with Rhiannon.*

As I step into the massive shower with more than fifty shower heads spraying me from every angle, my starving libido reminds me that luxuries like this aren't the *only* reason I wanted to exchange my exciting city life for a quiet one in the 'burbs. Another benefit is the daily interactions with a certain fiery redhead who happens to be Midnight Manor's housekeeper. But how I imagined things would be between us in a convenient cohabitating situation is far from reality.

Fiona and I were sneaking around together for several months leading up to the Ivy Moon Celebration Ball. Not because we had to but because it was fun. And honestly, I wasn't interested in anyone else's commentary about it. My brothers' or the press that hounds the Verran family like we're the embodiment of the second coming of their Christ.

But once I was announced as the future king, keeping it a secret became necessary. While the king is expected to be a lot more sinner than saint when it comes to his carnal appetites, there's also an expectation that he only be associated with highborn members of the court.

It's complete classist bullshit, but bucking thousands of years of monarchal tradition is easier said than done. All it takes is a single staff member telling their friend that "the future king is fucking the maid" and we'd be the topic of conversation at every breakfast table in the court.

Fiona would be cast as a social-climbing opportunist, and I'd be giving the Council grounds to doubt my competence and commitment to the Crown, and, by extension, the entire Verran line.

Now when we run into each other, we're hyperaware of getting caught acting as anything other than a royal and royal employee. Since living here, I've seen how much pride she takes in her job, but I don't care how well she makes my bed every morning. I'd rather have her messing it up with me, my body pressing hers into the mattress as I fuck her into oblivion, infusing my sheets with her intoxicating scent every night.

I groan and make quick work of soaping up my body to avoid an erection I don't have time for. I've worked out my frustrations so many times in this shower, my dick is going to start reacting the second I step inside if I don't get it some real action soon.

The problem is there's only one female I want, and it's proving impossible to have her even though we live under the same damn roof. But we can't risk anyone seeing us sneaking in and out of each other's bedrooms, either.

Needless to say, the past three months have been an exercise in near-constant sexual frustration for us both. There's only one area in the manor not monitored by security cameras. One room that's tucked far enough away from the main part of the house that the likelihood of being noticed is close to zilch, and it's completely soundproof.

The dungeon. The kind with a "red door." You get what I'm saying.

Fiona suggested it once early on, but I told her it was off-limits. More of a "fae truth" since it's only off-limits because I want it to be. I can't take her in there. I know enough about what she's into to know that she'd want certain things from me in that room that I can't give her. Things I haven't allowed myself to indulge in for more than a decade.

But that doesn't mean I haven't fantasized about marking her flawless skin with licks from my single-tail, whipping her into a euphoric state until I can see her juices dripping down her inner thighs…

Fuck. So much for avoiding an erection I don't have time to deal with. Bracing a hand on the stone wall, I change the water to the coldest setting and force myself to endure the frigid blast for a full minute before turning it off. I run the towel over my body in hurried strokes, then wrap it around my waist and head for the bedroom.

As I turn the corner, I run smack into a small female, then catch her on the rebound before she lands on her ass. The curtains aren't drawn on the wall of glass facing the rear of the property, so we're in full view of anyone who might be out there. I should release her, but I don't. Because every cell in my body is lighting up from the feel of her in my arms again.

"Fi." That one syllable sounds like I dragged it over hot coals in order to free it from my chest. The place where her warm hands are still pressed between us.

My eyes drink her in, cataloguing every detail to refresh the faded ones in my memory. Her long hair color is a brilliant copper that reminds me of the sky just as the desert sun begins to slip behind the horizon. She has it twisted into two loose braids that cover her ears and fall in front of her shoulders.

I want to undo them and thrust my fingers into the silky mass so I can trace the shell of her cute-as-fuck ears with my tongue.

I want to map out the dozens of pale freckles that dot her cheeks and trail over the bridge of her nose, to watch the pupils eclipse the amber of her eyes and crush her lips with mine.

Fiona finally has enough sense for the both of us and steps out of my hold, but she softens the tragedy with a saucy grin. "Apologies for my clumsiness, Your Majesty. I didn't see you there."

Your Majesty. She started using the new title right after Caiden announced me as the future king. And she's the only one I haven't corrected. Something about the way she says it fucking turns me on. The amount of times I've imagined her saying it on her knees in front of me is too high to count, and thinking of it now is making my mouth dry up.

Out of self-preservation, I smirk and give her a wink. "If you want to get handsy with my muscles, Fi, all you have to do is ask."

"Thanks for the tip, your royal arrogance, but I'm here to grab your dirty laundry, not your pecs."

"How about my—"

"Not your cock, either," she tacks on with an arch of a brow.

I open my mouth in mock offense, as though she didn't just read my mind. "I was going to say *dry cleaning*, you naughty girl."

"Naughty enough that I deserve a proper punishment in the dungeon?" Her eyes rake lasciviously down my bare chest and abs to where my towel is tucked low on my waist, then settle on the bulge already at half-mast and quickly growing.

"Fi…" I take a step closer, ready to devour her and fuck the consequences when three sharp raps pierce through the fog of lust clouding my better judgment. Cursing, I shove a frustrated hand through my wet hair, then point at her. "Don't move."

I cross the room and yank open the door, making sure to hide most of my lower half. Rian briefly bows his head. "Your Highness. Everyone's arrived and waiting for you in the study."

"Great. Tell Seamus I'll be down in—"

Fiona brushes past me carrying a basket of my dirty clothes. If Rian has any thoughts about the housekeeper being in my bedroom while I'm practically naked, he doesn't show it. Nor would any employee of the Crown, not in front of me. It's whether they voice those thoughts later that we have to worry about.

Pausing, Fiona is all business when she addresses me. "Thanks for letting me grab these, Prince Tiernan. I apologize if I held you up."

"Not at all, Miss Jewel. Next time, I'll have you grab my dry cleaning. It's been too long since I last gave it to you." I never thought I'd be using "dry cleaning" as a euphemism for my cock, but here we are.

She shoots me a death glare from behind Rian until he turns and grins at her. Smiling innocently, she gets her revenge in with a little word play of her own. "It would be my pleasure."

I barely stop the growl that wants out of my chest at the thought of her writhing beneath me. Instead, I return her smile and nod to dismiss her. A moment later, she disappears around the corner with my basket of laundry and the lust cloud she sucks me into every time she's near.

Able to think clearly again, I send Rian with the message

that I'll be there in five minutes and head to the large walk-in closet to quickly throw some clothes on. I need to get to that meeting. I might have a tendency to blow off Seamus's lessons on occasion—okay, semi-regularly—but even I understand the importance of needing to figure out what happened to Myrddin Kelly.

Dressed in a pair of dark jeans and an olive-green Henley, I make my way through the house to the study for the meeting about Myrddin's murder. Seamus is sitting behind the large desk that used to be Caiden's and will soon be mine, all of which seems unnatural. Caiden and Bryn are seated in the guest chairs and Finnian is leaning against one of the bookshelves.

There's an air of unease in the room. My brothers and Seamus are rigid with tension, while Bryn calmly holds her mate's hand. She's only been in our world a handful of months and probably doesn't fully grasp the severity of what's happened. Then again, as true mates, Caiden and Bryn can feel each other's energy and emotions. By staying chill, she's helping to quiet her husband's apprehension—or at least not make it any worse.

Seeing them together tends to take the edge off my resentment over my situation. Caiden's always been a closet romantic. He wanted the kind of meaningful fae bond with a mate that Celestial Court monarchs aren't allowed to have without the danger of possible imminent death. As long as he isn't king, they're free to live their lives without the threat of the blood curse hanging over them.

Finni's young yet and nails anything that moves, but I think he'll eventually want a mate, too. Me, on the other hand, I've always been quite content with the bachelor life and never understood why Caiden was so averse to the idea of a consort. I used to tell him if I was ever required to enter into a friends-with-benefits situation for the good of my people, "I'd happily do my duty and do it often."

But that was *before* a red-haired sex nymph started to consume every spare thought in my head. As of now, I have no desire to be with any female other than Fiona. But she won't be an eligible choice for a consort—she's not from a highborn family—and a king can only put off his duty for so long. Eventually the Council will start leaning on me to produce heirs, whether I'm ready to or not.

Caiden stands and meets me halfway to greet me with a brotherly embrace and a strong thump on the back.

We break apart, and my mood immediately lifts to see Bryn waiting her turn. Her blond ponytail shows off her newly acquired pointed ears, and her wide smile reveals the adorable gap in her front teeth along with her fangs, which are another recent addition to her features after she tapped into her full fae powers last year.

It's the extraordinary color of her eyes, though, that are unique to her alone. As the only fae born of both courts, her irises are a stunning mix of the Light and Dark signature colors. They appear as a bright hazel normally, but when she uses her powers, the individual colors separate and glow with green in the center surrounded by gold. I've never seen anything like it. None of us have.

She's an anomaly in our world, and yet even with her new fae appearance, she's still the kind, wholesome Wisconsinite we kinda-sorta kidnapped once—or twice—upon a time. No worries, though. She ended up staying of her own free will. Promise.

"Brynnie-Bear, get your cute ass over here and give your favorite brother-in-law a proper hug."

Bryn laughs and steps into my waiting arms as Finn snorts. "You *wish* you were her favorite."

Caiden chimes in. "Talk about my wife's ass again and see

if I don't kick yours."

Bryn steps back and rolls her eyes. "Will you guys ever *not* bicker like children?"

We answer in stereo. "No."

Like he's been doing for well over a century, Seamus refocuses us with a purposeful clearing of his throat. "Everyone settle in, let's get started."

I walk over to where Finn is posted up, wearing his usual athletic wear—dude is constantly working out or training with the Night Watch guys—that barely contains his frame. Our baby brother is almost fifty years younger than me, yet he's the largest of us by far. Standing at six foot seven with more muscles than Neit, the god of war, he's a fucking beast.

But for as big as Finnian is, his heart is bigger. Bryn calls him a giant teddy bear, much to his dismay and my delight.

He holds his fist out and I bump it with mine before lowering into the dark gray armchair next to him and addressing my family. "I assume we all saw the same news report." At the nods and mumbles of affirmation, I add, "Then I think I speak for everyone here when I say 'what the actual fuck?'"

Used to being in charge, Caiden speaks first. "That's the problem; we have no idea. Nothing like this has ever happened before that I'm aware of. Seamus?"

Our pseudo uncle shakes his head. "Not since our war in the mortal realm ended and the Treaty of Two Courts was signed."

Finn cracks his knuckles. "Yeah, well, that all went to shit when Edevane—"

"Also known as Talek the Twat," I interject helpfully.

"—tried to kill Caiden and Bryn last year. That makes him the number one suspect in my book."

Caiden rubs his chin with two fingers. "I don't disagree with you, brother. As our only known enemy, it makes sense that it would be him. Except..."

Seamus leans forward, clasping his hands and placing his forearms on the desk. "Except what would be the point of killing a single fae?"

"Maybe it was a message," Bryn suggests. "Myrddin managed one of our businesses. Maybe Edevane wants us to know he can get to us."

I frown. "Hold on. How *did* he get to us? No one from his court should've been able to enter the city, much less get all the way to Deviant Desires, without alerting the Night Watch."

After Edevane escaped, we had Erin Jewel—Fiona's mother, Bryn's aunt, and an incredibly powerful conjuring fae—cast a spell that acts like a security system around the entire perimeter of Vegas. If any member of the Day Court crosses it, the alarm is tripped and they're tagged with a locator spell that acts like a magical GPS, allowing us to track them down and investigate.

Or interrogate. Caiden, who earned himself the moniker of the Dark King for multiple reasons, is usually a fan of the latter, using tactics befitting his nickname.

"Correct, and the spell was never triggered," Seamus says. "Which means no Light Fae entered our territory."

"But if Myrddin wasn't killed by any of the Light," Finn says, "that means it was either a Dark, which has never fucking happened—"

"Or a familiar," I say, apprehension suddenly weighing me down.

Familiars are the small number of humans we trust enough to let into our inner circle. They don't know *all* our secrets, but they know enough to be dangerous, which is why we're extremely selective of who we bring in. Some are friends, like Robert. But most are people in advantageous positions who can help us remain a myth instead of a reality.

Our judgement has never been proven wrong before, and the thought that someone we trust could've outright murdered one of us burns like acid in my veins. Of everyone in this room—aside from Bryn, who up until several months ago thought she *was* human—I spend the most time with our mortal realm companions.

Humans are fascinating and complex in ways that fae aren't, even with our magic and preternatural abilities. I love how they take risks and act so precariously while knowing there are a thousand ways they can die on any given day. They're fun—especially in Vegas—and I genuinely like them.

"I don't know which is worse," Finn says, crossing his thick arms over his chest. "What do we do now?"

Seamus pins each of us with a serious look. "For now, we keep any and all information between the people in this room and Connor and Conall. Until we know more, we can't afford to trust anyone. I'll contact McCarthy to set up a meeting as soon as possible. He'll be able to give us the full scope of what the VPD knows and what they aren't sharing with the media."

Aleck McCarthy is the police chief of the Vegas Police Department. He's also fae. In addition to him, we have several officers and a couple detectives. Just because we've never had a fae murder doesn't mean we aren't sometimes involved in situations that garner police attention. Having people on the inside ensures we aren't outed as being *other.*

"Call me when you have the meeting set up and I'll clear my calendar for the day," Caiden says.

Seamus levels my older brother with a somber look. "I'm sorry, Caiden, but that's no longer your place. As the heir apparent and king regent, Tiernan and I will meet with McCarthy and fill you in after."

The only sign of Caiden's displeasure is the tensing of his jaw before he nods in acknowledgement. "Of course," he says, offering a tight smile. "I apologize. Old habits die hard."

Seamus holds a hand up. "No apologies necessary. We're all in a transitional period that takes some getting used to, but it will get easier with time. The sole focus must always be what is best for the realm. And that's something we all agree on, no matter our titles."

A pang of guilt hits my chest. Obviously I want what's best for our people. I just don't think that *I'm* it, and I don't know that I'll ever get used to being king, no matter how much time passes.

"Agreed, old friend," Caiden says. Bryn gives him a reassuring squeeze of her hand and a look that conveys a message only her husband can hear. His shoulders relax and the tension lines bracketing his eyes disappear as he places a kiss on her palm.

"I'll keep you all apprised if we learn anything new. Until then, get some sleep."

The others nod, but I mentally scoff at the directive, as I haven't seen a decent night's sleep since moving into Midnight Manor. Because being in close proximity to Fiona might be the best part about living here…but it's also the hardest.

CHAPTER THREE

FIONA

Leaning over a bowl of red grapes on the kitchen counter, I mindlessly pop the fruit into my mouth as I send my best friend a string of funny cat videos that have me quietly laughing in the dark.

Texting Bryn the highlights of my doomscrolling at three a.m. wasn't the plan when I went to bed five hours ago, but I couldn't sleep. Not even practicing my favorite deep meditation helped. It's certainly not the first time this has happened. If I were human, I'd be diagnosed with insomnia with the lack of sleep I've had the past few months.

Night after night, I dream of being taken by a certain rough and powerful male, my hands fisted in his chestnut-colored hair as he devours my neck and teases me with nicks from his fangs.

And night after night, I jolt awake just before we cross the big finish line, my body covered in a sheen of sweat and chest heaving like it was real and not a dream. The kicker? It *had* been real not that long ago. Because these sex dreams aren't fantasies, they're memories. Ones I block out during the day only to have them taunt me the moment I shut my eyes.

But if my subconscious insists on torturing me, the least it could do is *let me finish*. Don't get me wrong, I enjoy a good sadistic orgasm denial. Just not when it comes from myself. Now Tiernan, on the other hand, I'd love the chance to play masochist to his sadist someday. Unfortunately, every time I mention us getting kinky together, he shoots the idea down for one reason or another. But he always made me forget my disappointment by fucking me so good I also forgot my own name.

Gods, I miss fucking him.

Running into him yesterday, quite literally, has done one hell of a number on me. I can't even get to the dream stage thanks to the rampant thoughts plaguing me. My mind keeps replaying every detail of our close encounter on a constant loop. His golden eyes piercing mine, the muscles of his hard chest flexing beneath my palms, my spine tingling from the feel of his unrelenting grip.

If we hadn't been interrupted by Rian, there's a damn good chance I would've lost my good sense and caved. Gods know I've never been good at denying my natural instincts when it comes to him.

The first time he visited his brother at Midnight Manor after I was hired as the new housekeeper, I forgot all about the coffee table I was dusting and simply stared. He caught me, of course, and nailed me with his panty-melting half grin, then asked me if I wanted to polish *his* wood when I was done.

His snarky arrogance is what broke the spell, and I replied before thinking better of it. "Sure," I said, tipping my lips into a devious smirk. "Let me just go and grab the disinfectant spray first."

I immediately regretted my words, expecting him to demand my termination for daring to insult him, even in jest. Instead, he surprised me by laughing. That's when I knew he wasn't your typical royal. He was nothing like his older brother, that was for sure. Tier was *fun*.

He began showing up at the manor more often, and after weeks of flirtatious banter, Tiernan surprised me again when he grabbed my hand and pulled me into the pantry. We attacked each other without a second thought.

And then *holy shit*. Being a few years away from three-decades-old, I'm practically a baby among our people, but that doesn't mean I'm innocent like one. I'm still Dark Fae; deviance is in our very nature. Over the years, I've enjoyed sex with a lot of eager tourists—of a multitude of genders—but I'd never experienced anything like sex with Tier.

Calling it sex doesn't even begin to cover it. Filthy, carnal fucking, that's what it was. Each time was more wild and explosive than the last, like we were in competition with ourselves to up our game with every closeted encounter. Keeping them quick, dirty, and secret wasn't necessary, but it added an addictive adrenaline burst at the thought of getting caught.

And yet, for me, underneath it all, there was something about it that made it feel...*more*. That tiny, inconvenient kernel of truth is the proverbial pea under my stack of mattresses interrupting my sleep every night.

I scroll to the next video and absently reach into the bowl for another grape but hit bottom. Frowning, I look down to find it empty. "Oops."

Expelling a heavy sigh, I wince as I straighten, my body not happy from being hunched over in the same position for the last hour, then take the bowl over to the sink to wash it out. I'm so tired, my eyes are burning. Or maybe it's from staring at my phone too long. Fuck, I can't keep doing this.

I should probably ask my mom for help. As a powerful conjuring fae, she can cast a sleep spell or mix a potion that would put melatonin to shame. But I'm not ready for the inevitable lecture that comes along with admitting I was secretly banging the Rebel Prince and still would be if things hadn't gone from fun-secretive to *necessary*-secretive.

Going from spare heir to *the* heir made everything so much more complicated. I always assumed our closet dalliances would end eventually. I just thought it would be from a mutual decision, not one influenced by our stations.

Because a prince can fool around with whomever he wants. The *king* can't.

Either way, there's no point in continuing to poke at the scab. It is what it is. Wishing things were different won't do me any damn good.

Bryn's the only one who knew about Tier and me. She caught us coming out of the theater room in a disheveled mess the night of the Early Equinox Ball last September. At the time, she was Team Tierona all the way, but now she hates seeing me hang on to something that doesn't—or *shouldn't*— exist. She wants me to move on and find someone I can be stupid-in-love with like her and Caiden. Why do newlyweds always want to vomit their happiness onto everyone else? There should be a law against that.

Ooh, I should tell Tiernan about that. New kings get to make new rules and void old contracts and laws they don't like. Hell, while he's at it, he can just make it against the law for anyone to be happy, and then my misery will have company.

Sighing, I place the bowl carefully in the cabinet with the others. My mind might not be ready to move on, but my body is screaming for satiation. Even now, I can feel the ache building inside me again just thinking about it. "Gods, I need to get laid."

"Is that so?"

My heart practically leaps out of my chest, and it's a damn good thing I wasn't still holding the ceramic dish because it'd be shattered on the tile floor by now. His familiar, deep voice causes the adrenaline of shock to melt into a pool of heat between my thighs. An inconvenient reaction, since I can't hide it from his heightened sense of smell.

I never hear him move, but suddenly the heat from his body is radiating through the thin cotton of my sleep tank and boy shorts. We're too close and in a common area of the house. Instinctively, I take a step out to put distance between us, but he holds my shoulders to keep me in place. His soft breaths stir the baby hairs at my temple, and it's everything I have not to turn my face so his lips are pressed there as well.

"I can help you with that little problem, you know." Strong hands land on my hips and squeeze lightly, just enough to remind me of the way his possessive touch made me burn.

"No, you can't. The security camera—"

"I took care of it. When I saw you in here, I turned it enough that we're in a blind spot, but just barely, so don't make any big movements. Now, about that problem you mentioned."

I can't believe he moved a camera, and at the same time I don't know how much it matters. Blind spot or not, this is still risky business. We're not the only people in the manor. I should put a stop to this and go to bed. I will. Any second now...

"You *are* the problem, Tier," I say quietly as my hips push back until I feel his stiff cock brush my ass through our respective clothing.

His head drops, and he muffles his groan against my neck. "Fuck, I miss hearing you say my name, Fi," he rasps. "I miss lots of things about you. Want to hear them?"

"Yes." *Rhiannon help me.* My body's needs are overriding my common sense, but I don't have the strength to care. "Tell me."

"I miss seeing the scratches on my skin from your nails and fangs for days after we fuck. I miss seeing the desire flash in your eyes from across the room when my gaze maps out the marks I left on your body that no one else knows are there."

Pressing his front to my back, he obliterates what was left of the space between us. My breath catches, then escapes on a shudder as I melt into him, my eyes drifting shut with my head resting below his left shoulder. His hands skirt around to my front, and his fingers curl, digging into the softness of my belly, like a claiming.

Before I can stop it, a whimper slips through the tightness in my throat.

Tiernan's answering growl rumbles through me. "That sound. Gods, that sound drives me wild, you know that?"

My ability to form coherent thoughts abandons me the moment he slips a hand into the band of my shorts and slides his middle finger through the slickness between my lips. I chase his touch as he teases my entrance, then gasp when he pushes two digits deep inside.

"So fucking wet for me." He continues to thrust into my pussy, pulling more arousal from me with every withdrawal. "I was thirsty, so I came to the kitchen for some water. But what you have to offer is so much better. Bend over the counter, and don't make a sound."

He presses my upper body down until it meets the cool marble, then he drops to his knees behind me and drags my shorts to pool around my ankles. Apparently done teasing, he spreads my cheeks and dives in. His tongue laps at my arousal, delving between the folds, dipping into my entrance, flicking over my swollen clit, making my toes curl and stomach clench with the tension of my building orgasm.

I bite down on the heel of my hand to keep my screams at bay. Tiernan is relentless. He doesn't let up for even a second, devouring me like it's the last time he'll ever taste me, and it might very well be.

I'm so close I can scarcely breathe, his fingers flexing into the meat of my ass, and he presses his face in more to spear his tongue inside me, fucking me as I rock my hips back onto him to match his thrusts. He removes one of his hands to rub my clit with his knuckle. I lose myself to the pleasure enough that I *almost* cry out, and a teensy part of me is just reckless enough to get excited at the prospect of getting caught if I lose all control. But I won't.

Then he *growls* into my pussy, the vibrations rippling over my flesh, and I have to cover my mouth to make sure I don't as my orgasm detonates deep in the pit of my belly. The force of the explosion tears through me, lighting up every cell in my body and making my legs shake. He doesn't move until he's drank every last drop I have to give him and I'm completely wrung out. Then he stands to his full height and pulls me back against him again.

"That was refreshing," he says, his voice barely above a whisper. "Unfortunately, that only whetted my appetite for you, Little Red."

A smile curls my lips. The second time Tiernan and I met, he called me Little Red, claiming it was easier than trying to remember my name. I responded by noting his poor memory and horrible nicknaming skills, then said, "My condolences for Your Highness's small brain. At least you're pretty." He never stopped using it, and I never stopped pretending I hate it.

"That name is still stupid," I say lazily.

He chuckles. "See? I even miss the way you insult my intelligence." He nuzzles my cheek to guide my head to the side, giving him access to what he wants. When his mouth presses to the place where shoulder meets neck, I give in a little more, pulling on his hands until his arms are banded tightly around my middle. He groans in approval and noses my hair aside. "Mmm, and I miss these cute-as-fuck ears."

Suddenly, Tiernan freezes. I try to ask him what he's doing, but he claps a hand over my mouth. Then he pulls my shorts back into place, and his voice is barely audible when he says, "Someone's coming. *Go.*"

I don't wait to be told twice, but just before I exit the kitchen, I allow myself a brief glance back in his direction so I can commit this moment to memory. He's the most gorgeous male I've ever seen, human or *other*. Wearing only a pair of loose sleep pants that hang indecently low on his trim hips, the grooves on his chest and abs appear even more defined from the shadows cast by the soft glow of the cabinet lights.

Unlike his brothers' black hair, Tiernan's is a rich brown, like even that part of him needed to rebel. It's longer on top and sticking up in several directions right now, giving him a boyish appearance. The high angles of his cheekbones complement the cut edge of his jawline, and his usual groomed five o'clock shadow is more of a scruff at this late hour.

And, of course, completing his fae good looks are his pointed ears, ethereally bright golden eyes, and fangs.

Golden eyes and fangs. Oh my gods. I barely muffle the gasp from realizing my mistake, then bolt for the sanctuary of my room. Once inside, I lock the door, toss my phone onto the bed, and cross to the full-length mirror. Tucking one side of my long hair behind my ear, I slowly trace its rounded top with my finger before letting my hand fall at my side.

…and your ears. Gods, I miss these ears.

I'd always thought of that first time Tiernan and I tumbled into the pantry together as happening "without a second thought." For someone like me—someone inherently *different*—not thinking twice can be dangerous. But as soon as Tiernan's hand touched mine, it was as if nothing else existed. Not even my secrets.

Had I been thinking at all, I would've remembered why I have a *humans only* policy when it comes to intimacy: because I blend in better with them than I do my own kind.

It's common for fae to have sex with humans, but it's almost unheard of for it to result in a pregnancy. So much so that most fae think halflings are nothing more than myth.

However, I can personally attest that *I* am not a myth. I'm also not a halfling, but somewhere down the line on my father's side is human DNA. That's all I really know, and I'm fine with that.

I'm not ashamed of who I am, but being different for any reason is never easy. At best, you're whispered about behind your back. At worst, you're a target for every asshole with an inferiority complex. Which is why I choose to hide my features that are decidedly *un*fae.

So that first time in the pantry when Tiernan's fingers delved into my thick hair and brushed over the rounded tops of my ears, I held my breath and waited for the ridicule or rejection. Only it never came.

He kept his hands where they were and pulled back enough to look at me. Bright golden eyes dipped briefly to my fangs before returning to meet and hold my gaze, his silent question hanging heavy between us as his thumbs stroked over the smooth arches of my ears.

I answered with a shrug. "There was a halfling somewhere on my father's side. They're why my hair is always down or styled to cover them."

"That's a damn shame," he said with a grin, "because I think they're adorable."

It was a huge relief to know he didn't think less of me for having mortal blood, and it was clear he liked them by the way he often licked and nipped at the rounded shells. But I never got brave enough to be completely honest with him.

Staring at myself in the mirror, I regard my blue eyes and run the tip of my tongue across my straight, blunt teeth. Since I attempted to sleep before venturing into the kitchen, I'd already taken out my gold-colored contacts and the fanged caps I wear every day, unless I plan on being around humans.

I was ready to succumb to my needs with Tiernan a little bit ago, my sense of self-preservation all but forgotten. It may have been easy for him to dismiss a single human characteristic, but how would he react if he discovered just how different my mixed blood makes me? I'd rather not find out.

"You really do need to get laid," I tell my reflection. "Replace that godsforsaken sexy rebel prince with someone else, and *soon*."

Sighing, I climb into bed and replay those minutes in the kitchen with Tiernan on a loop until I finally drift off to sleep.

CHAPTER FOUR

FIONA

'm feeling much better this morning. A long yoga session followed by some meditation never fails to bring my body and mind back in line. With eyes closed, I sit on my mat with one folded leg atop the other and hands resting palms up on my knees. Drawing in another deep breath through my nose, I hold it for a count of three, then exhale through my mouth.

The corners of my lips quirk up when I hear Bryn shifting next to me on her own mat. She asked me to teach her "how to be all Zen and stuff," so she's been joining me in the MM's home gym three times a week for my morning routine. She caught on to the yoga quickly. The meditating...not so much.

"Good," I say in a soothing tone. "Now we'll do a body scan, checking in with each part individually. Start with the crown of your head—the roots of your hair, your forehead, and all the way around to the back of your skull. Focus on how those areas feel."

"Seriously? The roots of my hair?"

I can practically feel the arch of her brow and dubious stare boring into me. Biting the inside of my cheek to prevent a grin, I try to inject a touch of admonishment in my response.

"Bryn, you're supposed to keep your eyes closed and follow my instructions."

"Then don't give me ridiculous instructions," she fires back. I crack my eyes open the slightest bit to see her resume her meditative pose with a sigh. "I suppose my roots *do* feel a little tender today. Caiden fisted my hair so hard last night, I'm surprised I didn't wake up bald."

We hold our composure for all of two seconds before simultaneously bursting into laughter. Giving up on the idea of doing the body scan, I grab the small towel by my mat and wipe the sweat off the back of my neck. "No way I get my Zen back after that. Gods, what I wouldn't give for a little hair pulling. Or a lot."

Bryn takes several long swallows from her water bottle, then turns on her mat to face me. "Still not getting any new-king-nookie, huh? How you manage to resist the infamous Verran sex appeal is beyond me. You should both just come over to our house for a social visit and bang it out there."

I shake my head, wishing it were that easy. "Tier wouldn't go for that. Despite his complex feelings on his impending ascension, he knows what's at stake if anything got out about him not taking it seriously. His family legacy is important to him, so even as he hopes my mom will find a way to break the blood curse, he doesn't want to cast doubt about his competence among the people. Or his older brother."

I give Bryn a pointed look, and she gives my leg a quick squeeze, letting me know she understands that Tier's concerns stay between the two of us. "I get it," she says with sincerity. Then her bright hazel eyes twinkle with mischief. "Honestly, I'm just worried your lady-bits are going to shrivel up from neglect. You need an eggplant in your taco, STAT, girl."

The total one-eighty of the convo almost causes me to spit my water out. I manage to keep it all in except a dribble that I wipe away with the back of my hand as I bust out laughing.

We started a weird emoji language one time, and now we randomly throw it in, usually at the strangest times.

"We came pretty close last night. And I came *really hard* right before that."

Bryn pounces. "What? How is this not the first thing you said to me this morning? Spill the tea right now or I'll...think of something later, but it won't be fun."

Sighing, I lean back on my hands. "I was in the kitchen during one of my insomnia bouts. He was up to get a glass of water and suddenly he was just there. All I could smell and feel and hear was *him*. And the things he said..."

Bryn leans in, her eyes wide and attention hanging on my every word. Exactly how I used to be when she'd tell me about Caiden when things started heating up between them. "Oh yeah. I'm a sucker for dirty talk, too."

"It wasn't all that dirty, though. I mean, it wasn't suitable to repeat in front of children or anything, but it was only one chili pepper, if that."

She tilts her head to the side as though trying to solve a puzzle. "Was it the way he sounded, then? Do you have a voice kink?"

"No. Maybe? I think it's more of a Tiernan Verran kink, honestly."

"Okay, forget that part. What actually happened?"

Despite knowing we're alone, I give the gym a cursory glance to be sure before giving her the basic idea in emoji speak, ending it with, "Big tongue, waving hand, and then the trio of droplets." I remember how my legs trembled and almost gave out. "Like *five* trios of droplets."

Her jaw is practically resting on her chest. "Damn that's hot. Wait, so after all that, you still didn't get the eggplant? Don't tell me my wicked brother-in-law finally turned gentleman on you."

I snort. "Definitely not. He heard someone coming.

Probably a Watcher to check on the security camera he nudged to create a blind spot for us."

"Well, that blows."

"No, it ended up being a good thing." She frowns, probably unable to come up with a single reason I would say that after wanting to climb Tier like a tree the last three months. "I didn't have my contacts or fangs in."

"Oh, girl, I'm sorry," she says, sympathy lacing her tone. "I still think you should tell him. At least about those so you don't have to worry about always having them in around the manor."

Bryn is the only one who knows *all* the ways my halfling DNA makes me different—both physical and magical—and she couldn't care less. The fact that she lived as a human until recently means she doesn't have the same biases as most faekind. She's my first real friend, and as my mom's biological niece, she's also my cousin. I can trust her with my secrets.

I take a long drink of water, then shake my head. "I can't. Him knowing I have traces of human blood and rounded ears is one thing. But learning I have more in common with humans than I do my own kind is another." Sitting forward, I pick at the tiny loops of thread that make up my towel. "I couldn't handle it if he looked at me like I'm some kind of freak, Bryn."

She reaches over to give my hand a supportive squeeze. "He would never, Fi. Tiernan might come off as being no deeper than a puddle, but you know he's not as shallow as all that."

"I know, but it's hard to battle a lifetime of worry enough to open up to someone like him." I meet her gaze and offer a wry smile. "Plus, if my mom found out I told the future king about me after all she's done to help me blend in, she'd have a conniption."

Bryn winces. "Good point. I wouldn't wish Auntie Erin's wrath on anyone. She'd probably turn you into a toad for a week or something."

We laugh at that image, then I lead us through some light stretches on our backs. Pulling my knees into my chest, I turn my head to look at her. "How's married life treating you? Are you going to host an elaborate dinner party to lock in your reign as Queen of Suburban Housewives?"

Bryn pushes on my legs, causing me to fall onto my side and lose my stretch as I chuckle. "Hardly. I'm too busy with work to be pandering to Vegas's social elite. I do have something to tell you, though."

Her pensive tone worries me. Pushing up to a sitting position, I ask, "Is everything all right with you and Caiden?"

Still holding her knees-to-chest stretch, she looks up at me with a wide smile. "Everything is great, Fi. In fact, it couldn't be more perfect." Releasing her knees, she places her hands low on her abdomen. "I wanted to tell you first...we're having a baby."

My shock is quickly overcome with sheer joy as I fling myself down to envelop my friend in a squealing bear hug. Eventually, I stop crushing her with my excitement and pull her up to sit facing each other, our hands still clasped between us. "Tell me everything," I say. "Were you trying? How long have you known? How far along are you?"

"No, we weren't trying, but we hadn't thought to prevent it either. Even after my fae transformation, Caiden still often thinks of me as the human woman I was when we started our kidnapship."

"Your kidnapship?" I repeat with a chuckle.

"It's more accurate than courtship, don't you think?"

She's not wrong. Bryn was held hostage by Caiden for weeks after they woke up married and bonded to each other. Granted, he couldn't exactly let her go back home to Wisconsin, since any significant distance between them would've caused his death.

But it didn't take long for Bryn to enjoy her captivity

once the king introduced her to the many wicked pleasures inherent to the Dark Fae. Our sexual tastes naturally run on the depraved side of the spectrum, as one would expect of a people who created an entire city based on deviance and debauchery.

"Touché," I respond. "So basically, once you went full Darklight, your body was no longer acting human. But your hubby was still in the mindset of not wrapping his tool because he hadn't needed to before, and because bonded mates are able to conceive easily, you ended up with a bun in the oven. Right?"

"Exactly right. I think I got pregnant almost immediately, and I suspected not long after. I confirmed it the day we moved into our house and I told Caiden that night."

My jaw drops. "But that was almost three months ago! And you're just telling me? *Now* who deserves something not fun? I should revoke your BFF card."

"I know, I'm sorry. I wanted to wait until we passed the twelve-week mark before telling anyone. I know that my situation is different because fae don't experience the same complications, but I remember hearing my mom talk about how heartbreaking it was every time she miscarried. I needed to be farther along for my own peace of mind."

"Oh, honey, I completely understand." Emily and Jack Meara, the couple who raised Bryn as their own, suffered through years of infertility before my mom gifted them with a fae newborn spelled to appear as a human baby girl. "I'm honestly so damn happy for you. How's Caiden feeling about impending fatherhood?"

Bryn's mouth curves up as the love for her husband shines in her bright hazel eyes. "He's over the moon, Fi. Always placing his hand over my belly even though I'm not even showing yet, talking to the baby, telling them bedtime stories, and the nursery is already finished with at least two of everything we could possibly need and more." Her smile falters as she grows more serious. "But he's also a nervous wreck, and this whole situation with Myrddin has kicked his usual overprotectiveness into overdrive."

"I can't blame him. Nothing like this has ever happened before, and considering Talek Edevane is still ruling the Day Court from gods only know where, we have to assume he's just biding his time before making another play for the Night Court throne."

Shivers race down my spine. It's the first time I've voiced that fear out loud. I've been too afraid to acknowledge the fact that as the new king of the Dark Fae, Tiernan will be the one with a target on his back.

The only comfort I have is that Edevane is still bound by the Treaty of Two Courts that states neither king can kill the other "by their own hand or by their command." It's the reason he tried taking Caiden out by activating the marriage blood curse. So as long as Tiernan doesn't get accidentally mated, too, he should be fine.

But that doesn't explain why we've had our first fae murder in the history of our four hundred years in the human world. And if knowledge is power, we're at a huge disadvantage right now.

Seeing the worry crease my friend's face, I quickly change the subject. "Hey, want to go play a prank on the Woulfe boys? They keep digging in my honeysuckle beds, so I ordered some itching powder to teach them a lesson. I was thinking their gigantic dog beds by the patio firepit could use a couple sprinkles. Or ten."

Her eyes light up with mischief. "Let's do it. And we should bribe the Watcher in charge of the security cameras so we can see the fruits of our labor."

Laughing, I say, "Oh, absolutely. See? You may be half Light, but your Dark half is just as deviant as the rest of us. Now, let's go make the twins think they have fleas."

CHAPTER FIVE

TIERNAN

Sitting in the back of the Range Rover with Seamus, I take a fortifying sip of dark roast and wince when the desert sun finally peeks over the horizon enough to rudely pierce my bleary eyes with shafts of light.

"Well, one thing's for sure," I grumble to no one in particular as I lower my aviator sunglasses. "When I'm king, all court meetings before eight a.m. will be banned."

Conall glances at me in the rearview mirror. "Can't say I'd hate that."

Yawning in the passenger seat, his brother says, "Cosign."

"Perhaps if any of you bothered to go to bed at a decent time instead of playing your war video games, you wouldn't be such babies about meeting at daybreak," Seamus says in his famous tone that manages to scold without sounding like it.

Connor peers over his shoulder. "Normally I'd say touché, Dad, but Conall and I didn't spend last night playing *Modern Warfare*."

"We needed to run," Conall adds.

Their father's stern expression never changes, but his eyes soften as he gives them a curt nod. "That was wise."

Fae shifters, no matter what kind, have to regularly spend time in animal form. How often depends on the family line and the individuals. The twins could make it a couple weeks without any significant time spent as wolves. But then they needed a whole night to run through the desert and tap into that ancient magic. Any longer and their fae forms grew weak.

Seamus turns his fatherly look on me. "And your excuse?"

"You don't want to know."

"That usually means I *should*," he replies.

Shrugging, I tell him the truth while also not. "My three a.m. trip to the kitchen for a glass of water was followed by a long"—*cold*—"shower. Couldn't sleep after that."

Connor looks back at me and smirks. "You were in the kitchen awhile. Must have been thirsty, huh?"

He was the one who came to check on the skewed security camera. Though he hadn't seen anything, there was no mistaking Fiona's scent that still lingered in the room. I flash him a feral grin that says *shut your fucking face or I'll do it for you.* "What can I say? I take my hydration seriously."

Thinking about my encounter with Fiona is making me crave another taste of her. Those ten minutes with my face between her thighs, drinking down every drop she gave me, were possibly the best minutes of my life to date.

I can't decide if Rhiannon finally took pity on me and gifted me that time to take the edge off my desire for her, or if the moon goddess is toying with me by *only* letting me take the edge off. Because if I thought I was obsessed with having Fiona before, now I'm positively consumed by my need. My fangs are aching to drink more of her than just her arousal.

Fucking hell, get ahold of yourself or you'll be a walking sun dial when you get out of the car.

I don't think the pathetic excuse of having latent morning wood would pass muster with Seamus. As far as I know, he's not aware of my history with Fiona. But he'd have to be completely oblivious to not notice the sexual tension between us. He hasn't questioned me about it, though, which tells me he doesn't think it's an issue. *Yet.*

Conall, who's occasionally less of a dick than his twin, changes the subject for me. "I can't believe CV is going to be a dad. That's so cool."

Before we left Midnight Manor, Caiden came over and gave us all the news that Bryn's expecting. We burst into a round of congratulations and backslapping, and the pride on my brother's face was unmatched. But Seamus saw something more. "You're concerned," he said.

Caiden nodded. "The pregnancy is having unexpected effects. Her healing powers are stable so far, but her strength is increasing, and her power of suggestion is becoming unpredictable."

"Unpredictable how?" I asked.

"She can't always control it. Yesterday, we stopped at Nightfall so I could grab a few things from my office. I handed the keys to the valet, and Bryn jokingly suggested he take it for a joyride. The kid drove off in my Maserati."

Connor's hand flew to his chest like he was experiencing actual pain. "He *stole* your car?"

"No, he brought it back an hour later with an empty tank, but that's not the point. That unintentional use of her suggestive power, even as small as it was, completely drained her almost to the point of collapsing. As the only Darklight, there's no way of knowing how the baby will continue to affect Bryn the further along she gets."

Seamus pulled at his beard, concern in his eyes. "We must make sure someone is with her at all times."

"The only time I leave her side is if she's with someone I trust, and even then I'm not far. Obviously, I'll do what I can, but I wanted you to know why I may not be as involved with court matters for a while."

"No worries, bro, you take care of Brynnie and the baby. We've got this."

I can only hope I'm right, but I'm not going to say anything that shoulders my brother with more worry than he already has. So for now I'm going to do what I always did whenever I crashed a celebrity VIP party: fake it till I make it.

A buzz of energy passes through my body as we cross the threshold of the massive protective glamour cloaking the Dark Fae's most sacred place—the Temple of Rhiannon, where we pay homage to the moon goddess. A second ago there was only desert stretching as far as the eye could see, but it was all a clever mirage, hiding the massive structure half a mile in front of us.

Unlike Caiden, I've never held any special affinity for the ToR—the acronym started by the Watch that stuck as an abbreviated name. I respected it for what it is, but other than that, I never gave it much thought. But as we approach it now, a sense of pride and awe stirs in my chest. It truly is magnificent, and according to the elders, an exact replica of the temple in Tír na nÓg, where the Dark Fae hail from back in Faerie.

The black stone gleams in the sunlight, the spires on each corner stretching high into the sky as though trying to reach the goddess it's named for. The spell that hides the ToR from human eyes is visible in the air surrounding the temple, making it appear as a palatial mirage set in the middle of the Mojave.

Not only is the ToR our place of worship, it's also where the king conducts royal business, though traditionally it's never held during the day. Because, you know, *Night* Court. But special circumstances call for special allowances, and as much as I'm grumbling about the godsawful early hour, I'm fully aware this meeting can't wait for things like convenience or tradition.

We park near the back entrance, and the brothers check in over their comms units with other members of the Night

Watch inside, confirming that the ToR is safe for us to enter.

As we walk through the meandering halls toward the wing with the conference rooms, I remove my aviators and hook them onto the open collar of my blue suit shirt. With the sleeves rolled up and sporting khaki pants, this is as business-y as I get.

I'm not like Caiden, who probably sleeps and fucks in his designer suits. *Poor Brynnie.* I personally find anything dressier than casualwear stifling. Yet another unkingly trait of mine to add to the list.

We stop at the closed door to the main conference room. Conner briefly puts a finger to the comms unit at his ear. "Copy that." To Seamus, he says, "Chief McCarthy has been scouted three minutes out."

"Good. Have him escorted back as soon as he arrives."

At that, the Woulfe brothers lead us into the room. Because both of them are built like they could be starting linebackers for the Raiders, I didn't immediately realize we were interrupting a meeting already in progress. A meeting I knew nothing about. And by the look on Seamus's face, neither did he.

Seven males sit in the plush leather executive chairs around the large conference table, three on each side with one at the end. Their heads snap in our direction to aim various looks of displeasure at whoever dared to interrupt them. Until they see me and Seamus. Then they can't stand up fast enough. Bowing briefly, they offer proper greetings. I have to focus on not letting my lip curl in distaste, to keep my features smooth and unaffected.

These are the assholes who, for all intents and purposes, are running my life at the moment. The Dark Council. It's made up of the seven high lords of the Night Court, heads of the oldest Dark families. Their role within the court has been mostly honorific. Until now.

Now they have power. It's limited, but it's enough to make their dicks hard. Especially Hedrek Dolan, the Speaker of the Dark Council and the prune-faced putz sitting in the chair meant for the king. He's probably been creaming his pants since the night Caiden abdicated, making the DC operational for the first time in centuries. The fact that there's not a single female head of family in the bunch proves what a group of antiquated assholes they are.

Seamus clasps his hands in front of him and affects a smile that gets nowhere near his golden eyes. "Lord Speaker, what a pleasant surprise. I hadn't realized the Council was meeting this morning. Odd scheduling choice, this early, wouldn't you say?"

Hedrek makes a show of buttoning his fancy suit coat and returns a fake-ass smile of his own. "We were only trying to avoid taking the space during your normal business hours, Regent."

I arch a dubious brow. "If only there was some kind of scheduling interface accessible to all court leaders that would let us know when people were meeting and where."

Oops. Forgot to engage my filter on that one. Seamus doesn't dare say anything, but the way his shoulders tense next to me might as well be one of the head-smacks he gave me when I got a little too mouthy as a kid. *Message received, Obi-Wan.*

"Apologies, Lord Speaker," I say with zero remorse. "I know the digital age isn't easy for everyone to grasp. I'm sure it simply slipped your mind to check the Court Calendar."

I don't mention that I can't remember to check the damn thing either. Thank Rhiannon for Fiona. She's taken it upon herself to keep track of my schedule and make sure I don't miss anything important. Well, not by accident, anyway.

Thin lips creep up at the corners. "Indeed, Your Highness. I assure you it won't happen again. At any rate, we were just wrapping up, so the room is yours."

"Anything the Crown Prince and I need to be apprised of, Lord Speaker?" Seamus asks.

"No, Regent, but if that changes, I promise you'll be the first to know."

Damn, I want to punch the smarmy grin right off his fucking face. Nothing good ever comes from power-hungry assholes like him getting a taste of the control they crave. And I don't trust Hedrek Dolan not to be cooking something up behind our backs.

The members gather their things quickly and begin leaving, giving me a wide berth and avoiding eye contact. Before Hedrek leaves, however, Seamus calls him back. "We're about to meet with Chief McCarthy. He's going to fill us in on the recent events as he knows them. I'd like you to sit in on the meeting with us. It never hurts to have another leader who loves our people in the know."

The old crab-ass actually looks surprised and honored for all of sixty seconds before the blatant sense of entitlement returns. "I couldn't agree more," he said. "I'm happy to offer any assistance I can to the Crown during these tragic times."

I tuck my chin and mutter to Connor on my other side. "I think I just puked in my mouth." He clears his throat to disguise his laugh as Conall relays the message they must have gotten through comms. "McCarthy's here. Rian is escorting him back now."

I take advantage of those two minutes to use the Keurig on the wet bar in the corner to top off my coffee. As soon as the chief arrives, the mood in the room shifts, like he's a harbinger of bad news. Actually, he's not *like* that, he *is* that, and the weight of why we're all here suddenly seems too heavy to bear standing up.

He and Seamus greet each other with firmly clasped hands and the quick pleasantries old friends have when meeting under somber conditions. When they break away, McCarthy bows to me and nods respectfully to Dolan before Seamus gestures toward the table. "Let's get started."

He stands to the side of the head seat and meets my gaze. He's asking if I want to take my rightful place. I answer by taking the spot to the right of it designated for the senior advisor. *His* spot. Seamus lowers his big body into the king's chair and pretends we didn't just have a silent argument about seating arrangements, just as I'm pretending said argument wasn't a metaphor for things far greater than where I park my ass.

"Aleck," Seamus begins, "you have the floor."

McCarthy has a strong jaw and dark, serious brows that convey both his determination and his compassion. He looks every inch your typical TV detective, if you don't count the pointed ears and fangs, anyway. But if there's ever a *Law and Order: Special Fae Unit*, he'd be a shoo-in.

Scrubbing a hand down his face, the police chief sighs as though resigning himself to the reality of the conversation. "We had two more murders yesterday. Eoghan O'Leary and Cillian Valliant."

It feels like all the air is sucked out of the room as each of us tries to process the news. One fae murder was a shocking tragedy. *Three* is a harrowing godsdamn catastrophe. My insides vibrate with outrage at the senseless loss of our people. I can't begin to imagine how devastated the families must be, losing their loved ones so suddenly and violently like this.

Seamus's fist tightens almost imperceptibly on the table. "The head chef at Obscurity and the owner of Dark and Dapper."

Obscurity is an upscale restaurant on the south end of The Strip. Two years ago, the owner died and it went back to the bank. Caiden was in a bidding war with Stanley Leone, who enjoys collecting businesses as much as my brother and has been doing his best to gain a significant toehold in Vegas real estate for the last year or so. In the end, Caiden got the restaurant. Leone got big-mad.

Dark and Dapper is a bougie clothing boutique that specializes in custom designs. Cillian was the owner and the talent, but he ran the business with his husband. It's the only place Caiden gets his clothes, from his Court-wear, to his business suits, and even his jeans.

My lips curl into a snarl. "Another of my brother's employees *and* his personal tailor. That can't be a coincidence. But why? Why the hell would anyone be threatening Caiden now? He doesn't hold power in the Court anymore."

McCarthy holds up a hand, making me think I must look like I'm about to kill the messenger. "The threat might not be aimed at Prince Caiden specifically. It might not even be a *threat* at all. We don't know anything right now other than they all have him in common."

"The connection could be corporate or even Court based," Seamus adds. "The restaurant is owned by Onyx Inc but managed and run by Darks. And Cillian's shop is publicly known for outfitting Caiden with business suits, but Cillian also had a contract with the Court that catered to all members of the royal administration, including the Council."

Dolan raises a disapproving brow like a teacher silently scolding me for not doing my homework. "I'm more of an off-the-rack guy. Standing still while getting repeatedly poked in a sensitive area isn't one of my kinks. No judgment, though, Dolan, you do you." I wink suggestively as though I know all his darkest secrets, just to get a rise out of him. It works.

Aleck steps in to change the subject before Dolan blusters himself into a stroke. "That's correct, Regent, the connection could also be the Court and not Prince Caiden specifically."

He continues to provide details about the scenes. "Cillian's husband, Declan, said that Cillian left home about a quarter after six yesterday morning for his studio. That wasn't his typical routine, but he'd been excited about starting a custom gown for the Royal Mother to wear to Prince Tiernan's coronation.

"Declan arrived an hour later. He found Cillian just inside the studio doors in the same condition as Myrddin, badly beaten and stabbed. There was no sign of forced entry, and it appeared Cillian hadn't gotten started yet as no tools or fabrics were taken out in the back work area.

"Our guess is that the suspect—or suspects, plural— followed him in as soon as he opened the door and used a blunt force hit to the back of his head, giving them the element of surprise to get the upper hand before he could fight them off. The M.E. puts time of death around six forty-five a.m."

"And Eoghan?" I ask as the details spin in my head, trying to form a cohesive picture with answers, while my heart breaks for Cillian's husband.

"Obscurity has been closed all week for its annual deep cleaning. At the end of that week, Chef prepares a huge meal by himself and hosts an appreciation event for his staff at the restaurant before they reopen. The first ones to arrive just after eight p.m. found Eoghan in a pool of blood in the kitchen, which was a war zone. Looks like he put up one hell of a fight, but it wasn't enough. We found two different shoe prints and neither match the pair Eoghan was wearing, so there were at least two attackers, possibly more."

I frown. "How'd they get into the restaurant if it's closed?"

"One of his cooks said Chef always propped the back door open while preparing the food for the event because he didn't want the strong smell of disinfectant to permeate his cooking. The security alarm was unarmed at two-oh-nine that afternoon, so we know that's when he arrived, but it was a few hours before he was attacked. TOD is somewhere around five o'clock."

Seamus looks up from the legal pad he's been scribbling notes on. "Any other clues or details that might help lead us to the responsible parties? What about security footage?"

Shaking his head, McCarthy says, "Cillian's shop doesn't have any cameras, nor do the surrounding shops have any pointed in his direction."

"But the restaurant is rigged with cameras that cover every square inch, inside and out. The whole thing had to be recorded," I say.

"Negative. The feed is nothing but static. We found two items in the kitchen that were likely dropped in the struggle: a signal jammer which would have interfered with the signal for a wireless camera system, and a hag stone found near the body. Both were dusted for prints and came up clean."

Hedrek leans back in his chair. "A hag stone. That would mean the perpetrator is a familiar."

"Not necessarily," I bite out. "If they had to use a hag stone to see past Myrddin's glamour then, yeah, the perp is probably human. But that doesn't automatically make them a familiar."

"I disagree. That they knew how to subvert one of our oldest defenses speaks to the fact that they have intimate knowledge of the fae. That makes it more likely that it was someone we trusted."

I scoff. "I know you're not the best with modern technology, but I'm sure you've heard of a little thing called Google. It only takes seconds and a few keystrokes for humans to find hundreds of websites about fae. Sure, most of it's bullshit, but there's plenty that isn't. Try enough things and they're bound to get lucky eventually."

The lord stares me down from the other side of the table. "Possibly. Or possibly your habit of spending more time with the humans than your own kind has clouded your judgement."

Red tinges the sides of my vision. It's not easy to make me angry, but this asshole has a knack for pushing my fucking buttons. "Careful, Dolan. I won't always be in *this* chair, and you're speaking a little too freely for my taste."

His jaw tightens before he's able to force out the words. "Forgive me, Your Highness. I meant no offense."

When I don't immediately respond, Seamus taps my foot with his. "You're forgiven," I say through clenched teeth. What I don't say is that while I may forgive his insolence because I have to, I damn well won't forget it.

"Technically, it's too early to rule anyone out," Aleck says. "Even one of our own. Just because we've made it this long without a Dark versus Dark homicide, doesn't mean that's not what this is. The stone could've been planted to throw us off."

"Loath as I am to admit it, you're right, Aleck," Seamus says somberly.

"Anyone have any beef with the Romanovs?" All three pairs of eyes swing my way in surprise. "What? If we're looking at everyone, then we should be looking at *others*, too. The Romanov vampire clan is in Los Angeles. They're the closest ones to us and we know they're here on a regular basis. They own Blood Sport, the MMA gym on Fremont Street. So we start there, then look at the werewolves, djinn, sirens, et cetera."

Hedrek huffs in obvious frustration, like I'm a child speaking out of turn, doing him no favors where my mood is concerned. "I don't think so. In the four-plus centuries we've inhabited this realm, we've never had issues with *any* of the supernatural races."

"We've also never had one of our people slain under mysterious circumstances, so *I* think we need to investigate all avenues to eliminate the possibilities and narrow the suspect list." I look to Aleck, knowing he'll back me up. Not because I'm the future king but because I'm fucking right. "Isn't that how it's done, Chief McCarthy?"

"Yes, Your Highness, that's how investigations are conducted."

A flush creeps up Hedrek's neck. "To investigate such a thing would be an insult to the head of the Romanov clan, practically an accusation in itself, and could incite a war between our factions. Forgive me again, Your Highness, but I must insist—"

"You know, Dolan, I don't think I will. I'm fresh out of forgiveness, not to mention fucks at this point," I grind out. "Don't worry about Dmitri, I'll handle him."

"No," he says with impudence. "We will not approach the vampires unless or until the other leads don't pan out."

My lips peel back into a sneer, my fangs aching with the added adrenaline of wanting to clock this bastard where he sits. "And I say we will." *Check.*

The Speaker's spine straightens as he pulls his shoulders back and lifts his chin in a futile attempt to look down on me. *Me.* Forget that I'll soon be his king—at his behest, I might add—but I'm a godsdamn Verran, a member of the royal line. It's like watching a sackless weasel thinking he found his misplaced balls.

"If you wanted to make the decisions that affect our court, you could have ascended the throne when your brother abdicated instead of asking for time," Dolan says. "Are you saying you want to proceed with the coronation *now*, Your Highness?"

I force myself not to wince at the mention of the C-word and answer with a question of my own. "Regent," I say, never taking my eyes from Dolan. "Do you think we should question Romanov now or wait for an indeterminate date in the future?"

"Even if they are not responsible for the attacks, they may have heard something around the gym or other places they frequent that could prove helpful. Therefore, as long as the Crown Prince is *diplomatic* with his line of questioning..."

At the pregnant pause, I turn to see him giving me the *don't make me eat these words* look. "What?" I say defensively.

"I can be diplomatic."

"Then, yes, I believe it would be prudent to meet with them now."

Checkmate.

I barely refrain from sticking my tongue out or saying I told you so, but I do allow myself a haughty arch of a brow in the Lord's direction. Not that I'm all that excited about having to go meet with the vampire, but it needs to be done, and seeing Dolan's face turn mottled red with humiliation is worth it.

"Awesome. Now if you'll excuse me, gentlemen, I need to see a Woulfe about seeing a vampire."

CHAPTER SIX

FIONA

Today is my monthly mother-daughter mani-pedi session in the casino salon with my mom. Since it's always been just the two of us, we're extremely close. I don't think there's been a full week that I haven't seen my mom even after moving out of the house, and it's more likely that we see each other more days of the week than not.

She texted me from her Uber a second ago to tell me that they're approaching the manor, so I make my way down to the end of the drive and enter my code into the security panel to walk through the smaller door-sized gate set into the much larger one that closes off the property. The silver sedan pulls to a stop in front of me and I climb into the back seat with my mom.

"Hello, my love," she says affectionately as I lean over for a tight hug. Even with her glamour in place, her features are familiar and a comfort. Long, strawberry-blond hair is pulled back into a French braid with the bottom resting in front of her shoulder, and her honey-colored eyes aren't that different from their usual bright gold. Sometimes being with her when she's glamoured makes me feel closer to her, because it's when we look the most alike.

When we break apart, she hands me a travel mug of her special peppermint-nettle tea she's been making me since I was a kid. "Mmm, thank you, this is exactly what I needed today." Lifting the cup to my nose I breathe in the scent and let the nostalgia wash over me.

"Do they have you working too hard over there? Because I have no qualms about telling those Verran boys to take it easy on my baby, I don't care if they are the kings of this city."

I laugh, knowing full well she would never dare speak to any member of the royal family with such disrespect over something like my back hurting from too much laundry. "No, Mom, I'm fine. I enjoy my work there. I've just had a lot on my mind recently, so our regular date is a very welcome distraction."

"Well good, because this is my favorite day of the month. Now drink your tea before it gets cold."

I take a tentative sip at first, but when I realize it's not too hot, I take a deeper drink and let the warmth and mellow earthy flavors with mint flow through me like the comfort of an old friend. "What do you put in this stuff? I swear you make it with magic."

"I do," she says with a twinkling in her eyes. "It's called love."

I roll my eyes at her cheesy line, but it touches me all the same. "Any new developments on finding a way to break the blood curse?"

She sighs, her frustration at hitting so many dead ends evident in the way her shoulders sag. "I wish I could say yes. But anytime my research gives me even a glimmer of hope that there's a way to undo it, it's dashed soon after. I knew it wouldn't be easy, considering the magic the One True Queen wields is so powerful and not of this realm, but I hoped it wouldn't take this long. I won't stop trying, though. Until that curse is broken, anyone who wants to harm Prince Caiden could do so by going after Bryn."

I'm filled with pride as I watch new resolve fill her for her mission. Bryn is my mom's biological niece, born of her sister Kiera and her mate, Uther of the Day Court. Their love was a forbidden one, and their baby was never supposed to have existed.

My mom was with them in Joshua Tree the night they planned to run away together so they could live and raise their daughter in peace after she was born. What they didn't know was that Prince Talek Edevane, Uther's cousin whom he'd confided in, had turned on Uther and was hunting him and Kiera down to take them prisoner so he could steal the Darklight child.

Before they could escape, Kiera suddenly went into labor unexpectedly and gave birth to Bryn right there in the desert as Edevane and his Light Warriors could be heard bearing down on them in their loud trucks.

Kiera made my mom promise to keep Bryn safe from those who would harm her or use her for her unique powers, knowing that she and her mate were about to die.

My mom kept her promise and managed to spirit Bryn away before Edevane arrived, then placed her in the care of a loving young couple in Wisconsin who raised her as their own. And to hide Bryn's fae qualities, my mom placed a block on all her powers so that she would appear and act as human as her adoptive parents. It worked, until Edevane—who had risen to the place of king of the Day Court—manipulated Bryn into coming to Vegas and marrying Caiden, setting in motion everything that came to pass over the next few months that ended with the king abdicating his throne and Bryn becoming the first Darklight in existence.

With Caiden no longer the king, the threat on Bryn's life has lessened exponentially. Not to mention that she has powers stronger than most fae in this realm, and some she hasn't even tapped into yet. But that doesn't mean my mom won't continue to worry until every threat has been removed.

"You'll find it, Mom. I know you will."

She smiles at me and squeezes my leg. "You always have been my biggest fan, *mo stóirín*."

My little treasure. The nickname she gave me the day I was born never fails to warm my heart. "Why wouldn't I be? You've always been mine. You've never made me feel anything less than perfect, even though there are plenty of fae who would have rejected a baby like me."

"That's because you *are* perfect. In *every* way. No matter what happens in your life, I need you to remember that. My reason for helping you blend in while growing up wasn't because I was ashamed of what makes you unique. I only ever wanted to protect you."

"I know that, Mom. Us against the world, right?"

Her eyes shimmer with unshed tears. "That's right. Us against the world. Always."

The car pulls into the employee parking lot in the back of Nightfall just as I finish my tea. We thank our driver, who's an attractive man in his early thirties. I noticed him checking me out several times in the rearview mirror while we drove. Without my caps or contacts, I look like a normal human in his dating pool. Since my mom tweaks her glamour so that she appears old enough to be my mother, his full attention has been solely on me.

I briefly consider giving him my number and following through with my plan to get over Tier by getting under someone else. But I dismiss the thought just as quickly, pretending that it's because Mom is waiting for me and I don't have the time for random hookups right now anyway. Because even if I can't lie out loud, I can at least tell myself fibs in my own head.

The sun is setting over Vegas, giving it that ethereal glow

where the vestiges of natural light clash with the light from the neons. It's the time when the city starts ramping up, its tourists getting ready for the excitement of the nightlife. Despite no one being around us right now you can still feel the buzz of energy in the air.

"So what color are you going to go with?" I ask my mom as we walk toward the employee entrance of the hotel.

"I was thinking emerald green this time."

"A shade of green? I'm so shocked." Green is my mom's favorite color, so she always gets green, it just depends on what shade she's in the mood for.

She bumps my shoulder playfully, and we both laugh.

"How's it going, ladies?"

We're both startled to find five men stepping out from the shadows and walking toward us. "Enjoying your evening?"

A tremor of dread runs down my spine. I don't like the way they're looking at us, as though we're bugs pinned to a piece of wood that they want to examine and possibly pull the wings off. I grab my mom's hand and begin to walk faster, simultaneously doing a quick calculation. We're only ten feet away from the security door. That's about three seconds and then another three seconds to enter my access code to unlock it. With the way they're walking like they're on a Sunday stroll, we should have enough time to—

They change tactics so quickly, I don't even realize they've suddenly bolted until they have us.

"What the fuck?" I shout as I try to struggle free of their grip.

"Whoa, whoa, whoa there, take it easy. We just need to look into something, and then if it all checks out, we'll let you go and you can be on your way."

"I don't give a shit what you wanna *look into*," I snarl. "Get your filthy fucking hands off us."

We're both fighting to get free with no luck. This is one of those times where having super-strength would come in really handy. Then again, it apparently wouldn't help me even if I had it. My mom, being three hundred years older, is a lot stronger than someone my age and she's not faring much better right now, thanks to the time of day.

A Dark Fae's preternatural powers don't peak until after twilight, when night truly begins. When the sun's rays stretch past the horizon to usher in the dawn, our powers begin to wane again. Naturally, for the Light Fae, it's the exact opposite, which is why the kings always meet during the Equinox because the day and night hours are equal, giving neither court the advantage. Unfortunately, we have a huge disadvantage right now. My mom might still be stronger than a typical human, but the huge brutes holding her hostage are anything but typical.

The leader of this motley crew assesses us with more hate in his mud-brown eyes than I've ever seen. Probably in his early thirties, he's tall with an average build and thin blond hair that keeps falling over his forehead. He reaches inside his jacket pocket and pulls out a pale rock the size of his fist.

Carrying around a rock would be odd in itself, but this isn't just any rock. *This* one has a natural-made hole in the middle. This human has a hag stone, and from the smug grin on his face, he knows exactly what it's for. Fear floods my system as I see the recognition of what this means on my mother's face. He will be able to see that we're fae. And if they want to know whether we're fae, it isn't for anything good.

"Let her go," I say forcefully. "Let her go and you can do whatever you want to me."

"No!" Thrashing between the men who hold her, my mom tries desperately to gain the leader's attention. "It's me you want, not her."

"What? Fuck that—"

"*Fiona, stop talking!*"

My jaw snaps shut. She's never even raised her voice to me

before. Danger aside, it still shocks me into obeying.

"Go ahead," she says to the human. "Look through the stone. You'll see."

I don't have time to argue or ask her what she's up to before the guy does just that. He holds it to his face and uses one beady eye to look through the hole of the stone at both of us. Tucking the stone back into his jacket pocket, he points at my mom and says two words that turn my world upside down. "Just her."

"You want us to let this one go, then?" the guy holding my left arm asks.

"No, let her watch. Maybe it'll teach her a lesson that she should choose her company more carefully from now on."

The leader cracks his knuckles and approaches my mom as resignation and acceptance of what is to come settles over her beautiful face.

This has to be a nightmare. This can't actually be happening. Maybe all of these months of insomnia have finally caught up to me and I'm not really here with my mom, about to watch her fall victim to an attack of gods only know what. Maybe I'm really in my bed, safe behind the walls of the manor, and my mom is safe at home as well.

But if the test to determine whether one is dreaming is to pinch themselves, I'm failing, because the meaty hands gripping both of my arms aren't just pinching, they're digging into my flesh so hard, I'm surprised they haven't already drawn blood.

Which means this nightmare is of the living kind. A real one. And there's no escape.

My scream of protest is cut off by a sweaty hand covering my mouth. The thick fingers engulf the lower half of my face, pressing against the bottom of my nose almost to the point of cutting off my air.

The more I struggle, the tighter their hold gets. Tears fall in a steady stream down my face. My body shakes with my silent sobs as my mother locks eyes with me. "I love you, Fiona. Always."

The devil standing in front of her sneers. "Time to die, fairy," he says with disgust coating his tongue.

I scream so hard, it feels like my vocal cords are shredding inside my throat, but it doesn't change the outcome. He swings, his fist connecting with the fine bone structure of my mother's face. Her head whips to the side, blood spraying from between her lips.

My nightmare has begun.

CHAPTER SEVEN

TIERNAN

"Take a left up here," Connor says from the passenger seat. I put my blinker on and make the turn. We've been driving for five hours. Thankfully, Connor let me drive my own car instead of insisting on chauffeuring me in a security truck. I told him that if I didn't get to focus on something other than what was going on, I'd be too wound up by the time we got to Dmitri's, and there was a bigger chance I would do more than just insult him.

"You know what you're going to say to him?"

I shrug. "Haven't given it much thought."

"Well, that's understandable. It's not like you've had a lot of time to think about it."

"You know me, brother. I'm more of an improv guy. It'll come to me in the moment, I'm sure."

Connor snorts. "Yeah, let's just hope a fist in the vampire's face isn't what comes to you in the moment."

Yeah, that wouldn't be great for vamp-fae relations. It's not that we're enemies, but we're not exactly friends either. For the most part, each supernatural race sticks to their own kind as an unwritten rule. It's a delicate thing, and it wouldn't take much to tip the scales into war territory.

But Darks are being slaughtered, so my manners will only go so far before I don't give a fuck about diplomacy anymore.

"Well, that'll depend on how he answers my questions, won't it?"

I turn into the parking garage attached to the high-rise in downtown L.A. where the Romanov Clan's headquarters are. We park and don our human glamours as we make our way to the lobby, where a lone security guard sits behind the front desk watching some kind of comedy show on his cell phone. We barely rate a cursory glance before the comedian pulls his attention down once again. I wonder if Dmitri knows how lax his gatekeeper is. Then again, I think as I peer up at the camera pointed right at us, I'm sure there's a whole line of defense we can't see.

I ding the bell on the counter because I'm obnoxious like that and slightly irritated I'm being ignored. "Hi there. I can see you're incredibly busy, so if you wouldn't mind giving Mr. Romanov a heads up that he has guests, we'll get out of your hair."

"It is too late. Come back during business hours," he says in a thick Slavic accent, still not looking up. Now I'm *more* than slightly irritated.

"Ah, but it's only nine o'clock on a Saturday night, and you and I both know that his day is just getting started."

He scoffs, then starts laughing at something the comedian said. I reach over the counter and snatch his phone away faster than he can react, but it finally gets his attention. Glaring up at me, his blue eyes turn the color of spilled blood, his muscles tensing as though preparing to attack.

"Give me the phone, human, or you have seen your last sunrise." The guard peels his lips back to reveal razor-sharp fangs meant to neatly puncture or tear a throat to shreds. He's expecting me to run away screaming, but I remain unimpressed.

"Call your boss for us, and you can continue watching"—I pause to check the screen and look back at him with disapproval—"Louis C.K.? You know he's problematic, right?"

The guard roars, his patience reaching the end of its rope, and now he wants to hang me with it. Connor springs into action and reaches for the gun at his back, but I stop him. As soon as whoever is monitoring that camera sees a gun, all hell will break loose. So far it probably appears that we're simply having a conversation, and I aim to keep it that way. I promised Seamus I wouldn't start a godsdamn clan war. I'd like to keep that promise if inhumanly possible.

Dropping my glamour, I bare my own fangs in warning. Fae fangs aren't as long and narrow as the vampires' but they're just as sharp and deadly. "Ah-ah-ah," I say as he stops on a dime now that he can see who—or rather *what*—I am. "I wouldn't do that if I were you. In the words of the incomparable Ron Burgundy, 'I'm kind of a big deal' where I'm from. So, as I said before, please let your boss know that Tiernan Verran, future Rebel King of the Dark Fae, is here to see him."

All the vamp's fight leaks out of him like a balloon deflating, and his eyes slowly return to their original color. Picking up the desk phone, he presumably buzzes Romanov's penthouse while giving us serious side-eye. After a pause, he whispers low into the receiver for a bit. Connor and I share an amused look because we have no problem hearing the conversation and his side is rather rude. Finally, he hangs up and tells us to follow him.

He takes us to a private elevator, taps his badge on the access panel, and then uses it again on the inside to unlock the top floor. "Nice knowing you." As the doors close, he gives us a mock salute with a smirk.

"You know," I muse, "I don't believe he honestly meant that."

Connor's face breaks into a grin. "I think you might be right."

"His loss really. I'm a fucking delight."

"Now *that*, Your Highness, might be stretching it." We stand in silence for several seconds, watching the glowing numbers pick up as we ascend. Then he snickers. "The future Rebel King?"

I try to remain stoic, but I'm not successful. "I thought it sounded good at the time."

"It didn't."

"I'm still workshopping it."

When we reach the top floor, we're greeted by three vampires in the vestibule who I can only assume are the welcoming committee. They must really stand out in this city, considering the entire population sports year-round tans but they look like they just escaped from a maximum-security prison in Siberia.

The guy in the middle is wearing a suit, denoting him as the higher-up, while the ones flanking him are in black military-style T-shirts and cargo pants with AKs at the ready. A little much in my opinion, but most Russians aren't exactly known for their subtlety and Russian *vampires* even less so.

"Your Highness, to what do we owe this surprise visit?" the suit-wearing vamp asks.

"That's a discussion for me and Dmitri. Now, can you take us to him, or am I going to have problems with you like I did downstairs?"

"Not at all," he says with a grin, but it doesn't reach his eyes. "Follow me, please."

He shows us into the penthouse and leads us through the grandiose home of the head of the largest clan of vampires on the West Coast. There is a fortune in art displayed. I recognize the works of Michelangelo, Rembrandt, and Monet, along with some I've never seen before. Given Dmitri's age, it's possible they're original and exclusive pieces given to him directly from the artists themselves. I'm not an art buff, but even I would be impressed by that.

Finally, we reach the formal dining room. We both scan the space, cataloging details and looking for anything that might cause problems. Low overhead lighting, a floral centerpiece bookended by lit tapered candles, soft music playing from a record player in the corner, and a steak dinner on fine china in front of the empty seat adjacent to the man sitting at the head of a polished dark wood table.

Dmitri "D'yavol" Romanov is well over six foot and as broad as Connor. In his human life, he had been a *bogatyr,* a legendary Russian warrior similar to the Knights of the Round Table. He was ruthless in cutting down his enemies, earning him "the Devil" nickname. Intimidating in his own right, his pale-blue eyes remind me of polar ice caps and the scar bisecting his left eyebrow only adds to his prison-chic look.

From what I can tell, he appears to have maintained the physical discipline that made the *bogatyr* into such elite fighters. I have to wonder if he's still as honorable as their reputation suggests. Guess I'm about to find out.

Connor posts up at the threshold of the room so he can keep an eye on me while also looking out for anyone approaching.

"Sorry to interrupt your dinner, Romanov, but this couldn't wait. There somewhere we can talk?"

Dmitri smiles wide, his fangs glinting in the candlelight as he sits back in his chair. "Prince Tiernan, welcome. Have a seat, we will talk here."

"This conversation isn't for mixed company. It won't take long, then you can get back to your date."

"Nonsense," he says. "I must insist. I promise my *date* will not be an issue."

I look back at Connor to see what he thinks, and he just shrugs. *Real helpful, dude.* I'm about to suggest that we can wait in a study or another room until he's done eating when someone enters from the kitchen through the swinging door. I expect to see a chef or possibly a butler. The way Connor steps in front of me and pulls his gun says he's expecting a threat. The wry smile on Dmitri's face says he's expecting his date.

"Jesus, D, that's the last time you send me on a fucking scavenger hunt in your wine cellar—"

Everyone in the room freezes and my mouth drops open. We were all wrong. At least Connor and I were. But Dmitri looks pleased as punch that my *baby brother* just walked in from his kitchen holding what was likely a very expensive bottle of wine.

Connor and I speak simultaneously. *"Finnian?"*

"What the fuck are you guys doing here?"

"Us? What are *you* doing here? Wait, are you two dating? A fucking *vamp*, Finni? No offense, Romanov."

Dmitri arches his scarred brow and narrows his eyes slightly. "Some taken, Verran."

Connor gives me the *seriously, dude?* look, and I realize I already may have fucked this up. Finn scowls at me like I just insulted his personal bench press record. "No, we're not dating." Handing the bottle of wine to his host, he takes his seat and starts cutting his steak. "Dmitri has commitment issues not even Freud could crack."

Romanov shrugs, my earlier blunder apparently already forgotten. "Is true. Freud tried."

In a lame attempt to smooth things over, I say, "Okay, but you can see why I asked."

Finn's fork pauses halfway to his mouth. He looks up at me with confusion and the tips of his ears twitch in irritation. Connor and I pointedly scan the room, our eyes landing on all the signs. He seems to take in the setting for the first time and finally nods. "That's fair."

Dmitri gestures toward the seat across from my brother.

"Sit. We will talk."

Finn watches me lower myself into the chair as he chews a mouthful of steak and cuts his next piece so it's ready for the next bite. It's only now that I realize there are *three* ribeyes stacked and two baked potatoes on his plate. My little brother is a tank—always has been—and now I know why. The only time we really share any meals are business dinners with Caiden or when our mother guilts us into family time at her favorite restaurant, and he certainly doesn't eat like this at either of those events.

As Dmitri pours a glass of the dark red merlot, I say to Finn, "That's enough to feed a team of lumberjacks, brother. Got something you want to tell me? Should I be planning a double baby shower with you and Brynnie?" He gives me a droll look, picks up his water glass, and extends his middle finger as he takes a drink.

Dmitri chuckles and hands me the wine. "Ah, the fun of brotherly banter. It is something I envy. If I dared such a gesture with my sister, she would stab me in the heart with her silver dagger. It would not kill me, but it would hurt like a bitch."

I hear Connor clear his throat from where he's standing near the door again. Looking back at him, I watch as he gives a pointed glance at Finn, then Dmitri, reminding me there are mysteries to solve and questions that need answering.

"Right," I say, returning my attention to my brother. "Before I share my reason for being here, I think you owe me an explanation of why I found you casually eating dinner with the leader of the largest vampire clan on the West Coast."

Finn looks to his host as though he's asking permission to tell me—*his older brother*—about his business. And that irks me ten ways to hell and back. "Finni," I bark, pulling his attention back to me. "Tell me why you're here."

He swallows his food and holds my gaze. There's a flash of uncertainty there, and it reminds me so much of the little boy Caiden and I doted on. He's always been a people pleaser, our Finni. Trying to make everyone around him happy even if it was at the cost of his own happiness. And there was no one more loyal. I'm worried Dmitri Romanov is somehow exploiting that loyalty to get Finnian involved in whatever nefarious crap Russian vamps get up to.

"This calls for something stronger, yes?" Romanov crosses to an ornate liquor cart along the side wall and lifts the top from a black crystal decanter.

"Never been a fan of vodka. I'm good with this." I swirl the wine around my glass and take another drink as I keep my eyes on my brother.

"Is not vodka," he says, his thick accent making it sound like *wodka*. "Is AB-negative, the most rare blood type in the world. Very hard to find."

He pours it into a wine glass and the color looks the same as the liquid in mine, making my stomach turn. I set it away from me on the table. "Well, I *was* enjoying that."

Finn aims an amused smirk my way as he takes a huge bite of a loaded baked potato. "Now you know why I stick to water here."

"Thanks for the heads up, dick."

"Welcome."

Dmitri resumes his spot at the head of the table and shakes his head. "I do not understand you fae. What is the point of having fangs if not to aid in feeding from a vein?"

Historically, our fangs *were* used to feed off others. It was used as a war tactic, a way to harness another fae's magic for use in battle. But the One True Queen banished the practice centuries before we were ever exiled, fearing another power-hungry king or queen would collect enough magic to overthrow her.

That doesn't mean it's *never* done. Mates enjoy drinking from each other all the time. But even then, it's an intimate, often erotic act. We don't store their blood in crystal decanters to casually sip over some light conversation. That's just gross.

But since I'm doing my best not to insult the lord of the vampires, and we don't make a habit of sharing fae secrets with outsiders, I bring the discussion back around to my brother.

"The reason you're here?"

Finn glances at Dmitri, who gives him a slight nod. That he needs permission to tell me anything irks me, but I let it go. "I compete in an underground fight club for *others*, both here and in Vegas, in secret arenas beneath the boxing gyms Dmitri owns."

"You're fucking joking." When no one laughs, I drag both hands down my face and tell myself that flipping tables isn't a good idea. "Do you know how dangerous that is, considering who you are?"

"Of course I know, I'm not a kid anymore, Tier. And if you haven't noticed, I'm a lot bigger and stronger than most of the *others* in this realm. I only lose when I want to."

"Why the hell would you *want* to lose?"

"To gain favor with anyone who might have information on Dmitri's sister. She went missing six months ago."

"Fuck, Romanov, I'm sorry to hear that," I say sincerely. "I didn't know you even had a sister before today."

"She is not my *sestra* by blood, but we have been family for many centuries, long before the fae came to this world. Because your *brat*'s association with me has been kept secret, he is able to hear things I cannot. And I will do *anything* to find her and bring her home."

"I understand. And while I realize that my brother is his own person and can make his own choices, I speak for myself and our older brother when I say that if anything happens to Finn, we'll be coming for you."

Dmitri swirls his dinner around in the glass as he regards me for several tense moments. Finally, he dips his chin in a slight nod. "I would expect nothing less. Now, my patience and hospitality only go so far. It is your turn to answer why *you* are here."

"We've been having some unorthodox tragedies happening in Vegas. I was wondering if you knew anything about them."

"What sort of tragedies?"

"The sort where fae are being murdered with iron blades."

He studies me for several seconds before finally speaking. "Did you come to ask whether I have information? Or whether I am the one behind them?"

Finn freezes. "No way, Dmitri, we would never accuse you of that."

Dmitri never takes his eyes off me. "I believe that *you* would not accuse me, comrade, but I do not believe it of *him*."

"Tiernan," Finn says. "Tell him that's not why you came."

Keeping my gaze locked on the vampire, I answer my brother. "I'm here to eliminate him as a suspect."

"On what grounds? What could he possibly have to gain from being the one behind the murders?"

"Maybe he wants our city, Finn. He already has a toehold with his gym and secret fight club. Maybe he wants the rest of it, too. The point is, I don't know, which is why I'm here."

Dmitri drains what's left in his glass, then sets it carefully on the table. I don't sense an elevation in energy, or see any anger in his mannerisms, but that doesn't mean I trust what's going on inside his mind.

"If you had accused me of such a thing six months ago, I would have ripped your throat out where you sit," he says calmly. "But as you now know, I have had more important things to worry about than staging a coup against the Dark Fae. Besides, I already have a city. I have no wish for another."

I hear Connor's phone buzz from across the room as the leader of the Romanov Clan and I engage each other in a stare-off. Connor answers and speaks quietly to whoever is calling, but I'm too focused on watching for the slightest tick of movement from a male who has the speed and strength to rip my head clean from my body before I even know it's happening.

"All right, I think we have what we need. For the record, I'll be reporting back that you're not behind the attacks in Vegas. I consider myself an extremely good judge of character, and my baby brother—while too much of a bleeding heart at times—doesn't have a habit of getting in league with dishonorable individuals. If he vouches for you, that's good enough for me. Again, I'm sorry about your sister. I hope Finn can help you find her."

"Thank you, Prince Tiernan. I hope so, too."

Finn breathes an audible sigh of relief and checks the time on his sports watch. "If you guys are done giving each other the death stare now, I'm heading out. My fight's in two hours and I still need to get ready." We all stand up, and Finn comes around to give me one of his famous bear hugs. "Thanks, man. I'll be home tomorrow. Don't say anything to Caiden—I want to be the one to tell him."

"Let's maybe hold off on this one for a while," I say. "He has enough on his plate right now. Just don't get into a situation you can't get out of, you hear me?"

"I'll be careful, T. See you tomorrow."

Once Finn is gone, I extend my hand to Dmitri as an olive branch just to be safe. He accepts it, and I breathe a sigh of relief. Somehow, even with all the missteps along the way, I kept my promise to Seamus. I managed to avoid starting a supernatural war.

"Tiernan." The seriousness in Connor's tone puts me on alert. He steps in close, concern swimming in his eyes. "That was Caiden. We need to get back to Vegas ASAP."

"Did something happen with Bryn?" He shakes his head, and I know. Icy fear forms a lump so large in my throat I barely get her name out. "Fi."

"She and her mom were attacked. They made it to the hospital, but…"

A storm of volatile emotions rages in me and I square up with my friend. "But *what*, Con?"

"They had to call for Bryn. I'm sorry, that's all I know."

My stomach and heart drop all at once. As a Darklight, my sister-in-law has incredible healing powers. If the hospital called her in for help, it can only mean one thing.

Someone is close to death.

CHAPTER EIGHT

FIONA

"Fiona?"

"Mom? Oh thank the gods." I thought I'd cried myself dry hours ago, but at the sight of her awake, the waterworks threaten to start up again on full blast. Bolting forward, I reach for her hand closest to me. "How are you feeling? Should I get the nurse?"

I start to get up, but she curls her fingers around mine in a weak attempt to hold me in place. "Not yet. Just let me look at you, make sure you're all right."

I almost laugh at the absurdity of that. She has no reason to be worried about me. The worst I got were bruises on my biceps and the result of the punch to my cheek that knocked me out before they left my mom for dead and me unable to call for help until I eventually came to thirty minutes later.

My left cheekbone might have a dark purple bruise and hurt like a bitch, but compared to my mom when we arrived, I'm in flawless condition. I didn't even let Bryn heal me, insisting she use every ounce of her strength for Mom. "I'm fine, I promise."

She sighs, letting her eyes drift closed as she whispers a

tribute of thanks to Rhiannon. Her voice is raspy and she appears frail, reminding me that she's still injured despite nothing visible. Bryn's healing powers were able to do a *lot* to help the smaller issues like cuts, bruises, and even broken ribs.

What she'd had trouble with was the three-inch stab wound in Mom's stomach from an iron dagger. Bryn had reversed a similar fatal infliction for Finnian after he'd jumped in front of the Day King's blade to take the strike that was meant for her. She'd saved his life, managing to pull him back from the brink of death and seal the wound.

But that all happened within minutes. The iron had barely had time to infect him, whereas it had over an hour to do its damage to my mom. It took another hour of Bryn working consistently, using her Darklight power to mend her injuries and draw out the toxins left behind by the iron.

Like Finn, Mom was left with a permanent scar. A negligible price compared to death. I'd sobbed with immense relief and gratitude—to the gods, to Bryn, to all the doctors and nurses who'd kept her alive until my friend could arrive. But it was short-lived. Within minutes, her skin went from pink back to red. Then it began puckering and pulling at the seam until the sides started to bisect. It took three more times before it finally stabilized, nearly depleting all of Bryn's magic.

Caiden had tried to convince her to stop, worried for her health and that of their baby, but she'd refused to give up until my mom's body stopped rejecting the procedure. After that, she allowed Caiden to command that she rest on the condition that they go to the penthouse at Nightfall so she would only be minutes away if she was needed again.

"Mom, I need to check your wound, okay?" She nods. Rising, I pull the thin blanket down and gently part the open front of her gown enough to examine her abdomen. Exhaling the breath I'd been holding, I put her back together and tuck her in. Needing to be close to her, I sit on the edge of the bed next to her and pull her hand into my lap.

"It looks good," I reassure her with a smile. "One more title for Bryn. She started as my best friend, then my cousin, and now certified miracle worker. I should get her some business cards. What do you think?"

Something flashes over my mom's face, then she averts her eyes like she's staring out the window. Except the drapes are pulled closed, so there's nothing to look at. She swallows thickly and blinks rapidly against fresh tears welling in her eyes.

A million thoughts have raced through my mind since waking up next to my mom as she lay bleeding out on the pavement. Thoughts and images I've tried hard to lock away because if I allow them free rein right now, I'll break. Those things will have to wait until some undetermined time in the future when it's safe for me to unpack them, and because I've always been great at compartmentalizing, they will.

However, there's one thing I haven't been able to ignore. It's been incessantly scratching at the walls of my brain, demanding to be addressed. And I think it's the same thing plaguing my mom right now.

"Mom," I say, struggling to push the words past the lump in my throat. "How did you know he wouldn't want to hurt me?"

She turned her head and held my gaze for several seconds before sighing. "Because they're not hunting your kind."

"*My* kind," I muse, trying to understand what she meant. And then it clicked. "You mean because I'm part human."

"No, *mo stóirín*," she says softly as a tear finally spills free to roll down her smooth cheek. "It's because you *are* human."

There's a ringing in my ears, like I just left a rock concert where I spent the last two hours standing next to the speakers. That punch I took earlier must have caused some latent damage. I should ask for something to stop the shooting pain suddenly building behind my eyes. And I'm hearing things wrong. I must be, because there's no way my mom just dropped a nuclear-level bomb on me like that out of nowhere. She would never. And more than that—*it's impossible.*

I shake my head vigorously. "No, that—" A choking sob escapes before I swallow it back. "That doesn't make any sense. You're not thinking clearly, everything happened so fast, and you..."

I trail off, the look in her eyes telling me I can't wish this away. That the truth, however impossible, is still the truth. And yet, there's still a tiny thread of hope I'm holding on to, praying to Rhiannon that this is all a mistake. That I just have to get to the bottom of this mystery to solve it so the ending of this story will be in my favor. That I won't learn my entire life has been one giant lie.

"How?" I ask with a voice shredded with fear. "How is that even possible?"

"I vowed to my sister and her mate that I would keep their baby far out of Talek Edevane's reach, which is why I chose to block her magic and place her in the care of Jack and Emily Meara."

I knit my brows in confusion, unsure why she'd be telling me what I already know. "Because they'd been trying for years to get pregnant and it never worked, so you arranged it so they were able to raise Bryn as their own, making her a changeling—a fae baby raised in the human world unbeknownst to the parents."

"Yes, Bryn is a changeling, which was an act abolished by Queen Aine and made punishable by death. Before her reign over all of Faerie, King Ruaidri arranged for regular changelings to be placed in this world with human parents. Who he got in return were either used as servants or sacrifices to appease Balor, the demonic god of death."

"Sacrifices?" Out of everything she could have mentioned, human sacrifices wasn't one I expected. The very thought that anyone could do that, whether they were a different race or not, is horrifying. "Wait, what do you mean 'who he got in return'? I thought 'changeling' meant they changed from living as a fae to that of a human."

"No, *mo stóirín*," she says sadly, as though she's apologizing, but for what? For not teaching me the definition of a word we rarely use because it's become obsolete in the last thousand years? "They are called that because they are changed out for the human couple's baby."

I know she's trying to tell me something. I know it should be obvious. But my brain is smarter than my conscious mind right now, and it's doing its best to protect me. "That was the case back then, you mean, right? But not this time with Bryn. Jack and Emily weren't able to get pregnant, that's what you told me."

"Yes, I did, and it's the truth. They weren't able to get pregnant. But then they *were*. After all the years of infertility drugs and IVF, they finally conceived, and Emily carried their baby to term." New tears spill over my mom's cheeks as she swallows thickly and continues. "A beautiful little girl with red hair and eyes the color of the sky on a summer day."

I cover my mouth with my hand and shake my head in denial. No, this isn't right. The only thing I was sure of in life was who my mother was, that we were a team, just us against the world.

She reaches for my other hand, but I pull it away, unable to process her words and her touch at the same time. "I'm so sorry I never told you before," she says in a plea. "I didn't know how to tell you, and I was afraid you would demand answers I couldn't give you."

"Like who my *real* parents are. Because you couldn't let them find out that Bryn wasn't really their child. That would have risked her safety. Right?" She doesn't say anything because she *can't*. To deny it would be a lie. And fae can't lie.

"How? How has no one noticed that I'm human?"

"The peppermint-nettle tea," she says. "You weren't wrong when you said it was made with magic. It creates the temporary illusion of fae energy. As long as I made sure you drank it at least once a month, you read no different than any other fae. When you came of age, I added contraceptive properties for your protection."

"Because unmated fae don't need to worry about accidental pregnancies. Gods, you thought of everything. All I needed were some contacts, fake teeth, and to hide my ears." I shake my head and swipe angrily at my tears. I can't believe I didn't see it before. I've never had any powers to speak of, not even glamouring. No preternatural abilities either. "What about the way I heal? Whenever I got hurt as a kid I always healed right away. How could I have done that if I'm human?"

"When fae of different powers mate, their offspring will inherit one of their powers more dominantly than the other. But they still have small amounts from the other parent. Our father's conjuring abilities passed on to me and Kiera. But I have enough of my mother's healing power in me to fix very small things. Growing up, you never had any serious injuries. Cuts, scrapes, things like that. If you think back, you only healed once I touched you."

My mind pulls up memories from my past, showing me all the proof to back up her statement. It's true. There is literally nothing special about me. The only reason I believed I was fae is because no one ever questioned it—not even me.

"You told me I was fae but that there was human blood on my dad's side, which is what made me different. So how were you able to lie? Is that a magic spell, too?"

"No, there is no magic spell for that. I never actually told you that you were fae, just like I never actually told you that you are my daughter. I raised you, so what I was to you was never brought into question by you or anyone else. I told you there was human blood on your father's side, which is the truth because your father and all his ancestors were human."

"My inability to lie?"

At least she has the decency to look guilty as she admits, "That *was* a spell when you were little. But by the time you were a preteen, you didn't need it. You thought you couldn't lie, so you didn't."

I let out a humorless laugh. "Gods, you duped me with a string of fae truths." Standing, I begin pacing the room like a trapped animal in a cage. I feel like a shotgun went off in my brain and the buckshot is tearing its way through twenty-six years of memories so that the truth—the *real* truth—can rewrite my history, whether I want it to or not.

It's all been a lie. *Everything.* The most important person in my life is essentially my kidnapper. I will never know my real parents because they were killed by the Light King in an effort to isolate Bryn so she could be manipulated more easily for his own machinations against Caiden.

The life I was meant to have was stolen from me. All because of a power play between warring factions of a race that isn't even mine.

"I need to leave," I say distractedly. "I need time to process this and figure out what I'm going to do."

"*Mo stóirín*, please. I can't tell you how sorry I am about Jack and Emily. I planned on finding some small way of bringing them into your life, but then they had the accident and…"

She closes her eyes briefly and takes a breath to regroup. "There hasn't been a day that I haven't regretted not arranging for you to meet them sooner. But I can't regret taking you. You were their miracle baby, but you were also mine. I wasn't like my sister. I never wanted a mate or children. Our mother said I was born a free spirit, unable to be tied down by anything or anyone, and she was right. Until you."

"Fiona, I've lived the better part of three centuries, and it wasn't until I saw you in the hospital nursery that I longed to be tied down—to *you*. When I stood over your bassinet, you looked up at me with those beautiful blue eyes, and I swear to Rhiannon, you smiled. I felt like I'd finally found what I hadn't even known I was searching for. You *are* my little treasure. You are worth more to me than all the riches of Faerie and this world combined. You must believe me."

It takes a minute for my words to scrape their way past the boulder lodged in my throat, but I finally manage it. "I do. There's no way to fae-truth what you just told me. Your love for me is the one thing about my life I know hasn't been a lie. The rest..." My shoulder lifts in a weak attempt at a half shrug. I barely have enough energy to remain upright at this point. "It's a toss-up."

"I never meant to hurt you, *mo stóirín*. I'm sorry."

"I know that, too," I say thickly. "Rian's been assigned to be my shadow. I think I'll ask him to take me home now so I can get some sleep."

Normally, this is the part where we would hug and express our love for one another before saying goodbye. I've never not known how to act with my mother, but right now, we just stare at each other for long moments, me standing awkwardly on the other side of the room and her bound to the hospital bed.

She breaks the awkward silence first. "Fiona, I understand that this is all a lot and it's making you restless. And I know it's not fair to ask for any favors right now, but I'm going to anyway. Please don't make any big decisions about your future until I'm home and we can talk some more."

"Get some sleep. I'll let the nurse know you're awake."

Just as I reach the door, she calls out to me. "Fiona, promise me you won't leave."

I glance back at her. "I promise I won't leave."

Well, look at that, I think to myself as I walk down the hospital corridor with Rian close behind. *I guess I can lie.*

CHAPTER NINE

TIERNAN

On our drive back, Caiden kept us updated on Erin's status as Bryn continued to work on her. When he told me that Fiona hadn't been hurt, relief sliced through me, followed closely by guilt for being glad it wasn't the other way around. I broke just about every traffic law that existed between the City of Angels and Sin City and it still felt like an eternity in limbo before I passed through Midnight Manor's gate.

Caiden had offered to take Fiona with him and Bryn to the penthouse at Nightfall so she could get rest while remaining close to the hospital in case anything happened, but she'd insisted on staying with Erin in her room. So that's where I was headed until Rian texted and said she had him bring her home.

I don't waste the seconds it would take to park in the garage, I just throw it into park in front of the house and leave it running for Connor to take care of. Barely stopping myself before barging into her room unannounced, I take a deep breath, then knock softly on her door.

"Fiona, it's me. Can I come in?"

When she doesn't answer, I press my head against the

wood and clench my fists at my sides to keep from reaching for the handle. No matter how much I want to lay eyes on her to make sure she's okay, I shouldn't enter without her permission. Assuming she's sleeping, I force myself to take a step back. Then another. And another.

Nope, don't like that. I move forward a step. Three was too far, two feels better. I take a deep breath and blow it out. *Yeah, okay, two is good.* I'll just stay here in the hall until she wakes up, then. That's fine, right? I frown.

"Wait, is this creepy? Maybe this is creepy." I try to imagine how Fiona would feel, opening the door to find a fiercely stern male standing outside her room and staring at her door like he's been spying on her with X-ray vision or something. "Fuck," I mutter. "Definitely creepy."

Pacing. Pacing is a perfectly acceptable form of waiting. People do it all the time—in hospital hallways, outside board rooms, while waiting for—

A crash comes from her room. "Fiona!"

Racing inside, I follow the sounds and skid to a halt at the open bathroom door. The first thing I see is a dark purple bruise marring her perfect cheek, and rage boils in my veins. Healing slowly must be one of the traits she inherited from the halfling bloodline. Since Caiden doesn't know about Fiona's ancestry, he would have expected it to be gone by the time I got here. Still, I'm going to have a little talk with my older brother later about what constitutes "hurt."

I quickly scan the rest of her to determine if he left anything else out, but I don't see any other injuries. She's standing on the far side of the small room, wrapped in a towel that's tucked into itself above her breasts. Her red hair is more auburn when it's wet, standing out even more against the fair, freckle-dusted skin of her shoulders.

But it's her eyes that arrest me. Cerulean blue and filled with unshed tears make them look like the gods gifted her tiny pools of Caribbean water to look through. And even knowing it's a glamour, I can't help but favor this color over the golden one Darks share. Most don't bother changing our eye color, we just take the glow out of them, make them appear like they would if we were human.

But blue eyes have always suited Fiona better, in my opinion. Not that I'd ever tell *her* that; I'm a lovable asshole, not an *asshole* asshole.

"I'm sorry. My hands were wet and it slipped," she says. That's when I notice what caused the crashing sound. Between us, shattered glass blankets the light-gray tile with a pile of cotton balls plopped in the center. "It looked expensive. I'll pay to replace it or—"

"*Fi.*" I wait for her to meet my gaze. The poor thing looks lost, and all I want to do is pull her into my arms and hold her for a week straight until I'm absolutely convinced that she's all right. "Stay where you are, don't even lift a foot up. I'll be right back."

It only takes me a minute to grab a broom and dustpan from the closet at the end of the hall and return. "Hold on, I'm going to sweep everything into a pile, then I'll come get you, okay?"

She nods and watches me as I make quick work of the task, leaving the shards of glass and puffs of cotton in a heap by the wall. I'll get a cleaning service in here first thing to take care of the rest. Plus, they'll be able to fill in for Fi. She could use the time off, and I know she'll want to take care of Erin until she's at 100 percent, too.

Grabbing the fuzzy pink robe from the hook near the door, I cross over to where she's waiting. "Next step. We'll put your robe on, then I'm going to carry you over to the counter and rinse your feet off to get any glass dust that may be on you. Then I'll carry you out of the bathroom, leaving my shoes at the door so I don't track anything through the carpet. Sound good?"

She opens her mouth, but nothing comes out the first time. She clears her throat softly, then tries again. "Yes, okay."

Standing in front of her, I wrap the robe around her shoulders and hold it together in the front while she maneuvers her arms into the sleeves. Our eyes watch my hand as it slips between the sides to grab the towel and pull until it falls to pool around her feet.

Feet. Glass. Oh, right, I'm supposed to be helping. "Okay, hold on." Just as she finishes belting the plush material, I pick her up and revel in the way she feels cradled against my chest. Even after sweeping, the sound of glass bits crunching beneath my shoes tells me I was right in not letting her move.

I deposit her sideways between the two sinks, then lower her feet into the left basin. Once the water is warm, I use my cupped hand to pour it over her shins and all the way down to the tips of her chipped painted toes.

"Neon green?" I ask with raised brows. She's more of a pastel girl, I've noticed, the soft palette of her wardrobe in direct contrast to her bold personality.

"It was a joke I played on my mom at last month's mani-pedi day. She's always choosing shades of green, so I picked the gaudiest one they had. Then I told her how much I loved it and wanted us to match." A small smile creeps onto her face. "I kept up the act all day, making sure to point out our matching fluorescent green pedicures to everyone, even complete strangers. When I finally confessed, she ranted for a solid five minutes that she paid good money for an ugly pedicure, all so I could entertain myself. But then we couldn't stop laughing about all the times she had to pretend to like it because *I* pretended to like it."

"That was a good one," I say, chuckling at the image her story portrayed. Once I'm confident she doesn't have any stray glass that could cut her, I turn the water off and use a small towel to dry her. "My mom's great in her own ways, but

Morgan Scannell has *never* been the kind of parent you joke around with. You're really lucky to have the close relationship with your mom that you do."

Sensing a sudden shift in her mood, I look up to find her smile has been replaced with tears and a trembling chin. "Hey, hey, hey, come here, I've got you."

I pick her up, walk to the bathroom door, and kick off my shoes before continuing into the carpeted bedroom. I set her down gently on the edge of the bed and kneel in front of her. Brushing the hair away from her face, I'm careful not to touch the bruise on her cheek.

"I'm sorry I wasn't here for you sooner, Little Red. I left as soon as Caiden called, but I was all the way in L.A. with Connor." She sniffles and looks up at me through spiky, wet lashes. Something passes over her face at the mention of L.A., but then it's gone before I can figure out what it is. "I got here as quick as I could, but it wasn't good enough. I hate that I wasn't here when you needed me, Fi. I'm so sorry."

She shakes her head. "You don't need to apologize. I'm not your responsibility, and your life doesn't stop just because mine does."

"No, but wouldn't it be great if it did?" I offer her a crooked smile, hoping to lighten things a little. The corners of her mouth tug up the slightest bit, but the action doesn't reach those beautiful blue eyes. I study her intently, desperately wanting to solve her puzzle but feeling like I'm missing half the pieces. "Why the glamour?"

She shrugs. "Seems I'm stuck like this now."

I nod. "Sometimes our magic does that in times of high stress. It'll kick off on its own, probably after you get some sleep. Don't worry, though. I like you like this, too."

Sadness clouds her eyes in shades of gray. "What if I'm stuck like this forever? I bet you wouldn't like it then, would you?"

I stroke my thumb along her jaw. *Ah, sweetheart, if you only knew the truth.* "The answer doesn't matter because you *won't* be like this forever, I promise."

Her brow furrows and her shoulders sag as though she's disappointed in my answer. Does she not believe me? We stare at each other for several seconds, and it takes every ounce of restraint not to gather her up in my arms and hold on to her. But then she takes matters into her own hands and pulls me in for a kiss.

Instantly I react, pushing up on my knees and wrapping my arms around her small waist to pull her flush against my stomach. She hugs my hips with her thighs and hooks her heels behind me while twining her arms around my neck.

Her robe is doing very little to shield her body from me. With her legs splayed, I can feel the heat from her bare pussy through my shirt. The top has fallen off one shoulder, baring a creamy breast that beckons my hand to knead and mold. She moans and opens up to me, allowing my tongue to dive in and plunder the depths of her mouth, claiming it as my own.

Fiona fists my hair as she lifts her chin to give me access to her throat. I trace the vein that runs along the side of her neck and tease it with the tip of a fang, wishing I could taste her in a way no one else has.

"Tiernan," she whimpers.

What the hell am I doing? Reality dumps over me like ice water. *Fuck, I'm such a dick.* I slowly pull away and disentangle her from my body, then fix her robe for her. She gathers the two sides and pulls them more tightly around her, giving herself a hug in the process as she shuts down emotionally.

"Is something wrong?" she asks.

"You've had a long night. You should sleep."

"Right. Sleep." Her tone is wooden, almost hollow, but she doesn't give me a chance to think on it further before she moves up the bed and gets under the covers, robe and all.

I tuck her in, place a chaste kiss on her forehead, then gather my shoes.

On my way out of her room, I toss out parting instructions I hope she'll follow, but Fiona's always been too stubborn for her own good. "Get some rest, Little Red, and text me if you need anything later. I'll be here all day."

"Tiernan," she calls out just before the door closes. I lean back into the room, hoping she'll ask me to stay while also praying that she won't. "Thank you for…" She pauses, seeming to change her mind about what she wants to say. "For the assist in the bathroom."

I almost joke about finally getting to be her knight in shining armor. But the angry purple mark on her cheek reminds me of just how badly I failed her. When she needed protection, when she needed saving, I wasn't there.

But I will be what she needs in *this* moment, and all the moments moving forward. Right now, it isn't a lascivious lover or a court jester telling jokes. It's a friend, someone who won't take advantage of her when she's feeling vulnerable or deflect her pain with humor. Someone she can count on, no matter what.

"I'll always help you, Fi. Whenever and whatever you need, all you have to do is ask." I genuinely mean it, and she knows it's the truth. Because it has to be. "I'll see you in a little while, okay?"

She musters up a sad smile that about breaks my fucking heart. "See you in a little while."

CHAPTER TEN

FIONA

It's only been an hour since Tiernan left my room, and an hour and one minute since I lied for the second time in my whole life. I have no intention of seeing anyone today, least of all Tiernan or my mom. I need some time to think, to get away and process everything.

Except what happened with Tiernan. I don't want to *remember* it, much less process it. It was like one gut-punch after another.

He mentioned being in L.A. when Caiden called. I know it wasn't Nightfall or Night Court business. Since he moved into the manor, I've taken it upon myself to moonlight as Tier's kinda-sorta personal assistant. Unlike his older brother, the middle Verran requires an occasional kick in the ass to ensure he arrives to things on time, and there's nothing on his calendar until tomorrow. L.A. is one of his favorite party spots, so he was probably lap deep in women when he got the call. Not my concern, I know, but it doesn't mean the thought doesn't sting.

Then, when I asked whether he'd like it if I looked human all the time, he tried placating me with a non-answer—typical fae truth tactic—because obviously telling me the honest to gods truth would upset me.

And last but not least, in a totally spontaneous move, I practically threw myself at him, giving him exactly what he's wanted for months—what we've *both* wanted—but we never made it past kissing before he put a stop to it. That was the most *un*-Tiernan thing ever. Makes it kind of hard not to believe that he's just not attracted to me the same way without my fangs and contacts.

So yeah, I'm leaving. I won't go far. As much as I'd like to buy a one-way ticket to someplace tropical where I can lick my wounds on a beach while sipping Mai Tais, I need to be able to get back quickly if anything happens. Just because I feel the need to throw myself a pity party doesn't mean I've forgotten that fae are being hunted and put down like rabid dogs.

I pick up my carry-on and walk quietly down the hall to the stairs. It's not even seven a.m. so the house is still quiet. Or so I thought.

When I reach the first landing, I stop at the sound of voices coming from the living room down below. I recognize Tiernan's voice and of course Seamus's, but there are two others that I don't know by the sound of them. To get out of the house, I'll have to walk right by them, and I was trying to escape without anyone noticing. *Maybe they won't be long.*

I lower myself onto the bottom stair and tuck my suitcase against my knees as I listen. I should probably just go back to my room and try again later, but I'm curious as to why Tiernan is having a meeting this early in the manor.

"Chief McCarthy, thanks for agreeing to meet here instead of the ToR." That's Tiernan's deep timbre, and now one of the mystery guests is solved. "Fiona's resting now, but I want to be here in case she needs…anything."

Was that a pause I heard? Was he going to say "in case she needs *me*"? My brow furrows and I worry my lip with blunt teeth, having abandoned all pretenses and accessories for appearing as fae. Godsdamn it, even just hearing his voice again is cracking my resolve to leave, but then he had to go and be considerate and sweet, too. *Ugh!* Why can't he just be the self-centered rebel prince-slash-future king everyone thinks he is?

Seamus speaks to Chief McCarthy next. "Aleck, what new developments have there been since yesterday? In your message you mentioned the attack on Erin Jewel wasn't an isolated incident. How many were there?"

"Altogether, there were nine separate instances throughout the city. One of them was Lord Tynam of the Dark Council. Lord Dolan, here, was the one who found him."

The last voice in the room, which is apparently the speaker of the Council, is clipped with restrained anger. "They beat him so badly, he was unrecognizable. I knew it to be him from his family line's Armas ring they left on his finger. The detectives on scene confirmed his identity from his wallet that still held over a thousand dollars in cash. Somehow it seems worse that they didn't even bother to rob him."

"The fact they didn't gives us an idea of the kind of people we're dealing with, though," Chief McCarthy says. "They don't care about the money. Now, it could be that they're wealthy enough that a dozen C-notes and a ring with a ruby as big as a walnut doesn't faze them. But people with that kind of net worth aren't the type to get their hands dirty. Not directly."

"No, this is personal," Tiernan says. "Whatever their motives are, it's clear they want us to know that much. It's why they're not trying to hide what they're doing."

Chief McCarthy says, "Exactly. And that reveals a sense of entitlement, of righteousness. I think what we're looking for is an extremist group of some kind. Obviously, they have something against Dark Fae, but we need to know if it's *just* us. Since any contact with the Light Fae is temporarily prohibited, we're reaching out to the heads of the major families from the three biggest *other* factions in the U.S.—the Marceau pack in New Orleans, the Romanov vampire clan in Los Angeles, and the Amari djinn in New York. If they're experiencing anything similar, we could be looking at a national hunt of the supernatural, maybe even global."

I cover my mouth to muffle the involuntary gasp. The last great war between humans and *others* was in the early 1200s during the Mongol invasion of what is now Russia. Batu Khan, the then leader of the Mongols, invaded Russia believing that a vampire might change him and grant him eternal life. Instead, he and his entire army were wiped out by a united army of supernatural races who were assisted by the legendary *bogatyr* warriors. Most of the *bogatyrs* died that day as well.

Those who survived are now part of the supernatural world as vampires. Batu and his quest were mostly lost to history in favor of his much more successful and savage grandfather, Genghis. But as devastating as that was, it had happened in a concentrated area. What would it be like if we—I mean, *they*—are hunted all over the world?

Tiernan must have moved closer to the stairs because his voice gets louder. "I paid Dmitri a visit last night at his home in L.A. The vampires aren't involved, on either side of the conflict. He didn't know anything about what's been going on here."

That's what he was doing in L.A.? Shame leaves a bitter taste in my mouth. I shouldn't have assumed he was club hopping and partying with celebrities. He hasn't done that since shortly after learning he's to be king, and he definitely wouldn't be doing it now with his people in crisis. I know him better than that, but it's hard not to let my emotions color the lens I see him through sometimes. I need to make a conscious effort to stop doing that.

Well, I *would* make the effort if I was sticking around, but

I'm not. Even if I don't leave Vegas, I won't be coming back to work at the manor. The constant reminder that I don't belong to their world—that I'm *not* fae—would slowly kill me. Much like my sexual frustration has done while living under the same roof as Tiernan and being unable to touch him.

Jesus, Fiona, what the hell happened to you? The me from five years ago would have kicked my ass for being so pathetic. I've always been a masochist, but this is ridiculous.

"So th-that's it, then?" Dolan sputters like he's working himself into a lather. "That bloodthirsty mafia claims they're innocent and we're just going to take their word for it?"

"Respectfully, Lord Speaker," Tiernan says in a tone clearly *devoid* of respect, "in addition to my own intuition, someone I trust implicitly vouches for him and his clan's activity for the last six months. So either *you* decide to trust *me*, or you are welcome to visit Dmitri Romanov and inform him of your uncertainties. I'm sure the Council will vote in a suitable replacement for you as Speaker."

Seamus interjects casually, like Tiernan didn't just launch a thinly veiled threat at the Speaker of the Dark Council. "Hedrek, if we'd listened to you from the start, Prince Tiernan wouldn't have questioned Romanov at all for fear of insulting him. Now you contradict your original demand by suggesting we tell him that his answers aren't believable. Your former opinion was misguided, but your current one is reckless and dangerous.

"Thank you, Your Highness," the old wolf says to Tiernan. "We're grateful for your help with inter-faction relations. Isn't that right, Lord Dolan?"

I roll my lips inward to keep the chuckle bubbling in my chest from escaping. Suddenly I regret not sneaking down a few more steps and risking discovery just so I can see the puckered look on the high lord's face.

"Of course, Regent," he answers quietly. "I apologize for

my outburst, Prince Tiernan. I'm grieving the loss of an old friend and my emotions got the better of me."

I arch a dubious brow. I've never met him personally, but I've been at plenty of the same events as Hedrek Dolan, and I've never seen him act friendly with anyone, not even his fellow high lords. He mostly scowls and observes like he's silently judging everything in his line of sight.

"And for that, you have our condolences. Now that we agree that the Romanov clan is eliminated as possible suspects, we'll move on," Seamus says. "Aleck, based on what you know thus far, does this group appear to be targeting specific fae? Is there a pattern?"

"Before, I would have said yes. Until yesterday, all the victims had either been employed by the royal family or connected to them in some manner, with the locations being centralized near the Strip. But then their M.O. changed, virtually overnight.

"The number of instances more than doubled, and the victim pattern was interrupted. Seven of the cases are regular fae citizens who were found in locations farther out by about half a mile. If they continue with that trajectory, they'll be hunting in the suburbs within the week."

I hear a muttered curse that no doubt came from Tiernan, but Seamus answers. "Then it's time the Crown gives an official statement to our people. Let them know we're doing everything we can to put a stop to this and urge them to remain in their homes as much as possible, especially during the day."

McCarthy interjects. "If I may, Regent, I suggest we do more than urge. I think it would be prudent at this stage to issue a mandatory lockdown for all Darks and also familiars to be safe. Not everyone will comply, but the fewer walking targets we give them, the better."

"Agreed." Lord Dolan.

"Yes, Aleck, you're right, thank you." Seamus. "I'll write

something up and then send it to you for approval in case I miss any important details."

"And how is the Crown handling the ones we've already lost?" Dolan again.

"Their families are contacted immediately and offered assistance for anything they might need, including but not limited to providing security for their Remembrance Ceremonies, delivering ready-made meals to their home every week for a month, and paying for a year of family therapy sessions to help them process the trauma and grief."

The mention of a lockdown reminds me of how humans were affected all over the world when the pandemic hit. The fae didn't have to worry about contracting it, though, so for them it was business as usual.

Tiernan speaks up. "This lockdown won't be easy for them. We're not used to having to hide ourselves away. We've never been the prey, and that's going to grate like hell, so we need to make it as easy for everyone as we can.

"Financial assistance for those temporarily losing income, setting up an at-home system for anyone needing medical care, and providing online schooling for the kids so they don't get behind. I'm sure there are more opportunities to help that I'm not thinking of off the top of my head, so I suggest we have a committee dedicated to handling any aid that might be needed on both a universal and individual case basis."

"Excellent idea, Your Highness," Seamus says. His tone sounds like a mix between surprise and pride, making me smile. I imagine Tiernan's pseudo uncle giving him a look that says *see, I knew you could do this job* and him answering with a snarky *don't get ahead of yourself, geezer* eyeroll.

McCarthy adds, "For my part, I'm doing whatever I can to keep things out of the media while we work every angle we can think of. I've got all the fae in the department, and *only* fae, assigned to these cases so we don't have to hide evidence and we can speak freely with each other."

A cell phone rings only once before I hear a clipped, "McCarthy here." There are a few seconds of silence as the room—and I—wait to hear the news. "Send it over."

He ends the call and exhales heavily. "My team found an encrypted video on the dark web from a group calling themselves the NPO. They posted it in multiple recruitment forums for Nevada and the surrounding states. We decoded it to see if their message lines up with what's happening."

I lean forward and mentally echo Tiernan's, "And?"

"It's them all right. And it's a lot worse than what we thought."

"Put it up there," Tiernan says, and I see the TV above the fireplace turn on.

An image appears on the big screen, then the video begins to play. And for the next five minutes, I watch in absolute horror as the NPO details their plans to wipe out all fae-kind, first in Vegas and eventually *everywhere*.

CHAPTER ELEVEN

TIERNAN

"What in the hell did we just watch?" My question is to no one in particular. I'm not even sure I want an answer.

It can be summed up in one phrase: fearmongering propaganda.

The video didn't ease the viewer in with a casual introduction or friendly "howdy, neighbor." No, they dropped you straight off a fucking cliff, rolling graphic "caught-on-tape" footage of brutal attacks by creatures with inhuman strength and speed, their ears pointed and a flash of sharp fangs visible for a split second before tearing into their screaming victims.

The scenes were sickeningly graphic, the stuff of horror films and sweat-drenched nightmares. Except this was all very, *very* real. I've never seen a fae act so viciously for no reason; it's not in our nature.

When that portion was finally over, it switched to showing a group of nearly two dozen people outfitted in all black military-style gear, the kind you get at an army surplus store, and red faceless masks. Now that they had everyone's attention, it was time for the introduction.

A male, judging from the size and build, spoke using a voice modulator—probably for dramatic effect since the mask and gear made identifying him virtually impossible. He said they were the New Purity Order, and they had a singular mission: to act as the right hand of God and rid the world of the demons called fae like the ones seen slaughtering innocent humans.

I thought the scenes in the beginning were bad, but then it was time for the NPO to showcase their mission with footage of their retaliation.

Poor Cillian never had a chance when they jumped him from behind and didn't let up. And brave Eoghan fought with the ferocity of a cornered bull until eventually the iron infection from multiple wounds weakened him enough to give them the upper hand.

It was everything I could do not to vomit as I watched, but I didn't look away. The very least I owed them was to not shield my eyes from the pain and suffering they endured at the hands of evil until they drew their final breaths. And now that I know what was done to them, I can—and *will*—do the same to the ones who did it.

At the end, the leader said, "For the purity and preservation of the human race," and they all repeated it like good, little sheep. The final image was a still shot of a red banner with the words New Purity Order in bold type across the top and their logo in the center—a large hag stone with an eye looking through the middle and two daggers crossing behind it, the tips of the blades coated in blood—and at the bottom of the screen, instructions for how to reach them via an encrypted messaging system on the dark web.

Dolan's bony hand resting on the arm of the couch curls into a fist as he continues to stare at the image on the screen. "We watched humans doing what humans do best—destroy what they don't understand."

My stomach churns with acidic disgust as the need to shed blood—*their* blood—grows stronger with every passing minute. I want to reach through that TV and rip out every one of their throats with my teeth. "Those aren't humans," I say in a low voice. "Those are the monsters."

"They're a reincarnation." We all look at Seamus, whose focus is on the scar slashing across his right palm. The one he's given a hundred different explanations for to me and my brothers over the years. We know he got it from an iron blade—it wouldn't have left a mark otherwise—but never *how* he got it. "Or the group is, rather. The Purity Order began in Ireland in the late 1500s after a few drunk men had a run-in with a few trickster fae who offered them Faerie gold in exchange for use of their horses for the night. When the men woke up the next morning, not only were their horses still gone, but the Faerie gold—which we know isn't a thing—was nothing more than pieces of stale bread."

Lord Dolan furrows his brow. "I don't remember hearing anything about a Purity Order."

"I'm not surprised," Seamus says. "You were too busy playing court games with the other Lords, your sole focus gaining favor with the kings and queens of Faerie."

Ooh, burn. Seamus deserves a fist bump later for that one. "You're telling me they went all 'grab your torch and pitchforks' all because fae played a shitty trick and stole a few horses?"

"Yes and no. That *was* the only thing the tricksters did to the men, but after weeks of stewing about the incident with each other, the truth became bloated, the story exaggerated, until they believed their own lie that the fae had killed one of them when, in reality, the man had died the following week from a fever. Soon the stories they told each other spread to stories they told their families, their friends, and then strangers. It took less than a year for an angry mob to become a cadre of skilled hunters."

"All that to hunt down the occasional fae playing tricks on humans?" I ask incredulously. "That seems like overkill to me."

McCarthy leans forward, bracing his elbows on his thighs. "No, back then it was extremely common for fae to go back and forth through the veil, sometimes spending as much time in this realm as they did in Faerie. My grandfather told us stories about those days. That encountering fae back then was commonplace in Ireland, so much so that if you had a baby back then, there was a one in five chance you were raising a changeling."

Seamus nods. "Your grandfather was right, and the prevalence of these encounters eventually created two types of people—those who revered us and those who despised us."

"The Néit. I remember hearing about a new group of warriors the One True Queen appointed, but I assumed they were never called into action. I don't remember hearing about any of their battles or exploits," Lord Dolan muses.

Seamus rubs at his scar absently. "That's because we never operated in Faerie. Our sole purpose was to prevent the humans from entering through the veil."

My gaze snaps in his direction. "You were in the Néit? That's where that scar is from, isn't it? From fighting humans with iron weapons."

He nods once. "My brother Cedric and I were very young at the time, not yet twenty. But we were big, strong fighters, and we could shift. Your grandfather, King Domnall, sent us to join the fight that had started seventy-five years earlier and should have ended in at least half that.

"But the queen was stubborn, and it was an issue of pride. Before the Purity Order, our races enjoyed a mostly amicable relationship, even allowing certain humans who gained Aine's favor to spend as much time as they wished in Faerie without the consequence of going mad. The last thing she wanted to do was erase that legacy by sealing off the veil."

"How much longer did it take before the Néit won out? You said this is a reincarnation of the Purity Order, so you must have stopped them eventually," I say.

"No, we never did. For every one of them we cut down in self-defense, another five were newly convinced *we* were the monsters. Not even seeing proof otherwise swayed them.

"My brother had fallen in love with a young maiden. They managed to keep it secret for a year, until one day when her father and brothers came upon them holding one another in a field as they napped in the sun. It made no difference that Cedric was unarmed. Nor did it matter that she begged them not to harm him as she proclaimed her love through tears and screams."

Seamus rubs at his scar. "I felt the sword pierce Cedric's heart and ran to his aid, but I was too late. By the time I arrived, they'd killed her, too. I fought them in a blind rage, but I was alone against five. One of them almost managed to plunge his dagger into my chest, but I grabbed the blade just as the tip pierced my skin. I immediately began to weaken from the iron poisoning and was forced to shift to escape."

"Let me guess," I say. "They said Cedric was the one who killed her."

"Worse. They admitted to killing her. They claimed Cedric had bewitched her with his evil magic and the only way to save her soul was to release it."

"You're not serious."

"I wish I wasn't," he says solemnly. "And with every new generation, those beliefs and lies were passed down, creating even more of those who hated us. Finally, Aine came to terms with the reality that fighting the humans in the hope of restoring peace was futile.

"After one hundred years, she called us home and sealed off the veil, stating it would remain unpassable for two centuries past the death of the offspring of the youngest Order members.

Time," Seamus says. "The passing of time is how we eventually defeated the Order. It's how humans came to believe that we are nothing more than fantasy stories told over generations."

"Until now," McCarthy corrected.

Seamus inclines his head. "Until now."

I scrape a hand over my jaw, the stubble reminding me I haven't slept or even gotten to shower yet. "Okay, so do we think these guys have been operating underground all along and chose to come out of hiding to enact this big plan to wipe us off the map?"

"I don't think so," the chief says. "You saw them. Those aren't trained fighters or elite anything. The production quality of the video and that they're well-supplied with hag stones, technology, and iron weapons indicates they have funds, but I think the group itself is in the beginning stages.

"Extremist groups often start small with one or a few outliers with more radical thoughts than their peers. But with the right leadership and successful recruitment, those outliers can become an army. If we have any chance of preventing this from turning into a worldwide hunt for *others*, we need to stop them while they're still relatively unknown."

"Great, I'm on board. How do we do that?" I ask.

"We make contact using the instructions on the video and send someone in undercover to infiltrate the group. The goal isn't to take out the ones on the bottom—it's to find out who's at the top, who's bankrolling their operation and giving the orders."

"Cut the head off the snake, the body dies," I say.

"That's the hope anyway."

"How can we send someone undercover if they're using hag stones to see through our glamours?" Dolan asks, and for once we're on the same page.

McCarthy sighs. "That I'm not sure about. There's the obvious solution, which is to use a familiar of the Night Court.

But those propaganda videos of fae slaying innocent people will be hard to ignore, even for those who have been in our circle for years."

"I get that it looks bad," I say. "Hell, it looks worse than bad, but there's no way Darks are behind the attacks on the humans. For all we know, these could be rogue fae from one of the Elemental Courts in Faerie, right? Our familiars will know it's no one from our Court."

Seamus shakes his head. "I wish it were that easy. But fear makes humans unpredictable and susceptible to fearmongering tactics. It doesn't matter which Court the fae who committed the acts are from. To anyone with even the slightest doubt of our innocence, *all* fae will become the common enemy."

Cursing a blue streak, I shove my hands through my hair and stop pacing in hopes that my mind will work better if my body is still. What would Caiden suggest? Gods know I'm not experienced with crisis management. Maybe I should conference him in on the meeting. Fuck, Dolan would love that—me proving I can't hack this gig—and I'd rather choke on my own tongue than give him that kind of satisfaction.

Gripping the back of the couch, I hang my head between my shoulders and search for the godsdamned answers we need. An image of Robert comes to me, but I quickly shove it away. No way in hell I'm sending my closest human friend to infiltrate a violent group of extremists. "There has to be *somebody* we can trust to send in there."

"Send me."

My head snaps to the side, where Fiona is standing near the bottom of the staircase. It's only been a little more than an hour since I've last seen her and already I feel like I can breathe easier. She's wearing a pair of leggings and an oversized Nightfall sweatshirt, looking just as sexy as if she were in a cocktail dress. Vivid blue eyes stare back at me from a fresh face dotted with freckles I want to count with kisses.

Her red hair is pulled into a rare high ponytail that shows off her rounded ears, but with her glamour still in effect, they don't look out of place.

I clear my dry throat and force my brain to come back online. "How long have you been listening?"

"I heard everything and saw the video. You can send me into the group," she says again. "I'm the only one you can trust."

I glance down at the small carry-on suitcase next to her feet. "Going somewhere?"

"Don't change the subject, Your Highness." She says my title through clenched teeth, as though she'd love to call me a few other choice words that would be wholly inappropriate for a mixed audience such as this. "You have a problem, and I'm the solution."

"The solution is to send *you* into a group—that you can't even get into, by the way—who have more iron daggers than brain cells?"

"That's what I'm trying to tell you. I *can* get in. They'll never suspect me, I promise you."

"How will they not suspect you, Fiona? Tell me how that works."

"It just will. You'll have to trust me."

I shake my head. "No, not with something like this. If you want me to believe you, you'll have to tell me what kind of magic you have up your sleeve. Otherwise, no dice. I'm not risking your life for a maybe."

"*You* aren't. It's my life to risk, not yours." When that fails to move me, she glances at our rapt audience, then crosses to stand mere inches away. Looking up, she keeps her voice low. "Tiernan, I need you to believe me. It's *not* a maybe, it's a certainty."

"Tell me how, Fi." Sky blue eyes plead with me, making me weak in the knees. "Fine. Then the answer is n—"

"Because *I'm a human*, godsdamn it!"

The air is sucked out of my lungs, making it hard to draw my next breath. I can't believe she just shouted something I know damn well she doesn't go around telling people.

"Excuse us, gentlemen, Miss Jewel has had a very traumatic experience and isn't quite feeling herself." I place my hand at her lower back and usher her out onto the veranda, making sure to close the door all the way behind us. "Fiona, you didn't have to tell them that. And a little halfling blood doesn't make you a human, okay? I'm not sure why your glamour is stuck, but I'm sure it'll—"

"It's not stuck, Tiernan. It's not even a glamour, it never has been. *This is me.* What you saw before—what *everyone* saw—were colored contacts and custom-fit caps on my teeth to help me pass as fae. The reason those men didn't attack me last night is because when they used the hag stone, they saw me for what I truly am...*human*."

"You know if that were the case, we'd be able to tell from reading your energy."

"Not if a powerful conjurer spelled me to read the same as the Darks, you wouldn't."

Erin. "Jesus..." My mind is reeling, trying to reconcile everything I knew about Fiona five minutes ago against what she's telling me now. "I don't understand. Why pretend to be fae at all? Why not just tell me the truth?"

"Because until last night, I didn't know the truth. Bryn wasn't the only baby switched that day my mom placed her in Jack and Emily Meara's care. Turns out they already had a baby—me. So my mom took me and raised me as her own, never telling me the full truth until this morning."

She wipes away the tears before they can spill over. I can't imagine what she must be going through right now, finding out that literally everything about her life has been a lie. "Fi, I'm so sorry. I'm here for you if you want to talk or throw punches. Whatever you need."

"What I need is for you to let me find who's behind this so we can shut them down before anyone else gets killed."

"No way. It's too dangerous. We're not letting you infiltrate an unstable mob of weekend warriors who are armed to the teeth and have more ignorance than common fucking sense."

"Then let me go in as a stripper."

"I'm sorry, what?"

"The Devil's Door is a strip club—"

"I know what it is, Fi, it's Deviant Desire's rival club." It popped up about a year ago like some kind of copycat business and irritated the hell out of Caiden. They used the same alliteration for their name, created similar advertising, even tried to poach some of our dancers. But they've never been able to compete with Deviant, so we left them alone.

"I know," she says. "And that's where that video of the NPO was filmed. The guy who thought it was cool or funny to wear mirrored sunglasses over his mask gave it away. You can see the reflection of the center stage pole, and beyond that is part of the red neon of a sexy devil with horns and a tail hanging on the wall."

"Why are you so familiar with that club?"

"Because I dated one of the dancers for a while, and Sapphire and I are still friends. I know she could get me in there as another dancer. If they recorded their recruitment video in that place, then at the very least, someone in the group must have ties there. Maybe it's even their base of operations."

"Okay, let's assume for argument's sake that you're right. How does you dancing on a pole help us?"

"Because for the majority of their shifts, the girls aren't on the pole. They're on the floor with the customers. I'll be able to listen in on dozens of conversations every night. Believe me, no one is careful with what they say around strippers. Some of the things Sapphire overheard while giving lap dances would blow your mind."

Images of Fiona in barely there lingerie dancing seductively for a bunch of pervy, grab-ass humans has my blood pressure shooting through the roof. I open my mouth to tell her exactly what I think of her plan when another voice interjects.

"She's right, Tiernan," Seamus says from the doorway. "If they're operating out of Devil's Door, Fiona is our best bet to be able to gather information quickly. Anything McCarthy's team does will take time and doesn't have a high chance of success once it goes past virtual communication. We'll give her all the resources and protection we can. We'll keep her safe."

They're both right, I know this. But my gut is telling me this is a bad idea. If I'm the king on this chessboard, Fiona is the queen. While she might be the most powerful piece we have, the last thing I want to do is make her a sacrificial pawn.

Speaking softly, Fiona levels those baby blues on me. "No matter how hard I tried, I was never very good at being fae. At least give me the chance to be of help to you as a human. Please, Tiernan."

Fuck, that hurt. She may as well have struck me with an iron blade of her own with that plea. I can't say no to her after that. I doubt I ever could. "All right," I relent at last. "But I'm going to be with you *every step of the way.* And if there's even the slightest hint that they're on to you, we pull you out and think of something else. Deal?"

Fiona nods. "Yes, deal."

"Then let's go back inside and tell McCarthy we're sending in a stripper to take out the New Purity Order."

CHAPTER TWELVE

TIERNAN

"Okay, Robert, go over it with me one more time."

My old friend gives me the side-eye from the passenger seat of the Range Rover. We're parked down the street from Devil's Door. Fiona's interview for her dancing job is in half an hour, so I asked Robert if he would do a small recon job for me.

"Just because I'm old," he says, "doesn't mean I can't remember simple instructions."

Fiona, who is sitting in the back seat, snickers. I shoot her a look, and she rolls her lips inward to stop herself from all-out laughing. Adjusting the Raiders ball cap I'm wearing, I glance out the tinted windows to make sure no one's paying us any attention, then turn back to Robert.

"I'm not implying you can't remember simple instructions. I'm making sure that we're all on the same page, so everything goes smoothly. These fuckers are no joke. They're armed and unstable, and there's nothing more dangerous than that."

As soon as we settled on this plan, Seamus, McCarthy, Fiona, and I spent all day and night working out the details to make sure everything would run smoothly. We decided on working two angles—Fiona as a dancer and McCarthy's team working to identify the people in that video.

I'm hoping they come up with answers soon so I can pull Fiona off this operation. But it's unlikely the cops will get NPO to spill any information over the net. They'll insist on vetting any interested recruits in person and in a public place where they can use a hag stone from a distance to identify whether a prospect is who they say they are. And the number of humans we're willing to trust with our lives at the moment is all of two, so that's not an option.

Robert reaches over and pats my shoulder. "I know, Tiernan. Don't worry, Fiona is going to have her interview, and I'm going to report back to you on everything I see. They'll never suspect a horny old guy looking around in a room full of exotic dancers."

"All right then." I give him a single-ear Bluetooth headset and a cell phone to slip into his pocket, then I call it and show him how to answer using the earpiece. "Good. This is why I asked you to wear a suit. You'll blend in as just another businessman taking calls at a strip club. I'll have you on speakerphone so we can hear you. Then, when Fiona goes in, I'll be in contact with her using the spy-wear earpieces McCarthy gave me."

He eyes the small box holding the tiny earbuds with all the longing of a boy dreaming of being 007 someday. Smirking, I tell him, "Sorry, old man. I would've let you use them, but considering your advanced age, people would probably assume a dementia patient wandered off and call social services on you."

Fiona gasps. "Tiernan, don't be such an ass. Just for that I hope you stub your toe every day for a month."

My friend laughs heartily at that. "I may never forgive you for not introducing this gorgeous woman to me before. She is an absolute delight. Fiona, dear, I hope you'll join Tiernan the next time we get a chance to resume our matches. The addition of your company would be a welcome change from only dealing with this arrogant bastard."

"Matches? Do you guys play tennis?"

Robert scowls at me. "Have you never even talked about me? What am I, your dirty little secret?"

I roll my eyes and sigh. "Always so dramatic. It's not that I don't talk about you to people. It's just that Fiona and I never..."

Leaning in from the back seat, she says, "We never did any talking. Our encounters were brief and extremely nonverbal. In fact, if anyone was a dirty little secret, it was me. Right, Tier?"

Her smile is playful, but her words have bite. Something I'll need to address with her later. "Neither of you is my dirty little secret. Now, can we start this mission before it's past Robert's bedtime?"

Robert unbuckles his seat belt. "Just for that, I'm going to drink all your whiskey when I get home."

"Yeah, yeah. Get out already."

"Fiona, it was lovely finally getting to meet you. I can see why the prince is so taken with you. Be careful in there."

She places a hand on his shoulder and smiles warmly. "Thank you, Robert, you're so sweet. You be careful, too."

He winks at her, then gets out of the truck. Fiona climbs into the front seat as I call his phone and put it on speaker. Robert answers, lets me know he hears me, then walks in the direction of Devil's Door, the strip club where we think NPO is either operating from or at least has ties with.

Setting my phone on the dash, I open the small box McCarthy gave me and fit one of the tiny devices into my ear. Then I give the other to Fiona. "Anything goes sideways in that interview, I'm coming in after you."

"I'll be fine. Sapphire was more than happy to accept your

offer for a week's paid vacation. She told the manager she needed time off to take care of her mother but had a friend from out of town ready to take her place until she returned. This is just a formality so he can see me with his own eyes. I'll be in and out."

"*This* is just a formality, but then you have to dance in front of an audience, all while trying to gather information about this group without causing suspicion and getting caught, or worse."

"Whoa, slow down already, geez. Let's not borrow trouble from tomorrow and just stay chill, all right?"

Pulling my shit together, I give her a lazy smile that belies my true feelings. "I don't know what you're talking about, I'm completely chill."

Fiona shakes her head, then gets lost in the scene outside the windshield of tourists and locals living up the nightlife in this city my family built. It's my legacy and one of the most impressive, sought-after cities this side of the veil. But it might as well be an endless stretch of corn field for as much interest as it holds for me, because I can't stop staring at her.

The *real* her.

We haven't had a chance to talk since yesterday when she shocked the hell out of me with her revelation. But it wasn't for lack of trying.

Every time we had a minute alone, she found a way to circumvent the topic before I could even ask how she was doing, telling me without words to leave it alone, so I did. Fiona's strength and independence are some of the traits that attracted me to her in the first place. If she needs to process things on her own, I'm not going to push her to share more than what she's comfortable with.

As for me, once I recovered from the initial shock, I accepted the new information about her in record time. I don't know if it's because I knew about her ears and already thought at least part of her was human, or if I just don't give a damn whether she's fae, human, or garden gnome—she's still the same Fiona to me, and that's all that matters. "I've always loved your blue eyes, you know. Even when I thought they weren't real." I keep my voice low in the quiet of the car, not wanting to disturb this rare moment of truce between us. "They're even more stunning now that I know they are."

She turns her head to look at me, half of her face in shadows and the other washed in a pink glow from a neon sign outside. "I'm not sure what to say to that," she replies, her words stained with hints of sadness. "I guess I haven't decided how I feel about them."

"What do you mean?"

"I wasn't ashamed of them when I thought they were a kind of defect as a result of not being a pureblood. Yet now that I know I'm human and the color is perfectly normal..." Shrugging, she returns her gaze to the front. "I'm almost disappointed in them. Like they're the ones who betrayed me, not my mom."

Without thinking about it, I reach across the center console and thread my fingers through hers, staying silent to give her room to sift through her thoughts.

"No matter how much I want to be mad at her—how much I want to blame her for this overwhelming feeling of displacement—I just can't. She's all I've ever had. I love her too much. So instead, I'm mad at my eyes." A soft, self-deprecating laugh escapes with a shake of her head. "I know, it's ridiculous."

I spin my cap around backwards and lean in to close the physical distance between us even if emotionally she's a mile away. Cupping the side of her face, I guide her until she's looking at me. "Fi, how you feel is never ridiculous. And it's okay to be mad at your eyes. I'll show them enough love until you're ready to love them, too."

"It's really annoying how you always say the right things."

The corner of my mouth tilts up. "I know."

"I guess that's what a hundred and fifty years of seducing other women will get you."

Staring into her eyes, I whisper, "What other women?"

Our faces are close enough to feel our breaths mingling. I've never wanted to kiss her more than I do in this moment. To show her how special I think she is, with or without magical capabilities. She probably thinks it was another practiced line, but she truly makes me forget everyone who came before her.

My lips graze hers with the ghost of a touch, not wanting to press for more but unable to resist her taste. Her eyes fall to my mouth for a weighted beat before flicking back up to mine, her long lashes casting shadows on her cheekbones. "Tier..."

"C'mere," I grate out before pulling her in with a hand at her nape and crushing our mouths together in a passion-drenched kiss.

She makes that soft mewling sound of capitulation that drives me wild as she opens to me. My tongue sweeps in to dominate hers in a fevered dance we've perfected over dozens of times of physically charged clandestine encounters. I'm ready to haul her ass across the center console when she palms my stiff cock through my jeans. My brain short-circuits as a pained groan rumbles from my chest—

"You kids know I can still hear you, right?"

I curse as reality crashes back in with the interruption. We break apart and Fiona devolves into a fit of giggles. I wince as I do my best to adjust the uncomfortable situation in my pants, then pull my cap on the right way again.

"Watch who you're calling a kid," I grumble. "I've been around more than double what you have. If anyone is a kid in this friendship, it's you, sport."

"Yeah, but when you put your average lifespan up against mine, you might as well be a pimply-assed teenager compared to me. Which makes me the elder, so I'll call you what I want."

"How long have you guys been friends?" Fiona asks.

Robert's light chuckle comes through the phone's speaker. "Oh, it's got to be around fifty years now, I'd say. That sound about right?"

"Fifty-two, if you want to get technical. How far away are you from Devil's Door?"

"About a block and a half. I'm not exactly power walking over here, you know. Just because I have a new hip doesn't mean I'm Speed Racer."

"You're fine," I say, glancing at the time on the dash. "As long as you're inside before Fiona's interview is set to start, that's all that matters. After you've been in there for a few minutes, I'll drop her off out front."

"Oh sure, the young person gets valet service, and the geezer has to walk five blocks."

Fiona chuckles, and that makes me smile as I answer. "If you were wearing five-inch heels, I would have dropped you off in front, too."

Fiona interrupts Robert's grumbling. "So then tell me the story of how you guys met and why you play each other in tennis matches."

Now it's my turn to laugh. "Not tennis, sweetheart. We play chess."

She arches a brow in surprise. "You play chess? As in *chess*?"

"Do you have a problem with chess?"

She shakes her head. "No, of course not. I just never pictured *you*—party boy extraordinaire—as someone who could focus long enough to play a game of strategy without solo cups and ping pong balls involved."

Robert laughs uproariously, to the point where I'm concerned he might actually start hacking up a lung. "I happen to be an excellent chess player," I say. "Isn't that right, Robert?"

"Only because you had the best teacher around. And even

after fifty years you still can't beat me more than twice in a row."

"Did you meet at a chess match somewhere?"

"Sort of," I say. "Robert was playing a tournament at an outdoor park where I happened to be passing by. It caught my interest, so I picked a spot underneath a shady tree and watched. Robert won the whole thing. He was impressive."

"And also scatterbrained," Robert added. "I wasn't paying attention when I went to cross the street and I almost got hit by a car. Tiernan used his super speed to get to me in time to pull me back out of the way. Course, at the time I assumed he must have been close by. He didn't come clean with me for five years."

Fiona's jaw drops. "Oh my gods," she says in awe. "You pulled an Edward Cullen? You really have a thing for him, don't you?"

I could almost hear Robert's confused expression coming through the earpiece. "He pulled a what?"

"Nothing, old timer. It's not a reference you'll understand," I say in the direction of the phone. Then I dish out some sarcasm to Fiona. "Yeah, I was emulating the persona of a fictional character who wouldn't be created for several decades that day. That makes total sense."

She places an elbow on the console and rests her chin in her hand as she grins. "Do you secretly wish you were a vampire, Tiernan?"

Leaning in, I hold her gaze and drop my voice an octave. "Why, Fi? You wanna role play with me? Let me tap into the sweet, pulsing vein in that pretty little neck of yours?"

Her lips part on a soft gasp, drawing my gaze and making me ache to taste them, to trace the soft pillows with my tongue before claiming her. I drag my eyes back up to hers, heavy lidded with pupils eclipsing the blue of her irises. *Gods.* I've never wanted anyone so badly as I want Fiona.

"Save your weird sex games for later, Tiernan. I'm here."

Fiona and I pull away, and the mood turns serious. "Okay, Robert, just walk me through what you see. Remember, we want to know what kind of security they have. That includes manpower and cameras if you can see them."

"Walking through the front door now." We hear a door open and muffled music with a heavy bass line. "Whoa, look at you two beefy guys. I bet no one tries to mess with either of you, huh?" Fiona and I look at each other and shrug. Two guys on the outside isn't so bad. So far so good. We hear Robert pay the cover charge to get in and be given instructions on the rules of the establishment. "I just go through this next door here?"

"Wait," a male voice says. There's a sound of two knocks and what seems like wood sliding on wood.

Robert comes back in with commentary. "Oh wow, would you look at that! That's the biggest, weirdest peephole I ever did see. What is that, a rock with a hole in it wedged inside your door?"

"Okay, so we know they have a hag stone in the second entrance testing for fae. That right, Robert?"

"Yup, that's what it is all right. Oh good, I get to go in now. Thanks fellas, I appreciate it."

I start the engine of the Range Rover, getting ready to drop Fiona off for her interview. "You're doing great, old friend, now just pick a seat and pretend you're looking at all the pretty ladies. When I park again, you can tell me what you see and I'll write it down for McCarthy."

Fiona opens up her purse and grabs a tube of lipstick. She pulls down the visor and uses the mirror to apply another coat of red that accentuates her full pouty lips. She's wearing more makeup than usual, playing up her role for her new job.

I'm not used to seeing her this made-up, and it strikes me that in its own way it's just another glamour. Something to change her appearance so that others see her the way she needs to be seen. And suddenly I want to wipe it all off, to get rid of anything that disguises the real her. So that for the first time in her life, she doesn't have to hide who she is, because who she is naturally is *perfect*.

"We should go," she says. "I don't wanna be late and make a bad first impression on my new boss."

I clench my teeth so hard they nearly grind into dust. There isn't a single thing about this plan that I like. Not the fact that she'll be dancing naked in front of drunk assholes who have a hard time remembering to keep their hands to themselves, and not the fact that she's going to be snooping around trying to find information we can use to take down NPO.

"Tier, you're making that face again."

Robert pipes in. "Is it the one where he looks constipated? He does that every time he thinks too hard."

"Anything more out of you that isn't security based and I'll tell your daughter it's time to start looking at assisted living."

There's a slight pause and then, "I never shoulda given you Wanda's number."

Muting the phone to keep my friend out of this part of the conversation, I answer Fiona. "I wasn't making any face."

"Yes, you were. It's the one you get when something is happening you don't like. I'm telling you I'm going to be fine. Right now, I'm just talking to the guy. After that, I'll be asking some discreet questions and dancing on a stage." My jaw pops at the mention of that last thing and she notices. "Wait, is that the part that's bothering you? Me dancing?"

"Jesus, Fi, every part of this is bothering me. But yes, you having to dance naked for this bothers me. You shouldn't have to expose yourself like that, it's not fair to you."

She lets out a humorless laugh. "If you'd ever played with me like I wanted, you'd know I'm an exhibitionist. I have no issue showing my body to people who want to see it. So, if that bothers you, it's *your* hang up, not mine."

An exhibitionist. *Fuck.* As I pull into traffic and drive toward Devil's Door, I swallow hard, imagining her in a proper BDSM scene, restrained and exposed to an audience while I perform unspeakable things to her to make her come undone. My cock twitches and my balls start to ache with the need to have Fiona like that, on display and undeniably mine.

And yet, at the same time, my palms get clammy and my stomach twists into a knot. I haven't done anything like that in ten years. Not since a sub was hurt under my care. That was the last time I picked up a whip for a scene. That was the last time I did a scene at all. Since then, I've relegated myself to "normal" sex only and kept my kink beast caged.

When Fiona brought up exploring more than just closet sex together, she assumed I don't trust her with that part of me. But the truth is, I don't trust *myself* with *her.* It was bad enough hurting Julie, and we weren't anything more than play partners. If I ever hurt Fiona like that, the guilt would slice me in two.

Oblivious to my dark thoughts, Fiona continues to rant at me. "But even if I was uncomfortable taking my clothes off in front of strangers, I would still do it. I will do anything it takes to bring these bastards down who hurt my mom and killed so many others."

Gods, the fire within her burns as bright as her red hair, and no matter what I try, I'm helpless to be drawn to it. "I know you would, Fi. And you're right, I made assumptions and was projecting my shit onto you. I apologize."

"Accepted."

"Good." I park the truck in front of the club. "Okay, sweetheart, go knock 'em dead. I'll be right there with you the whole time. You need anything, you just say the word, and I'll get inside before you even finish."

She gives me a small smile and a nod, then exits the vehicle and sashays her sweet ass up to the doors. I want to stay here and watch her until I can't see her anymore, but I can't risk anyone recognizing me. Even with the hat and the tinted windows, it's not impossible if you look hard enough.

Pulling away, I tell Robert to start talking. "And keep an eye on our girl."

"Copy that."

CHAPTER THIRTEEN

TIERNAN

"You're on in five, Candy."

"Thank you, Donnie, you're the best," Fiona says with exaggerated enthusiasm.

Sitting in a surveillance van with two of McCarthy's best IT guys isn't my idea of a good time, but at least tonight I have eyes inside the main area of Devil's Door and we'll be able to see Fiona instead of just hearing her through the comms unit. I can't see her yet, though, because she's in the back getting ready. While it bothers me that I don't yet have a visual, I guess it's a good thing there are no cameras in the area where the dancers get dressed.

Leaning back in my chair, I cross my arms over my chest and keep my eyes on the screens monitoring the activity in the main room. "I can't believe you chose Candy as your stage name. Was Trixie taken already?"

"Actually, yes," she says quietly so as to not draw attention to the fact that she's talking to no one. "Plus I liked the costume idea."

The muscle in my jaw ticks. "What costume idea?" When she doesn't answer I say, "Fi, what costume idea?"

"Now why would I ruin the surprise when you'll be able to see for yourself?"

Ouch. Her words were sharp enough to cut. Clyde and Evan pretend they're not listening, but that would be impossible with the three of us crammed in here like sardines.

There's no getting around Fiona's irritation about my insistence on having eyes on her inside the club. Last night was her first shift and even though we could communicate with the earpieces, I couldn't handle being in the dark. So I went to McCarthy and told him we needed to get visuals somehow, either by placing our own camera inside or tapping into theirs.

Fiona thinks I'm being an overbearing ass, and she's right. But no amount of her ire is going to stop me from doing everything possible to make sure she's protected. However, because I don't have a death wish, I'm not *telling* her what "everything" entails. Like the fact that I visited her mother this morning and asked for a favor.

Erin's still in the hospital and extremely weak, but the doctors say her health is improving a little each day. I was surprised to hear that Fiona's only checked on her via short phone calls. Instead, she's been taking advantage of knowing she can lie now. She told Erin she couldn't visit because she's too busy with the undercover operation. I know that's not the case, but I didn't contradict her statement to Erin. I'm pretty sure she knows the truth anyway. Moms usually do.

I knew it was a long shot, but I wanted to know if there was anything she could do to trick the hag stones so I could pass as a human with my glamour–something we would have asked our resident conjurer as a way to protect our people had she not been attacked before we even had the chance.

Erin told me the cloaking spell that's used to disguise the ToR could be made into a potion, but due to the iron poisoning weakening her powers, she could only risk enough for one vial and couldn't guarantee its potency. I told her anything was better than nothing in case I need to get to Fiona without raising suspicions.

She gave me a list of ingredients and instructions on how to brew the potion, then I brought it to her to perform the spell. She warned me again that it wouldn't last for more than a few hours, and then I left with the promise that I would keep her daughter safe.

There are four monitors in front of us showing different angles to cover every area of the mainstage and audience. So far nothing out of the ordinary has happened, but the night is still young, and I have the small vial of Erin's potion in my pocket as my "break glass in case of emergency" failsafe.

The woman on stage ends her song and quickly gathers the loose dollar bills before exiting through the back curtain. I crack my knuckles to release the tension in my fingers, if nothing else, as I wait for Fiona to make her appearance. Last night was torture only being able to listen to the song and all of the cheers and catcalls from the obnoxious audience watching her. Now that I can see the people, I'm not sure it's going to be any easier. She hasn't even stepped on stage yet and already I want to pummel every single one of them.

The DJ announces Fiona as the next dancer and starts her song, "Pour Some Sugar On Me" by Def Leppard, and the crowd goes wild. I lean forward and brace my elbows on my knees, keeping my eyes glued to the screen showing the long stage with a pole centered at the end of it.

The black curtains in the back explode open as she pushes her way through and struts down stage to the beat of the music. My jaw slackens and my eyes damn near bug out of my head. She's dressed as a sexed-up vintage candy striper. Her outfit is a white corset paired with a fluffy pink and white striped mini-skirt, complete with the mile-high platform shoes that clack loudly on the polished floor. A long white wig with bangs pulled into low pigtails gives her an innocent look that contradicts the vixen persona now spinning around the gleaming silver pole.

When she takes a six-inch-long sucker out of her pocket and sticks the whole thing in her mouth, then pulls it out slowly as she slides her back down the pole until she is kneeling on the floor, I hear a choked sound from my right. Snapping my head to the side, I look over to see Clyde and Evan with their eyes glued to Fiona.

"There are three other screens you can be watching," I growl. "I suggest those are the ones you focus on."

They answer in tandem. "Yes, Your Highness." Then they busy themselves with checking on the technical shit I know nothing about.

Watching her is like the worst kind of torture. Or maybe it's the best kind. My body and mind can't agree. My jeans are becoming uncomfortably tight, and the thoughts swimming in my head of all the dirty, filthy things I want to do to her the way she's dressed right now are making me crave things I haven't done in a really fucking long time.

On the flip side, seeing the crowd lust after her, believing they can have her for a price, seeing everything she has to offer a lover, makes me murderous and territorial as hell. I want to mark her. I want to claim her. I want to go in there and haul her off that stage, throw her over my damn shoulder like a Neanderthal, and take her home.

How did we get here? Six months ago, we were fucking all the time whenever we had the chance. It was a game; it was fun. Then my station at Court changed, and so did everything between us. As king of the Dark Fae, I don't have the luxury of being with anyone I want.

But that was only true when we thought she was fae. Is that necessarily still the case now that we know she's human? I guess that depends on what we want from each other and how long we want it for. Eventually I'll need to take a consort to provide heirs for the throne, but Fiona won't be around in another hundred years.

That thought punches me square in the chest. I'd lose her sooner rather than later. Robert's the only human I've dared to get close with for that very reason. I've tried pretending what I feel for Fiona is just physical, but every day I fall a little more for her. Her spirit, her fire, her bravery, everything about her speaks to me.

As hard as it would be to say goodbye to her, wouldn't it be worth it to spend the time we *do* have together? Maybe we could have a normal life together. Or whatever normal is for a fae king and a human wife.

Wife. I've never thought of that word in context with myself before. And now that I have, I feel like it's branding itself into my mind. Marrying Fiona wouldn't activate the blood curse because she's not fae. I could conceivably marry her. *What makes you think she'd want to marry you? What do you have to offer her?*

That question plagues me as I continue to watch Fiona dance, peeling off her skirt and eventually her corset so that the only thing she's wearing while spinning on that pole is a pale pink G-string and her heels. My heart pumps fiercely in my chest and my cock aches to be buried inside her. I want to suck on her cherry nipples and feast on the sweet juices of her pussy.

No, not want. *Need.* But there's nothing I can do about it now. I'm stuck in this godsdamned van another five hours until the end of her shift while she does her best to gather intel between sets.

When she hits the last beat of her song and the crowd goes wild, I just barely manage to keep myself in my seat as I watch her accept men sticking dollar bills in the waist of her G-string before she gathers the rest and exits through the back curtain.

The sound of her heavy breathing comes through the

speaker. "Did you notice the three guys in the corner table who weren't paying attention to the show?"

"You had every person in that room creaming themselves and you're worried about a couple of guys who weren't into it? That's vain even for you, Fi," I say teasingly, even as I search the monitors for the men in question. Anyone who wasn't paying attention to her performance either can't see or is preoccupied with things that have nothing to do with strip shows.

Evan points to one of the monitors. "There they are," he says.

One of the dancers approaches the table, clearly looking to entice them with a lap dance, but they dismiss her with hardly even a look. "Yeah, we see them. They just turned down a dance from a curvy brunette in a red leather bustier."

"That's Ruby, and no one turns her down. She's the most popular girl here." I recognize the sounds of metal hangers clanging as she does a wardrobe change and the various makeup items clacking on the vanity as she uses them. "I'm going to swing by their table and see what they're up to."

I sigh and push a hand through my hair. "All right, we'll be watching. Just be careful."

"Careful is my middle name."

I watch as she emerges from the back room dressed in the white corset and G-string and walks casually between the tables toward the back corner where the three oblivious men are sitting. "Somehow I doubt that," I say absently, unable to take my eyes off her.

She glances up at one of the cameras, looking straight at me. "How would you know? You've never asked."

It's a flip remark, probably meant as a joke. But it jabs me like a needle. She's right, I haven't asked. As much as I know about the kind of person she is and how attracted I am to that person, I don't know many details about her life or her past.

And she doesn't know much about mine. Our encounters have always been quick and focused on the physical.

Ignoring the fact that we have an audience in this vehicle, I get close to the microphone and say, "You're right about that, Little Red. But don't worry. That's about to change."

She falters briefly, telling me my words affected her. Hopefully, in a good way. But I don't have time to find out, and now is not the time anyway. The guys and I watch closely as she approaches the table.

"Any of you boys want some attention?"

Fiona slides a hand across the shoulders of the man closest to her. For a second it looks like he's about to turn to her and accept her offer, but the guy across the table catches his eye and gives a shake of his head. Shrugging Fiona's hand off, the first one says, "Not tonight, babe, we're busy."

Fiona pouts while twirling a pigtail as she straddles the guy's leg that's sticking out in the aisle. "Oh, come on, baby, everyone deserves a little break."

"Bitch, I said *no*." He shoves her hard enough to make her stumble backward into another of the dancers, who manages to keep Fiona upright. Violence sparks through me like a bolt of lightning. I shove to my feet with a throaty growl, forgetting where I am, and end up hunched over the technical equipment with my back pressed against the roof of the van.

"Take it easy, Hulk, I'm okay," Fiona says to me as she puts herself to rights again, then squeezes the hand of the girl who prevented her from falling. "Thank you, Penny. No, I'm good, I promise. No need to get anyone."

Penny must have made some kind of subtle offer we can't see from the cameras to get security, which makes me realize not one of the muscleheads standing around the room made any sort of move to interfere. I'm going to have every one of their names by the end of this and then I'm going to—

"Um, Your Highness?" I look down at a nervous Clyde. "If

you wouldn't mind sitting. It's just, we don't want the vehicle to rock and draw attention..."

"Right. Sorry." I lower my bulk onto the stool again and focus on Fiona. "Okay, Fi, see if you can chat up one of the bartenders. They usually have their fingers on the pulse of everything going on around them. They're observant and people are always chatty with—"

She grabs a tray of drinks and a rag off the bar. "I'm going back to that table."

"What? No, you're not."

"They're involved in this somehow, I know they are."

"Fine, then we'll wait for them to come out and I'll have a chat with them."

She moves expertly around the tables, the tray held up on one hand. "And say what? 'Hi, you guys wouldn't happen to be going around murdering fairytale creatures, would you?' I'm sure that'll work great."

"Caiden's very influential."

Fiona smiles and finger waves at a gawking man in his sixties without ever breaking her stride. "Not with people like this. Fanatics put the cause over themselves."

"She's right," Evan says, resituating his ball cap on his head. "They're taught that dying for the cause makes them heroes and martyrs. There are probably a few in the whole group who wouldn't withstand that kind of...um, questioning...but odds of you getting the right ones are slim."

I rub a hand over the stubble on my jaw and run through my options. I can't get in there to run interference, and Fiona isn't about to listen to me, so all I can do is sit in this godsforsaken van and watch everything unfold. Truth is, I don't have *any* options tonight. But tomorrow...

Fuck it. I won't be able to relax until I have someone on the inside who can watch her back and step in if shit goes south. Their hag stone security checks won't reveal anything supernatural on *others* that aren't fae, which works in my favor. I need someone strong, lethal, and on the darker side of morally gray.

Someone like Dmitri Romanov.

I know getting in bed with the Devil will cost me—Dmitri doesn't do anything for free. But if it means keeping Fiona safe during this operation, I'll gladly sell my soul.

Decision made, I finally relent. As if I have a choice. "Fine. What do you plan on doing?"

"The one in the leather coat is obviously the leader, or at least the leader among the three of them. He's been texting with someone since he got here. I figure it must be an important conversation, so I'm going to swipe his phone."

Every muscle in my body tenses. "And just how do you plan on doing that?"

"You'll see."

CHAPTER FOURTEEN

FIONA

"The hell I will! Not until you tell me your plan." There's a growling monster in my ear, but I ignore it as I run a quick calculation of what I need to do to make this a successful mission. "Godsdamn it, Fiona, are you listening to me?"

"Do I ever?"

I swipe the phone off a table from a customer too busy drooling over Ruby's tits inches from his face to notice a little petty theft. Then I hold it up to my ear and start arguing dramatically with my fake boyfriend as I approach my targets.

"What do you mean, you're leaving me for Cherise? How can you do this to me, Johnny? I've given you everything. *Everything!*" I stop right next to them, my tray of drinks balancing precariously on my hand. "That's *my* dog. Don't you fucking dare—"

I stomp my foot for emphasis and "accidentally" tip the drinks into Leather Coat Guy's lap. He scoots his chair back and holds up his hands, scowling at the mess I've made of his pants. I note that his phone is on the table, which is where I need it to stay.

"Oh my God, I am so sorry!" I set my stolen phone next

to his then take the bar towel and start dabbing at his clothes, apologizing profusely via explanation of my crumbling love life. "I mean, I just can't believe he'd call me at work like that, you know? He's such a fucking asshole."

Sniffle, sniffle, watering eyes. Damn, I'm a natural at this lying stuff.

Leather Coat Guy tries to stop my blotting attempts, but I pretend I don't notice and keep going until he finally gets irritated enough to snap at me. "That's enough! Just get out of here already. Christ."

"Shit, I'm sorry, okay." I drop the towel over the phones and continue to apologize as I quickly pick up the two rocks tumblers from the floor. Then I pick up the towel with *both* phones inside and dump everything on the tray to make my hasty retreat, praying he's flustered enough that it takes him a while to realize he's misplaced his cell.

I replace the one I borrowed as I walk by and breathe a sigh of relief that my hasty plan worked. Now that I'm done, my adrenaline is through the roof and I'm starting to shake.

"I can't believe you just did that," Tiernan says into my ear. If he said anything to me while I was working for my Oscar nomination, I didn't hear it. But now I hear him loud and clear, and the ominous tone in his voice is doing things to me that will make wearing only a G-string very inconvenient. "I'm going to belt your ass so hard, your tears will form puddles."

Oh gods. The tiny scrap of material covering me is no match for my body's reaction to his words, and with every step I take I can feel the slick wetness between my thighs. "You shouldn't get in the habit of making empty promises, Your Majesty. Meet me out back."

I hear a barked command to shut down the connection to my earpiece and the sound of a van door sliding open before it cuts off. The tightness in my stomach eases once I make it to the back room where the girls get ready. I abandon the tray on a vanity and take the phone still wrapped in the bar towel with me. Three dancers are doing their makeup and one is changing into her costume. Luckily, all four have been friendly with me.

"Ladies, I'm taking a john break. Be back in five, hopefully longer," I say with a wink.

I'm met with a round of "go, girl"s and "get him, honey"s as I slip out the heavy door that leads out to the alley behind the club. As soon as it shuts, I'm grabbed from the side and pulled into the shadows by a very tall, very angry fae prince.

"What the fuck is a john break?"

Gotta love supernatural hearing. "It's when someone meets a john out back for extra fun and extra cash. Now they won't use this exit for their smoke breaks or whatever else. It's like calling dibs on the alley. It's honestly a very considerate sys—"

Tiernan grabs my face and crushes his mouth on mine.

I fist the front of his shirt and hold on like he's a rodeo bronco that could buck me off at any second. His tongue expertly stokes the flames of my desire until he's swallowing my moans and answering with ones of his own.

"I think tapping into the cameras was a mistake," he says as he trails kisses down my neck. "Watching you dance drove me insane."

"And what did you think about my candy prop?" He's using a glamour, so I can't see the pointed tips of his ears, but I have their shape memorized and trace their edges with my fingers before plowing my hands into his thick hair. A shudder runs through his body as he groans against my skin.

"I think you somehow cosmically connected your candy to my dick. Every time you licked it or sucked it into your mouth, I swear I could feel your wet heat and talented tongue on my cock."

"Speaking of..." I undo his belt and open the fly of his jeans in record time, then wrap my hand around his considerable length and pull it out where I can stroke it freely. "We're in a camera-free zone. I think it's time we finish what you started in the kitchen that night."

He hisses in a breath and thrusts into my hand. "Grip it harder. Shit yes, just like that, *fuck*." He nips at my jaw and wedges a hand between my thighs, pushing the tiny scrap of material to the side to tease my entrance, making me whimper with need. "Mmm, you're absolutely drenched, sweetheart. This all for me?"

I nod, my breaths quickening as I stare up at him through my long, false lashes. With his free hand, he smacks my bare ass cheek before gripping it hard. "Say it."

Moaning, I comply. "It's all for you."

"That's good, Fi. Very good," he says huskily. "You've earned a reward."

He sinks three fingers deep into my pussy and starts fucking me. I throw my head back and grab onto his shoulders for support. "Oh gods…"

I keep pace with my own hand as I jerk his thick cock. "That's it, Little Red, give it to me," he growls into my ear.

The sounds our bodies make echo off the bricks in a sordid symphony that turns me on even more. His shaft is slick with precum, allowing my hand to glide easily even with how tightly I'm squeezing him. When I focus my attention on the fat tip with short, fast strokes, I feel him grow impossibly larger, and the tortured groan that escapes him satisfies me to no end.

Until he turns my own medicine on me, kicking his efforts up several levels.

Curling two fingers forward inside me to hit my G-spot, Tiernan changes the direction of his thrusts from up and down to back and forth, moving faster and harder. The tension inside me builds and builds until it feels too large for me to contain and I'm dancing on a knife's edge, waiting to tumble over.

"Oh gods, oh gods, oh gods," I mumble, my voice pitching higher with each repetition.

"Do it, Fi, let go for me. I want you to drench my hand, want it running down your thighs. I want the scent of what I do to you so strong that every fucker in that place knows you've been claimed. Come for me, sweetheart."

"Tier!"

Time stops as the tension in my belly finally snaps, and my world shatters into a million tiny stars. But he doesn't give me time to float on the high. Digging his fingers into the flesh of my ass, he lifts me up and sandwiches me between his hard chest and the brick wall. A second later he lines himself up and impales me on his thick cock. The force of it makes me throw my head back on a gasp. He presses his face into my neck and growls as he gives me time to revel in the delicious feeling of being stretched by him.

"Fuck you're tight."

I sink my fingers into his hair. "And whose fault is that?"

"You complaining, Fi?" He drags the tip of a fang up to the sensitive spot beneath my ear then laves it with his tongue.

"Hell no. Now fuck me."

Tiernan doesn't need to be told twice. He withdraws almost completely before thrusting in to the hilt. I arch off the wall on a hiss, the bricks scraping my bare skin. As he's always done in our many tight-quartered liaisons, he makes a quick adjustment for my comfort and places one of his hands between my upper back and the wall. Then he sets a feverish pace.

As much as I want to enjoy every detail of this rare encounter, there's no separating them. Everything is a blur of sensations. His mouth ravages everywhere it touches—my lips, my throat, my shoulder. I fist his hair and dig my nails into his nape.

The world around us fades away except the here and now

with our bodies joined and our pleasure mounting. This is raw, unadulterated sex. Yet somehow, it doesn't feel as trivial as that. The way we move together, the way we respond to each other, it's like we're communicating on another level when we're like this. Like our innermost selves are twining together in a dance only they know, one that feels so...*right*.

All too fast, my second orgasm sneaks up on me. I don't want to give in, I don't want it to end.

"This isn't the end, Little Red, it's only the beginning," he rasps out in reply to what I apparently said out loud. I'm not sure what he means by that, but his next words ensure I forget what he said entirely. "Gods, I've missed the way your sweet cunt squeezes my fucking cock. Need to feel you, baby."

I drop my forehead to his and whimper as my climax balances on the edge. "Oh fuck, Tier."

"That's it. Come for me, Fiona, come for me *right fucking now*."

My entire body seizes with the force of my orgasm. My thighs grip his hips tighter, my fingernails bite into the back of his neck, and my heartbeat pulses around his cock. His roar echoes in the alley, and then I feel the satisfaction of his hot seed lashing the walls of my sex.

He drops his head to my shoulder, the sweat from his brow mingling with the sheen on my skin, as we work to catch our breaths. Slowly, the shattered pieces of me fall back together and my pulse returns to semi-normal. Tiernan carefully unseats me and lowers me until I'm able to stand again, albeit with the help of the wall behind me.

Still in a daze, my eyes follow his hand as it delves between my legs. He collects our combined arousal, then rubs it over my swollen folds and inner thighs. I lift my gaze to find him staring at me. Not where his hand is, but at *me*. Neither of us says anything. We don't need to. His actions are speaking louder than any words could. He's marking me as his. It's as much of a claiming as one can do in a dark alley behind a strip club.

When he finally pulls my tiny panties back into place and puts himself to rights, I find my voice again. Trailing a finger down the center of his chest, I give him an impish grin. "When I'm done tonight, let's go back to your penthouse. Now that we're not mucking up the Night Court hierarchy by the future king having relations with a lowly fae commoner, we can have a proper scene and sex that doesn't have a five-minute time limit. It'll be a revelation."

I chuckle, expecting him to laugh with me. Instead, his expression grows serious and he casts his eyes downward. "I don't think that's a good idea, Fi."

My smile falls. "Why not? There's no rule against the king being with humans. It was Caiden's preference not to for security reasons, but obviously I'm not about to spill any fae secrets."

"Come on, give me a little more credit than that. It doesn't have anything to do with security *or* me being the king."

"Okay, then what is it?" He shifts his weight from one foot to the other, another very *un*-Tiernan thing to do. I've never seen him uneasy before. It's like he's nervous to tell me the truth. *Oh no...* "Gods, I'm so naive sometimes. Here I am thinking that the *one* silver lining to me completely losing my identity and learning I'm human is that it fixes the complications our stations caused when we thought I was fae. But if there was a station lower than the one I had before, it's being human, isn't it?"

His brows knit together over the straight bridge of his nose. "What? No, Fi. Jesus, why would you think that being human makes you less in my eyes?"

"I think the better question is, why wouldn't I?" I push the phone onto his chest, forcing him to grab it or risk it falling. "Have the guys in the van get what they can off this and then one of them needs to bring it back to me. I'll hand it to the bartender and say I found it on the floor."

I spin on the heel of my platform Pleasers and stride toward the door as he calls out for me.

"Fiona, wait."

"Hurry up with that before they realize I'm the one who took it."

Once inside, I blink rapidly to beat back the angry tears threatening to spill over. I have another set to get ready for, and Tiernan Verran isn't worth ruining my makeup.

CHAPTER FIFTEEN

FIONA

Sitting at one of the vanities in the back room at Devil's Door, I apply my makeup while paying close attention to everything going on around me. There's a ton of activity between the girls changing costumes and getting ready, one going on stage while the other's coming off, and the occasional waitress coming in to bring various drinks or messages from patrons.

This is my third night here, and I've gotten to know some of the girls pretty well. Others aren't the kind to play nice with the New Girl. Normally I'd meet snark with snark, but I'm here to get information, and the only way to do that is to get on everyone's good side, so I'm killing them with kindness like a true Southern Belle.

Trixie, who is my favorite by far, sits down at the vanity next to me. "Hey, girl, I heard you had a john break last night. How'd it go?"

I think about what happened between me and Tiernan the night before against the alley wall. It started out with so much promise, hot and needy, desperate to get each other off. Was exactly like what we used to have with each other, and I've missed that. But there's so much more we could be enjoying if we explored our kinks together.

Unfortunately, he doesn't feel the same.

I don't think he trusts me. I'm not even entirely sure what it is he doesn't trust me *with*, it's just a gut feeling I have. I would bet Tiernan's baggage is trust issues and now he's gun-shy when it comes to relationships of any kind that take more effort than a handful of minutes in a closet or other seedy location.

Was I hurt when he rejected me last night? Yes. But I'm getting quite comfortable with the idea of emotional pain. I packed it up and tossed it in my own mental closet. And that will be my baggage to unpack at a later date. A much later date.

Smiling at Trixie, I say, "It went exactly as I expected it would."

I can tell from her expression she isn't sure whether that's a good or bad thing, but when I continue to smile, she makes the only assumption she can. "That's great! And now that your john-break cherry has been popped, you're part of the family."

I'm not sure Trixie could have used a worse turn of phrase. I grew up thinking my mom was my family, and by extension, the Dark Fae. Now I know that neither is true, and the people who should have been my family are gone. I have no family, yet this sweet girl wants me to feel welcome and a part of their sisterhood.

Telling myself not to cry, I fight back the warmth gathering behind my eyes. "Thanks, Trixie."

"You're welcome," she says. "Hey, can I borrow your bronzer? I can't find mine for the life of me."

"Oh yeah, here you go." She thanks me and starts applying the makeup. "Trix, do you know if there's a basement or some kind of cellar in this building?"

She frowns and pauses in her stippling. "Not that I know of. Why do you ask?"

Because if the text messages we got off Leather Coat Guy's phone are right, there's a group of fae females being held prisoner in some basement room with iron bracelets on their wrists to keep them weak.

I was determined to bring these bastards down before, but now I'm consumed by the idea. The thought of what those females are going through—from being held captive plus the constant drain on their powers and painful burns caused by the irons—makes me sick to my stomach.

But I can't tell Trixie any of that, so I give her a bogus story I came up with about being addicted to ghost hunting shows and going into basements to try and connect with spirits.

She tells me emphatically that she does not share my love for ghosts and hopes like hell there are no creepy basements under our feet. "Yeah, I suppose you're right. Getting scared while spinning on a pole upside down could cause some major injuries," I say with a laugh to ease her nerves. She joins in and then gets up to go change into her next costume, leaving me alone with my thoughts.

"It was a good idea to ask her," a deep voice says in my ear.

So much for being alone. He's been quiet most of the night so far that I almost forgot he was listening in. Tossing down my lipstick, I sigh in frustration. "Doesn't matter if I can't get the answers we're looking for."

"You will, Fi. Just keep asking around—someone has to know about a basement or lower level. And keep using that ghost hunting story. That was clever."

"Don't be too impressed, took me all night to come up with it. I'm heading out to the floor, so try to keep the commentary to a minimum."

"Understood."

I can hear the disappointment in his tone, but I don't comment on it. Things have been tense between us since last night when he shut me down. But instead of being mad at him, I should be thanking him. Somewhere along the line, I decided I want more with Tiernan than what he can give me. Even if he'd said yes, and he finally allowed us to truly explore each other sexually, that's as much as we'd ever have together.

I'm not going to settle for being on the fringes of anyone else's life ever again.

Walking into the main room, I scope out who might know a bit more than Trixie about this building. Then I remember what Tiernan said about bartenders and head straight back, managing to avoid the customers trying to flag me down by giving them the *just one minute* gesture, like I'm too parched and need a drink first before performing.

I find an open spot between customers, one facing the bar and the other with his eyes riveted on the stage, and signal to Joey, the bar manager. I've talked to him a few times and he seems like a decent enough guy. He tosses the bar towel onto his shoulder and greets me with a smile. "Hey, Candy, what can I get you?"

"Hiya handsome. I'll have a vodka and energy, hold the vodka please."

He chuckles as he cracks open a Red Bull and pours it over ice. "Need a pep in your step tonight, huh?"

I slap my palms on the top of the bar for emphasis. "That's an understatement. When I got home last night, I binged that new *Ghost Hunters* series instead of sleeping. Have you seen it?"

"Can't say that I have, no." He slides the glass to me and adds a straw.

I suck down several gulps like I wish I could mainline the stuff. "Oh man, that's so good. You know, I try to visit as many haunted spots as I can whenever I travel. With all the mob activity in this city over the years, I bet Vegas is just *crawling* with disgruntled ghosts. Hey!" I lean over the bar as far as I can, which isn't much, and wait for Joey to mimic me. "Is there like a basement or anything here I can explore?"

His amused expression shutters and his brown eyes narrow on me slightly. "Why would you think there's a basement here?"

Interesting. I give him a disarming smile. "I don't know, don't most places have basements?"

Joey straightens as he uses the towel from his shoulder to start drying a glass. "Nah," he says with a weak grin. "No basement here. You best hurry up with that drink and get back to work before Donnie comes back through."

The guy facing the bar to my left turns sideways and looks down at me from his considerable height. Piercing pale-blue eyes lock onto mine as he holds up a crisp one-hundred-dollar bill between two fingers. "It would please me very much if you would join me and my comrades at our table, *chestnyy*."

There's no mistaking his Russian origins, not only from the accent and the foreign word he called me, but the visible black and gray tattoos on his neck, chest, and the tops of his hands. His dark hair is styled perfectly and complemented by a nicely groomed beard. There's a scar that bisects his left eyebrow, creating a juxtaposition of bespoke violence with his well-cut suit that fits his broad shoulders perfectly. And the way he holds himself says no matter what the situation, he's in control.

I have a suspicion as to who this is, and if I'm right, I'm staring at one of the deadliest beings to live — or *sort of* live — in the last five hundred years, give or take a century. When I fail to form words or even blink, he takes pity on me. "Come, *chestnyy*, I will bring your drink. You will need your energy to entertain us, yes?"

He winks, then points to a table where two more Russians look like they're sitting in as extras for a mafia movie. Pasting on a bright smile, I pull myself together and walk in front of him toward his buddies while speaking as low as I can get away with. "Tiernan," I say sharply. "You wouldn't happen to know anything about a certain vampire being here, would you?"

I can practically hear him wincing through the tiny earpiece. "Relax, Fi—Dmitri's just there as backup. I made it very clear this is an eyes-only job."

"Oh, you misunderstand, Your *Highness*," I bite out. "My issue is that you keep micromanaging this operation like you don't think I can handle it. Giving the Russians lap dances, on the other hand, I have no issue with."

"Fiona, do *not* test my patience right now."

"Then don't *tempt* me," I fire back.

A deep laugh comes from behind me just as I reach where the *others* are sitting. Dmitri places my Red Bull on the table, then sits in the chair as regally as if it were a throne. "I think my friend does not want to watch you dance for me."

Tiernan growls. "We're not friends, we're parties with a mutual interest, and if he touches you, we'll be a lot less than that."

All three vampires chuckle and share a look like someone just told a joke.

"You can hear him?" I ask.

"Of course," he says matter-of-factly. "His kind has good hearing. Ours is better."

Donnie passes behind the Russians and arches a brow. Translation: *I'm not paying you to talk to the customers.*

Affecting my Candy persona, I twirl one of my white pigtails and bat my heavy-with-falsies eyes. "You want some sugar, Sugar?"

"*Da.* I have a big sweet tooth. In fact, I have two of them." He winks and smiles wide enough to flash me his lethal fangs. As I place my hands on his shoulders and straddle his thighs, I can't help but return his smile. For as scary as he's supposed to be, he has a charming side to rival that of the male growling in my ear.

I begin dancing, moving my hips suggestively, leaning in

so that the swells of my breasts above my corset are enticingly in front of his face.

"You are good at this, *chestnyy*. It is no wonder you have not been found out yet, even with your strange questions about basements."

"What does that word mean that you keep calling me?"

"It means fair one. Appropriate for one who is beautiful as you."

"He's a dead man," Tiernan says.

Dmitri answers him. "Yes, I have been that for a very long time."

"Well, as fun as it's been listening to both of you, Joey's reaction only solidified my suspicion that there's a lower level of some kind in this building."

"You are right," Dmitri says. "There is a private club downstairs. The main entrance that leads there is through the adjoining building with a high level of security. But I believe I have heard of another entrance used by some of the girls who also work down there."

If it's a door that the girls are using, then it must be somewhere in the back room where they get ready. I don't even think to say goodbye or thank you before power walking to the dressing area, ignoring the cheers and jeers and commands of the patrons to attend to them. I take a deep breath and say a little prayer to Rhiannon that the room is empty, then step inside. Praise the moon goddess, there's not a soul in sight.

I turn around in a slow circle, examining the area. I'm trying to think if I've seen anyone going in behind a clothes rack or—wait a minute. Has that black curtain always been hanging on the wall? A rack of shoes sits in front of it, and if you don't really analyze it, it looks like it just could be a strange choice of decor. Or like there's a window behind it that needs to be covered up so that no one can peek inside.

Or...like it's hiding a door.

Unsure of how much longer I'll be alone, I jog over in my five-inch Pleasers and pull back one side of the curtain. It's thick and heavy black velvet, like a stage curtain that goes from the ceiling all the way to the floor, and sure enough, there's a thick steel door behind it. I try the doorknob, but it's of course locked. I squat down and look at the lock to determine if it can be picked easily by a novice like me. Maybe if I use my hair pins…

"Hey! What the hell do you think you're doing, Candy?"

My heart jumps into my throat as I stand and spin around to find Donnie, the stage manager. He's holding his clipboard and glaring at me suspiciously. "I'm not doing anything. Just looking around at the new job site. You know, taking a breather and stuff."

"You are either full of shit or dumb as a box of rocks," he says. "Either way, not my job to care."

I breathe a sigh of relief like I just had a stay of execution. I'm about to thank him—although for what I don't know— and head back out to the main room when he lifts the tiny microphone on the cord of his headset and says, "Hey, boss, I caught Candy snooping in the back room by the curtain. Yeah. Right now? Okay, we're on our way." He drops the mic and arches a brow at me as he jerks his head in the direction of the main room. "Let's go. Boss wants to talk to you."

My stomach drops, and my pulse starts to race. *Stay calm, Fiona. Just keep playing the part of the curious new employee with a passion for ghost hunting. You can talk your way out of this.*

Donnie leads me back into the main room. I glance over at Dimitri and see him answering his phone. He's watching me intently and saying things I can't hear, but I assume he's speaking with Tiernan, who must have me on mute because I can't hear what he's saying, either. The vampire gives me a nod as if to say he has my back if I need it, and then Donnie leads me up a set of stairs to the loft, where the manager's office overlooks the club from behind large panes of two-way mirrors.

"I can't get a visual in there, Fiona—there aren't any cameras. But the Russians are standing by. If you need a distraction to get the hell out of there, say the words 'I'm fine' and they'll start a brawl the manager won't be able to ignore. Got it?"

Because I know he can still see me, I nod, but I'm not worried. I only met Frank once on the day of my interview. He was what I would expect of a man running a strip club. I don't think he listened to a word I said, instead letting his eyes do the deciding for him on whether I was pole dancer material. But that was as far as it went. He never even shook my hand, and the entire meeting lasted five minutes.

But when Donnie knocks on the door and is given permission for us to enter, it's not Frank sitting behind the desk waiting for us. Well-dressed and clean-shaven, he's a brown-haired businessman in his late forties, above-average height, and athletically slender, if that's a thing. Whoever this man is, he's way more intimidating than Frank, and he looks like he has all the time in the world to question a suspicious employee.

"Hello, there. My name is Stanley Leone, and I own this club. What's your name?"

"Candy."

He arches a dubious brow but doesn't press me for the truth, not that I would give it to him anyway. It's not like I filled out any paperwork for this gig. Since I'm supposedly only filling in for Sapphire, I agreed to work on tips alone.

"Thank you, Donnie, I'll take it from here." I keep my eyes forward, resisting the urge to watch my safety net leave. The loud music from downstairs floods the room as the door is opened and then muffled again with the resounding click of it being closed. "Candy, I understand you were trying to get into things not meant for you to get into."

"I know, and I'm sorry. I have a strange obsession with ghost hunting and thought maybe it led to a basement I could explore." Thank Rhiannon for the ability to lie through my blunt fucking teeth.

He steeples his fingers in front of him and tilts his head to the side. "Now why is it I don't believe you?"

Damn it. Apparently telling the truth your whole life makes you a shitty liar. Tiernan comes through like the proverbial devil on my shoulder. "Double down, Fi. He can't prove you're lying, so just stick to your story."

I open my mouth to do just that, but something about this man stops me. There's a shrewdness in his eyes that says he can see through people's bullshit. And if he owns this club, then maybe he has something to do with the captive females, or at the very least has ties with the NPO. So, at the last second, I take a different approach.

"You're right, Mr. Leone, that's not the real reason."

"Fiona—"

I continue as if I don't have a pissed-off prince in my ear. "The truth is I heard there's a private club that some of the girls get to work at downstairs, and it piqued my curiosity. Private club means more money. More money means nicer things. And unfortunately for me, I have extremely expensive taste."

Leone leans forward in his chair, placing his folded hands on the desk and studying me with a predatory grin. "Now *that*, I believe. Do you happen to know what kind of private club I run?"

I hear Tiernan curse my name and then the white noise from my earpiece cuts off, meaning he's muted himself again. "I've heard some things," I hedge, hoping that if I guess incorrectly, I can chalk it up to misinformation.

He strokes his chin in thought, then seems to make a

decision. "And based on the things you've heard, if I were to hire you, show me a position that would be required of you. Literally speaking."

Tiernan comes back on. "Fucking hell, Fiona, it's a private BDSM club. Dmitri says the girls who work there are subs for hire."

Okay, so it's not exactly an easy gig like waitressing or anything, but at least I know what Leone is looking for. With as much grace as I can manage in these shoes, I lower to my knees, sit on my heels, place my palms up on my thighs, and settle my gaze on the floor.

I hear Leone stand as he gives me a few appreciative claps. "That was lovely, Candy. I'm impressed. You may look up," he says.

I lift my head and have to swallow the rising bile at the feeling of being in a submissive pose like this to anyone other than someone of my choosing, someone I trust, which is certainly not the man in front of me. It's been a long time since I've indulged this side of myself, but there's just something about Leone that throws up my internal alarm.

"How would you like to start working downstairs tonight? We'll give you a trial run and see how you do."

I hesitate, going through all the possibilities of what I might be expected to do once I get down there. But what he's offering is an all-access pass to everything I've been searching for, including the missing girls.

Tiernan speaks instantly. "Don't even think about it, Fiona. Tell him you'll consider it, tell him you've changed your mind, tell him—"

"I would like that very much, Sir."

A slow grin slips onto Leone's face, obviously pleased with my use of an honorific title with him, even though he hasn't done anything to earn it. "Then let's get started."

CHAPTER SIXTEEN

TIERNAN

"Fi, can you hear me? *Fiona...*" Nothing but static comes through the speaker. "Fuck!"

I slam my fist into the side of the surveillance van, causing a sizable dent in the metal. Clyde and Evan barely even react, having grown used to my outbursts every time Fiona defied me over the last few days. I've never been this emotionally volatile in all my one hundred and sixty-five years, but leave it to a petite redheaded female to drive me to the brink of madness.

"Everything in here is useless now. We had no visuals and now we don't even have her on comms. Isn't there anything else we can tap into that helps her?"

The guys are already typing furiously on keyboards, what looks like a bunch of gibberish code filling up the screens. Clyde looks up briefly. "We're trying right now. The security system for the underground club is connected to the one we already hacked into, but it was hidden behind multiple complex firewalls. Since we didn't know the other club existed, we never looked for it."

"Shit, I don't know if we'll be able to get through," Evan says, his brows knitted in concentration. "I mean, we're good, but we're only Vegas-PD-good. Whoever built this system is like *black hat* kind of good. Everything we're trying is blocked a nano-second after we get it open."

Cursing under my breath, I go back to my call with Dmitri as I climb out of the van. "Romanov, tell me you know how to get us in there."

"You still have emergency potion?"

"Got it right here." I pull the small vial from my jeans pocket.

"Take it and meet me in front of Hell's Kitchen next door."

"Keep trying, guys. Call me if you get anything." I slam the door shut and down the contents, wincing at the bitter taste as I jog down the block where Dmitri is already waiting for me. "Where are your comrades?"

"They remained inside in case we cannot find her and she manages to get back upstairs."

"Not finding her isn't an option."

He holds a key card up to the panel with a red light at the top. The light switches to green and there's a click. "Then you had better hope that potion works fast."

We enter a gutted-out restaurant. The tables are all pushed to the outer walls with chairs upturned on top of them, and the only sound is the faint buzz of the fluorescent lights. The wood floors that were probably polished to a shine in the past are now dull but clean.

Our footsteps echo on the boards as we make our way to the back where the kitchen is. "Devil's Dungeon is through the old cooler. Security makes sure only members and their guests who are approved ahead of time go in."

"Okay, cool, so you'll use your compulsion and—"

"No compulsion. I cannot use it."

I narrow my gaze on him. "Performance anxiety?" His response is a droll expression, telling me it's none of my fucking business. Sighing, I say, "Fine. Then how am I getting in?"

"Adam works Sundays. He will allow you in."

"How do you know that?"

"I play with him on the occasion I find myself in town. He gets much out of pleasing his Master." The serious Russian's mouth quirks up on one side like he's recalling past scenes. "He is very good boy."

"Let's hope that doesn't change."

He holds his hand up when we reach the swinging doors that lead into the kitchen. Through the round windows we can see the large cooler with the words Devil's Dungeon in red neon over it. And guarding it is not one but *two* bouncers who look like they eat nails for breakfast. Their suit shirts and pants are stretched to the point of being in danger of splitting if they move the wrong way.

"*Der'mo.*" Dmitri signals for me to follow him away from the kitchen and around the corner into a hallway for the restrooms.

"Why'd you say 'shit'? Are neither of those beasts Adam?"

"*Nyet*, they are not."

Perfect. "The one guy was holding something that looks like an iPad," I say. "What's that for?"

"To pull up my information before they allow me access downstairs."

"Including whether or not you have approved guests?"

"*Da.*"

I hit a button on my phone and call the guys in the van. "Evan, can you get into Romanov's membership file and add me in as an approved guest with a photo and alias? I need to be someone out of town and filthy rich but not anyone who would be well-known by the general public."

"That shouldn't be a problem. Give me a minute." Several seconds of key clicking feels like an eternity before he finally says, "I've got it. You're Dante Ricci, an Italian-American Formula 1 race car driver for the Ferrari team, partying with your friend in Vegas before the new season of Grand Prix races begins."

Romanov and I share a quizzical look. "That's somehow both super random and oddly specific, but okay," I say quietly. "We good?"

"Should be good to go in another sixty seconds. I'm sending you a reference photo for your glamour."

I end the call and use the photo he texted to affect my new persona. With Erin's potion, the glamour won't be stripped away by the hag stones, so I'll remain Dante Ricci for as long as the spell lasts.

"All right, the plan is to get in, get Fiona, and get out with as little disruption as possible. I know your clan's motto is typically rip throats out first and ask questions later, but that's not how we do things here, Romanov. If things go sideways for any reason, the goal is *zero* human casualties. Got it?"

He shrugs one shoulder. "Sounds very boring, but is your rodeo, Verran."

"That it is." I give him the nod to lead us back, then we push through the swinging doors and enter the gutted kitchen. There's nothing left but the four walls and doors for the attached storage rooms.

Dimitri suddenly transforms from serious and scowling to pouring on the charm like he did when I showed up at his home in Los Angeles. "Good evening, gentlemen. Lovely night for a session, is it not?"

The guards' eyes widen before they share a brief look. The one on the left holds up a hag stone and peers at us through the hole in its center. Then points his finger directly at me. "He's fae!"

"So much for your magic potion."

"Now's not really the time, Romanov," I snap, right before both beasts lunge for us. "Guess we're doing this the old-fashioned way."

We throw punches in a coordinated attack. All we need to do is knock them out long enough for us to get to Fiona and get out of here. Our powerful right hooks land at the same time, whipping our opponents' heads to the side, saliva spraying from between their lips...and that's it. They don't crumple to the floor unconscious; they don't even stagger backward.

However, they *do* turn back smiling without a care in the world, like neither of us had any more force behind our strikes than a grade schooler.

I stare in shock. "What the fuck?"

But there's no time to ponder the answer to my question because all hell breaks loose. Four larger-than-average males fighting in close quarters is chaotic at best and a total shitshow at worst. Punches and kicks land over and over, and friendly fire is unavoidable when your target ducks at the last second and your partner is directly behind them.

When my fist accidentally connects with Dmitri's temple, he shouts a growled "Enough!" His movements are a blur and in the next second, two bodies lie on the floor with their heads twisted sickeningly the wrong way on their shoulders.

Breathing heavy, I push a hand through my hair. "What did I fucking say before?"

Romanov straightens his shirt. "You said no killing humans. They were too strong to be human."

I drag a hand down my mouth and jaw. "Yeah, okay. But then what are they, and how are they reading as human?"

"I do not know." He takes out his cell and fires off a text. "My men are on their way to collect the bodies, so they are not discovered. If they find any answers, they will let us know."

"Good enough," I say, not really giving a shit anymore. I only want to get downstairs to Fiona. Apparently, Erin's iron poisoning affected her enough that her spell didn't take at all. If anyone else has a hag stone they want to use in my direction, this randomly-specific glamour won't do me any damn good.

Dmitri pilfers an access card from one of the mysterious guards and holds it to the panel on the wall. It beeps with a green light, unlocking the huge metal door. I pull it open, and we enter into what used to be the kitchen cooler.

Straight ahead is an arched doorway that leads to a red stairwell with a winding flight of stairs. As we follow them, we get to a vestibule that looks like it could be a waiting room in any high-end corporate office with leather couches, modern glass coffee tables, and even a minibar and water cooler.

There are also two doors on the far wall. The one on the left says "Succubi" and the one on the right is labeled "Incubi."

"Wow," I say flatly. "They really committed to the whole Devil and Hell theme."

"It is cliche, yes, but it is done well."

We go through the Incubi door into a luxury locker room where members can change into their kinky gear and prepare for a night of fun. It's large and well-lit with plenty of space to move around. There are rows of lockers, a comfortable seating area, and several large mirrors. The walls are adorned with BDSM artwork, and the floors are covered in plush black carpet except for the tiled shower area.

"I have some leathers you can wear and a mask."

"Mask?"

"This is very exclusive, invitation-only BDSM club for Vegas's rich and powerful. Some do not worry about their reputations, like me. But most wear masks to protect their identities. No cell phones allowed past the locker rooms, regardless. There are public play spaces and private rooms."

"It can't be that exclusive if my brothers and I weren't invited."

"I know this will come as a shock, but not everyone loves the Verran Kings of Vegas."

I catch the leather pants he tosses at me. "Including you?"

He shrugs. "I like the youngest one. I have not yet decided

on the older two. Time will tell."

"I don't need your adoration, Romanov, just for you to hold up your end of our deal."

"And so I am," he says, removing his suit shirt to reveal an upper body almost completely covered in black and gray tattoos. "As I expect of you when the time comes."

"I'm a male of my word. You call, I'll be there."

He nods, satisfied with my answer. The deal we made is open-ended and unspecified, meaning he can cash in my IOU at any point in the future, near or far, and for any reason. It's weighed heavily in his favor but I don't give a damn. All that matters is Fiona's safety while we work to bring down NPO. That's his job in all this, nothing else.

As soon as we're both dressed in dungeon-appropriate gear—leather pants, no shirts, and me with a half mask—we place our street clothes and phones in the locker and close it up. "Let's go find your woman."

The main area of Devil's Dungeon is dark and erotic with red walls and black-painted concrete floors. The ceiling is adorned with multiple hard points for suspension work and there are stations throughout holding a variety of toys, whips, and restraints. With no windows, the only light is from red lamps and clusters of large candles around the black leather furniture where people can relax and socialize or watch the scenes playing out around them.

Bass-heavy music is pumping through the speakers, but unlike upstairs where it's at ear-bleeding levels, it's low enough that a safe word can be heard. Not to mention all the moans and cries of pleasure, the echoing cracks of paddles or hands striking bare skin, and the unmistakable sound of flesh meeting flesh in a hard fucking.

If I was here under different circumstances, everything about the environment would call to that darker side of me that's been buried, tempting it to claw its way to the surface for the kind of carnal fun it used to enjoy.

"What I don't understand is if this is a kink club, where do the hired girls come in? Does Leone run some kind of rent-a-submissive business model?"

"Only partly. Most of the members come with their own partners or hook up with other members here. But they also have the option of hiring a play partner in one of several types of roles, not just subs. Everything is done with consent and practiced safely, as assured by the dungeon masters on duty."

"Did you know Leone owned both Devil's Door and Devil's Dungeon? We didn't even know the dungeon existed, but when we tried to find out who owned Devil's Door, it was just a shell company with no trail to follow."

"No, I did not know who owned either. It was never my concern. I did not frequent the club upstairs, and I only attend the dungeon when I am in town. Most of my play happens back in Los Angeles where I spend the majority of my time." He nods suddenly in the direction of a small group of members. They're standing around Fiona, who's now wearing a white bra and panty set and white half mask, appraising her like she's fucking livestock.

Red eclipses my vision and my nails begin to lengthen into sharp points. My fangs ache to tear into anyone thinking for even one second that they can have what's mine. I take a step forward, but Dmitri stops me with a hand on my chest. His stern expression is one I recognize, as Caiden used it often with me and Finni when we were younger and in trouble. *Let me handle this.*

Trusting the vampire lord doesn't come easy to me, but I'm the one who brought him in to help protect Fiona in the first place. And if nothing else, I know he's a man of his word. Drawing in a steadying breath, I give him a clipped nod and follow his lead.

"Ah, a new girl," Dmitri gushes as we approach the group.

"This is perfect. You see, my friend? I told you I would make sure you had a good time tonight. This place has the best submissives Vegas has to offer, and by the looks of this sweet thing, it just got better. Dungeon Master, I would like to gift this new angel to my esteemed friend."

Fiona's head is angled down in proper submission, so she can't see me—and even if she could, I don't *look* like me—but she can recognize my voice. "She's positively stunning." The tension melts from her posture, confirming she knows I'm the one here with Dmitri.

Leone's lips peel back in a poor attempt at a smile. "I'm sorry, Master D, but Mistress Alma was the first to request her as a playmate for her pet."

A woman who looks in her late fifties and dressed in a leather body suit flicks her platinum blond hair behind her shoulders and stares us down. At her feet, on the end of a metal leash, is a man in leather shorts, harness, and collar with a puppy-play mask. He cocks his head to the side, and I hold my hands up to assure him I'm not judging. However, if his mistress gets in my way of taking Fiona, I won't be held responsible for what I do to either one of them.

"Perhaps my pet and I will grow tired of her in a few hours," Mistress Alma says, giving Fiona another perusal as though trying to gauge her value. "Your friend may have her then, Master D."

"That is a generous offer, Mistress, however my friend is leaving town and only has a few hours to play this evening." Dmitri turns back to Leone. "He is a well-established master at many international clubs, but he has grown bored of them and their available subs as of late. I wasn't sure here would prove any different for him, but he is very taken with this new beauty. If he has a good experience, he is sure to spread the word about Devil's Dungeon in his many travels."

Leone arches a brow of interest at me. "Do you travel for

business or pleasure, Master..."

"You can call me Master Dante." *It's not my name, but that's what you can call me.* "And I'd say it's definitely both." *Sometimes Caiden drags me along on business meetings in New York, sometimes I'm partying in Hong Kong.*

Clever half truths can only take me so far, so I don't indulge his curiosity more than that. Thankfully, my partner in crime steps in with an assist.

"My friend is too modest to boast. He is an accomplished Formula 1 driver and travels all over the world to compete in Grand Prix races. Very exciting. And after he is done racing, he makes time for *personal* enjoyment at local clubs."

"Well, Master Dante, we're delighted you chose to seek your enjoyment here at the Dungeon during your visit. We have many lovely submissives to choose from. I'd be happy to show you—"

"*No,*" I say sharply. Too sharp, from the way Leone is now studying me. Reining in my frustration, I try another tactic: bruising his ego. "I'm sorry, I understand that as the DM on duty you're just trying to do your job. Perhaps I could speak with the manager or someone else in charge to plead my case."

"I'm as in charge as it gets, Master Dante." A smug grin lifts the corners of his mouth. "I own this club and the one above it. Plead away."

"Money is no object."

"Nor is it for Mistress Alma or any of the other members here," he says, unmoved.

I look over at my competition, who's studying her claw-like nails out of boredom, clearly confident in the outcome. Fiona has taken to picking at the skin of her thumbs. If I don't settle this in the next few minutes, I'll be tempted to grab her and run out of here. But that's not an option; we need to find those girls, so I have to get us out of this.

"Then would you be interested in VIP tickets to the Grand

Prix race being held here in Vegas this fall, complete with pit passes and a personal tour?"

That gives him pause, and the look in his eyes tells me I've got his attention. He can be interested in the exclusive package all he wants. I never said I'd give it to him.

"Master D mentioned you're a well-established master," Leone says, continuing to scrutinize me. "Do you have a specialty?"

Finally, I'm able to give a straight answer. "Whips."

The close-lipped grin he gives me is about as patronizing as a pat on the head. "Ah, I see."

My gaze narrows. "Do you?"

"Of course," he says, "but while they require a certain amount of skill, I thought you might specialize in something less common than floggers."

"Single tails," I grind out between clenched teeth.

He pauses. "Pardon?"

"I'm an expert with single tails. Bullwhips, snakes, flickers, dragontails. You name it, I wield it."

His eyebrows shoot skyward, and even my competition's head snaps in my direction. Leone appraises me with another once-over like this somehow paints me in a whole new light.

"Very well, Master Dante, you win," he says with a used car salesman's enthusiasm. "I accept your VIP offer and award you Candy."

Mistress Alma stalks off in a huff, her pet scampering after her. I barely hold back a sigh of relief as I take Fiona's hand, anxious to get her out of here. But we don't take more than two steps when Leone adds, "On one condition."

"And what's that?" My scarcely seen temper is on a hair trigger at this point.

"It's rare that we get anyone who specializes in the art of whips. I'd like you to give us a demonstration. After that, you may play with her wherever you wish, including one of our private rooms."

The private rooms. If the girls are anywhere, there's a good chance they could be in that area of the building. And if Leone thinks we're playing privately, he won't be breathing down our necks. It's our best chance at finding them.

All I have to do is indulge his request.

My stomach drops. The thought of doing a public whipping scene with Fiona makes me uneasy, especially since we've never played before. I catch Dmitri's attention and he gives me the barest acknowledgment. He's thinking the same thing, silently telling me I need to do this.

Putting on my best indulgent smile, I say, "I accept."

CHAPTER SEVENTEEN

TIERNAN

I do my best to block out the small crowd gathering and give Dmitri a short list of whips to retrieve for me, then I focus on readying Fiona. Instead of using something stationary and confining like the St. Andrew's Cross, I choose a pair of wrist cuffs hanging from chains attached to a hard point in the ceiling. This will allow me to move around her freely and check in on her emotional state more thoroughly.

Taking advantage of the expectation that I would have a private conversation with the sub I intend to play with—especially one I supposedly don't know—I speak just above a whisper next to her ear so only Fiona can hear me.

"If you're not good with this, just say the word and I'll figure another way out."

"No, don't. He's already suspicious because you and Dmitri were so insistent about me. I'm glad you showed up when you did. I didn't think he'd push me onto someone the second we got down here. I thought I'd have time to be on my own to poke around."

"Believe me, I'm going to address your recklessness properly later."

"We need to find those missing girls," she whispers.

"We will. But first we need to get through this and away from scrutiny. I'm going to make this scene short, taking you through the stages as quickly and safely as I can. But make no mistake, the scene will be *very real*. Do you trust me?"

Blue eyes meet mine. "I do."

I have a hard time thinking I deserve a female's trust after what happened with Julie. That Fiona didn't even hesitate makes me feel ten kinds of things that are so entangled I can't tell them apart.

"I know you're a masochist, but do you have experience as a whip bottom?"

"With floggers, yes. I've watched single whip scenes but never bottomed for one."

The knot in my stomach tightens. "We're not going that far. Dmitri's grabbing a deerskin flogger, leather cat o' nine, and a dragontail. What are your hard limits?"

She shakes her head. "I don't have any that would come into play for this."

"Good. We'll use the traffic light system. Green means you're fine and okay to continue, yellow means pause and check in, red is your safe word that stops everything and the scene is over. Understood?"

"I know what the traffic light system is, for gods' sake." I can tell she's about to brat-out and roll her eyes, so I remind her that we're being watched with a sharp raise of my brow. She immediately corrects her attitude, though I know for a fact it's only because of the situation we're in. "Understood. *Master.*"

I have to stop my lip from curling. That title might work well for Dmitri, but I was never fond of it. I preferred the common "Sir" when playing with subs before. Simple, impersonal. But neither of those feel right coming from Fiona.

"You may use that for now. We'll need to agree on

something different in the future."

Her eyes widen behind the mask. I'm just as shocked at my words, at what they imply. But now that they're out there, I don't want to take them back.

Leone clears his throat loudly where he stands waiting with the others. The time for secret conversations is over. The room is waiting for a show, so it's a show they'll get. Raising my voice to a normal level, I start the scene.

"As of now, little sub, you are mine to do with as I please." I reach up and test the chains holding her arms overhead, then recheck the cuffs, ensuring they're tight enough she can't slip out while still allowing for proper circulation. "Tell me your safe word."

"Red, Master."

From the corner of my eye, I see Dmitri return with the items I requested. "Very good. Let's begin."

Everything I do to her from this moment on is part of the scene. Every touch, every word, every look will be intentional. Calculated. It's a seduction of the mind as much as it is of the body, easing her into a headspace where her submission becomes a gateway to mental euphoria and heightened pleasures through the careful pain I inflict.

Unhooking her bra in the back, I grab onto a shoulder strap with both hands. I hold her gaze as I tear it in half. She draws in a sharp breath, and satisfaction rolls through me when her pupils begin to eclipse the blue of her irises. I do the same with the other strap then toss the ruined garment aside. It frustrates me to leave the half mask and white wig on her. After all this time, I'm finally getting to see Fiona the way I've dreamed of—restrained and under my control—and the parts that make her *her* are hidden.

My eyes are drawn to her exposed breasts, and I blatantly stare at her rosy nipples as they tighten into needy little buds. I slowly map them out with my fingertips, reacquainting myself with their teardrop shape, tracing over the faint blue lines of her veins, and grazing their tips with my thumbs.

Her belly sucks in on a quiet gasp before a whimper escapes from the back of her throat. That's when I realize that it doesn't matter if her face and hair are covered; I could be blindfolded and recognize the feel of her body beneath my hands and the familiar sounds she makes when I touch her.

I grip the back of her neck with one hand while the other trails down her body to tease her clit with slow circles through the small triangle of her G-string that's already damp with her arousal. Groaning my appreciation, I add a bit of pressure and watch her muscles melt and her eyes drift closed. "Good girl. Stay focused on me, on my touch."

I nod to Dmitri, and he steps forward and places the handle of the black flogger in my outstretched hand. The handle is made of sturdy wood, wrapped in black leather for a comfortable grip. I give it a few test twirls in a figure-eight pattern and am satisfied with the balance. The twelve-inch long falls are soft and supple, yet will provide a satisfying smack. I trail them up her stomach and over her breasts, letting the sensation and anticipation of what's to come wash over her. Then it's time to move on to the next phase.

Taking a steadying breath, I begin my first whipping session on a person in a decade.

Tapping into my skill and muscle memory, I move the flogger in a figure-eight pattern, working solely from the wrist and keeping my distance so that the falls lightly graze one breast, then the other. I repeat the fluid motion again and again, warming up the skin by bringing her blood to the surface, which releases the endorphins that allow pleasure and pain to comingle.

I change areas on her body, spending a couple minutes on her stomach before pausing to brush the long hair of her wig in front of her shoulders so I can warm up her upper back and finally the perfect globes of her ass.

Once she's comfortable, I switch the flogger out for the cat o'nine tails. It looks almost the same, except the nine falls are individually braided and knotted at the ends. It provides quite a bit more sting and takes a lot of care to wield properly.

Continuing to move around her, I gradually increase the intensity as she gets used to the sensation, making sure I don't spend too much time in any one area. I pay close attention to her breathing and the color of her skin, watching to make sure it doesn't turn red, which is a sign it's overworked.

She's responding beautifully. I let her soft moans and whispered pleas for more sink into me like a balm for my wounded soul. Fiona is more perfect like this than I ever imagined, and it's becoming difficult to not want to push myself to see how high I can truly make her fly.

Eager to take her to the next level so I can watch her come undone for me, I signal to Dmitri that I want the dragontail. There are different variations, but this one is a four-inch-wide soft leather strip that tapers to a point at the end of the three feet in length. It's a unique whip that isn't commonly known, which makes it more of a novelty. Yet it's not hard to use with a little bit of practice. It's a similar motion to snapping a towel.

The pointed tip of the tail flicks over Fiona's body, and with every lick of pleasure-pain, her arousal builds until she's panting with desire and moaning in need. Her entire body begins to quiver as I push her closer to the edge of her climax.

Suddenly Leone's grating voice penetrates our bubble. "I certainly hope you're not planning on ending the scene without showing us your skill with the bullwhip, Mr. Ricci. Your dragontail work is impressive, but it's not quite as rare as getting to witness a true master with a single tail."

I could kill the bastard for interrupting Fiona's head space, let alone mine. I know he knows better than to interrupt a scene; he's swinging his dick around, reminding me he's in control of our situation.

I spare a glance back and can practically see his wheels turning. I should've let him hire Fiona out and then handled the problem with Alma, even if it meant hogtying and gagging her and her pet before shoving them into a closet.

But my inability to keep my cool forced Dmitri to act so out of character that now it seems Stanley can't shake the feeling something is off. If I can't show him that I'm as experienced as I claimed, there's a good chance he'll pull on that thread of doubt until our whole story is unraveled.

Dmitri must realize the same thing, because he's already retrieved a four-foot bullwhip for me and pressed the coil into my hand. "Can you truly do this?"

I meet his pale-blue gaze. Real concern for Fiona is there, and my respect for the vampire lord grows exponentially. "Yeah," I rasp out. "I can."

"Then give him what he wants so you can take her to a private room. He won't be able to deny your duty to administer aftercare."

Keeping hold of the handle, I let the rest of the whip fall to the floor and flex my hand, focusing on the feel of the braided leather pressing into my palm. I have a whole rack of whips at home—multiple versions of the different types used in BDSM with different lengths, weights, and materials. Luckily, I have a similar one to this and am very adept with it, so there will be less room for error.

For the first time, I'm glad I forced myself to practice regularly over the years as a twisted version of self-imposed punishment and exposure therapy. Because of that, I'm confident in my skill. I should be fine as long as I don't let my head mess with me.

No, *fuck* that. There's no *should be* about it. I would rather flay the skin from my own body than risk harming Fiona. So *I will* be fine. I will be present in the moment, I will stay focused on my submissive, and I will take care of her—first with my whip, then with my hands.

Because Romanov is right. The sooner I give Leone what he wants, the sooner I get us out from under his microscope. It's time to stop running from my past…and pray to Rhiannon it doesn't catch up to me until I'm far enough away that Fiona isn't caught in the blast.

CHAPTER EIGHTEEN

FIONA

I'm not sure how long it's been since our scene was brought to a halt by that asshat Leone, but even a second is too much. He's lucky I'm floaty in subspace enough to not want to murder him where he stands. I can't promise the same about Tiernan, though. I'm not so far gone that I don't see the tension in his shoulders and the way the muscles in his jaw are working as he approaches me.

He hangs the whip around his neck and strokes my hip with one hand while cupping my face with the other. "How are you doing, Little Red? Feeling okay?"

"Yes, Master, I feel really good." Lowering my voice to a whisper, I ask, "What about you? Something's wrong, I can tell."

His Adam's apple bobs in his throat, but it's the only indication that he's struggling to respond as he lets his hands roam over my heated flesh. "Nothing is wrong. I apologize that we were interrupted, but I'm going to take care of you. I'll bring you right back to where I had you, then push you further until you fly for me." Two fingers pinch my nipple in a vise and pull. I gasp from the sharp bite, then moan as the pain zings down to my aching clit. "That's a good girl, just like that. Stay focused on me and don't move. Think you can do that for me?"

"Yes, Master."

"Tell me your safe word."

"Red, Master."

His hands move over my back and down to grip my ass cheeks as he speaks low next to my ear. "Now swear to me you'll use it if you even get to yellow. Swear it, Fiona."

That he switched to my name throws me off for a second, so I don't immediately answer. He gives me a swift crack on my butt to get my attention. "I will." He pulls back to briefly look into my eyes, and I can see a hint of doubt swimming in the golden-brown pools of his glamour. "I swear it," I whisper.

Satisfied, he nods once, then walks away from me, swinging the whip out in an arc in front of him to push the crowd back far enough to give him the room he needs.

He begins by using a warm-up technique I've seen Tops use before, using a side arm motion to wrap the end of the whip around my thighs, hips, and upper back. The anticipation of when he'll switch to the more serious straight-on approach is killing me. He's moved behind me, so I can't see him, but there's a break in his rhythm. A moment later I feel his hand skim down my back, over my cheeks, and up my hips.

Then he appears in my field of vision. His eyes lock onto mine and hold my gaze as his hand continues to roam. "What color are you?"

"Green, Master," I whisper. Fingers graze my clit through the drenched material covering my aching pussy, causing me to mewl and press forward into his touch.

"Good girl. Almost there, Little Red. Let my whip guide you to that place where you soar for me," he says, taking his hand away. Once again he disappears from view, and all I can do is wait...

Crack!

My entire body jolts from the sting of the popper as it snaps against the center of my right cheek. It's closely followed by a matching snap to the left side, then he continues with erratic patterns of placement and rhythm so I can't anticipate when I'll feel the next strike or where.

The sensation of the single tail biting into my flesh as Tiernan expertly wields it is exhilarating. Surrendering myself to his will, to his whip, is quickly becoming a drug I know I'll crave long after the last lash. I'm in a state of blissful ecstasy as the pain and pleasure meld together and my orgasm barrels toward me like a runaway freight train, my pussy wetter and wetter with each strike he administers.

My eyes drifted shut at some point, so I don't realize he's moved until I hear the crack of the whip in front of me a split second before I feel a flame lick over my clit that detonates my climax. Throwing my head back, I scream as the full-body orgasm rips through me, my limbs shaking as I come harder than I ever thought possible.

My eyes are too heavy to open, but I know the moment he's close. The warmth of his body melts over my exposed skin, and his scent permeates the air around me. Then another large, shirtless man crowds my back and wraps his arms around my waist, lifting slightly to relieve the tension on my restraints.

"You did so good, *chestnyy.*" *Ah, Dmitri.* I should've known he'd be the only one here Tiernan allows to touch me. "Relax and your Master will take care of you."

I manage to grunt in acknowledgment as Tiernan reaches up to undo the buckle on my left cuff. When my wrist is free, he slowly lowers my arm to my side, then gives my shoulder a quick rub before repeating the process for my right arm.

Tiernan scoops me up and cradles me against his chest. "Hold on, baby, I'm bringing us somewhere private to take care of you."

I manage to crack my eyes open, the urgency of before creeping back to the surface. "The girls," I whisper.

Tiernan looks at Dmitri who nods. "During your scene, I sent someone to save a room for you. Through those double doors, down the hall, third room on right. You take care of her and I will look for Adam, see if he knows anything. When you're ready, come and find me in the main area."

"Thanks, man. See you soon," Tiernan says, then follows Dmitri's instructions. As soon as he closes and locks the door behind us, Tiernan carries me over to the large bed and places me in the center. I try to scoot under the covers, but he stops me. "Not yet, sweetheart, I need to check you over first to make sure you're all right."

I attempt to bat his hands away. "I'm fine, Tiernan. I just want to get cozy and snuggle as I come down. Come and get cozy with me."

His hands roam over the places on my body where the different whips worked over my skin. But his touch isn't seductive or even affectionate, it's clinical, methodical, and the furrow on his brow is intense. "Tiernan, what's wrong?"

"Turn over so I can check your back," he says, trying to push me onto my side.

I resist. "Tiernan—"

"Fiona, stop fucking fighting me on this!"

Both of us freeze, my eyes wide as I take in his manic state and realize something is definitely wrong. Regret washes over his features and he drops his head to grab fistfuls of his hair.

"Fuck I'm sorry. I never should have agreed to that scene. I fucking *knew* better than to open the cage, but I just couldn't resist, could I? Like a godsdamn addict ruining ten years of sobriety the minute someone offered me a hit."

I'm totally stunned, but when he turns to get off the bed, I scramble up to my knees and stop him. "Whoa, hold on. Tiernan, talk to me. What's going on? What are you going on about?"

I grab his face with both hands and force him to look at me, grateful he no longer has his glamour up so I can see the real him. Pain swims in his golden eyes, and it cleaves my heart in two. I think he's experiencing Dom drop—an extreme emotional drop, similar to what subs can go through after a difficult or highly intense scene—so whatever it was that I saw bothering him right before he switched to the bullwhip, his brain is amplifying it by a thousand right now.

"Why don't you come get under the covers with me and we can give each other aftercare while we talk. Please?" When I suspect he's about to turn me down, I brush a section of his hair back from his forehead and lightly trail my fingernails over his scalp.

He closes his eyes briefly, then nods and helps me get us both settled beneath the warm blankets. I rest my head on his chest and sink into the comfort of his arms around me. I almost wish I wasn't floaty from subspace so I could fully appreciate the weight of this moment that I've been dreaming about for months—being in a bed and cuddling with Tiernan after doing a scene together. I should probably pinch myself, but if this *is* only a dream, then I'd rather not wake up.

"Tell me why you're so worried you hurt me, Tiernan. I didn't safe-out, so you should know I'm fine," I say, absently drawing circles through the light dusting of hair on his pecs.

"Because the last time I did a whip scene, the sub didn't use her safe word…" He audibly swallows. "I ended up hurting her."

"What happened?"

"Julie. She told me she had plenty of experience as a whip bottom. With my skill level, I didn't want to take the time necessary to train someone, so it was my rule to never play with first timers. We discussed limits before the scene; she said she didn't have any and that she had a high pain threshold."

I don't interrupt him, but now I know why he seemed

shaken earlier. We had an almost identical conversation. It'd be impossible not to have that trigger the past.

"I restrained her facing away from me on a St. Andrew's Cross. I started slow and easy and worked my way up from there, as always. Over the course of an hour, I checked on her multiple times. Every time she said she was green, and I was careful not to overwork any one area.

"It was going great. I was in the zone, and she was handling it beautifully. After another green check-in, I focused my efforts on her cheeks and pushed things to the next level—breaking the skin. She took three strikes before finally screaming in pain. Even then she didn't use the safe word. But I'll never forget the sound of her anguish in that scream.

"I rushed to release her from the Cross and when I gently lowered her to the bed, she curled into the fetal position on her side. She wouldn't look at me and flinched every time I touched her. I had to bring in another Dom to administer aftercare. I felt like a fucking monster. It was my job to take care of her, and I not only failed in that, I was also the one who hurt her."

"But you didn't do it intentionally, Tiernan, and she kept giving you the green light—literally. So I don't understand, how did it even get to that point?"

"Months after it happened, Julie came to see me. She apologized and told me it wasn't my fault. That she'd wanted to play with me so badly she lied about her experience and limits. She admitted that things stopped being fun for her when I transitioned to the dragontail but she continued giving me the green light out of pride, and even after I moved on to the bullwhip."

"Oh my gods," I whisper, hurting for this man who lived with the thought he'd recklessly caused harm to another. "Did it help that she absolved you and apologized?"

"On the surface, yes. But I'd already spent months torturing myself about it and vowing to stay away from BDSM altogether, so the damage had already been done in that respect."

"That's why you never wanted to do anything more with me," I said.

"It wasn't about not wanting to. Fuck, Fi, there was nothing I wanted more than to have you like that. It was about not trusting myself. And a Dom who doesn't trust himself is a danger to any sub he plays with. I couldn't take that chance with you."

"But now you have," I say, looking up at him. "And you know that I can take what you dish out and still crave more. I don't have the words to describe how amazing that felt, Tiernan. I was never even close to yellow, I swear to Rhiannon. If you ever give me the chance to go under your whip again, I'd do it in a heartbeat."

"Fi..."

He whispers my name like it's a plea or maybe a prayer for something neither of us wants to examine. We know it's there, smothered by heavy layers of duty and tradition and recent revelations. But unearthing it would only allow us to stare at what we can't have, bringing us nothing but harsh realities and heartache.

"Before we go any further, hear this. I have *never* thought less of you, Fiona," he says earnestly. "Not before when I thought you were a fae with halfling blood and not now that I know you're human."

I don't think I realized how badly I needed to hear Tiernan say that. Emotions clog my throat and blur my vision, but I hold it all back as he continues.

"I get that things might be different for us outside these walls. But right now, in here, you're mine. Say it."

I wish there was a world in which we didn't need qualifiers. But I'm greedy enough that I'll take whatever sliver of time Rhiannon grants us. "In here, I'm yours."

"Mine," he growls before claiming my mouth.

His hands roam, igniting a fire wherever they touch as he deepens the searing kiss. Sliding between us to stroke my pussy, his fingers find my most sensitive spot and make me shudder in pleasure.

Rolling me onto my back, he follows and presses me into the mattress with the seductive weight of his muscular frame. I gasp as he starts to explore my body, his hands and mouth leaving a trail of fire wherever they touch. He teases my nipples into hard buds before making his way lower, kissing and licking his way to my throbbing clit. He flicks it with his tongue, causing me to moan and writhe.

When I'm on the brink of orgasm, he stops and moves up to slide into me in a single, deep thrust. I cry out at the all-consuming pleasure, the feel of him stretching me to capacity deliciously overwhelming.

As always, the desperation of our need for one another rides us hard. He doesn't pause or break stride as he pistons his hips again and again, impaling me on the length of his cock with a wanton fervor.

"Gods, yes," I moan. "Harder. Fuck me harder."

Growling, he pins my wrists above my head with one hand and encircles the front of my throat with the other, squeezing the sides just enough to make me feel his possession. "Who do you fucking belong to, Fiona? Who commands this tight little body and makes your cunt drip with desire?"

I stare up into his glowing amber eyes and, despite having the power to lie, I speak the truth. "You, Your Majesty. It's only ever been you."

"You're godsdamn right. Now come on your king's fucking cock like a good girl."

Moans escape me as the tension in my belly twists and twists, my sensitive nipples grazing his chest with every thrust, causing frissons of pleasure to ripple through me. The hand on my throat slips between us, the rough pad of his thumb rubbing my swollen clit, and it sends me off like a rocket with him immediately following.

We ride out the aftershocks together, his strokes slow and lazy as we catch our breath and stare into each other's eyes. Neither of us want this moment to end, but it isn't ours to keep.

Tiernan lies down and pulls me back against his chest, curving possessively around me like a child with his new toy. "You're mine," he whispers again…only this time, there are no qualifiers.

In the safety of the darkness, my fool heart answers, "And you're mine." But I don't think he hears me because his breaths are already deep and steady.

The exhaustion from the adrenaline dump and rigorous sex must have sapped him of the last of his energy. I wonder if Dmitri has had any luck finding information about the girls. He told us to meet him in the main room, but I hate to disturb Tiernan if there's nothing to be done yet. I chew on my bottom lip as I think over my options, then make a decision.

I know Tiernan didn't mean to fall asleep, and he'll probably read me the riot act later, but I don't need to wake him up just to check in with Dmitri. If anyone asks, I'll tell them my master has sent me to collect his friend for a little menage-a-trois action. Hopefully he's made headway regarding the location, then we can either grab Tiernan or do some recon ourselves first, then get Tier for the rescue.

Yeah, that's a solid plan.

Moving slowly, I carefully extract myself from Tiernan's hold and make use of the spare clothes I spotted on shelves near the door. Although *merchandise* would be a more accurate word. Stacks of T-shirts, tanks, hoodies, and more are available in multiple sizes, all in black with the red logo and name of the club.

Keeping in mind that a sub is more likely told to walk

around naked, I choose a pair of boy shorts and tank top. If anything, I'll claim he got territorial after the public scene. With one last look at the sleeping giant, I slip out of the room and close the door quietly behind me. I go left, toward the main play area, when I hear a sound in the distance coming from the other direction that stops me in my tracks. I hold my breath and wait to see if I can hear it again…but there's noth—

There! I spin around and stare at the door at the end of the long hall. The sound of a feminine voice shouting for help.

This time I don't think. I just *run*.

CHAPTER NINETEEN

TIERNAN

I wake up with a jolt, like my own brain kicked me in the head trying to alert me that something is off. It was right. The bed next to me is empty, and so is the room I brought Fiona to after our scene.

Fuck, I can't believe I fell asleep. The drop combined with the mind-numbing orgasm I had from being inside Fiona knocked me out like a sucker punch from a heavyweight fighter. A quick glance at my watch tells me I couldn't have been out for more than five minutes, thank gods. But that doesn't bring me a whole lot of comfort considering Fiona is *gone*.

I don't even have to guess why. She's looking for those girls, exactly like I was supposed to be doing before my past trauma snuck up on me and kicked my ass. And as soon as I find Fi, I'm going to spank hers for not waking me and instead running off like a fucking rogue agent.

It only takes me seconds to pull on my pants and boots, re-glamour myself as Dante Ricci, and exit the room. To the left is the main area of the club, so I go right.

"Verran."

I look to see Dmitri striding toward me, so I double back

and meet him halfway. "Fiona went off on her own."

"I know where she is," he says. "Come."

Spinning on his heel, he leads me in the opposite direction at a clipped pace. A sick feeling settles in my gut, but I don't risk saying anything as we wind our way through the members socializing or playing out scenes in the play area. When we get to the Incubi locker room, he pushes through the door, and I follow. "She's in here? Where?"

He turns to face me, his expression solemn. "No, she is not here. She was taken."

"What the fuck do you mean *taken*? Taken *where*?"

"That I do not yet know. I looked for Adam but he is not here. In fact, I do not recognize any of the security guards. But I heard them talking on their radios. They caught her just as she found the females. As soon as I heard, I called for backup then came to find you."

"Perfect, let's go." I turn to go back into the club, but Dmitri stops me with a hand on my shoulder.

"No, we cannot go in there without first devising a plan and exit strategy. We will leave now and come back when we have those in place."

"I'm not leaving here without her, Romanov, so you can fuck off if you want. You'll have to kill me or knock me out. We both know you won't kill me, and in a head-to-head fight, you're not strong enough to knock me out."

"I know this," he says a bit too casually. "Is why I called for backup."

Before I can ask him what the hell he's talking about, my baby brother steps out from behind a row of lockers. "Sorry, T."

Then the asshole sucker punches me and the world goes dark.

· · ·

For the second time tonight, I jolt awake in a bed that's not my own. At least that's what I assumed until I realized that the bed I'm in is mine; it's just not the one I've been sleeping in for the past three months. This is the one in my penthouse apartment where I lived before moving into the manor. I kept the place out of a misguided hope that I'd eventually be back.

How the fuck did I get here? I was at the Devil's Dungeon with Fiona... *Oh gods.* It all comes rushing back. The intense scene, the incredible sex, falling asleep with her in my arms. Waking up to her gone and captured by the NPO. And before I could even tear the place apart to find her, Dmitri and Finnian conspired against me, and it was lights out from there.

I roar as the fear and rage explode inside me, propelling my upper body forw— *What the fuck?* Before I make it a foot off the mattress, I'm yanked back down from the chains and thick leather restraints around my wrists that shackle me to the hardpoints above my headboard.

"Finnian!"

Caiden strolls into the bedroom in his usual unruffled manner. "Glad to see you're finally awake, brother."

My mouth drops open. He says it like I decided to come in here and take a godsdamned nap. "You could've woken me up at any time, asshole! Fucking unchain me!"

"Not yet. In the state you're in, you'll end up going off half-cocked and we can't have that."

"Who's we? Are those traitors Romanov and our baby brother here, too?" They enter the room and flank Caiden, one looking decidedly regretful and the other in his usual RBF— Resting Bastard Face. "Well, if it isn't the Devil himself and Judas Iscariot. Do I have that right? It's been a while since I read the Christian fairytales."

Finn crosses his arm-cannons over his chest and scowls. "Just for that I'm not sorry anymore."

"You will be when I return the favor."

Caiden cuts in before we get into one of our usual banter wars. "Kill the theatrics, Tiernan. We've been working on a plan to get Fiona and the other females back. If you promise to play nicely, we'll let you out and be part of the team. But if you plan on storming out of this house like a one-man army the minute we release you, then you can just cool your heels on that bed."

I turn my head to look away from the men standing in front of me so they can't see me struggle to swallow around the fist closing off my airway. Caiden moves to the open door. "Give us a moment please, gentlemen."

I hear the *snick* of the door close, then Caiden approaches and begins unbuckling the cuff on my right wrist. I don't say anything, and I don't move as he makes his way around, for fear he'll change his mind. As soon as my left leg is free, I swing my feet over the edge of the bed and hunch over to fist my hair with my elbows braced on my knees.

Concentrating on taking slow, deep breaths to keep myself calm, I ask, "How did you know I wouldn't run?"

Caiden sits on the bed next to me, his clasped hands resting on his thighs. "Because as much as you want to storm the castle, you know the right decision is to stay and plan. You might be a rebel in many ways, Tiernan, but in the moments that matter, you do what needs to be done for the good of those you care about."

I don't know what to say to that, so I don't. Guilt racks me, clouding my judgement and creating a dank hole for old wounds to fester. I can't help but blame myself for what happened to Fiona. I let the shit from my past interfere with protecting her in the present. And if anything happens to her—if she's hurt in any way—it will be more than I can bear.

After what we shared at the club, my feelings for her slipped into the deep end. I pulled her into my arms and told her she was mine, and I fucking meant it. For as many years as she has on this earth, I want us to spend them together.

Except now she might not even have days, *much less years, thanks to you.*

"Caiden..." It's a poor attempt at a plea for help, but it's all I can manage to get out.

My older brother places a hand on my shoulder and squeezes. "We *will* get her back, whatever it takes. I swear it to you." As though he's instilled me with his own strength, I'm finally able to compose myself and rise. He stands with me. "Let's go see if Romanov's contact has called back."

We join the other two in the living room, and I accept the olive branch of a glass of Devil's Keep from Finnian. He gives me a wry grin. "You get one free punch to make it even."

"Tell me we have a plan in motion and I'll wipe the slate clean. Finding Fiona is all I care about."

He nods. "We're working on it."

A cell phone rings on the coffee table and Dmitri presses the button to connect the call. "Adam, what have you found out?"

It must be the security guard who Dmitri had the occasional D/s dynamic with at Devil's Dungeon. The man's voice comes through over speaker phone. "I think you were right, there was a group of women here. I found some evidence of glitter and a broken five-inch heel in an old storage room that shouldn't have had anything in it. I don't know how long they were there, but there's no sign of them anywhere in the building now."

Caiden rubs two fingers over his chin. "They knew Fiona was looking for the girls, so they would naturally assume that whoever Fiona is affiliated with is also looking for them and now her. The most logical thing to do is move them to a new location. Do you have any idea where that might be, Adam?"

"I can think of two places he owns that could work. There's a warehouse out in West Vegas that was used to store all the furniture and equipment for the Dungeon while it was under construction. To my knowledge, it's been empty since the club reopened. There's also an old hotel out on Route 582 toward Boulder City that he's renovating with plans to turn it into a casino and flip it for profit."

Caiden nods to Dmitri and pulls out his phone, turning away to make a call of his own. Before Dmitri can end the call, I say, "Adam, why weren't you working your normal shift last night?"

"Mr. Leone let all the bouncers go and replaced us with guys from a private firm to work the security jobs." Dmitri and I share a look, remembering how unnaturally strong the guards were. "Is there anything else I can do for you, Master D?"

Dmitri answers in a tone that's almost soft. "I will call if I need something. Thank you, Adam. Master is pleased."

"It's my pleasure, Master."

I quirk an eyebrow at him. He sits back in the leather chair and arches one of his own. "What? I like good boys who are eager to serve."

Finnian puts his hands up. "No judgement here, man. I am wondering, though, if you plan on putting a collar on that."

He lets out a dismissive hiss. "Of course not. He is married to his Top, and I have no interest in ever collaring a sub. When you are immortal it is best to never create ties. I have only ever had one constant companion."

The Russian grows solemn, and I know it's because he's thinking about his sister who's been missing for the better part of a year now. I feel for Dmitri. It's only been hours for me, and I'm practically climbing the walls with Fiona missing. When all this is done and we've dismantled NPO for good, I'll do whatever I can—pro bono that doesn't have to do with him calling in his favor—to help Finn find Dmitri's sister.

Caiden ends his call and addresses us. "I gave Conall the locations Adam mentioned. He and Connor are going to investigate in wolf form. If Fiona and the other females are in either of those two buildings, they'll know. If we get lucky with one of them, they'll gather as much intel as they can—entry points, guards, security cameras, lay of the land, et cetera."

I blow out a breath, hating that I have to do more waiting but knowing this is the right call. "What do we do in the meantime? I can't just sit here."

"We go back to Midnight Manor," Caiden says. "The guys will report to Seamus as soon as they have any information. Then we can take things from there." He must see the worry carving itself onto my face. "The guys won't take long, they're splitting up to save time, each taking one of the locations. We'll be making our next move soon, Tier."

"Yeah, okay. Let's go," I say.

All four of us push to our feet. "There was one more thing. Conall said Dolan is at the manor on official Dark Council business. He's moving your coronation up from the original date to much sooner."

My nails sharpen with the spike of anger burning through me, the points threatening to break the skin of my palms as my hands curl into fists. "How much sooner?"

Caiden pins me with an ominous look. "Effective immediately."

CHAPTER TWENTY

FIONA

I usually enjoy being tied to chairs and other furniture, except when the reason that I'm tied up is because I'm being interrogated by a large man with a wicked backhand-bitchslap combo.

"Just tell me what I want to know, and this all stops."

I peer up at the man through hooded eyes, the physical toll on my body making me more exhausted than I have ever been in my life. But I won't talk. Not because I've been trained in anti-interrogation skills like some badass in the military, but because telling them anything will only cause more death and put the people I love at risk. It will put *Tiernan* at risk.

"I want to speak to the manager. The accommodations and hospitality at this hotel are not up to my standards."

The seven females behind me whisper to each other from where they're huddled in the corner. None of them have been beaten, thank Rhiannon, but they haven't been treated well either.

When I found them at the club, I was shocked at how gaunt they appeared. What little they were wearing from their last shift at Deviant Desires was dirty and torn in places. One of the girls' heels broke off her platform shoe and she twisted her ankle. It's now swollen and bruised. Normally she would have healed in an hour. But due to the iron cuffs on their wrists, the girls are weak and sick.

Charlie—that's what I heard one of the others call him—uses the back of his hand this time to punish my insolence. My head whips to the side and pain lances my lip as it splits open and blood sprays from my mouth. *Fucking hell, how does Finn do this for fun?*

"*Ow.*" I test my swollen lip with the tip of my tongue and wince. "That's going in my Yelp review."

In the beginning, I wasn't so daring and bold. But I learned that no matter if I was polite or silent or pleading, Charlie still hit me. So after a while, I shoved all my fear and pain into a tiny little box and locked it away. All that left me with was the snarky side of Fiona, who my counterpart here does *not* appreciate.

"Who were you working with? Who else knows about the girls?"

"Look, Charles—may I call you Charles?—I told you before, I don't know what you're talking about. It was my first night in the Dungeon and I was looking for the bathroom."

Charlie bends over and gets right in my face. "Listen, you little bitch, my orders are to work you over without making too much of a mess of that pretty face. But there's more than one way to skin a cat, and I'd be happy to work you over in another way. You catch my meaning?"

"Go ahead," I say as I laugh. Deliriousness is starting to set in, but that's probably not a bad thing in this situation. "From what I can tell, I don't think I'll feel a thing. If you catch *my* meaning, Charles."

That makes the girls laugh quietly among themselves, but it's loud enough that it still echoes in this empty warehouse room. My left eye is almost completely swollen shut, but my vision is good enough to watch his face turn red. I give him a lopsided grin and I can almost see his anger building like steam in a kettle, the pressure growing and growing until at last he explodes.

He roars at me, only inches away, and there's a split second where his face transforms. His brow becomes more prominent, and his upper and lower canines elongate as his face morphs and twists into a vicious snarl.

I rear back as far as the chair allows. But by the time I do that, there's nothing unusual about Charlie at all. My mind races, trying to determine if my mental state combined with slightly blurry vision would cause hallucinations. I don't *feel* impaired enough for that. But what the hell do I know? This is my first—and hopefully last—interrogation.

"Charlie! You've done enough."

Stanley Leone walks into the room, his dress shoes echoing on the concrete floor. Two of his big goons are with him and go straight for the girls. Their terror is palpable with how they cower and cry. The goons—the sick fucks—seem to get off on the fear.

"Give us some privacy," Leone demands, not taking his eyes from me.

Tweedledum and Dumber pull guns from their shoulder holsters and force the girls to move toward the door. Abby, the one I've figured out has been acting as the matronly leader to the others, is helping Wanda limp along with her swollen ankle but gathers enough courage to challenge her tormentor. "What are you going to do to our friend, you fucker?"

Leone laughs, still never taking his eyes from mine. "You're mistaken. Candy, here, is *my* friend, and we're just going to have a little chat. Like friends do. Isn't that right, Candy?"

I force myself to tear my gaze from the biggest threat in the room to reassure Abby. "I'll be okay." As the echo of the door slams shut, I pray to Rhiannon that I didn't just lie.

"Where are you taking them?" I demand through clenched teeth.

"Don't worry, they're not going far. I just wanted to have a private boss-employee chat." I snort at that because he knows by now that I'm not an exotic dancer from out of town named Candy. Then to Charlie, he says, "Go make yourself useful somewhere else."

Charlie gives me one last dirty look. As he passes Leone, he gives him a wide berth but makes up for it with a scathing glance on his way out. Charlie seems like he has a real problem with authority. "He'll never climb up the henchman ladder with that attitude."

Shit, did I say that out loud? Yep. Super delirious.

"You would be right if there was a henchman ladder. Lucky for him, his family and I are in a mutually beneficial arrangement. So, while I am the one running the show, I'm not currently in a position to punish him as I would one of my own. Yet, anyway."

Laying on the sarcasm, I give him a droll look. "Awesome. We're finally at the 'villain monologue' portion of our show."

His expression sours. "Watch your tone. I don't need Charlie to do my dirty work for me."

"Just tell me who you are and what you want already. You obviously know about fae, and I'm assuming you're the one who started the New Purity Order that's doing its best to wipe fae from the planet."

"Not all fae. Only the infernal Darks."

"Why us—I mean *them*? You can't seriously intend to murder an entire court of innocent people because of some real estate pissing match between you and Onyx Inc. for who has the most pieces on the Vegas chess board."

His laugh is patronizing, as though I couldn't have suggested anything more ridiculous. "While I do have several ancient bones to pick with the Verrans, I couldn't care less about this city. The only real estate I'm interested in is on the other side of the veil."

Stanley's appearance shifts, the middle-aged smarmy used car salesman dissipating to reveal a younger looking, fit male with emerald-green eyes and pointed ears peeking out from his shoulder-length blond hair. The smarmy look is still there though. Some things abs just can't fix.

A smug grin spreads across his handsome face, revealing lethal fangs. Though I've never seen him in person, I know exactly who stands before me.

"Edevane," I whisper in disbelief.

"King Talek the Tenacious of the Faerie Day Court, at your service."

He performs a shallow bow as though introducing himself at High Court. As though he's nothing more than a proper royal with impeccable manners and not a deranged sociopath who has laid waste to so many people in my life—Uther and Keira, Jack and Emily, and he attempted to kill Bryn multiple times.

Hate seethes from my pores and burns with every breath I take. "Your service sucks, asshole," I snarl. "And you pronounced Tyrannical wrong."

"Careful now, or I won't tell you a bedtime story...Miss *Jewel.*" My lips part on a gasp. "Yes, I know who you are. Once we caught you trying to help our merchandise escape"—he *tsks* like I'm a child he's grounding—"it was easy enough to find out. Sending Charlie in was simply punishment for your deception."

My mind races trying to figure out how he could have escaped detection with my mom's tracking spell in place all over the city. And how is he reading as a human? Dmitri and Tiernan would have recognized him as *other* in the Dungeon...

Then it hits me. "You have a conjurer helping you."

He smiles widely, flashing his fangs. "Guilty. It wasn't easy to find one, considering they so selfishly keep their powers to themselves."

"It's not because they're *selfish*," I snap. "It's so that monsters like *you* can't use them to do monstrous deeds. It's for self-preservation and to protect potential victims. Being a conjurer is as much a curse as it is a gift."

"You would know, wouldn't you?" He cants his head to the side, his calculating stare making my skin crawl. "Fiona Jewel, the unremarkable human child swapped out for a powerful fae changeling. What was it like being raised by a mother with so many special powers while you yourself had none? And to add insult to injury, she let you believe you were a defective specimen of a superior race instead of telling you the truth: that among your kind, you are quite exceptional. I can see why the Heir Apparent is so taken with you."

He touches his fingers to my chin. I jerk back and glare up at him. "Don't fucking touch me."

Chuckling, he holds his hands up as though he's responding to my command and not doing whatever the hell he wants. Then he slips them into his pockets and winks at me. "Bear with me, Miss Jewel, I think you'll really appreciate this story."

"I seriously doubt it, but go ahead. Enlighten me so I can laugh when you get to the punch line of your joke."

"We'll see who's laughing at the end. But first we must start at the beginning—the night you and your changeling were born." As he speaks, Edevane begins to slowly walk around me as though giving a lecture at UNV, but I keep my eyes forward, refusing to indulge him by craning my neck around to keep him in my sights. "Back then I was the crown prince and leader of the Light Warriors, waiting not-so-patiently for my father to die so I could rectify his grave mistake when he made peace with our enemies, the Darks."

"Right, because no one wants to live in peace. What a shitty idea *that* was," I deadpan.

He whips around to face me, his green eyes blazing. "The Darks *do not deserve* peace."

Matching his fury, I shout, "Why? There's been no contact between the courts, apart from the kings' meeting once every decade, since the treaty was signed. What the hell did they ever do to piss you off so bad?"

Like someone flips a switch, he composes himself into the picture of a totally rational male once again. "That I will not share. As you are not fae, it does not concern you, *human*."

Okay, ouch. Smirking, I fire back. "Then I'll have to assume it's because you're butthurt that the Darks built a city where people go to *live*. And you built Phoenix, where they go to die."

A slow smile spreads across his face, but it doesn't look right. It's hollow and cold. A shiver trickles down my spine. I counter it with a hardening of my jaw and squaring of my shoulders as I glare at the bastard.

"Let's get back to the story, shall we?" he says cordially, like we're having a chat over tea. "When my cousin told me he'd fallen in love with a Dark female and they'd miraculously conceived, I knew Lugh was smiling down on me. To have a Darklight with mind control powers meant I could bend *all fae* to my will, including my weak-willed father.

"However, as you know, the child was taken before I caught up to Uther and his mate at Joshua Tree. I learned of the sister and presumed she was the one who'd taken the baby and hidden her in the human world."

Hidden away with my *parents and living* my *life.* I shake that thought away before it can dig its thorny barbs into my heart. I have no hard feelings toward Bryn. She was as much a victim in this as I was, our fates intertwined since shortly after our birth.

"I knew if I found the sister, I could find the child, but she too seemed to disappear off the face of the earth. She was either dead or a conjurer able to mask her location, so I focused my search on the child. It took more than twenty years and teams of investigators before we found her, and even then, I wasn't one hundred percent sure she was the one until shortly before bringing her to Vegas."

The blood in my veins turns to ice. "You killed Jack and Emily on the *off chance* that she was the Darklight?"

He shrugs. "If you want to make an omelet..."

I lunge forward, pulling at my restraints until my muscles scream in protest. "They weren't eggs, you fucking asshole, those were her parents. They were *my* parents!"

"If it makes you feel any better, those weren't the only ones I killed trying to find the changeling. I left quite the wake of destruction in my search, but all those deaths can be lain at your mother's feet. If she had minded her own business, you would have stayed where you belonged and none of those people would have died."

"They didn't *die*, you *killed* them," I croak. "And if you did all that so you could have a Darklight help with your evil plots, why did you manipulate Bryn into marrying Caiden if you planned on killing her in order to kill him?"

My stomach rolls, and I have to take a deep breath through my nose so I don't start dry heaving. If I never have to say the word *kill* again, it'll be too soon.

"I was always going to use her to assassinate the Dark King—that was all part of my 'eye for an eye' plan, which is another story for another time—but if she'd had use of her full powers, I simply would have taken her away from him. He would have died because of the distance all the same. But once I realized her powers weren't able to get through whatever block was placed on her, I had no use for her beyond getting a small amount of her mind control powers to eke out enough to persuade Verran to bond with her."

A chilling calm blankets me as I sit back in my chair. I take in the carefree way he moves, the air of someone without a problem in the world. He speaks about killing innocent people the same way I would discuss what I want to eat for lunch. "You're a fucking psychopath."

He smiles wide, showing me his fangs and reminding me once again that I have none. "Psychopaths are merely misunderstood geniuses."

"Agree to disagree. And anyway, what does all of that have to do with you starting the New Purity Order and kidnapping Dark females?"

"Ah," he says, taking up a leisurely pace around my chair again. "In regard to the females, revenge is costly, and unfortunately my funds are running low. I'm selling them on the supernatural black market to a buyer willing to pay top dollar for them. The rest, however, has to do with your mother. Which is why it was so fortuitous you fell into my lap, because now you can carry my message to her."

My heart stops, and I wish time would do the same. I don't want to know what he's about to tell me. Because whatever it is, I have a sickening feeling it will turn my world upside down. Again. "What message?"

"Patience. I'm getting there. Now, even after finding the changeling, I didn't know who your mother was, if she was alive or dead. Until the Meeting of Two Kings. Imagine my surprise when I stood on top of the bluff and watched the Darklight embrace her true self, guided by a female claiming to be Keira Jewel's sister, making *her* the conjurer I'd been unable to find for twenty-six years. And now I could finally make her pay for the trouble she caused me."

I huff out a disgusted laugh. "So while you continued with your genocidal plans to become the fascist dictator of the fae, you went on a little side mission to kill my mom for fucking you over when she saved her niece from becoming your magic puppet, is that it? Well, your little band of murder-y men couldn't get the job done. You failed, asshole. *Again*."

"Ahh, now we're getting to the good part," he says gleefully. "You're not thinking big enough. You assume because she's alive that I failed, but you're wrong. You also think the attacks on the Dark Fae are separate from my revenge plot against your mother, but again, you would be wrong.

"You've no doubt learned of the original Purity Order back in Ireland. The only thing that stopped it was the fae's ability to retreat into Faerie long enough for fact to turn into fiction. But what do you think will happen if the Dark Fae have nowhere to retreat? The humans will continue to grow their hate, and they'll never stop hunting with their hag stones and iron blades. Until eventually there are no more fae to hunt and in another century or so, they'll be forgotten altogether."

"Did you forget that *you* are fae? And what about your people, don't you care about them?"

"I won't be around to see the fallout, and it's not a question of whether or not I care. This is the reality all fae face. Unless…"

"Unless what?"

"Unless your mother stops the New Purity Order before that happens. *That* is the message."

"She won't murder anyone, regardless of what they've done. She's not you!"

Edevane grins. "That's what I'm counting on."

Frustration and fury consume me. "What the fuck are you talking about?"

He glances down at his bare wrist. "It's been lovely chatting with you, Miss Jewel, but I'm afraid that's all the time we have for today."

I'm helpless to do anything other than stare at his back as he walks away from me. When he reaches the door, he turns to look at me one last time. "Oh, I almost forgot. Now that you've heard the punch line, remind me again which of us is laughing." I want to scream, to make baseless threats and vow vengeance against him and everyone he loves. But I do none of those things. I'm frozen in shock, numb with fear. "That's what I thought."

Chuckling, he locks me away behind the steel door, leaving me with nothing but my thoughts and sickening dread for what's to come.

Something tiny moves in the corner and catches my eye.

Correction: my thoughts, sickening dread, and a little gray mouse.

CHAPTER TWENTY-ONE

TIERNAN

As soon as we arrive at Midnight Manor, Dolan is waiting in the foyer to formally request a private audience with the heir apparent. Unable to trust that I wouldn't say something Seamus would force me to apologize for later, I signal for him to follow me to the study, where I take a seat behind the large desk and wait.

Hedrek clears his throat and stands rigid like a statue with his hands clasped in front of him. "Your Highness, the Council has decided that we cannot wait any longer. The time for you to ascend is now. Our people need a ruler."

"They have a ruler. Seamus is Crown Regent, which for all intents and purposes means he is the king until I ascend. I assure you, he's the better choice anyway. I still have more than two months until the agreed-upon date. And once we've saved Fiona and the other females, I'm going to spend every second of that time hunting these bastards down until I've turned every last one of them into buzzard food."

"Absolutely not," he sputters. "The future king cannot go on a manhunt for a murderous faction who are looking to kill every fae they come across. You need to remain under

protection at all times. Of everyone, it is *you* who must obey
the curfew. The idea of you acting like a common vigilante is
completely preposterous."

"No, what's preposterous is the idea that you think
I'm going to sit on my ass behind a high-security fortress
while more of our people are being picked off every day. If
something happens to me, I have another brother who would
make a better king than me anyway, regardless of age. And
if something happens to *him*, you'll have Caiden and Bryn's
child to continue the Verran line. So, you see, Lord Speaker,
the fate of the Dark Fae does not hinge on me alone. We are
a kingdom with two contingency plans."

"That was only one, Your Highness," Hedrek says.

I hold up my hand and tick them off with my fingers.
"Finnian. The baby."

"I'm afraid not. Prince Caiden's baby will not be of pure
Dark blood and therefore will be ineligible to rule."

"You've got to be shitting me," I spit out. "Because of
Bryn's Light blood, my brother's child will be denied their
birthright?"

"Night Law clearly states that only a pureblood Dark may
sit upon the Midnight Throne. Prince Caiden's offspring will
not have any such birthright. The moment he abdicated he
ensured his direct bloodline would no longer rule; instead, it
will be yours."

Clenching my jaw, I inhale deeply and let it out before
speaking. "I'm not going to debate anything with you right
now, Dolan, especially not about the legitimacy of my brother's
child. I'm also not ascending the throne until we put a stop
to these attacks."

"Your Highness, we have no way of knowing how long it will
be before that happens. And by postponing your coronation,
it sends the message that the next king will do what *he wants*
rather than what *they need*. And what they need is a son of

the great King Braden sitting on the throne."

Caiden's words to me back at the penthouse echo in my mind. *You might be a rebel in many ways, Tiernan, but in the moments that matter you do what needs to be done for the good of those you care about.*

It may never have been my job to care for our people in the way it was my brother's and father's, but I *do* care about them. Doesn't caring for them mean I do whatever I can to keep them safe from a violent hate group?

"However," he continues, clearing his throat, "due to recent events, and out of respect for your father, the Council has decided to allow some time to tie up any..." Dolan inserts a pause big enough to drive a truck through. "...*loose ends* you might have before committing to the responsibilities and duties befitting a Night Court King."

He's talking about Fiona. This stodgy, two-legged Shar-pei is daring to insinuate that I'd just roll over and put an end to everything with her because the Dark Council doesn't approve. I've already made my decision to enjoy as many years with her as we have, and I won't suffer his bullshit about carrying on the royal line before then. But he doesn't have to know that.

"How *much* time?" I ask.

"The coronation will take place at the next full moon on the fifth of February."

That's three weeks away. All I have to do is save Fiona and the others while taking down a faction of murdering racists multiplying like cockroaches—because I'm not sitting out on that mission no matter what Lord Wrinkles says—and convince Fi that even though we can't have the life we wanted, we can still have what we want for the rest of *her* life, and if the DC has a problem with it, they can suck my big, manscaped kingly balls.

Sure, I can do that in three weeks. No sweat. Just don't check my armpits.

"Fine. In three weeks I'll ascend. Now, if you'll excuse me, I need to join the others."

He steps to the side to block my path, and I level him with a threatening glare for his boldness. "Apologies, Your Highness, but I—I mean, *we*, the Council—must insist that you sign this coronation contract."

Motherfucker. "Why do we need a contract now if we didn't before?"

"We feel it's prudent under the extenuating circumstances, Your Highness. The contract is to prevent the finish line from moving."

"Funny, considering *I* haven't moved it once." Dolan's wrinkly face morphs into some semblance of a sheepish grin, but he doesn't attempt to deny or defend against my statement. I hold my hand out for the contract and I'm surprised to find it's not a single sheet or two at most. I know legal jargon is a whole lot of word salad, but ten pages is a whole salad buffet.

My phone vibrates on the desk with a text message, but I ignore it to thumb through the contract, searching for the highlights. I note where the date of the coronation is set for the fifth and skim past all the details about the event itself, like who attends, who presides over the ceremony, and even what I'm supposed to wear.

Blah, blah, turn the page…blah, skimming, turn the page… skimming, skim—

"What are these?" I demand, my words laced with acid.

"The Council voted to include three additional stipulations."

My eyes pin him in place, daring him to make the slightest move and see how the violent beast inside me reacts. What little propriety I possess is now shredded beneath its claws. "What kind of fucking stipulations, Dolan?"

"If you'd like some time to look it over—"

My phone buzzes on the desk again, and again I hold off checking it. "I have more important things to do than proofread your security blanket, so do me a solid and fucking lay it out for me."

"The first states that you will not engage in any dangerous activities involving anything to do with the New Purity Order. You may be involved in strategizing, of course, but any actions taken against them, including aiding in the rescue attempts of those taken, is strictly prohibited."

I grind my teeth together, knowing that he likely started with the least provoking demand. "Go on."

"The second states that on the night of your coronation ceremony you are to choose either Lady Maeve or Lady Deirdre as your consort."

My blood starts to boil. I don't know either of them well other than they're both highborn females, daughters of two of the Council members. Shocker. "Why would I need to name my intended consort if I don't intend on taking one for at least a century?"

"Because of the third stipulation, which states that you and your chosen consort must conceive shortly after you ascend to bear the court an heir within the first full lunar calendar of your rule."

The rage bomb inside me detonates. "Are you fucking serious?" When he doesn't respond, I place my fists on the desk to lean in, curling my upper lip back from my fangs. "Let me see if I have this straight. You and your buddies are pissing yourselves because you don't want me to be with a human for however long she has on this planet. One who, need I remind you, was raised as one of us and has since been *kidnapped* because she put herself in danger to help *save our people*. Racist much?"

"I assure you, Your Highness, it has nothing to do with race."

"Says the male who won't let Caiden's offspring rule because they have a small percentage of Light in their blood."

His pasty cheeks flush red, but whether it's from embarrassment that I called him out or from anger for the same reason, I don't know, and I don't give a shit.

"With all due respect, Your Highness, our situation has changed. The Treaty of Two Courts has been violated, and the Crown has had multiple threats against it these past several months. We can no longer afford the luxury of waiting decades or centuries for a king to settle down. We need pureblood heirs to ensure the royal line as soon as possible, it's as simple as that."

"No, it's not. And you can all fuck right off. I'm not signing this."

I grab my phone and eat up the distance to the door in a few long strides, eager to get away from him and this conversation.

"Prince Tiernan," he calls out, stopping me in my tracks. "If you choose not to sign this contract or, if you do but do not abide by its stipulations, the Dark Council will have the authority to take over the realm and appoint a new royal line for the Night Court, effectively ending the Verran line's reign… permanently."

Stabbing me in the chest with an iron blade would've been less painful than hearing that. More than a thousand years of tradition and duty settles on my shoulders, nearly crushing me under the weight. I may have wanted to make a name for myself in the Night Court history books, but not as the guy who fucks everything up after a millennia of successful Verran rulers.

The Council's giving me a true Sophie's Choice; they've set me up so that I can't win no matter what I choose. Either I fail my duty as a Verran and destroy my family's legacy…or I fail myself and destroy the chance for a future with Fiona.

My heart is a two-ton brick in my chest as I force myself to take the steps back to the desk. Staring at the contract, I remember something my father once said. *A successful negotiation is when both parties walk away feeling as though they've lost.*

"I'll sign this on one condition," I say, my tone emotionless at the knowledge of what I have to do.

The reality is that there *is* no choice. If I give the Council the opportunity to rightfully appoint a new line in our place, it's not only my family's reputation that will be at risk—it's also the welfare of the entire Night Court. With someone as self-serving as Dolan on the throne, there's no telling how our people will be treated.

Dolan was right about one thing. The king's job is to put their needs above his own, and Verrans have *always* done what was right for our people. That includes today.

"I'll agree to your terms if we strike the first stipulation." They may have found a way to keep me from having a life with Fiona, but I'll be damned if they prevent me from ensuring she has a life to live. "If something happens to me, the Crown will go to the next Verran in line, as it would under any other circumstances. It goes to Finnian, regardless of how you or anyone else feels about his age."

He hesitates, probably thinking about having to give the rest of the Council the news, but at last, he nods. "Agreed."

Picking up a pen, I flip to the last page and scrawl a hasty signature in black ink on the appropriate line, then wait impatiently while he does the same as the representative for the Council.

"Are we done here?" I ask, my voice deadened.

"Yes, Your Highness. The Council and your people humbly thank you and look forward to a long and prosperous rule under your leadership."

He bows his head in deference like we just had a polite chat about what hors d'oeuvres to serve at the ceremony. If I don't get away from him in the next few seconds, I'll have to stash a body and think of an excuse for the blood stains on the carpet.

"I'm going to give you a little piece of advice, Lord Speaker." Dolan straightens and bravely meets my gaze. His bravery is misguided. "Make yourself as scarce as possible at Court. And I do mean *scarce*."

Seeing the panic in his dull amber eyes offers a modicum of satisfaction. As I cross the room a second time, another text alert vibrates in my hand. Finally, I allow myself to read the message, and the burning rage of the last fifteen minutes is washed away with cool relief.

We found them.

When I get to the living room, I join my brothers, Dmitri, Seamus, and McCarthy just as the twins enter from the hall. Caiden and Seamus give me the same questioning look. I know they want details on what happened between me and Lord Dolan, but I just shake my head. We'll discuss it later. There's only one thing that matters right now. "What did you find? Where are they?"

Connor slips a hair tie from his wrist and begins putting his hair up while he talks. "They're in the abandoned warehouse. There's not much activity inside from what we could tell, but any windows that it does have are boarded up, so we couldn't get a visual. There are at least ten guards scattered around a hundred-yard radius from the building and four on the roof, one for each direction."

Conall continues. "There are two main entry points on the ground level, both with two guards. They're strapped with assault rifles, but they're not standing at attention and their guns are just hanging on them. Either they're not trained, or they just don't give a fuck."

McCarthy chimes in while taking notes. "If we're lucky, it's both. That would make it a much easier rescue mission, that's for sure."

"I'm not sure about that," Connor says. "Because here's

the weird part."

Over to Conall. "Besides the fae females from Deviant, we didn't get a read on any *others* within a five-mile range. All the energy was completely human, except we scented—"

"Werewolves. And judging by the strength of the scent, the number is somewhere around *many* with a capital M."

"Werewolves?" Caiden's brow furrows. "From the Šunktokeca pack in the Dakotas? They're the closest established pack."

Conall shakes his head, the ends of his hair brushing his shoulders with the movement. "No, they're from Gage Marceau's pack down in New Orleans. Which could explain how they masked their energies."

Connor nods. "Voodoo magic."

Seamus paces while stroking his beard, brows pinched together in thought. "That still doesn't explain anything. Why take the girls in the first place, and then Fiona? And how does all this tie into the sudden creation of the New Purity Order and all the attacks? Is this all their doing?"

Finnian cracks his knuckles from where he's sitting on the couch, glaring into the middle-distance. "Does it matter? Unless they've been kidnapped, too, they're a part of it all." He lifts his head and locks eyes with mine. "Which means if they get in our way, they die."

Finally, someone on my level of thinking. Finni might be the most tenderhearted Verran brother, but when it comes to defending and protecting his own, he's by far the most vicious.

"Agreed," I tell him with malice coating my tongue. "And I want you leading the charge, little brother."

CHAPTER TWENTY-TWO

FIONA

I don't know how long it's been since Edevane left me in this room. I've tried to stay awake, to stay alert, but as it turns out, getting smacked around and then having the details of an evil plot dumped on you is exhausting. Several times I've drifted off, but I don't know for how long. There are no windows in here, just concrete walls, a concrete ceiling, and a concrete floor. I don't know if it's morning or midnight, if it's been hours or days. I've had a splitting headache for an eternity, I can't see out of my left eye, and my bottom lip feels like a collagen injection gone wrong.

But for as much pain as I'm in, both physically and emotionally, I haven't cried. I'm not sure why. I'm not trying to be strong or brave—there's no one here for me to be those things for. Edevane never brought the girls back in. I hope to gods they're okay. I hope they haven't been shipped off to somewhere else, to wherever the next step is in a supernatural trafficking ring.

"I failed them, Squeaky." The little gray mouse looks up at me from where he's perched next to my knee. I'm sitting on the floor with my back against a corner to help keep me upright. I guess since I haven't moved much since slumping into this position, he's deemed me safe. He's not very talkative, but he's a good listener. I suppose if those traits flip around, I should be concerned about my mental health. Until then, it's just nice to have another living thing in here with me.

"I shouldn't have run off by myself like that. We probably could have saved them had I just gone back in and told Tiernan what I heard. I was never good at being fae. Turns out, I'm not great at being a super spy either."

Squeaky twitches his nose and flicks his tail lazily. I think I might be putting him to sleep with my boring conversation. Suddenly he freezes and sits up on his hind legs. His ears angle back and then he scurries away into a hole in the wall.

"Squeaky, where are you going? Was it something I said?"

I get my answer in the sound of gunshots in the distance. I don't know whether to be elated or fearful as my heart hammers in my chest. Charlie bursts in, his eyes wild and piercing as he grabs me by the arm and hauls me up to my feet.

"What's going on?" Moving faster than I can keep up, he practically drags me across the room. I nervously keep my gaze on the large gun in his other hand, making sure he doesn't raise it toward me. "Where are you taking me?"

"Shut up! He might consider you collateral damage, but I think you're just collateral. If I can't use you as a bargaining chip, I'll use you as a shield. Either way, you're going to help me get out of here alive."

He pulls me into the hall and takes a right. I can hear the fighting much louder now. Shouted orders and the report of bullets echoing. His fingers bite into my arm as he picks up the pace, forcing me to stumble after him in my weakened condition down a flight of stairs. When we reach the main floor, my eyes widen in horror.

The cavernous warehouse has been turned into a war zone. Spray patterns of crimson stain the pale concrete walls and floor, even the large pillars that stretch up to the vaulted ceiling. It looks like the space was used as a canvas for an abstract painting of death and carnage.

It's easy to tell who is who based on what they're wearing. Charlie's men are in camo-colored fatigues versus the all-black tactical gear and masks of the Night Watch. Relief floods me to see that out of the dozen or so lifeless bodies, only two are Watchers. Then the relief is flushed out and replaced with grief at who they might be. *They might not be dead, they may be able to heal, or maybe they're only unconscious.* The possibilities are precious little comfort, but I latch onto them like lifelines.

"C'mere. We're going out the back." Charlie positions me in front of him and pushes me across five feet of exposed battlefield toward an entryway. I cover my head with my arms as best I can and let out a yelp when the wood frame explodes by my face just as I pass it.

Charlie curses a blue streak as his grip on me jerks hard. We flatten our backs against the wall as soon as we're in the hallway that's identical to the one on the second floor where we came from. My breaths saw in and out of my lungs to the point I think I'm hyperventilating, and my right cheek feels weird. When I prod the area, I hiss from the sting and pull out a sliver of wood the length of a toothpick.

Warm blood trails down my face from the wound, but I'm better off than Charlie, who's examining the hole in his shoulder. *What the hell are you doing, Fiona? RUN!*

I bolt off the wall and run as fast as I can down the hall, not knowing where I'm going or even caring. My chances on my own are better than his plans for me, but I don't get very far before he yanks me back by my hair. I scream in pain and twist under his arm to start fighting back now that the shock has cleared. I haven't taken any fighting lessons with Finnian like Bryn has, but *Miss Congeniality* is one of my favorite movies.

I step on his foot as hard as I can, but my bare foot is no

match for his motorcycle boot. Undeterred, I throw an elbow into his crotch, which he manages to thwart, making me mad as hell. He wraps his arms around me, pinning mine against my body, rendering me unable to attempt any other attacks.

Kicking and screaming, I do my best to disrupt his hold on me as he picks me up and walks like I'm nothing more than a squirming toddler.

"Knock it off, you crazy bitch!"

"Fiona!"

A Watcher at the end of the hall yanks the black mask from his head, and my knees almost buckle at the sight. *Tiernan.*

I've never seen him look so feral, like he was raised by actual wolves and not a respectable wolf shifter. His fitted long-sleeved shirt is sliced open in three places—left shoulder, right forearm, and right rib cage—revealing bloodied wounds already in the process of healing. Chestnut brown hair stands in wild spikes, his golden eyes are ablaze, and the tips of his pointed ears are flushed red from anger.

But it's the wicked snarl and bared fangs that promise tremendous pain and suffering to anyone who gets in his way.

Charlie swears and raises his gun.

"Tiernan!" Lifting my knee, I thrust my heel backward as hard as I can and finally nail the bastard square in the crotch. He releases me on a gasp, doubling over and holding his balls in one hand. But it's the other hand I should've paid attention to—the one holding *the gun.*

I hear it go off a full second before the fire rips through me, the lingering burn echoing his warrior's roar thundering in the hall.

A blur of reddish-brown fur streaks past my vision, taking Charlie with it. His shout of surprise quickly turns into tortured screams, accompanied by snarling, snapping teeth, and the gruesome squelching of freshly-torn flesh. It's the soundtrack of nightmares and I'm not even fazed. Probably in shock...

My legs give out. I brace myself for impact, but just before I hit, strong arms wrap me up in their embrace. His familiar scent comforts me as he lowers us to the floor with me cradled against his chest. I drop my gaze to his hand pressed over my abdomen and blanch at the blood steadily seeping from between his fingers. *Well, damn...not good...*

"Fuck, Fiona, what the hell were you thinking? I'm the one who heals from bullet wounds, not you."

"Heard them say...bullets...iron-tipped."

A river of lava carves a tunnel through my body from front to back. It feels like my organs are being cauterized, ripped open, then cauterized again, over and over. It's the most excruciating pain I could've imagined multiplied by a thousand.

Don't think about it, don't think about it, don't think about it...

Tiernan clenches his stubbled jaw. "I don't care if they're made of hellfire. You never fucking do that again, you hear me?"

The chant must be working because I don't hurt as bad now. Staring up into his misty eyes, I do my best to smile and whisper, "Yes...Your Majesty."

A cold, wet nose nuzzles my cheek. I turn my head to see Connor in wolf form crouched on the floor next to me. His rust-colored fur is darker and glistening wet around his muzzle and chest. He looks at me with sad eyes and whimpers. "S'okay, buddy. You did good. Thank you."

I'm vaguely aware of Tiernan shouting on speaker-phone with someone. It isn't until I hear the words "Give her your blood" that I make the effort to pay attention.

"I can't, Seamus. She's human, remember? We have no idea what that'll do to her."

"You may not, but I do. If you want her to live, give her your blood *right now*, before it's too late!"

"Fuck!" My vision is blurry, but my hearing still works. It sounds like he drops the phone, then I hear material ripping. A moment later, Tiernan's wrist is above my mouth, with steady drops of blood splashing onto my lips. "Open up, Fi. I need you to drink."

My brain feels fuzzy, and I don't respond right away, so he takes matters into his own hands and presses his wrist to my lips, forcing his blood into my mouth to slide over my tongue and down the back of my throat. Lifting me up to hold me tighter, he presses his cheek against my temple and speaks softly into my ear.

"I swear to the gods, Fiona, if you die on me, I *will* follow you. I will find you in whatever afterlife exists for humans, and I will drag your cute ass back to the land of the living, even if it costs me my soul's place in Mag Mell."

His vow is the last thing I hear before the black void eclipses my world and everything in it.

CHAPTER TWENTY-THREE

TIERNAN

Last night's rescue mission led by Finnian ran like a dream…until it turned into my own personal hellscape.

All in all it was a success—our team came away with very few serious injuries and no deaths, despite the iron-tipped bullets, thanks to the Kevlar and tactical gear we wore, and we intercepted their attempt to traffic the fae dancers from Deviant and got them home safe to their families.

But Fiona had been shot and lay dying in my arms. The fool woman took a godsdamned bullet that was meant for me. My desire to strangle her even as I prayed for Rhiannon to spare her life had been overwhelming. For as long as I live, I'll never forget the way the color drained from her pallid skin and the blue of her eyes seemed to dull as her blood formed a pool on the floor beneath her.

If Seamus hadn't known that the magic in *my* blood could possibly be enough to reverse the damage…I would've lost her. She wouldn't be lying here beside me, her breaths soft and even as I watch for any signs of change.

After she slipped into unconsciousness last night, I brought her to my penthouse so she could recover in the privacy and solitude the manor wouldn't have. Glancing at the bedside clock, I hold back a sigh of frustration. It's going on twenty-four hours now, and I started worrying at hour two.

Seamus suspects it took a lot for her human body to heal itself, so now it's taking the time to recover from the effort. Either way, I haven't left her side since bringing her here, and I won't until she wakes up.

Stretched out in the bed next to her, I stare down at her beautiful face and continue stroking her hair and tracing her features with the tip of my finger.

"How about this one. If you wake up for me, I'll find you the Heart of the Ocean, that gigantic diamond necklace from *Titanic*."

I pause, willing her to respond. She doesn't. I press a kiss to her temple, then I keep talking.

"No, huh? Let's see, so far you've turned down a new Ferrari, a trip to the Maldives, a tap-dancing pony, and now a fictional diamond necklace. You know, not for nothing, Fi, but Caiden says Bryn is super easy to please when they negotiate for things. Figures you'd be this stubborn; gotta be the red hair. That's all right, I'll think of something you want."

"Egg...plant."

I snap to attention, bracing up on my elbow and cupping her face with my other hand. "What was that, baby? Say it again."

"Eggplant," she whispers, her voice raspy from unuse.

My brows knit together as I stroke her cheek with my thumb. "Fi, I don't understand. You want an egg—" The corner of her mouth quirks up the slightest bit as her lashes flutter open, revealing those beautiful, crystalline blue eyes. I smile so big my cheeks hurt. "Are you saying you want *my* eggplant? You saucy little wench. Had I known offering you my cock would get you to wake up, I would have done it forever ago."

Her smile falters. I can almost see the events trickling into her memory as the mood goes from teasing to somber. "How long have I been out? The girls?"

"Almost twenty-four hours now, and yes, the girls are all fine. We managed to intercept them right as they were being loaded into a truck for transport. As soon as we cut the iron bracelets off, they began to heal. Everyone is back to one hundred percent, and Seamus has been fielding calls from them checking on you. They told us how brave you were."

"Wasn't so much bravery. More like dealing with the consequences of fucking up. I had to hold out as best I could and hope you were better at planning rescues than me." She lowers her eyes to the comforter and picks at the edge. "I shouldn't have forced you to let me help. I only made things worse."

"First of all, no one forces me to do anything." *Except for the fucking Council.* But I can't think about how they've singlehandedly ruined any chance I have for happiness right now. "Second, what you did *was* incredibly brave. We wouldn't have even known about the girls if you hadn't gotten the phone that night. You put yourself on the line—and on a *pole*—to take down the NPO. You got shot for fuck's sake."

She frowns like she'd forgotten that tiny little detail. Shoving the blanket down, she lifts the bottom of the Pink Floyd T-shirt I put her in to peer at the place the bullet hit. I rub my thumb over the small silver scar on the left side of her lower abdomen. It's all that remains of the wound that should have taken her life.

"How?"

"Seamus knew what to do. His brother fell in love with an Irish woman during their time fighting the Purity Order. Even though she wasn't fae, they shared blood regularly like a normal mated couple. After a few months, she started to feel younger and even appeared healthier, more youthful. They determined fae blood essentially regenerates a human's damaged cells. But it has its limitations. We think it worked only because I was able to give it to you right away. Another few minutes and you would've..."

"You can say it. I would've died."

I don't say anything in response. I can't bring myself to acknowledge the elephant in the room. I'll walk around that fucker all day and pretend it doesn't exist as long as it means not having to think about what could've been.

Apparently, she doesn't have the same problem. "It's going to happen sooner rather than later, Tier. I'm human. We don't have a very long shelf life, comparatively speaking."

The way she says that so matter-of-factly, with no snarky tone, not even a half-hearted smirk, throws up a red flag in my mind. Something's off about her. I was so relieved when she woke up—making a joke, no less—that I didn't notice how hollow her words sounded. I've never known Fiona to say anything without the vibrancy of emotion behind it, whether good, bad, mad, or sad.

Then again, she *did* just wake up from an incredible ordeal that almost cost her her life. I suppose something like that is bound to take it out of even the most animated of people. Some quality TLC—Tiernan Loving Care—and she'll be right as an evening rain.

"Come on, sweetheart, let's get you in the shower. The hot water will ease your tension and help you feel like yourself again."

She doesn't express much excitement for the idea, but she also doesn't argue with me as I lead her into the bathroom. I turn on the water to let it warm up as we undress, and I make sure that my eyes never stray from her face. This isn't about sex; it's about making her feel cared for and safe. Because she is.

As we step into the spacious shower stall lined with gray subway tiles, I wish I had a large jacuzzi tub for us to soak in together. At least there's a built-in bench she can sit on if she feels too tired to stand.

Once I make sure the water temperature is ideal, I situate her under the spray and begin a regimen of washing her long hair and body. I take my time with each step, massaging her scalp and kneading her tight muscles.

But my intention of helping Fiona to relax doesn't seem to be working. In fact, she looks like she's getting worse. Her movements are few and far between, letting me turn her in place or tip her head forward and back. Sometimes she closes her eyes for long periods of time and others she appears to stare straight through whatever's in front of her. It's like she's descending inside her own mind and becoming less aware of her own body.

I try not to worry, but it's not long before I lose the battle. Cupping her face in my hands, I gently guide her gaze to meet mine. "Fi, talk to me. I can't read your mind, sweetheart. Tell me what you're feeling."

"Nothing," she says plainly. "I feel nothing."

"What do you mean?"

"I feel…numb. I wasn't worried I was in danger. I didn't cry or pray. I wasn't scared or upset when I was dying, and I'm not happy or relieved now that I haven't. I'm not anything. I just…" She shrugs, like she can't describe it any differently. "I don't know, I just *am*."

No one I know has ever been more full of life than Fiona Jewel. Seeing her like this is a different kind of death, and I'll die myself before I let this stand.

"Close your eyes for me." She does, and I pinch her upper arm. Not hard, but hard enough to notice. "Did you feel that?"

She opens her eyes and frowns. "Feel what?" I do it again, but this time she sees me do it. "That I felt."

"Try again. Close your eyes." I reach down and pinch her inner thigh. "Anything?"

She looks up at me. "No."

Christ, she's not even worried about not being worried. "I think I know what's happening; I've read about cases like this before. Our brains are extremely good at protecting us from trauma. Except yours is doing *too* good of a job, and it's starting to affect your nervous system."

"I wouldn't call anything I've gone through a picnic, but I wouldn't call it *trauma*, either."

My eyebrows fly up. "Fiona, in the last week alone you and your mother were attacked and she almost died. Then she told you you're human, causing you to realize your biological parents were murdered before you ever knew about them, making you feel displaced and betrayed. Then you were captured, beaten, and almost died yourself."

She frowns again with the spot over the bridge of her nose pinching together. "Oh…well, when you put it like that…"

"Sweetheart, I'm not putting it like anything. That's just the Cliff's Notes version, surface level stuff." I tuck her wet hair behind her adorable ears and frame her face. "The reality of experiencing all that goes much, much deeper."

Fiona blinks, her spiky lashes dotted with tiny droplets of water. "I'll be fine, Tier. I always am."

The corners of her mouth curve up in the worst interpretation of a smile I've ever seen, and it makes me angry. Not at her, never at her. But at the circumstances that put her in this almost catatonic-like state, that stole the life from her soulful blue eyes. I'm not a psychologist, a therapist, or even good at giving advice. But there's one thing I *am* good at, and it's making her *feel*.

Pitching my voice lower into my Dom register, I ask her, "Do you trust me, Fi?"

Her pupils dilate the slightest bit. It's not much, but it's enough that I believe her when she answers.

"I do."

CHAPTER TWENTY-FOUR

FIONA

Tiernan traces my lower lip with the pad of his thumb. I feel it because I see him do it. I'm not sure if I would if my eyes were closed, though. The realization that I didn't know he was lightly pinching me before is unsettling. Or rather, I know it *should* be unsettling. But when I try to examine how I truly feel about it, all I come up with is indifference.

I'm standing beneath the shower spray, the water at my back and steam billowing around us. The only light is from the dimmed fixtures over the mirrors, bathing the room in a warm glow, like candlelight without the flickering. My sense of touch might be faulty, but my sense of sight is making up for it by drinking in the stunning image before me.

His hair is dark brown when it's wet with slight waves that frame the pointed tips of his ears, and the longer stubble gives him the sexy rakish look he's so well-known for. At almost a foot taller than me, he towers over me, and I have to crane my head back to meet his fervent gaze. But I'll risk the sore neck every time as long as I can drown in his fathomless gold depths.

"We're going to do a scene, Little Red," he says, his voice dark and rumbly. "It will be simple—no toys or whips. I'll start off light and build the intensity until you regain sensation without the benefit of sight. Are you in agreement with my plans?"

"Yes," I say.

He tips my chin up farther with the side of his forefinger and levels me with an expectant look. "Yes, what?"

"Yes, Your Majesty."

He drags his fangs over his lower lip like he's dying to sink them into me. It's a fantasy I've had more times than I can count. I wonder if I would feel his bite.

I don't get the chance to find out. He tells me he'll be right back, then turns and exits the shower. The view of his muscular back and tight ass is the silver lining of him leaving. He's only gone for a few seconds, though, and when he returns, he's holding the black belts from the two robes hanging in the bathroom.

Tiernan places my hands together and uses one of the belts to bind my wrists together, testing for tightness without preventing blood flow. I glance up and notice a hook currently holding a bath puff but is obviously made to hold a *lot* more.

"What's your safe word?" he asks as he tosses the ball of mesh in the corner.

"Red, Your Majesty."

"Good girl. Let's begin."

He turns me to face the wall, then ties the other as a blindfold over my eyes. Once it's secure, he raises my hands and uses the hook to hold my arms in place over my head. I focus on trying to hear his movements through the sound of the water hitting the shower floor, but he's either not moving or not making any noise when he does.

"Can you feel if I'm touching you right now?"

I try to stretch my senses out, to do a body scan like I do when I meditate and take note of how each part of me feels. After a few seconds, I sigh. "No."

A hand twines around the length of my wet hair and yanks my head back. I draw in a sharp breath from the unexpected force and a squeak of surprise escapes me. Tiernan's lips brush the shell of my ear as he speaks. "You forget yourself, Little Red. That's not how you address your king. This is a proper scene, and you will treat it as such, or I'll keep you in a constant state of arousal just shy of coming for the remainder of the day. Have I made myself clear?"

For the first time since waking up in his bed, something sparks inside of me. Like his dominance struck a match and now there's a tiny flame of sensation that can turn into something bigger or be snuffed out altogether. And suddenly, I'm desperate for it to grow into more.

My voice is breathy with need. "Yes, Your Majesty."

"Pulling your hair made you feel something. Your nipples tightened, so we're getting somewhere. I suspected I'd have to tap into the harsher touches to get your body's attention. Let's get your inner masochist purring again."

There's a light nip on my earlobe. I have no way of knowing whether it was actually light or if he gave me a new piercing, but I revel in the soft tingles that ripple over my scalp from it all the same, and I'm eager for more.

Blunt fingernails dig in at my sides and drag across my abdomen in opposite directions. "Ohhhhh." I moan and arch into the sensation. He growls in appreciation for whatever he sees.

"That's it," he encourages softly.

The smack of a wet hand connecting with wet flesh echoes off the tile, then a glorious heat radiates out from my ass cheek. I thought I was indifferent to lacking my sense of touch, but now I nearly weep in relief. Allowing my bonds to hold my weight, I relax into the pleasure-pain of each new strike of his palm.

When he turns me around to face him, he adjusts the

spray of the water to hit my breasts. He twists and tugs on my nipples, uses his nails to score my stomach and upper thighs, drags the tips of his fangs up the side of my neck. Then he uses a foot to kick my legs wider apart, giving him unfettered access to my pussy.

A fingertip circles my swollen clit, dips into my entrance to gather my arousal, then goes back to torturing my— *SMACK*. I hiss in a breath as flames lick over my folds and I cry out in rapture. "*Oh gods!*"

Tiernan cups his hand over my pussy and holds the heat in as it seeps into my body. "That's it, let it flow through you. Feel how the hot sting melts into a warm caress, like two sides of the same coin." Finally, he slides two digits into my sex, stretching my walls as he scissors them inside me. Needing more, I mewl and move my hips, shamelessly fucking myself on his fingers. "Atta girl, Fi. Make yourself feel good. I want to watch you come undone for your king."

A myriad of sensations light me up like a supernova, and I do exactly as my king commands while screaming his name. My entire body shakes with the force of my orgasm as he continues to slowly pump his fingers and run his free hand over my breasts and belly.

When the last of the aftershocks ebb, he removes my blindfold. Light floods my vision and then I'm staring up into the face of a very sexy, very satisfied Dom. "You did so good, baby," he says, reaching up to unhook me and untie my wrists. "How do you feel now?"

"Alive." My answer makes him smile. His plan worked. I still have a lot to process and work through, but his method of reminding my body what it's like to feel through the pleasure-pain it craves worked. As soon as my wrists are free, I wrap my arms tightly around his neck. "Alive, but not satiated."

I press my hips forward, trapping his thick erection between us. He hisses in a breath and the black of his pupils eclipse the gold as his desire changes from one of benevolence to that of a hungry predator. With a low growl he hoists me up and sits on the bench so I'm straddling him. "Then use me until you are, Little Red. Take what you need. I'm fucking yours."

Raising up on my knees, I guide the head of his cock to the entrance of my tight pussy, already slick with a fresh wave of arousal at hearing his command, at hearing he's *mine*. Slowly, I sink onto his thick erection, reveling in the way he stretches me, fills me, completes me. "Oh gods," I rasp. "I love how you feel inside me."

"That makes two of us." He grips my hips in his large hands and holds me in place. As if I would ever want to leave.

I lean forward and claim his mouth in a heated kiss. As our tongues delve and dance, I begin to rock my pelvis back and forth in his lap, grinding myself on his stiff cock. We swallow each other's moans, then take gasping breaths before going back for more.

My muscles tense as I chase the powerful orgasm that threatens to consume me in a rapturous conflagration. His hands grip me tighter, fingers digging deliciously into my flesh but still letting me set the pace, letting me take what I need. And what I *need* is *everything*.

We break apart and lock eyes as my movements become more frantic and desperate. His feral beauty is a sight to behold. Stubbled jaw clenched, teeth bared, muscles taut— he's my sexy, wild king, and even if I could live to a thousand, I would never tire of looking at him.

"Fuck, you're squeezing me like a godsdamn fist," he grates out. "That's it, sweetheart, grind on my cock until you come."

"Tiernan...I'm...*oh gods...*"

I let out a throaty cry as my climax crashes over me like a tsunami. Tiernan buries his face in my neck and groans my name. My sex convulses on his cock as he spills himself deep inside me, branding me as only he can.

Framing my face, he pulls me to him for a languorous kiss filled with every emotion we dare not speak. Then I tuck myself against his chest, close my eyes, and revel in the sensations his hands elicit as he takes care of me until I drift off to sleep.

CHAPTER TWENTY-FIVE

FIONA

I was mostly still asleep when Tiernan pulled his T-shirt over me early this morning and kissed my forehead before tucking the covers over me again. The past few days must've really taken it out of me because I was too tired to ask why he was dressing me and not coming back to bed.

The next time I drift toward consciousness, I feel someone rubbing my back in gentle circles and hear a feminine voice softly calling my name. "Wake up, mo stòirìn."

"Mom?" My eyes flutter open to see her sitting at the edge of the bed and staring down at me with a smile, just like she used to do when she woke me up for school every day. Except she looks different than she did back then: frail and almost muted, like she's on the tail end of suffering from a violent illness.

I rush to sit up and throw my arms around her neck. "Thank Rhiannon, you're okay."

She hugs me back and her familiar scent envelopes me with a feeling of security I knew as a child. "I'm fine," she says, squeezing me tighter. "I was so worried I'd lost you. When they told me you'd been shot..."

I hear her sniffle and pull back to see her golden eyes filling up with tears. Mine instantly begin to water, and I've never been more grateful to cry at the drop of a hat. I have Tiernan to thank for saving me—both from the brink of death and from falling into a numbing abyss.

"I know, but I'm fine. See?"

I lift up the T-shirt to show her my scar but end up showing her a lot more than that. Raised pink welts stripe the tops of my thighs from where Tiernan raked his blunt nails over me, and I'm sure there are plenty more in other areas of my body. I quickly pull the shirt down, but the look my mom is giving me says it's too late.

With a sheepish grin, I say, "I know it sounds strange, but it was actually more of a therapy session."

"I don't care what it was, as long as it means you're here."

"Speaking of which," I say, curious as to how my mom ended up at the future king's private residence.

"Prince Tiernan sent a car for me. When I got here, he showed me through and then left for the manor to meet with his brothers and the Regent." Worry fills her eyes, and this time I know it has nothing to do with my near-death experience. "We haven't really had a chance to talk."

I nod. "Why don't you go see if you can figure out how to make us some coffee or tea, whatever he has here. I'll find something to wear and join you in a minute."

She points to a large bag near her feet. "I brought you a change of clothes from the things you left at home. Also your favorite mug from when you were little with a box of the gourmet hot chocolate you love."

"Ooh, I'll have some of that instead. Thanks, Mom."

"There's also a thermos of peppermint-nettle tea, sans magic," she adds with a wan smile.

"Is that because I don't need it anymore, or because you're not strong enough to do the spell?"

Brushing some hair out of my face, she tucks it behind my ear. "I'm so glad you're okay. I'll meet you out in the living room."

I try not to let her omission bother me as I get dressed and go through my morning routine as best I can in a strange bathroom. After pulling my hair back into a ponytail and using the new toothbrush Tiernan set out for me, I head out to the living room to have our first heart to heart since she turned my world upside down.

I join her on the couch, and she hands me a mug of the hot chocolate. She's made it just the way I like with a single ice cube, so it's not too hot when I take several generous sips. Sighing, I sink into the comfort of its warmth and the plush cushions behind my back.

"So," she starts in that tone that moms have when they're about to be nosy. "Am I sensing something between you and Prince Tiernan? Other than the 'therapy' session, I mean. I had my suspicions about the two of you having fun together before, but the way he's acting now makes me think it might be something more."

I chew on my lower lip for a bit, unsure of how to answer. But she misreads my hesitation. Lowering her gaze to her own mug, she says, "I'm sorry. Perhaps you feel it's no longer my place to ask you such personal questions. I hope one day you'll be able to forgive me for deceiving you."

Guilt fills me, weighing me down like a lead balloon. "I think I forgave you before I ever walked out of that hospital room. I'm not saying that I'm not still hurt, but I can understand why you did it. And maybe if I had never met and become close with Bryn, I'd resent the situation more. But I'm glad you kept her safe and that she had a loving home...like I did."

She lifts her head, hope swimming in her eyes. "Thank you, mo stòirìn. I understand you need time to process things in your own way, you always have. Just know I'm here for you, and I love you."

"I love you, too, Mom. Us against the world; that hasn't changed." We share watery smiles and a quick hand squeeze. "As for me and Tiernan, we have…strong and complicated feelings for each other. I'm not sure what the future holds for us, but I know we're trying to figure it out."

Remembering last night and how he broke through my emotional dam, I'm overwhelmed with a certain feeling I'm too afraid to put a label on even in my own mind. "He saved me." *In more ways than one.* "I didn't know if I'd ever see the outside of that warehouse again."

She swallows thickly, her emotions written on her face. As hard as it was for me to sit with her in the hospital and not know if she would survive the attack, I can't imagine how she must have felt not knowing what was happening to her only child, whether I was alive or dead. I reach for her hand again, and this time I hold onto it.

"I'm okay, Mom," I say softly, doing my best to reassure her.

Nodding, she gives me a weak smile. "Do you want to tell me what happened?"

I sift through what I remember, unsure if there's anything I'm willing to tell her that won't further upset her. I'm not about to give her the gory details of how Charlie—may he rot in hell, the fucker—used me as a punching bag during his interrogation. Joke was on him, though, because somehow, I held out. Even pissed him off enough that he—

I draw in a sharp breath as the finer points of my time in captivity rush to the surface. An image of Charlie's face partially transforming flashes in my mind.

"Werewolves." I slowly set my mug on the coffee table, not trusting my shaking hands with anything breakable. "I need to tell Tiernan the weres are involved."

"He knows. When the twins tracked you and the others, they could scent them. They're from the NOLA pack, but we can't figure out their connection to Leone. And they were hiding their energies, likely with Voodoo. Leone might not even know they're *other*."

I shake my head. "No, Mom, it's so much worse than that." Shoving my fingers into my hair, I dislodge my ponytail. "Shit, I can't believe I didn't remember this sooner. We need to call Tiernan—where's the phone?"

Before the ensuing panic attack takes hold, Mom pulls my hands into her lap. "Fiona, look at me. *Look at me.*"

My gaze stops bouncing around the room in search of any kind of communication device and settles on the pair of eyes I know better than my own. They're the ones that have pulled me out of nightmares and said "I love you" a million times.

They're my home.

"Good," she says. "Now take some cleansing breaths with me. Come on." I follow her lead and we complete three deep breaths together. "Better. Now, can you tell me what you just remembered before we make any calls? It might help to organize your thoughts first."

Icy dread sits in the pit of my stomach as I recount everything I learned in that concrete prison, talking to a madman. I tell her that Leone is the Light King in a glamour and cloaking spell. That he has a conjurer helping him, which is why the werewolves—who are working *for* him—aren't reading as supernaturals either.

And then I tell her the worst part: that *she* is the reason he created the NPO. How he realized who she was at the Meeting of Two Kings and vowed to destroy her for spiriting Bryn away all those years ago.

"When I tried to throw it in his face that his attack on you failed, he implied it happened as planned. He wanted me to tell you that you're the only one who can stop the NPO from spreading like a cancer and wiping out all the fae in this realm. But if he hates you so much, what does not killing you accomplish? And why create a hate group if he's hoping you'll stop them? *None of it makes any damn sense.*"

My mom releases my hands and appears to almost go inside herself as she slowly stands and walks toward the floor-to-ceiling panoramic view of the city. "Because it's not enough for him to simply eliminate an enemy. He wants to inflict the maximum amount of mental anguish." She stares out at the city through the large pane of glass for a count of nine heartbeats, but I can tell the second her focus switches from the distance to her own reflection. "It's time to call Prince Tiernan. I know how I can stop the New Purity Order."

Hope sparks in my chest. "How?"

Turning, she faces me with tears in her eyes, and my newborn hope is snuffed out by the return of icy dread pricking my skin.

"By sacrificing myself."

CHAPTER TWENTY-SIX

TIERNAN

Standing just outside my room at Midnight Manor, I lift my glass of Devil's Keep and take a healthy swallow as I stare at the lights of the Vegas skyline in the distance. Being that it's late January, it isn't the warmest this late at night, but I chose only to throw on a pair of sweatpants after my shower. The slight chill from the breeze against my bare chest and feet with my still-damp hair keeps me focused and helps me think.

Since we issued the court-wide curfew, there have only been three fatal attacks. It's three too many. Only one night left, then we end this.

Preparing for tomorrow has been a week of hell. We were either planning, strategizing, or discussing plans to strategize for our big move against the NPO and their leader, who we now know is none other than Talek Edevane.

Part of me says I should've known he was the one behind the group of genocidal maniacs, and it's been eating me that I didn't. But as Caiden pointed out, with all the securities we had in place, plus him and his werewolves reading as humans, there's no reason we would've jumped to that conclusion. Conjuring fae are rare, and conjurers powerful enough to mask so many, so completely, are unheard of.

It's just our luck Edevane would have one like that at his side, and adding insult to injury, he did a damn fine job of taking *our* conjurer out of commission. Erin has such a small amount of magic left. If she burns it up taking out the NPO, there's a good chance it'll kill her.

Tomorrow will not only be risky, there's no guarantee it won't also prove fatal. We tried to come up with a better plan—one that at least gave us better odds of everyone walking away in one piece—but if there's a better plan out there, I couldn't find it.

We've prepared all we can at this point. All that's left is to pray that Rhiannon is looking out for us, and that what Erin's giving up won't be for nothing.

When I wasn't in meetings this past week, I had to deal with Hedrek-fucking-Dolan. He's crawled so far up my ass about the coronation it's a miracle I can walk. The one good thing about ascending is that I'll finally be able to extract him from my ass *and* my daily life. Once a king is on the throne again, the Council will go back to being mostly ornamental, and I'll only have to suffer his presence at official court events.

But that doesn't get me out of what I have to do now.

Bile churns in my gut as I scroll through the contacts in my phone until I get to the Ds. I stop on "Dickhead" and hit the button. He picks up on the first ring as though he's been waiting for my call.

"Good evening, Your Highness."

I don't bother with pleasantries. I just give him the answer he's been waiting for. "Lady Maeve."

"Excellent choi—"

I end the call and immediately feel sick. I toss back the rest of my drink, hoping it helps. It doesn't, of course. But eyeing the bottle of Keep, I estimate there's enough left to get me blind-ass drunk. It won't help me forget my betrayal of Fiona and any future we may have had together, but it might dull the stabbing pain in my chest that feels like it's tearing me in two.

I don't know how I'm going to tell Fiona; it's all happening too fast. For the past three months, I felt like I've been driving at top speed with no brakes toward a concrete wall. I've known crashing was inevitable, but it was still several miles out. I knew I had time to come to terms with my fate.

Then, out of nowhere, Dolan and the Dark Council drop a boulder the size of a house directly in front of me and expect me to smile as I make impact. I'm doing my fucking best, but there's only so much a male can take, even if he's a royal.

Maybe some fresh air and moonlight will help ease my turbulent thoughts. Pouring myself another two fingers of Keep, I wander out onto the second level balcony. The sound of a fire crackling down at the other end of the manor reaches me. Fiona is sitting in front of the outdoor fire pit, her heels on the edge of the cushion with her arms wrapped around her knees as though trying to prevent herself from falling apart. Looks like I'm not the only one with turbulent thoughts tonight.

Before I even realize I moved, I find myself standing in front of her. "Care for some company?"

She lifts her head to peer up at me. "As long as you don't mind me being *bad* company."

"Nothing about you could ever be bad, Fi." I take a seat next to her on the couch and offer her my glass. After a brief hesitation, she accepts it and takes a generous swallow of the whiskey before handing it back.

"Thanks."

"Welcome." I should tell her now; it's the perfect opportunity. And yet there's something about the timing that doesn't seem right. Or maybe that's simply my justification for chickening out.

"What's on your mind, Little Red? You look like you're

contemplating the world's mysteries."

"No, just my own."

"Wanna talk about it? I've been told I'm a good listener."

She snorts. "By whom?"

I pretend like I'm trying to think of someone until she giggles softly. Mission accomplished. "Look, we all know I'm good at everything, so listening won't be any different." The sound of her light laughter is like a balm to my soul. I wish I could bottle it so I could hear it whenever I wanted. "Seriously, though. What's wrong?"

She grows serious again, the worry lines between her brows becoming prominent as she stares into the dancing flames. "I feel...unmoored, I guess. Like I have one foot in each of the worlds, but I don't belong in either." She turns to look up at me, her blue eyes swimming with raw emotion. "I don't know what to do with that."

I'm overwhelmed with the need to prove her wrong, to prove that she *does* belong somewhere. *With me.* Grabbing her face, I kiss her with everything I am and everything I feel for her. She immediately surrenders, opening for me and inviting me inside, just as she always has. I groan into her mouth and pick her up to straddle my lap. Her hands grip the back of my neck, and the bite of her nails makes shivers dance down my spine.

"Tier, I need you. Please—"

"Ssshhh... You don't have to beg me for a godsdamn thing, Fi. I'll happily give you what you need and more."

Wrapping my arms around her waist, I stand and head for her bedroom for the simple fact it's the shortest distance to a bed. Once inside, I hit the button that activates the wall of windows to slide closed, then I lay her in the center of the mattress and follow her down.

I make quick work of undressing her and shedding my sweatpants. She reaches for my cock, but I capture her wrist and pin it above her head as I kiss her. I need to make this night special, to give us a memory that will last the rest of our lives, even if what we have together ends tonight.

Pulling back, I hold her gaze as I trail open-mouthed kisses between her breasts, pausing to briefly suck each nipple into turgid peaks, then continue down her stomach to dip my tongue into her belly button, then kiss down her mons until I reach Mag Mell on earth.

My mouth instantly waters from the intoxicating scent of her arousal, and there's no hope for me drawing this out. She bends her knees and spreads her legs, offering herself up to me. The petal-pink folds of her slick pussy glisten in the low lamplight, and I can't resist any longer.

Pressing a quick kiss to the insides of her thighs, I lower my head and seal my lips over her soft flesh. Her moans of pleasure mix with my groans as her sweet taste bursts on my tongue. Gripping the globes of her ass for purchase, I begin to feast.

Fiona throws her head back, arching her body and almost breaking my seal, but I move with her and enjoy the ride. "Oh my fucking gods. *Tiernan.*"

As much as I loved it when she used the Majesty title, I love hearing her say my name in the throes of passion even more. I imagine we're living a different life: that we're bonded and happy, and this is just a normal night for us.

Reaching between her legs, she fists her hands in my hair. The harder she pulls, the more I devour her. My tongue delves into her tight hole and thrusts, drinking her juices down like it's lifegiving water from the gods.

Nothing else compares to this—the way she reacts to me, her sounds, her scent, her flavor, her gasped pleas in my name. Everything about her is fucking sublime, and I will never want another female like I want Fiona. Never.

"Tiernan, *please.*"

I growl against her flesh in answer, making her cry out and clamp her thighs around my head as she rides the waves of her first orgasm of the night. "Gods, Fi, you taste so fucking good." I lift up enough to dip two fingers into her tight pussy. I twist them, then drag them back out, satisfied when they come out coated in her. I hold her blue gaze as I suck her come off my fingers, moaning at how good she tastes.

"Come up here," she says, pinching her nipples.

I don't have to be told twice; this is one time I'm happy to take an order. Climbing up her body, I brace myself above her and let her do the honors. She reaches between us and my gaze follows her movement as her delicate hand wraps around my engorged cock, making me hiss.

"Fuck," I grind out through clenched teeth. She starts to stroke me from root to tip and back again, slowly with a firm grip that drives me wild. "Sweetheart, if you keep that up, I'm going to finish on your stomach before I even get inside of you."

"Well, that won't do," she says softly. "Because there's nothing I want more right now than to feel you deep inside me. I want to lose track of where you end and I begin, Tier."

Angling my cock down, she lines me up at her entrance. At the first kiss of her heat on my sensitive crown, I suck in a breath and use every ounce of restraint I have to hold my position. She reaches up and pulls my face down for a passionate kiss, then stares into my eyes and whispers, "Make love to me, Tiernan Verran, future Rebel King of the Dark Fae."

My throat tightens with truths I can't bring myself to utter. Not in this almost-perfect moment with this more-than-perfect woman. So, for possibly the first time in my long life, I don't say anything. Then I push my hips forward, groaning as I invade and stretch her hot pussy inch by punishing inch until I'm fully seated.

Resting my forehead on her shoulder, I focus on my

breathing and wait for her to adjust. Her breasts press against my chest as she takes a deep breath of her own, then relaxes beneath me—her body's version of saying "green."

We move as one, as though we've made love a thousand times before. I know it would be wrong, but the desire to sink my fangs into her and share my blood with her is almost overpowering. The animal inside me is godsdamned selfish, and it wants to mark her. Brand her. *Claim her.*

But I fucking can't. Not tonight, not ever.

Shoving those morose thoughts aside, I focus on this time I do have with her and thank Rhiannon for each blessed second.

Kissing her deeply, our hands roam over each other's bodies: nails scoring, fingers flexing, tongues tangling. Eventually we break apart to lock eyes as I continue to slowly pump into her. On every withdrawal, her slick pussy squeezes my cock in the sweetest of death grips, threatening to send me to the Otherworld well before my time.

"Remember this night, Fiona. Know that you belong to me, just as I belong to you. Now and always, no matter what."

She cups my jaw in her delicate hands and gazes up at me with her heart in her eyes. "Now and always."

With that, I adjust my angle and hit the spot inside her guaranteed to make her fly. On my next thrust, she cries out a keening, "Yes, oh gods, right there." Keeping the pace slow and steady, I thrust home, again and again, each time driving us toward the crest of a mutual climax.

"Fuck yes, Little Red. Come with me. Wanna feel—*ah gods!*"

"*Tiernan!*"

Light flashes behind my eyelids as her pussy grips me like a vise and hurtles me over the edge with one final drive home. My cock pulses in time with her heartbeat as I empty myself inside her, painting the swollen walls of her sex with my seed. Branding her one last time the only way I can, just as she's branded herself on my soul.

"Tiernan, I..." Her blue eyes mist over as she splays her fingers into the hair at my nape. "I..."

I stop her with a kiss before she can say it, because I'll hurt her when I don't say it back. I can't. "You're fucking perfect, Fi," I whisper to her as I tuck her hair behind the rounded shell of her ear. "Whether fae, human, or *other*, everything about you is—and always has been—fucking perfect."

Lying next to her, I pull her back against my chest and hold her to me with my body curled protectively around hers. We don't speak as we stare out at the view of Vegas, the city of sin that carries on every night as though it's the last night it'll ever have. It's hard not to draw a parallel between that...and this.

Soon, her breaths even out, her body sags into the mattress, and I know my time is up. Everything changes for me—for us—the minute I step out of this room. And I've never resented something more.

Careful not to disturb her, I disentangle from her hold and slip out of the bed to pull my sweats on. Blinking back the moisture pricking the backs of my eyes, I press a kiss to her adorable ear and make my way quietly to the door.

Just before I go, I allow myself one last look. Then, leaving Fiona and my broken heart behind, I give up the life I want to accept the life I have.

CHAPTER TWENTY-SEVEN

TIERNAN

"What do you think our odds are that this flashy thing works?" I ask Romanov, who's sitting with me in the bar area of the Nightfall ballroom we always use for Night Court events. The large space is completely empty except for the two of us. Crystal chandeliers hang from the ceiling around a huge skylight that slides open to allow the night and Rhiannon's moon inside for the Dark Fae ceremonies and celebrations.

Tonight, however, this opulent ballroom will be Ground Zero for our showdown with the Day Court king and the New Purity Order.

We're here early, so I grabbed us bottles of Redbreast whiskey and Beluga vodka and we've been pouring ourselves drinks while we wait to take the edge off the nerves. Luckily, *others* have incredibly high tolerances, or we'd be smashed by now.

Dmitri frowns. "What is flashy thing?"

"You know, from the movie *Men in Black*. Will Smith calls the thing that wipes people's memories the flashy thing." The vampire lord gives me a blank look. "You know, for a guy who's been around for-fucking-ever you know very little about the world you live in."

He shrugs and pours himself another shot. "I know what is important for me to know. And now I know 'flashy thing' is another way of saying 'boring plan.'"

The Russian was plenty vocal about his opinion that there wasn't enough bloodshed with our plan. Since he's only here as support, his vote didn't count.

"Believe me, I think they're getting off easy, too," I say with barely restrained rage. "But slaughtering them would only prove we're the monsters they say we are. They might not be stellar examples of the human race, but chances of them becoming murderers were probably nil until Edevane brainwashed them into thinking they were doing it to save humankind."

Romanov grunts then takes his shot. "Fifty-fifty."

"What?"

"Chances of the flashy thing working. I give it fifty-fifty."

I pause in lifting my glass of whiskey and look over at him. "I wouldn't take any jobs as a motivational speaker if I were you. The least you could've done was lie."

"That is the difference between us. You fae wish you could lie, so you go out of your way to be deceitful. I, on the other hand, can lie all I want but choose to be truthful."

"Holy shit, you're right. How's that for back-asswards?" I muse. "So wait, you *never* lie. Like, never?"

"Never. Things are what they are. There is no point in saying otherwise."

I fucking hate how right he is, and now I'm realizing that by not being truthful with Fiona about the coronation contract and the situation I'm in, I've done a disservice to us both. Regardless of how much I wish things were different, they're not. And ignoring the ugly truth in favor of a pretty lie will only make things worse when everything is brought to light.

Which means I need to have a very serious talk with Fiona tonight when all of this is finally done.

Sighing, I finish the rest of my drink and check my watch. The jumbled knots in my stomach I've had since this morning tighten even more. "Almost show time. Let's get into position."

About an hour ago, every member of the NPO showed up to their headquarters at Devil's Door for a mandatory meeting afterhours with their leader, one Stanley Leone. They'd received the encrypted message through their usual channel on the dark web, courtesy of Evan and Clyde. Only when they arrived, there was no leader and no meeting.

Instead, they were met by a dozen of Dmitri's clan members holding AK-47s. Not that vamps need firepower, but it's easier to scare humans *and* keep them calm when you threaten them with what they already understand—scary Russian mafia guys with scary big guns. No need to make the humans piss themselves by introducing them to their worst nightmares. They think *we're* bad; the fae are like Golden Retriever puppies compared to the Romanov vampires. Sparkling vegetarians they are *not*.

After they were rounded up, McCarthy and his unit bound and brought them over to Nightfall via paddy wagon caravan. Now they're cooling their heels in the private sector attached to the ballroom with their armed escorts, waiting for the main event to begin. Which should be any second now.

I left a message for Edevane—on his Stanley Leone business voicemail of all places—saying I wanted to meet one-on-one to broker a deal with him. I of course didn't get the courtesy of an RSVP, but I gave him the time and place, so now we see if he takes the bait. My money is on yes. He's too arrogant to think we can outsmart him, and the opportunity to rub his accomplishments in our faces is too great a temptation.

I take my place in the center of the room and shake out my hands. For the last week, I've had this thrum of extra energy in my veins as I've worked to prepare for this moment. Everything is riding on this plan to work, and I only have *one shot* to get it right. If I can't stop the NPO tonight, there's no chance we prevent an all-out war between humans and fae. No pressure or anything, though.

Great, now my heart is pounding like a fucking jackhammer.

"Relax, comrade, you will do fine."

My eyebrows shoot up as I look over my left shoulder to where Dmitri is standing. "Did you just call me your comrade? You going soft on me, Romanov?"

"My part of our deal was satisfied when your woman was rescued. I do this as your ally."

"You mean *friend*. Come on, you can say it."

He glares at me. "Do not push it, Verran. And stop fidgeting."

"I can't help it. My skin feels like it's too tight," I say as I undo the top two buttons of my shirt. It was Caiden's idea that I borrow a pair of his fancy black suit pants and shirt to give the appearance of someone who should be taken seriously. I thought it was a good idea at the time, but now it just feels like it's trying to suffocate me.

"He is coming," he says, checking there's an iron-tipped round in the chamber of his Glock.

"How do you know?"

"I smell the wolves."

"My guys?" The twins were ordered to escort him to the ballroom and keep guard in the hall while we conducted our business.

"*Nyet.* Weres."

So he didn't abide by the "come alone" stipulation. "Good."

The double doors swing open. The Light King, no longer bothering with his Leone glamour, struts in with two werewolves of the Marceau pack from New Orleans. As soon as they're inside, Connor and Conall nod that they've got all the exits covered just in case, then pull the doors closed behind them.

"Edevane, why am I not surprised to see you have a hard time following instructions? I bet you're not real good at coloring inside the lines, either, are you?"

"A little hypocritical, wouldn't you say?" He gestures to Dmitri behind me.

"What, him? Nah, he's just job shadowing. It's 'take your vampire to work' day at school. Isn't that right, 'Tri?"

"Fuck off, Verran."

I smile wide. "He's kidding, he loves that nickname. Anyhoops, let's get down to business, shall we? Here's what I was thinking. You call off your little NPO buddies—tell them you made a mistake, or they've been Punk'd, whatever, I'll let you worry about the details—and in return, I won't imprison you until your eventual death forever from now. Deal?"

Edevane stares at me like I've lost my mind—to be fair, I'm not entirely sure I haven't—then begins to chuckle with mild amusement that builds into a crescendo until he's all-out laughing enough to wet himself.

"Did I say something funny?" I ask.

"More like *everything* you said." His laughter dies down as he regains his composure. "I can't believe your brother abdicated his throne to *you*. You're not king material. You're nothing more than a joke, just like the ones you so enjoy telling."

His barb pokes at my insecurities as intended, but it's not the focus of my ire. The energy flowing through me spikes with my wrath. "He was *forced* to abdicate because you kept trying to kill his mate!"

"Yes, well, as the humans are fond of saying, all is fair in love and war. He never would've found his mate if it hadn't been for me. It seemed like a fair trade off to give them a few weeks together before I sent them both to Mag Mell."

"Do you plan on calling off your NPO dogs, or not, Edevane?"

He grins the grin of a used car salesman—one meant to draw you in before chewing you up and spitting you out with a sky-high loan you can't afford. "Not."

"That's what I figured. Romanov?"

Dmitri speaks into a walkie to his second-in-command. "Alexei, *privedi ikh*."

Alexei opens the security door in the back of the room for a glamoured Finn and Dmitri's other men to usher in the dogs in question. A couple dozen men in their second-rate military garb, duct tape around their wrists and over their mouths, spill into the main room. Their confusion and fear are palpable and seeing Edevane doesn't clear anything up for them. They don't recognize him without his Stanley Leone glamour.

They *do*, however, notice our pointed ears, near-glowing eyes, and fangs, making us both their sworn enemy—*fae*.

"Well, this is an interesting turn of events," Edevane says with an amused chuckle. "I certainly hope your big plan isn't to kill them in front of me. Not much of a revenge scheme."

"No, that wouldn't be. And there's no point in telling them the truth because they'll never believe that you're the one who's been pulling their strings while walking around in an Edgar-suit this whole time."

I pause and look at Dmitri. "That's another *Men in Black* reference. You really should watch it, it's great." The arch of a scarred dark brow is his only reaction. "Fine, geez. Everyone's a critic."

"If you're not going to kill them," Edevane says, "what's your plan?"

"Sorry I'm late. I hope I didn't miss anything."

Everyone looks to where Fiona is pushing her mom in a wheelchair from the back corridor. "Not at all, Erin." When she reaches my side, I take her hand and squeeze it gently.

"You're right on time."

Edevane *laughs*, pointing at Erin who's noticeably in a weakened state. "This is delightful. I realize I planned this, but I thought for sure you'd hold issue with one of your own sacrificing herself. Using what little power she has left to wipe their memories will likely kill her in the process. Then again, I didn't leave you much choice."

"That's correct. We didn't have *much* choice, but we did have *a* choice. Erin is here merely as a spectator today. Seeing as you had such rude plans for her, I thought it only right she gets a front row seat to your demise."

I nod to Fiona, signaling that it's time to move her and her mom to the other side of the room. She doesn't hesitate, knowing that things are about to get hairy. Then I turn my attention back to my enemy and target.

Edevane props an elbow up on his other arm and strokes his chin. "Curiouser and curiouser."

"Indeed," I reply, giving him my best Cheshire Cat grin. "Are you familiar with chess, Edevane? I'm sure you're aware it's a game of strategy. Oftentimes a player calculates what they believe to be the perfect combination. They mentally plan every move and how their opponent will respond to those moves, ultimately giving the player the upper hand, or possibly even the victory."

Undoing the buttons on each cuff, I begin methodically rolling my sleeves up to my elbows. "But *sometimes* their opponent will pull out a surprise move. One that forces an immediate and unplanned response, thus ruining their plans. When that happens, it's called a Zwischenzug."

"Is there a fucking point to all this, Verran?"

It's the moment of truth. The moment I find out what I'm made of. Whether I'm truly just the good-time Verran who excels at charming business partners and partying with celebrities, or if maybe I'm the Verran everyone—including myself—has been underestimating my entire life.

Earlier today at Midnight Manor, as I mentally prepared myself, the people I care most about in this world were there to offer their support and words of encouragement.

Strike first and strike hard, T. And don't let any of his trash talk get into your head.

Hurry up and get this over with so we can get back to our chess matches already.

My hormones are all over the place, and if you get so much as a scratch on you, I will freak the fuck out. So don't get hurt, do you hear me? *Okay, I love you, go kick some ass.*

Your father would be proud of you, Tiernan. As am I.

We'll be right outside if you need us, but you won't. You're gonna smoke him where he stands.

My special boy, I always knew you were destined for greatness. Please be careful.

Come back in one piece, brother. You have a court to rule and my kid to uncle.

There's no one I've believed in more. You've got this, Tier.

Fiona... My gaze seeks her out, locking onto those crystalline blues. They act as my touchstone and keep me grounded. Placing a hand over her heart, she silently repeats the declaration we made last night.

You will always belong to me, and I will always belong to you. No matter what.

She mouths, "*You've got this*," and her unwavering faith touches me more than she'll ever know.

In front of her, Erin gives me an encouraging nod, reminding me of the guidance she gave me all week as I trained tirelessly for this day.

Erin was prepared to do the selfless thing and sacrifice herself for the greater good of all faekind this side of the veil. But there was no way I was allowing that to happen.

Edevane was right about one thing. With the damage the

iron poisoning did, using the kind of power it would take to wipe specific memories from two dozen humans would've killed her. But if someone in the prime of their unnaturally long life were to drink her blood and carefully siphon the last of her conjuring magic, they'd be able to wield her powers without consequence.

So that's exactly what I did. *Here we go...the moment of truth.*

I signal the Marceau werewolves, and they grab onto Edevane's arms to hold him in place. Shock registers on his face as he realizes he's been betrayed, though I'm not sure why he's surprised. Marceaus are only truly loyal to those in their pack. For anyone else, it goes to the highest bidder. Funny thing about buying loyalty: there will always be someone willing to pay more.

"My *point*, asshole," I say, snarling, "is you thought you had the perfect combination of moves to exact your revenge..."

I open my senses and feel the energy of everyone's confidence in me flow through my veins and infuse the very marrow of my bones. Tapping into the power thrumming inside me, it swells more and more until it fills every cell and crackles like electricity beneath the surface of my skin, ready to be unleashed.

"But you underestimated your opponent, and I'm throwing down the mother of all Zwischenzugs."

CHAPTER TWENTY-EIGHT

FIONA

My stomach is in knots as Tiernan channels his new powers: powers he acquired by siphoning through the act of drinking a conjurer's blood. An act forbidden under penalty of death in Faerie. An act that stripped my mom of all her conjuring magic.

An act that ultimately saved my mom's life.

The air in the ballroom feels charged with electricity, the tiny hairs on the back of my neck standing on end. I'm so nervous I think I might get sick. There was no way for Tiernan to test this plan to the extent he'll need to do it now. The amount of magic this spell will take to pull off at this magnitude will burn through everything he was able to get. If this doesn't work the first time, it won't work at all.

I reach down, and Mom instinctively grabs onto my hand, squeezing it tight. "He's going to be fine, Fiona," she says. "He can do this."

"Right, I know." I nod, mostly to myself because no one else is looking at me. Then my focus is drawn to where Edevane is thrashing around. "Oh wow, bad guy is *pissed*."

"I'd say so, yes."

Talek the Tyrannical, as I've come to call him, has turned five shades of red since the NOLA guys switched teams. He struggles to get free from their grasp, but winds up looking ridiculous. Fae are strong, but one fae isn't nearly as strong as two werewolves. Especially the ones from the Marceau pack. Those guys are just built different.

"What the hell do you think you're doing, Verran? You think you can use her powers to stop me? You have no idea—"

One of the weres takes a kerchief from around his neck and shoves it deep into Edevane's mouth with a muttered, "Finally."

Tiernan angles his body so he can see Edevane and the group of NPO members, who are now visibly shaking in their combat boots. Energy crackles above him as he slowly raises his hands and builds enough power to (hopefully) erase all memories and knowledge of fae existing from the humans.

As for the Light King, he's getting his memory of the night Bryn was born removed. If he doesn't remember killing his cousin and his mate over their newborn being taken and hidden away, then he won't remember his search for Bryn or his revenge against my mom. And if we're really lucky, wiping those memories will end his desire to either rule over or destroy the Night Court.

Finally, with his arms stretched out to the sides, Tiernan chants the spell he spent all week learning forward and backward.

"Tríd an veil ní fheiceann tú a thuilleadh.

Ní mise, agus ní aithne dhúinn.

Glacaim do chuid cuimhní cinn, déan dearmad cad atá caite.

Glacaim do chuimhní cinn agus cuirim go deireanach iad."

Through the veil you no longer see.

Not I, nor we are known to thee.

I take thy memories, forget what's passed.

I take thy memories and make it last.

The humans all cringe and groan like someone is giving them massive headaches. I've never had someone suck out my memories, but I imagine it's not fun. My mom says it won't take long, and that when it's over, they'll most likely fall unconscious from the toll it takes on them.

However, Edevane isn't cringing with pain. He's shouting like he's pissed as hell and trying to disrupt Tiernan's chant. I hope to gods he's too focused to hear the ranting. If the spell is interrupted or messed up in any way before the process is finished, it's all over.

"How long will he have to do this?" I ask my mom, squeezing her hand a little tighter.

She has to practically shout to be heard over all the noise. "He's able to feel for the memories he's targeting while saying the spell. When he no longer feels them, he'll be able to stop. It shouldn't be much longer."

He completes the chant three more times before stopping. As predicted, the humans crumple to the ground in boneless heaps, seemingly unconscious.

Tiernan's arms drop before he bends at the waist to brace his hands on his knees like he's in danger of collapsing after completing his first marathon.

"Tiernan!"

Getting the all-clear from Finn, the Woulfe brothers come in to handle Edevane as planned, but I rush over to Tiernan, my heart in my throat at the thought of him being hurt. Kneeling in front of him, I search for any signs of discomfort or physical damage. We had no way of knowing how wielding a power as strong as conjuring would affect him. Especially as the royal line hasn't had more than basic fae magic since the exile.

"Hey, are you okay? Are you hurt?" Perspiration dots his brow, and his eyes remain closed as he tries to catch his breath.

Concern drops like a brick in my stomach. Caiden and Bryn are tucked safely away in their penthouse upstairs, waiting for us to join them after everything is done. But if he's hurt, we need to get him to Bryn now. Brushing the damp hair away from his face with trembling fingers, I try again. "Tier, please answer me. I need to know if you're okay. *Say* something."

His lids open and I'm relieved to see his golden eyes are as bright as ever. "Fi…"

"Yes? What is it? Tell me," I blurt out, desperate to know what he needs.

"I'm a perverted fucker, but even I won't expect you to get on your knees for me with your mother in the room." My mouth drops open as I realize what he's implying. "I mean, she's right over there, sweetheart."

Recovering from my shock, I narrow my eyes and give him a nice, hard shove. Unfortunately, as he's going down, he grabs hold of my wrists and takes me with him until we're splayed on the floor and laughing. It might seem like a weird time to act like a couple of teenagers at a slumber party, but immense relief after weeks of dealing with life-or-death situations will do that to you.

A throat clears loudly, interrupting our playful shoving match. Hedrek Dolan, who insisted on watching the events unfold in the safety of the security room, is standing over us. If you looked up "judgy" in the dictionary, you'd see a picture of his scowling face.

"Congratulations, Your Highness, but perhaps you could rise and oversee the things that still need to be taken care of? This is hardly the proper way to behave. What would your future c—"

Tiernan throws up a hand and stares the elder down as though he were the one on the ground and not Tiernan. "Yes, Lord Speaker, I know. What would my future court think of their future king acting like a youngling in such a serious situation? I forgot myself briefly, and I apologize. It won't happen again."

Hedrek sniffs in response before walking away. I frown as I stare after him and ponder the strangeness of their exchange. "Jesus, he came out of nowhere."

Tier's upper lip curls in disdain. "He's like my godsdamn shadow. I wouldn't be surprised if he had a detailed log of every time I took a shit."

"Ew, Tier, *graphic* much? Anyway, why would he even pose the question about what the court would think? He'd have to tell them for that to even be a concern."

I'm surprised Hedrek doesn't have smoke wafting up from the hole Tier's burning into the back of his head. "Oh, he'd tell them, all right. He gets way too much joy out of making me miserable."

Something in the tone of his voice sounds off. But when I look over at him, he flashes his signature lopsided grin at me and winks. "So, how'd it look? Was it awesome? I should've had you record it. Wait! The security cameras, we'll have footage from every angle. I'll have Bryn edit it like a movie trailer—"

I can't help but laugh. "Slow your roll, Scorsese. Let's wrap things up here before you start writing your Oscar speech."

"That's fair. Come on, Little Red." Tiernan pushes to his feet, then offers his hand and pulls me up. "Let's go gloat to the Big Bad Wolf..." We turn around and come up against two giant walls with man-buns and identical glares aimed at their friend. "...who clearly isn't a real wolf because *wolves* are awesome, and *he* is not. That's what I was going to say."

I pat his arm. "Nice try."

"Yeah, well, I wouldn't go gloating too much," Connor says. "We have him in iron cuffs, so he's weakened and detained. But—"

"The memory spell didn't work on him," Conall finishes in

that twin thing they often do. "Erin thinks his conjurer must have placed a protection spell on him."

"Shit. I'll call Caiden."

"No," I say. He looks down at me, his brow furrowed. "Tier, it's fine to ask him if you truly need his guidance, but Caiden isn't on the throne anymore. In a matter of days, it will be *you*. Trust in yourself the way *I* trust in you. The way we *all* do."

Something flashes across his face I can't quite read. If I had to name it, it would be sad gratitude. But that's a strange combination and doesn't make any sense.

"She's right, bro," Conall says.

Connor claps him on the shoulder. "Say the word and it's done."

Tiernan scratches the stubble on his jaw as he thinks. "It's not the outcome we wanted, obviously, but we can't release him into the wild if he's going to continue to be a threat. And we can't kill him because of Aine's Fun-with-Curses."

"And because, unlike him, *we* are not cold-blooded murderers," I add.

"Right, that too," Tiernan says. "Let's go talk to him, shall we? His fate will depend on him."

As we walk toward where Finnian is guarding the Light King in the far corner of the room, I finally take in the scene around us.

The Marceau boys are nowhere to be seen. Since they had no dog in this fight, once their part of the deal was done, the mercenaries for hire probably hightailed it out of here, eager to get back to the bayou and their pack.

Over by the group of NPO members, McCarthy oversees his part of the operation. They're implanting a tiny tracking chip into each person in the back of their neck, right at their hairline. They'll be closely monitored for several months to make sure the spell sticks and they're not causing trouble. After that they'll only get checked on occasionally, with an alarm set to go off on McCarthy's phone if more than two of them ever gather in the same place.

Once they're tagged, the VPD will transfer them to the waiting vehicles out back and drop them off at their respective residences in the middle of the night. They're all getting planted evidence that makes it look like they're coming off one hell of a Vegas bender. Regardless of if they've mentioned fae to anyone, the members will have no idea what they're talking about. Eventually, it will all turn into mere stories that were told, just like the rest of the fables and fairy tales.

Mom is graciously pretending to listen to Dolan's inane chatter while keeping a close eye on the bastard who tried to orchestrate her suicide. Knowing her, she considers that the very least of his crimes. Kidnapping fae, ordering her daughter beaten, multiple attempts on her niece's life, and murdering both her niece's adoptive *and* biological parents—who were also Mom's sister and brother-in-law—are far more serious crimes to her, and he's gotten away with all of them.

Until now. Tiernan's plan worked, and as a result, Talek the Tyrannical will finally answer for everything he's done.

"There he is," Edevane says from his place on the floor. "The second-rate future king of the second-rate Celestial court."

Tiernan's lips peel back in a feral grin, fangs glinting. "Says the king shackled in iron at my feet."

He gives a half shrug. "A temporary setback."

Tiernan crosses his arms over his chest and glares down at our captive. "The spell didn't work on you. Is that because of your conjurer?"

"I'd have to be pretty stupid to come to a meeting with my enemy without a little extra protection, don't you think? I didn't know the were-mercs could be bought off so easily, not with what I was paying them. I should've known better than to work with a bunch of backwoods greedy fucks. That was a miscalculation on my part. How much did you offer them?"

"That's between me and Gage Marceau."

Edevane's eyebrows shoot up. "You spoke with the alpha? I'm impressed. He's harder to access than the Pope."

"Got any more revenge plots you care to share with the class?"

"No."

"No, you don't have any, or no, you don't want to share?"

"I'll tell you what," he says with a smile, "you take these cuffs off me and let me walk out of here, and it'll be a surprise."

"Yeah, that's what I figured. Since I can't kill you, we'll do my second choice. How does life imprisonment with no possibility for parole sound?"

"Where, in the state prison? Something tells me it'll cause a lot of suspicion when one of the prisoners actually lives for the several hundred years he's been sentenced."

"That's true, it would. Which is why my father had the foresight to build several cells beneath our temple. Very nice, made of iron. Fit for a fae king."

Finnian grabs Edevane by the arm and hauls him up to his feet. "I'd be happy to escort our guest to his new quarters, brother. In fact, I'd consider it a personal favor to be the one to lock him up and throw away the key."

"Ah, Finni, you know I've never been able to say no to you. You're my favorite brother. Don't tell Caiden."

Edevane grows somber. "Remember this moment... You're going to regret it."

Tiernan matches him in tone, his expression hardening. "You could say that about a lot of moments in my life. But this moment isn't one of them."

Finn rips a piece of duct tape off from a roll and slaps it over the prisoner's mouth before hauling him out of the ballroom. Within the hour, the one responsible for so much pain and so much death will be behind bars until he takes his last breath in this realm.

I wasn't prepared for the deluge of emotions that would overtake me the minute it became real. I exhale a shuddering breath as tears stream down my face.

"Hey, hey, hey, Fiona baby, what's wrong? You're supposed to be happy right now."

"I am," I say between halting breaths. "I'm so happy and relieved, and I don't think my body knows how to handle it." I try laughing, but it isn't easy through the sobs.

"Come here. Let it all out. This is way better than being numb. You cry all you want, sweetheart. I've got you."

He holds me against his chest, and I do let it all out while he rubs comforting circles on my back and whispers sweet things against the top of my head. Being in his arms is like the icing on our victory cake. Nothing could make me happier than being with him like this right now.

"Your Highness, congratulations on apprehending the Day Court king."

I pull out of Tiernan's arms and swipe at the wetness on my cheeks, trying to compose myself in the presence of the speaker of the Dark Council. Once again, Hedrek Dolan has managed to ninja out of nowhere and ruin a moment between us.

"Thank you, Lord Speaker," Tiernan says. "I presume you'll be heading back to the council to give them the good news."

"Indeed I am. I will also tell Lady Maeve of your brave heroics. She will be pleased to hear her king is alive and well." Giving me the barest of nods, he says, "Goodbye, Miss Jewell."

Then he exits stage left, leaving me reeling from this new plot twist. I don't even have to ask Tiernan what Dolan meant by that. The look on his face says it all.

I ball my fists at my sides to prevent them from shaking, but there's no stopping the way my insides are trembling. It feels like my heart has been cleaved from my chest, and I'm certain if I look down, I'll see it carelessly discarded at my feet. Because the one I trusted to take care of it...didn't.

"When were you going to tell me?"

He swallows hard. "Tonight," he says in a low voice. "But I should have told you before. I'm sorry I didn't. I have no excuse other than my own selfishness. You would have pulled away again the second you heard about the contract and I—"

"A contract? What is it that you agreed to exactly?"

"I agreed to name my consort the night of my coronation. And to provide the court with an heir within the first year of my rule."

Bile creeps into my throat imagining Tiernan with another female. Imagining Tiernan with their baby. "Is that what you want? To have children with Lady Maeve?"

He steps in close, fisting his hands at his sides. "Of course it's not, Fi. You know exactly what it is I want. But that doesn't mean I can have it. I've avoided accepting my responsibility for too long, and now I have to do what's right for my people. That's all there is to it."

"What about what's right for you? Doesn't that count for anything?"

"Not when you're the king." Frustration makes the muscle in his jaw tic. "I wouldn't be the male you care about if I didn't do the honorable thing."

"That's true. But sometimes the honorable thing isn't what you think it is. Just because something always has been doesn't mean it always *should* be, Tier."

"Believe me, I fucking know. But what I think doesn't matter. The council has me by the balls, and if I don't abide by their rules and contract, millennia of Verrans sitting on the Midnight Throne will come to an end, and there's no doubt in my mind it'll be the Dolan line that gets appointed as the new Night Court royals. You know I can't let that happen."

My heart breaks for him. It breaks for us, and for the life we'll never have. But mostly I'm pissed as hell. At the Dark

Council, at antiquated laws and bigoted views. And I'm pissed at Tiernan for not fighting for us, not even a little.

I do my best to hold the angry tears at bay and take a step back to extract myself from his magnetic pull. "You know, this is probably for the best. I think we started confusing great sex for other things. I mean, what do we really know about each other? Not much when you think about it. For example, you don't know my middle name, and I never thought the Rebel Prince would roll over for a bunch of geriatric blowhards trying to run his life."

"Fi…" He steps forward, but I retreat another step. Fisting his hands at his sides, he speaks low through a clenched jaw. "Godsdamn it, Fiona, what would you have me do?"

"*Find another way.*"

"There *isn't* another one!"

"Then I guess there's nothing left to say." I swallow past the fist-sized lump forming in my throat. "What's it called in chess when neither player can win?"

His shoulders fall. "Stalemate."

Nodding, I take another step away from him. "Stalemate. That seems rather apropos, don't you think?"

Tiernan moves like he wants to follow me, but the warning look I give him stops him cold. He rakes a hand through his hair, making it stick up in different directions and giving him that boyish appearance I love so much. "I will never stop wanting you, Fi. Not for as long as I'm breathing."

Wanting. Not needing, not loving. "I might be a Vegas girl, but not even I would take that bet," I say with a wry smile. "Goodbye…Your Highness."

Then I walk out of the room and shoot my mom a text to let me know when she's ready to leave so I can come and help her. Until then, I'll go out to the car and wait.

Much like I'll be waiting the rest of my life for my heart to be put back together again.

CHAPTER TWENTY-NINE

FIONA

It's been four days since our victory over Edevane and the New Purity Order. So far, every member has gone about their lives business-as-usual with no mysterious meetups or strange rants about supernatural beings. There's been no chatter on the dark web, no propaganda videos popping up, and no one carrying hag stones. Tiernan's plan worked, and my mom was spared.

Now that it's safe to venture out again, she and Bryn have dragged me out to Nightfall for "a relaxing evening at the spa." But the side glances they keep giving me when they think I'm not looking prove there's more to this than just a regular GNO. It's obvious they're concerned about me, and I guess I can't blame them. If either of them were in my position, I'd feel the same way.

After the way things ended with Tiernan that night, my daily yoga and meditation practices haven't helped me find my Zen like usual. Like wisps of smoke that you can see but not hold in your hand, it eludes me every time I think I almost have it, and the feeling of not being centered is discomforting.

I've managed not to compound that by resigning and

moving into my old room at Mom's. Unfortunately, the lack of physical proximity hasn't lessened how much time I spend thinking about the future king and what we've lost.

I keep telling myself that the depth of my heartbreak is disproportionate to that loss. It's not like we were ever a couple in the true sense. And there was what, all of a day or two where we thought we *might* be able to have *some* kind of life together?

Even that wasn't going to be all rainbows and roses. We would've faced a lot of scorn from the Council members and possibly even the people. Not that they've ever cared whether their kings indulged in depravities with humans, but to be in an exclusive relationship with one while putting off their duty to provide heirs with a fae consort is a different thing altogether.

Not like any of that matters now. Stop torturing yourself. It's done and in the past. Start focusing on your future. Wherever that is.

"Wherever *what* is?" Bryn asks from off to my left.

We're in the final stage of our pampering party. Our fingers and toes have been done, our bodies massaged and detoxified, and now we're reclining in leather chairs, wearing soft robes and sipping on champagne—or sparkling grape juice for Bryn— as the estheticians mix up some concoctions in the next room to apply on our newly derma-planed faces.

I look over at Bryn. "What?"

She huffs, her legendary patience on a short leash thanks to the pregnancy hormones. "You said, 'Wherever *that* is.' What did you mean by that?"

I said that out loud? Great. Now my internal monologue is on the fritz. "Even if I *did* say that—and I'm not saying I did—I didn't sound like an angsty teenager when I did it."

Unhelpfully, my mom answers from my right. "Yes, you did. On both counts."

Arching a brow in her direction, I quip, "You're supposed

to be on my side, here."

"I am, *mo stóirín*." Her amber eyes soften on me. "We both are. It's why we're worried about you."

Bryn tags in. "You haven't wanted to talk about what happened between you and Tier. You told us what was said, but not how you're feeling about it all. And I know sometimes it's easier to try and convince ourselves that we're fine. But that only lasts for so long. It's like this sparkling juice," she says, picking up the green bottle from the bucket of ice between us. "The cork might be on there super tight, but if you shake it up enough, all those teensy, little feelings-bubbles will pop that sucker off and erupt into a huge mess."

There's a long silence as Mom and I stare at her with twin expressions of confusion. "That was a *horrible* analogy," I finally say. "What's the expiration on that bottle? I think the juice is fermented."

"Bryn, darling, maybe put the bottle down, hmm? There's a lot of condensation on it."

She rolls her eyes and lifts it higher as she uses that hand to gesticulate. "I don't know what you guys are so worried about, it's fi—*shit*." The bottle slides out from her grip and plummets to the floor. I squeeze my eyes closed and angle my body the other way to protect myself from flying glass...

But the crash and ensuing spray of shrapnel never comes.

Turning back, my eyes grow round as all three of us stare at the bottle hovering in mid-air, inches from the floor. "Auntie Erin? You have telekinetic abilities you didn't tell me about?"

"That's not me, sweetie. I think it's you," my mom says, her tone full of wonder. "Or rather, the *baby* using powers *through* you."

My jaw drops. "Try lifting it back up, Bryn." She scrunches her brow in concentration, then the juice slowly rises until it reaches her outstretched hand. Grabbing onto it, she carefully places it back in the bucket. "That was *so cool*," I say. "Try moving something else."

Mom clears her throat loudly, drawing our attention to the three women approaching with bowls of what looks like mud and a small plate of cucumber slices. We dutifully follow their instructions to lie back and relax as they adjust our chairs into a zero-gravity position and apply the cold mixture to our faces.

Once I'm completely slathered in the stuff, my attendant holds up two thin cucumber slices. "For puffiness and swelling." She places them over my closed eyes, then leans down to whisper, "You can use this remedy at home, too."

I lift the corners of my mouth in a tight smile. "Good to know, thank you."

Yep. Nothing like getting subtly told by a beauty professional that you look like you've been crying for the last seventy-two hours. Not that she's wrong, but still.

As soon as the ladies leave the room and close the door behind them, Bryn doesn't miss a beat. "Look, Fi, shitty analogy and freaky baby powers aside, my point about bottling up your emotions stands. And I'm still waiting for the explanation of the 'that' you were talking about earlier."

Taking the cucumbers off my eyes, I toss her a droll look. "Anyone ever tell you you're like a damn dog with a bone?"

She pops off her own and returns the look. "My husband, daily." Then she starts eating the cucumbers.

"*Gross*, B. Those were on your face that just had a ton of products slathered on it," I say with my nose scrunched up.

"Girl, I am starving. Like *all* the time. I wouldn't care if I'd picked these off the floor at this point."

"We just had lunch an hour ago."

She raises her eyebrows at me. "Did you miss the part where I said *all the time*? Now spill."

I sigh, resigned. "My future. I'm not sure where it will be."

Bryn frowns. "Why would it be anywhere other than here, in Vegas, with your family?"

Family. A few weeks ago I wasn't sure I had any real family. I felt betrayed and forced to play an unwitting fraud in my own story. Now that the worst of my hurt is over, I know Bryn is right. My family *is* here, and it's comprised of those who have been in my life all twenty-six years up to some I've known for only the past six months. But...

"I can't stay here, not for a while at least." I swallow thickly past the knot in my throat. "I can't watch him be with someone else, even tangentially. I haven't seen him in days, and yet I swear I can feel him, like a low hum in my veins, and it's too painful."

Bryn reaches over to squeeze my hand. "Then what are you planning on doing?"

"Thought I'd do some traveling. See the country, maybe even the world. I figured a little wanderlust therapy would do me good."

"I can't believe you want to go on a walkabout right when I'm turning into a hormonal—and apparently *magical*," she says, giving her belly the stink-eye, "catastrophe waiting to happen. What about the baby shower? You'll come back for that?"

Visions of celebrating something I'll never have with Tiernan cut me too deep. "It depends on where I am, B. But I'll definitely visit when the baby's born."

"You'd freaking better. I don't want to have to show them their baby book someday and answer the question of why their godmother isn't in any of the pictures."

My jaw drops, cracking the mud on the lower half of my face. "Godmother?"

"Oops. I was supposed to wait for when Caiden and I could speak to you together." She waves her hand dismissively. "Whatever, I'll blame it on pregnancy brain."

"I don't understand. Why me?"

Her brows pinch together. "You're my best friend, Fi. There's no one else I want as my baby's Faerie Godmother.

Also? Never in my wildest dreams did I think I'd get to say that with a straight face. Six-year-old me is legit dying right now."

"Bryn, I'm so touched, but…" Emotions swell in my chest and my eyes get misty. "I don't think it's a good idea. I'll only be around for a fraction of their life. You should choose someone fae."

Bryn's expression softens. "Fiona, regardless of time, *you* will give them a thousand times more love and guidance than anyone else can. We may not be related by blood, but you're my sister in every way that counts, and you're going to be the best aunt our baby could ask for. There is no one else—only *you*."

"She's right, Fiona."

"Of course I'm right. I mean, who should I ask instead, Lady freaking Maeve? As *if*. She can take a long walk off a short—"

My mother clears her throat loudly and gives her niece the look I know so well. Bryn rolls her lips between her teeth to keep from finishing her thought out loud, then mutters, "My bad. I get a bit hangry."

I press my fingers to my mouth so Mom doesn't see my struggle not to smile. Hormonal Bryn is kind of fun. Except when she cries. Which is frequent lately. So, okay, she's *sometimes* fun. And hearing her go off about Maeve is more satisfying than I want it to be. There's honestly nothing wrong with the highborn female—from what I know, she's very lovely—but I can't help hating her a little just knowing she'll have the life I want.

Although, that's not entirely true, either. Maeve will be Tiernan's consort, not his wife or his mate. She won't live in the same house and won't sleep in the same bed. For all intents and purposes, they will be partners in parenting and nothing more. A fact that almost makes me sad for her. And it definitely makes me sad for Tiernan.

It must show on my face, because the mood is somber again when Bryn speaks. "I'm going to miss you, Fi. Where will you go?"

"I don't really have a plan. I've never been out of the Vegas area, though, so there's plenty out there to see." I hesitate only a moment before adding, "I'd like to go visit Jack and Emily's graves, if that's okay with you."

Tears fill her eyes as she gives me a watery smile. "It's more than okay. I hate that they were taken before you had a chance to know them. It's not fair."

"It's no different than Uther and Keira being taken from you. That wasn't fair, either."

My mom grabs my hand and squeezes, then I do the same with Bryn, connecting us all. "You were both robbed of knowing your parents in this world. But that doesn't mean you can't ensure you'll be with them in the next."

I turn to Mom and frown. "Can we do a Remembrance Ceremony this late?"

She nods. "There are no time limits placed on connecting with our ancestors or loved ones."

My heart warms in my chest for the first time in days. Bryn sits up in her chair so she can see Mom better. "What's a Remembrance Ceremony?"

"It's a mix between a funeral and a celebration of life. A ritual that sends them off to Mag Mell and connects our souls to theirs, so that we may find each other once again in the afterlife." She gives me a pointed look. "But they are always performed on New Moons, which means you'll have to stay until the end of the month."

I know that my mother truly does want to perform the ceremony for us. But part of me can't help but wonder if she didn't think of it as a way of keeping me around a little longer. I suppose I can't blame her for that either. "Okay," I say. "I'll stay until after the ceremony. But I'm not going to the coronation tomorrow night."

There's only so much pain a girl can take.

CHAPTER THIRTY

TIERNAN

I finish my 500th lap in the pool at Midnight Manor and brace my arms on the edge to catch my breath. For the past week I've been doing multiple workouts a day to try and keep my head clear, to distract myself from focusing on the one thing I can't afford to think about: losing Fiona.

At this rate, in another month, I'll be bigger than Finnian. At least then maybe I can beat him in an arm wrestling contest for a change.

Tomorrow is the full moon, which means C-Day is already here. It's funny, I always thought Caiden was being dramatic about having to take a consort.

Now here I am finally ready to ascend and take my place as the ruler of our court, but the last thing I want is a FWB situation for the purpose of procreating. Or any reason for that matter.

The sound of female laughter floats to me on the breeze, and I close my eyes for a minute and let myself imagine it's Fiona. That she's laughing at something I said and telling me how ridiculous I am. Maybe she's teasing me about my bromance with Edward Cullen or reminding me how ridiculous she thinks her nickname is. I'd pick her up and throw her over my shoulder to carry her to the pool and jump in. She'd get feisty and threaten my manhood, but then we'd start making out like wild animals. You know, if wild animals made out.

"Dearest and wise brother-in-law, would you be so kind as to come over here and settle an argument for us?"

"No fair using flattery, Beauty. I know it doesn't seem possible, but his ego *can* get bigger, it has no limit."

Pushing up on my hands, I hop out of the pool and walk to where my brother and his beautiful bride are sitting in a lounge chair facing the view. Taking a seat on the chair next to them, I push my wet hair back and force a good-natured smile onto my face. "I'd like to say that's a lie, but obviously it isn't. What's the argument?"

"My highly intelligent, usually logical—"

Caiden interjects, "Don't forget uncommonly sexy."

"—husband," Bryn continues while giving him the stink-eye, "says that our baby should start *sword wielding lessons* at the age of *three*. Can you please tell him how completely asinine that is?"

"For you, I can absolutely tell him how asinine that is," I answer carefully. But she's been in our world long enough to catch on to fae-speak.

She narrows her eyes at me. "You can say the words, but would you believe them?" she asks. I press my lips together.

A smug grin creeps onto my brother's face. "Told you. That's how we were raised. Every Verran child picked up a sword by their third year. A small sword, mind you, but a sword nonetheless."

He speaks true, of course, but that doesn't mean Bryn still can't win this fight. She looks between me and her mate, then back at me, her hazel eyes scrutinizing. Catching her gaze, I raise my eyebrows, letting her know she still has a move she can play.

Finally, her green-and-golds light up and she addresses me again. "Tiernan, sweet brother-in-law mine."

I grin wide. "Yes, Brynnie-Bear?"

"Do you support Caiden's insistence that we should carry on the incredibly dangerous and highly unnecessary tradition of teaching our toddler to wield a sword? *Or...*"

She pauses for dramatic effect for my brother's sake, because he already sees the writing on the wall. "Do you support *my* insistence that there is absolutely no reason why our baby would need to learn how to sword fight before learning their ABC's and *therefore* we should abolish that ungodly tradition?"

"Why, Brynnie, I'm so glad you asked. Since it is my choice on who I support, regardless of personal experience and/or beliefs, I do believe I will support *you*," I say enthusiastically.

She raises both arms overhead and whoops in celebration. I laugh and clap, proud she was able to best my brother in a fae game of Word Gymnastics.

He glares at me in mock disappointment. "Traitor."

"Told you, I like her better."

She sticks her tongue out at him, making me laugh even harder, because if I know my brother—and I do—he's going to come up with very creative ways to punish her for that later. "Man, I can't wait to spoil that kid so fucking rotten. I'm giving them espressos and a puppy right before I bring them home from spending the day with their Uncle T."

Now it's Bryn's turn to glare in my direction. "I'd think extra hard about any torture you put us through. We'll be able to turn it right back around on you soon enough when you have kids."

My good mood pops like the fragile bubble it was, and it's impossible for it not to show. It's not the thought of having kids that upsets me. It's the thought of not having them with Fiona.

"Shit, Tiernan, I'm sorry. I wasn't thinking."

"Brynnie, it's okay, it's not your fault I'm a sad sack."

She opens her mouth, no doubt to berate herself and apologize profusely—and possibly even cry if recent hormonal events are anything to go on—but my brother stops her. "Since we're staying here tonight, Tiernan is insisting we take my old room. Go and run us a bath and before the tub is full, I'll be in to join you, okay? I think it's time I offer the Crown Prince some kingly advice."

Bryn traps her bottom lip, clearly at odds between her emotions and his instructions. Caiden uses his thumb to free her lip, then gives it a tender kiss. "Go on, Beauty. He isn't upset with you, and if he is, I promise to toss his ass back in the pool before coming inside."

She finally relents, but not without throwing her arms around my neck and squeezing the breath out of me first. Rubbing my throat, I try to reconcile the chokehold with the little thing disappearing into the house. "Fuck, she's gotten strong."

"And as of yesterday, randomly telekinetic."

"Damn. That freaking you out?"

"More than I let on. I mute my energy around her so she doesn't feel it. She has enough to worry about, she doesn't need my shit on top of it."

I release a heavy exhale. "Fuck, I'm sorry, Caiden. I've been so wrapped up in my own shit, I never stopped to think about yours."

"Nor should you. Your shit's way bigger than a little Darklight fatherhood anxiety. I'm the one who's sorry. I should have had this conversation with you long before now, but better late than never." He gestures to the pool bar behind us. "Want a drink?"

"What kind of question is that?"

"A rhetorical one, apparently," he says wryly. We head over, and I park my ass on one of the stools. Caiden walks around and grabs two rocks glasses, setting them on the bar top between us. "Tomorrow's a big day. How do you feel?"

Crossing my arms over my chest, I watch him pour the whiskey and fight my natural instinct to fire off a sarcastic answer. If I want the people to take me seriously as king, I need to practice not saying the first thing that comes to mind all the time.

"Admittedly, it's a lot. I'm not even official yet, and it's like the weight of every Dark's life is sitting on my shoulders, you know?"

My older brother smirks. "I might know something about it."

"I suppose you do." I chuckle as we clink our glasses together, then I take a sip and revel in the smooth heat sliding down my throat. "I guess I never realized the kind of pressure you were under. You always seemed to take everything in stride."

"That was my training. Father prepared me for the role my whole life, including how to appear to have my shit together, even if I didn't."

"That's what I mean, man. You had over a hundred and fifty years to get ready for this, I've had four and a half *months*. By all rights, I should be running for the fucking hills. Don't think I didn't consider it."

He leans his hips back on the countertop behind him. "I'd be more surprised if you hadn't. There isn't a fae ruler in history who's been put in your position. Anyone would've considered running, including myself. But—and I say this not only as a supportive brother but as someone with experience— you're going to be an amazing king, Tier. Better than me *or* our father."

I snort out a self-deprecating laugh. "Yeah, I'm every fae's dream king. I'll be lucky if they don't run me out of town within the first year."

I hold out my glass, and he pours me another two fingers. "What is it that has you so worried?"

"Come on, Caiden, I'm nothing like you or Dad. I'm not professional, I rarely think before I speak, and sometimes I enjoy being contrary just for the fun of it. Nothing about me says 'kingly,' not even the way I dress. Bottom line, no one wants a rebel for a king."

"Let me tell you something. If I'd still been king when all this was going down with the NPO, I probably would've let Erin go through with her plan because while tragic, it was the most logical solution to lose one versus all. We would've gotten the same results, but at what cost? Erin would have lost her life and Fiona her mom. That's what doing things 'by the book' gets you.

"But you refused to put anyone else in harm's way. You said 'fuck the book' and thought outside the box to come up with a better way. It was ill-advised, risky as hell, and worst of all, put *your* life—the life of the future king—in danger. And it *worked*, Tier. You saved Erin's life and the lives of all our people by stopping Edevane and the NPO *your* way.

"So, if you ask me, sometimes a rebel king is exactly what the people need." He raises his glass. "Cheers, brother."

He doesn't wait for me to clink and drink with him because I'm too busy letting his words tumble around in my mind. Yes, I insisted on finding another way, one that didn't require one of our own to fall on a sword held by a sociopath—but that's only one thing. A single incident doesn't speak to the probability of whether I'll be a good king for the next several centuries.

"What about Fiona?"

Jarred by the hard left the conversation just took, I grab the whiskey and pour myself another drink. "Bryn said she's sticking around until the New Moon, then she's leaving Vegas."

"Think if you tell her you love her that she'd stay?"

Love. I haven't allowed myself to think that word in

relation to Fiona out of self-preservation. But I love her so damn much I can't think straight most days. If the gods exist, this bone-deep agony will fade. But if that's how I measure my faith, I suspect that soon I'll believe in the gods as much as I believe in fairy tales.

I shrug, then drain my glass. "Doesn't matter because I can't tell her. I won't ask her to be my dirty little secret while publicly being tied to Maeve. She deserves more than that."

Caiden sets his empty glass down and comes around the bar to stand next to me. "I'm sorry, brother. If I'd had any other way…"

"Don't apologize for keeping your mate safe, Caiden. And I don't want you to think that I'm not ready for this, because I am. If the last few weeks have taught me anything, it's that I have the capacity to be more than a rebellious spare heir. I just need to remember to act like it. But our legacy is secure, I promise. I won't fuck this up."

"I never thought you would," he says, placing a hand on my shoulder. "Rebel or not, Tier, I believe in you, and you should, too."

CHAPTER THIRTY-ONE

TIERNAN

C-Day.

The day I've been dreading for four months is here. Oddly enough, I'm no longer dreading it for the same reasons I was. I used to think being the king of the Dark Fae was the worst possible job someone could have. All the responsibilities, the pressure, the necessary events and appearances. None of it sounded like a good time to me because that's all I used to be concerned about—a good time.

But over the last few weeks, something shifted in me, and last night's talk with Caiden only helped to solidify my newfound confidence in my ability to rule. I no longer fear the responsibilities or pressure that come along with being king.

What I fear is the half-life.

Caiden was right not to want a consort. I never put much thought into our parents' relationship, but the more I look back on it, the more I remember things that were missing. Like affection and companionship. *Love.* Those were things my parents couldn't have with each other, not if they didn't want to activate the blood curse.

But even more than hating the half-life, I hate that I

hurt Fiona and forced her into the same situation because of my selfishness. Because I refused to face reality in favor of believing we had a chance.

Bryn told me Fiona plans on traveling after the Remembrance Ceremony at the end of the month. I'm hoping I can see her as much as possible, even just as friends, before she leaves. Unfortunately, she's avoiding me so far and I don't know if she has any intention of stopping that.

The ballroom at Nightfall is full of our subjects of every age and walk of life. I meander through the crowd, followed at a respectable distance by Connor and Conall. I stop and talk to those who wish to speak to me, listen attentively, and respond appropriately. I'm charming and sincere and gracious. But all the while, I'm searching for a crown of red hair, adorably rounded ears, and straight white teeth inside a brilliant smile that lights me up inside.

"Your Highness, may I say that you wear my mate's design well," Declan, the husband of Caiden's tailor we lost in the attacks, says with his head bowed and hand on his heart. "I am humbled and grateful that you wanted to honor Cillian's memory."

I place a hand on his shoulder, the familiar gesture encouraging him to lift his gaze and speak freely with me. "It's me who's humbled and grateful, Declan. That he was already working on a design for me means a lot. I only wish he was here to see how great he made so many of us look tonight."

"Thank you for putting out that call. I don't think I realized how many people at court frequented the shop, but it's amazing to see them wearing his designs tonight. And the tribute patch you requested... I have no words, Your Highness."

He's referring to the patch I asked him to make and sew onto the left breast pocket of my coat. It features Dark and Dapper's logo, Cillian's name, and the words *síocháin sa dorchadas*—peace in darkness—which is our version of "rest in peace."

And that's not the only tribute in place tonight. Every single fae we lost to the NPO attacks has a banner on the wall with their picture, name, date of birth, date they passed on to Mag Mell, and their family Armas. It was my first order of official business; it's important that everyone know we will not forget them.

"He deserves the recognition," I say to Declan. "He served the court well with his talents."

"He would have loved seeing all his work on display at once like this. Of course, his ego would have gotten too big to fit through the doors, so he probably wouldn't have seen it anyway."

Declan laughs with tears in his eyes and I offer a comforting squeeze on his shoulder. "I hope you'll consider taking over Dark and Dapper and continuing the contract with the court."

"I'm flattered you would ask, Prince Tiernan, however I must be honest with you. I worked for Cillian on the regular orders and learned a great deal from him over the years, but I don't have the experience he did. He had a real gift, one that cannot be matched. I'm afraid my work would be a disappointment by comparison."

"I understand why you might feel that way, but if there's one thing I've learned in the last few months, it's that when push comes to shove, we often rise to the occasion. There's no pressure, but I'll help you with whatever you need—employees, design classes, whatever—so you can keep the shop open and let Cillian live on in the quality clothing you provide our people and the people of this city."

Declan places a hand over his heart, his emotions clear in his eyes. "I would like that very much, Your Highness. Thank you."

"My pleasure," I say with a smile. "I'll stop by sometime next week to discuss it further. For now, take advantage of the free champagne and the incredible food prepared by Eoghan's kitchen staff."

He says he will and I move on, once again searching for the person I want to see most tonight. Then I catch a glimpse of the next best thing. Erin is standing with Bryn and Robert—who's allowed to attend as a familiar—over by the appetizers. If I need to find my sister-in-law, all I need to do is search for the buffet table. I walk with purpose in their direction, and thankfully no one tries to interrupt me.

"Ladies, you look positively stunning tonight. Robert, you don't entirely suck either."

"If I wasn't already buzzed on the bubbly, I might take offense to that," he says with a goofy grin. I decide not to lecture him on the drinking since it's a special occasion and I'm in a benevolent mood.

Erin dips into a shallow curtsy. "Thank you, Your Majesty." It's a bit premature, but hearing her say the title Fiona used with me only strengthens my need to see her. "Ready to make it official?"

"Ready to get it over with," I say a little too honestly. "Is Fiona here? I was hoping to see her tonight."

Two pairs of eyes, one golden and one hazel, look at me with pity. My heart sinks as Erin places a gentle hand on my arm. "I'm sorry, Tiernan. I tried to get her to come. She's just not ready."

"It's okay. It's not like I can blame her. If I had to watch her claim someone else as her life partner, I'd do a lot worse things than stay away."

Bryn narrows her gaze past my shoulder where the dais is. "This is such bullshit. I'm sorry, but you two belong together. This is all because of that pompous, wrinkly—"

Erin shoves a lobster-stuffed mushroom into her niece's mouth, then gives her a small plate of more. "Keep eating, darling."

Bryn gives her a sheepish grin and a thumbs-up as she eats

the large mushroom. I can't help but chuckle at her pregnancy antics. I should probably feel sorry for my brother with the roller coaster he must live on trying to keep up with her mood swings. But I don't.

"Thanks, Brynnie-Bear, but we don't always get what we want. Especially when you're the king."

Robert snaps and points at me, his eyes alight with wonder. Or too much champagne. "It's your blood, isn't it?"

Arching a brow at him, I check the level of his glass. "I think it's time you lay off the sauce, old man."

He scowls and waves his hand. "Bah, I'm fine. It's my next guess for the magical Fountain of Youth. The thing humans can take to live as long as fae is *your blood*."

I cut my gaze over to Erin and Bryn, both of whom are frozen in wide-eyed shock. They give me barely perceptible shakes of their heads, telling me they didn't let the cat out of the bag. Since I can't lie, I lay the sarcasm on. *Thick.* "Yep, you finally guessed it. It's totally our blood. Because that's not gross at all." I roll my eyes and chuckle for good measure. "What do you think we are, vampires?"

Deceiving one of my oldest friends doesn't sit right with me but telling our secrets to *others* or humans—even familiars like Robert—is forbidden. The sarcasm trick works, though, so I don't have to worry about breaking one of our biggest rules on the day it becomes my job to enforce them.

"Yeah, I suppose you're right. That wasn't one of my better guesses," he says. "I'll figure it out one of these days."

Thankfully, his critical thinking skills seem to have been dulled by the champagne. Sober, he would've called me out on that bullshit non-answer in a heartbeat. "I can't wait to hear what you come up with next, my friend."

Connor lets me know that it's time for the official ceremony to begin. I excuse myself and make my way to the front of the room and up the stairs of the dais.

Hedrek Dolan and Lady Maeve are seated on the far end. She is the picture of demure beauty, whereas the look on the Speaker's face is an odd mix I can only describe as smug annoyance.

Next is the Royal Mother, also known to me and my brothers as plain old Mom. She looks as regal as ever, her posture perfect and chin raised. Her expression remains stoic, but the shimmer of tears in her eyes is the same as her whispering how proud she is.

On the opposite side, Finnian is seated on the outside, followed by Caiden, then Seamus, all of them looking on with support and confidence in me I'm not sure I deserve. But it gives me the final push I need to move into position.

A High Priestess is standing in the center, ready to begin the ceremony. I approach her, then go down on one knee and bow my head. I remember my brother in this position not even twenty years ago. I was so proud of him that day. It was a day of his fate being fulfilled, the role he'd trained for his whole life becoming a reality. He looked so distinguished and noble, so calm and sure.

I remember thinking I could never do what he was so willing to do. And now I wait on bended knee, eager to follow in his footsteps and our father's. To prove that the Verrans belong on the throne because we are the best choice for our people.

The ceremony itself doesn't take long, and it's performed entirely in the old language. I force myself to pay attention, keeping my thoughts from straying, as they're wont to do these days, and before long, it's over.

The High Priestess speaks her final blessing and places the crown atop my head. Made of heavy metal, its weight is not insignificant. But it wasn't the physical weight I'd been worried about for so long, it was the metaphorical kind.

I thought for sure that the heft of being responsible for

every life in the Night Court would crush me the moment the crown was placed on my head. But it doesn't feel too much at all. It's not too light and it's not too heavy. In fact, it feels just right. I'm like the fucking Goldilocks of the Dark Fae.

I almost laugh and imagine telling Fiona later about my errant thoughts and how we could live happily ever after since we're both fairy-tale characters now—as Little Red with No Riding Hood and Your Majesty Goldilocks.

Except as fast as I think about telling her, I remember that I probably won't get a chance to because I fucking ruined everything. And suddenly the well of laughter dries up.

The priestess must have officially announced me as the new king because the room is full of applause and the occasional shouted cheer from Robert, who could give a flying fuck about being proper. Gods, I love that human.

I rise and face my subjects for the first time and the moment is bittersweet, but the pride I have in being the next ruler of our people grows inside me like a living thing and pushes away the pain, at least for now.

Lifting my hands, I signal for them to quiet and let me speak. I didn't prepare anything ahead of time. Caiden almost always did; he liked to gather his thoughts, mull them over, and reshape them if needed. He said Father taught him that a prepared king is an inspiring king. Which I guess is like the royal version of the Boy Scouts motto or something.

But I've never been a fan of homework or planning ahead. Spontaneity is where I live, off-the-cuff is my specialty, and reading rooms is my superpower. It shouldn't be any different whether it's an audience of one or one thousand, right? *Let's fucking hope not.*

"Thank you, everyone, and thank you for joining me on this cool February evening to witness my coronation. I promise to make this short so we can get back to the food and festivities. However, since this is my first time doing this, it probably won't be all that pretty. So I'd appreciate it if you go easy on me; my safe word is pineapple.".

"Ha! That's a good one." Well, at least Robert gets my humor.

Apparently, he's the only one, though. A quiet murmur ripples through the crowd, their collective uncertainty coating the back of my throat and making it dry. I'm almost tempted to pull a one-eighty and do my best to emulate my father to put them at ease.

But my conversation with Caiden last night made me realize that to do that would be disingenuous, and I won't spend the rest of my life pretending to be someone I'm not. Someone who's formal and stiff and regal to a boring fault. That doesn't mean I won't take my role seriously; it just means I'm going to keep the mood light and fun while I do.

"Let me start by stating the obvious here. I'm not like any king you've had in the past. Hell, you're the ones who dubbed me the Rebel Prince before I was two decades old. So, if you're unsure of how this is going to go, I get it. As far as royals go, I'm kind of a wild card, and betting on me probably feels like risky business. But if there's anywhere in the world that knows how to beat the odds to win, it's the city *we* built."

Lots of nods and murmurs of acknowledgment. It's an improvement. I'll take it.

"I know I wouldn't have been your first choice to ascend after my brother, and I can't blame you for that because not even *I* would've chosen me. But thanks to the Dark Council's gracious offer to give me time to acclimate to the idea of being your king, I've grown and learned a lot these past months. I may not have been born for this role, but I have one very important thing that's in your favor. I'm a Verran.

"No one else in this court has more love for the Dark Fae than the Verran family line. Our duty to you is ingrained in our very DNA. You are not in service to us, it's us who are in service to you. It's why the king sets time aside every month to meet with you in person, to hear your complaints, to celebrate your wins, to grieve your losses.

"But I'm far from perfect, people. I mean, like, seriously godsdamn far. So, if at any time you feel that I'm not living up to the legacy of my family, I want you to call me out on it. You don't even need to wait for a special meeting at the ToR. See me in line at a food truck? Tell me you have a bone to pick with me. I'll listen to you right there and then I'll buy you lunch so we can discuss how I can do better over some tacos and a beer.

"On the flip side, if you think I'm doing something well, toss those comments my way, too. If I don't hear about it, I won't know what to keep doing. Also, I can always use a good ego stroke."

Laughter floats to me from the now smiling faces, boosting my confidence. Except now I have to do the part I've been dreading. Looking over to the right, I see Lady Maeve sitting next to my mother, perfectly poised, beautiful, and everything someone could want. Unless that someone is me.

Dolan gestures for me to continue, and it feels like he's pointing a gun at me while snarling "or else." I'd like to shove all ten pages of that contract up his ass, but I take a cleansing breath and remind myself what happens if I don't play his fucking game. Too bad we're not playing *my* game. I'd smoke him at chess.

Turning back to the crowd, I reluctantly make my next move, forced as it is. "In my first official duty as king, I'd like to announce that I've chosen a consort with whom I'll provide the court heirs to continue the Verran legacy as kings or queens of the Night Court of Faerie."

Sounds of intrigue and surprise ripple through the room. As I wait for it to die down, a flash of burnished red in the back pulls my gaze. My heart stops. Fiona is there with her hair pulled up into a bun and wearing an olive-green sweater, dark jeans, and Uggs. Definitely not coronation attire, but she's never looked more beautiful to me.

Seeing her standing by herself next to the double doors reminds me of the last time we attended a party in this ballroom. It was the night of the Ivy Moon Celebration, also known as the night my life changed forever. We met up in a closet down the hall to have sex, then snuck back in together as Caiden was giving his speech and announced he was abdicating the throne.

It was the first time Fiona referred to me as "Your Majesty." It'd been said in jest, but knowing what it eventually turned into brings up a lot of complicated feelings anytime someone uses it. Which is going to be a problem now that it's my official honorific.

Thanks to my preternatural sight, I can see her clearly from this distance. The sadness swimming in those twin crystalline pools puts me in a chokehold. It gets worse when she spins on her booted heel and disappears through the doors. It's like watching my heart walk away, and I'm helpless to stop it.

Godsdamn it! What good is being the king if you're bound by antiquated laws that don't—or shouldn't—have any relevance anymore?

Wait, why *am* I bound by them? The king doesn't have to answer to anyone, not even the Dark Council. I was so worried about needing to act a certain way and follow the path of every Verran king before me to be a good ruler for our people that I didn't pay attention to what everyone's been telling me.

Just because something always has been doesn't mean it always should be.

You said 'fuck the book' and thought outside the box to come up with a better way.

The thing humans can take to live as long as fae is your blood.

I think about the contract and the language it uses. *The heir apparent...* But I'm not the heir apparent anymore. I'm the king, and since the new king has the power to void any previous contracts or rulings as they see fit for the benefit of all Dark Fae, I'm no longer bound by the very contract I signed before I ascended.

Holy shit.

"Everyone, I'm making a change to today's program. Not that we have programs, but bear with me, here."

Dolan shoots to his feet, his face turning ten shades of red. "Your Highness—I mean, Your Majesty—this is highly unorthodox. Please continue with naming your consort for the court."

"You're right, Lord Speaker, this is unorthodox. But the court needs to get used to it because that's going to be my style of ruling." Addressing the crowd again, I say, "If you'll all excuse me for just one minute, five at the most, there's something I need to do. Then I'll be back to wrap things up so we can get to the fun part of the evening."

I jump down off the dais, and the crowd parts down the middle for me. Connor and Conall step from their positions to follow me, but I wave them off. "I'm not going far, guys. I'll be in Rian's sight outside." *I hope, anyway.* Then I start jogging toward the exit.

"Your Majesty, *please*! You cannot do this!"

I stop at the doors where Robert is now standing, holding a fresh glass of champagne. He gives me a questioning look, silently asking if I'm all right. I answer with a wink, then turn back to face the fuming lord standing at the edge of the dais. "Are you familiar with the game of chess, Dolan?"

Hedrek purses his lips together and continues to glare. Robert takes a sip of his drink. "I don't think he does."

"No worries," I say loud enough for my voice to carry throughout the room. "While I step out for a minute, Robert here can tell you what a Zwischenzug means."

My friend and chess mentor busts into uproarious laughter. "It means you're *fucked*."

The attendees have a multitude of reactions, running the gamut from amusement to shock. I hold back my own laughter (barely) and do my best to give Robert a stern look. "You're cut off."

Still laughing, he says, "Worth it."

I really do love that human. Shaking my head, I push through the double doors and go in search of my queen.

CHAPTER THIRTY-TWO

FIONA

Shit, shit, shit.

Speed walking down the hall, I berate myself for not sticking to my original—or second or third—plan of staying far away from the coronation ceremony. The prick of hot tears blurs my vision and the lump in my throat is making it difficult to breathe. Up ahead I see an oasis, somewhere I can let myself break down and put myself back together before facing the world again.

Thanking Rhiannon for the reprieve, I duck into the utility closet and press the lock button so I'll have a warning if anyone in maintenance tries to get in. Flipping the light on, I sit on a stack of upturned five-gallon buckets and sag in relief against the wall. I close my eyes to stem the tears and focus on dragging in slow, deep breaths through my nose.

Gods, he'd looked so amazing on the dais. Bespoke in a custom-tailored ceremonial suit—a black shirt and pants with a fitted royal blue vest featuring wide lapels and black brocade, finished off with a dress coat that molded to his muscular frame and split into longer tails in the back. The Midnight Crown fit him perfectly, its symmetrical points on the bottom encircling his head with the three-dimensional triangles of various lengths rising up at flared angles.

Magnificent and commanding, he appeared every bit the king he is, but unlike his predecessors, he abandoned the stiff, professional demeanor for naturally charming and approachable. He was still just so *him*.

He was perfect.

I knew watching the coronation wouldn't be easy, but I couldn't stay away. I told myself I was only coming to support him like I would with any friend of mine. As soon as the ceremony was over I would leave and that would be that.

But then he started speaking, and hearing the deep timbre of his voice soothed me as nothing else has since the night he made love to me. So I stayed.

Big mistake, because part of that speech was announcing Maeve as his consort. Even then, I tried to be the mature adult I am and suck it up. But I lost that battle the second our gazes locked from across the room. Then I fled.

Knowing another female will have, in part, the life I want with Tiernan hurts like hell, and the piece of me that loves him couldn't witness their big announcement as a non-couple couple.

Except the piece of me that loves him is also so fucking proud of how far he's come since last October when Caiden announced Tiernan would become the new ruler. Five minutes before that, Tier told me—in this very closet—he never wanted the kind of responsibilities his brother had as king, that he was perfectly content being the Rebel Prince.

But sometime in the last month, he grew to embrace his new destiny and rose to the occasion, and I've never loved him more.

"Fiona?"

I shoot to my feet and stare wide-eyed at the door like I can see him standing on the other side of it. "Tiernan, what the hell are you doing out there?"

His words are colored by his signature lopsided grin. "Sweetheart, I think the better question is what are you doing *in there*?"

"Gods, Tier, you can't pull shit like this in Hour One. Get back in there."

"I will as soon as you come out. I need you to hear something."

I worry my bottom lip with my teeth and cross my arms over my middle as though it will help me stay together as I try and think of what to do. "I can hear you fine like this, so tell me and then you can get back to your Lady Maeve."

Wincing, I slap a hand over my mouth. That's not what I meant to say. *People. Then you can get back to your* people. *Way to go, Princess Petty.*

"She's not my anything, Fi. I'm not taking a consort, not tonight or ever."

I freeze. "But how? The contract..."

"I'll explain everything if you just open the door." My mind is racing almost as fast as my pulse. "Come on, Fi, let me in."

"I can't," I say, shaking my head. "What if this is some cruel auditory hallucination and I open the door but you're not there? I couldn't handle—"

The knob groans in protest, then snaps before the door swings open and Tiernan steps inside. I'm so relieved he's real, I don't even think before letting him wrap me up in his arms. Pressing my face into his chest, I inhale deeply, his familiar scent comforting me as much as his embrace.

"Gods, I missed you, baby. Don't ever freeze me out like that again."

My old nemesis, aka Reality, steps back in to remind me that Tiernan and I are nowhere near Happy Couplehood territory. Cursing, I step out of his arms. "I didn't freeze you out, Tiernan. You *chose someone else* over me. Don't turn this around as though it's my fault."

"You're right. I'm sorry, that was the wrong thing to say. It *was* my fault. You told me to find another way, and I didn't think I could. I thought being a good king meant doing everything exactly how the ones before me did it." He frames my face with his large hands. "But you were right, Fi. Just because something always has been doesn't mean it always should be. And there's so much that needs to be changed, changes I intend to make. Starting with us."

"Us?"

"Yeah, us. I love you, Fiona. I love you infinitely more than I love myself, and you know how much I love myself," he says, his boyish grin revealing a hint of fang.

A myriad of emotions flood my eyes. Tiernan Verran said he *loves* me. Not wants, not needs. *Loves.* An admission I would've thought an impossibility a few short months ago, but one I fantasized about anyway. And now it's happened.

"Okay, this is the part where you say it back and spare my fragile ego."

"Oh sorry," I say, laughing through my tears. "Yes, of course I do! I love you."

I barely finish saying it before his mouth descends on mine. His tongue sweeps inside on a groan as he wraps me in his arms and pulls me flush against him. My fingers grip the nape of his neck as I rise on my tippy toes, needing to be as close to him as humanly—or faely—as possible. When we finally break apart, he glances at his watch and winces. "Come on, we need to get back in there."

Digging in my heels, I pull him up short. "I still don't understand. How can there even be an us? I thought you signed a contract."

"Let me worry about Dolan and the contract." Tipping my head up with a finger under my chin, he stares into my eyes. "Do you trust me, sweetheart?"

My heart swells, and I answer him the same as I always have. "I do."

A huge smile breaks across his face. He kisses the top of my hand, then leads me out of our closet—yes, it will forever be known as *our* closet—and back down the hall to the ballroom.

As we enter through the double doors, everyone in attendance stops talking and turns to watch us walk through the middle of the crowd. I feel incredibly self-conscious and underdressed, but there's nothing to do about that now.

Tiernan leads me up the stairs and onto the dais, never once letting go of my hand, even as he begins to address his subjects. "Hi there, everyone. Thanks so much for waiting. Before I ran out of here, I told you I was going to be naming my consort, who was obviously going to be Lady Maeve, as she's already up here."

The people standing below us whisper to one another, but they never take their eyes off of us, not wanting to miss a second of the soap opera unfolding on stage.

"But here's the thing," Tiernan continues. "I'm not in love with Maeve; in fact, we barely know each other. The role of consort is not glamorous, nor the honor we make it out to be. Lady Maeve," he says, turning to speak directly to her, "you deserve to be mated with a person of your choosing. Someone who loves you every bit as much as I love Fiona Jewel."

I jump a little when the noise level in the room spikes with collective shock. But that's not nearly as bad as the shriek of outrage that comes from Hedrek Dolan. He stalks over, shaking some papers in his fist. "Did you forget about this? It's the contract *you* signed—"

"When I was the heir apparent, yeah, I know. The thing is, when a new king takes the throne, he's allowed to make whatever changes he deems fit for the best of the people. And this contract is officially null and void." Tiernan rips the pages in half and hands them back to the now sputtering Lord

Speaker. "And so are you and your little band of merry males. I'm disbanding the Dark Council as it is and will be installing a new, diverse Council made up of Darks representing different backgrounds and specialty lines. Their job will be to communicate with the people and speak to the Crown on their behalf regarding how we can better support our subjects."

"Absolutely not! You cannot do whatever you want, this is preposterous!"

"Hey, Dolan, I have a riddle for you. What do you get when you ask a Rebel Prince to ascend the Midnight Throne?"

From the crowd, a familiar gravelly voice shouts, "You get a *rebel king*!"

Tiernan doesn't take his eyes off Dolan as he points in his friend's direction. "Robert gets it."

"Zwischenzug!" Robert cackles, and I have to cover my mouth with my free hand to stop from laughing myself.

"Connor," Tiernan says to his friends. "Can you call someone to give Lord Dolan a time out?"

Connor speaks into his comms unit and a second later, a Watcher hops onto the dais and firmly escorts Hedrek down the stairs and through the ballroom. But the best part is when everyone starts to clap and cheer. Smiling, Tiernan waves and calls after them. "Remember, the rule is one minute for every year of his age, or he won't learn."

Once he's removed from the room, and the crowd settles, Tiernan's demeanor changes. He's more serious and sure of himself, like how I saw him during the weeks we spent fighting against the NPO.

"The kings who came before me—including my brother and father—were phenomenal rulers, and I aspire to be every bit as good as they were. But I also aspire to be *better*, because a lot of our ways are outdated and need an overhaul. In the coming months, I plan on making some changes, the biggest of which will be a fae-human integration.

"We've been living in the human realm for over four hundred years, and while we've assimilated into their world, we've never accepted that we're a part of it. We continue to set ourselves apart from them, as though they're somehow lesser. But that's never been the case.

"I know this might be controversial to some, considering what we went through these past few months. But just as we wouldn't want to be judged on the heinous actions of the Light King, we can't judge all humans on the actions of those in the Purity Order, past or present."

Tiernan looks down at me and smiles, and I realize I've been staring up at him in awe—like everyone else in the room—as he detailed his plans to bring the fae and human worlds together. Pride and love fill me so completely, I think I might burst. I'm utterly speechless.

"To do this well, it will no doubt be a huge undertaking. But luckily, I have the perfect person to help me with this endeavor," he continues. "Fiona Jewel, a human raised as a member of the Dark Fae, is uniquely suited to this mission, as she cares deeply for both races. Which is also why she will make an excellent Dark Queen."

"*What?*" I slap my hand over my mouth. Guess that speechless problem is fixed. Gaping up at him, I admonish him under my breath. "Don't you think that's something you should've *asked me first*?"

He frowns, his brow furrowing. "I didn't ask you to marry me?"

My jaw drops. "Uh, *no*. Pretty sure I would've remembered that."

Looking out at the audience, he chuckles nervously. "Everyone hold tight again, I need another minute." He maneuvers us so that he's in front of me, blocking me from view. Then he gathers my hands and gazes into my eyes. "Fiona Lynn Jewel—yes, I learned your middle name—there is no one else I want to walk through this life with. You belong to me, and I belong to you, now and always."

"Tier, I..." Emotion clogs my throat and tears blur my vision.

"You belong by my side, Fi...as my queen."

"You're serious."

"As a human heart attack. Which you won't ever have because of the blood bond we'll share." He strokes a finger down the side of my throat. "We'll be able to live a very, very long life together. What do you say, sweetheart? Will you be my wife, my true mate, and most importantly, my queen?"

For the first time in a week, my heart is finally back where it belongs—with his. He's giving me everything—his trust, his blood, his love—and I'm going to spend centuries doing the same for him. Tears well in my eyes, and for once, I don't bother to blink them away.

Not trusting my voice, I nod. He gives me a swift and passion-filled kiss that leaves me breathless and dizzy. Then, facing the crowd once again, Tiernan raises our joined hands into the air and shouts the most human thing ever. "She said *yes*!"

The ballroom erupts with thunderous applause and cheers. If the skylight wasn't already open to connect us with the night and the full moon, the glass probably would have shattered. Tiernan signals for the music to start, effectively ending his speech and getting the celebration underway.

Pulling me into his arms, he leads us in a dance. Gazing down at me, he smiles wide, showing a hint of his sexy fangs. He looks so pleased with himself I can't help but laugh. "What are you thinking about?" he asks.

"I'm thinking it's not a bad first day for someone who didn't want the burden of responsibility or power."

"I've learned that neither is a burden when used for the forces of good," he says with a wink. "Plus, I plan on delegating most of it. I need to free up my time for pleasuring my queenly wife-mate."

I laugh again. "Your *what*?"

"Never mind, I'm still workshopping it. My point is, I hope you don't have any plans for the next hundred years or so, because I don't think I'll be ready for us to come out of the manor's dungeon until then. So many whips, so many delicious ways to inflict pleasurable pain, Little Red."

Tiny, winged faeries take flight in my belly as I imagine all the possibilities. "Looking forward to it, Your Majesty."

As he effortlessly changes our direction, I'm struck by the magnitude of my love for him. "I'm so proud of you, Tiernan. You're going to make an excellent king."

Dipping his head, he kisses me tenderly. "In chess, the king is useless without the queen, and the same is true in life. I'm nothing without my queen by my side. As long as we're together, we can't lose."

EPILOGUE I

FIONA

"Thank you," I say to Robert as he hands me a glass of whiskey from the tray Tiernan is passing around for everyone. Then he reaches for his own glass but Tier pulls it away at the last second.

"The doctor told you to quit, old man."

"Shut it, *Your Majesty*. We're here to celebrate life, so that's what I'm gonna do, and I'll be drinking the good stuff like everyone else while I do it."

Tiernan rolls his eyes and hands the glass to his friend. The small crowd gathered with us in Joshua Tree snickers at the casual and utterly unaffected way Robert addresses the king.

I've grown to adore Robert in such a short amount of time and it's going to be hard when we eventually lose him. One of the first things Tiernan implemented after he ascended was a system in which fae could request that certain humans be made trusted familiars and brought into the Night Court fold. If accepted, they're given the choice of whether or not they want to use a blood bond as a means for living a much longer life.

Tiernan was so excited to finally offer Robert the

"Fountain of Youth" he'd been asking about for decades. Tier never dreamed his friend would turn him down, explaining that he's lived a good life and is more than satisfied with the time he's been given. It's been hard for Tiernan to accept, but he respects Robert's decision. The only thing that's changed is that now Robert is free to come and go at the manor as much as he wants, which means more chess matches and more shit talking, just as it should be.

The new moon in February is a symbol of healing for the fae. It is a beacon that assures us that Spring is just around the corner, bringing with it new life. It is also a night of immense power for the Darks, which is why we've chosen tonight for our ceremony. Though Bryn and I have been looking forward to today, now that it's here, we've both felt a bit somber, so the levity Robert provides is appreciated.

Seamus clears his throat and signals Tiernan. I watch as all the people most important to us gather in a circle surrounding me and Bryn, my sister in all ways that matter. Aside from Tiernan, Seamus, and Robert, Caiden, the Woulfe brothers, Finnian, and my mom have all joined us to celebrate the lives of our parents, both fae and human.

Once everyone is in place, Seamus begins the Remembrance Ceremony.

"Is tús nua é bás. Síocháin sa dorchadas." *Death is a new beginning. Peace in darkness.*

The second birthday, as the fae refer to it. Though long-lived, fae do die, and when we—*they*—do, it is believed that it's the beginning of a new life in Mag Mell, the paradise of the otherworld. It's where we all go to one day be reunited with our loved ones.

The ceremony Seamus is helping us to perform today is one as ancient as Faerie herself. It's one that will connect both my and Bryn's souls to Kiera and Uther and to Jack and Emily, so that one day we will find each other again. Hopefully, in about four hundred years or so, when my and Bryn's second birthdays are celebrated by our loved ones, we'll finally be reunited with our parents in the afterlife.

Seamus begins a prayer to Rhiannon in the ancient fae language, melodic words I don't understand yet feel as though my heart has no trouble translating them. My mom steps forward, misty-eyed, carrying fae lights for both Bryn and me. Tonight's difficult for her, too. Between hiding Bryn to protect her then raising and protecting me, she never had the opportunity to say a proper goodbye to her sister.

"I love you, Mom," I say, accepting the light and getting misty too.

"And I, you, *mo stóirín*."

She takes her place again in the circle as Seamus finishes the prayer. Then he lifts his faerie light and releases it into the air saying, "Go dtí go gcasfar le chéile sinn arís."

The others repeat it and follow suit. Then it's our turn.

Bryn and I lock gazes, our faces lit by the flickering flames inside the paper lanterns. Her glowing green and gold eyes, fangs, and pointed ears peeking out from her blond hair. My regular blue eyes, blunt teeth, and rounded ears that are holding my red hair back from my face.

We are true opposites, and yet, six months ago when we met, we were essentially living each other's lives. She thought she was human, I thought I was fae. We were both wrong, and now we've switched places again, the same as we did at barely a day old.

But though we've reclaimed our original identities, who we were raised as are still huge parts of who we are. And we both live in the world of the Dark Fae, mated to two of the Verran Kings of Vegas and Kings of the Night Court of Faerie, a land none of us will ever see but still feel connected to.

Raising our lights up, we release them into the moonless sky and say in unison, "Go dtí go gcasfar le chéile sinn arís."

Until we meet again.

I reach for Bryn's hand and she pulls me into a side hug as we watch the faerie lights float up toward Mag Mell and our parents, until we can't tell our lanterns apart from the twinkling stars helping to guide their way.

The formal part of the ceremony over, we break formation and build a fire while drinking more whiskey, laughing, and listening to stories about the celebrated couples. I do my best to participate, but my eyes keep straying to the sky, wishing I knew for a fact whether I would ever see them again.

But I guess that's why they call it faith.

Tiernan steps up behind me and wraps his strong arms around my waist. I melt into his tight embrace on a contented sigh as he kisses the top of my head then the shell of my right ear. "You'll meet them again, sweetheart. I promise."

A smile curves my lips. We both know he can't really make that promise, but because he believes it wholeheartedly, he's allowed the words. And I love him all the more for it.

Turning in his arms, I clasp my hands behind his neck. "I know. But until then, I figured I might spend the next four-ish centuries with you, if that's all right."

"Sweetheart, if you tried to leave, I'd lock you up in the manor's dungeon and keep you there for my kinky pleasure. I don't know if you know this, but we Verrans have a history of holding our mates hostage."

I laugh. "Then I guess it's a good thing I don't plan on leaving."

His expression grows serious. "You better not, because I'm nothing without you, Fi."

Gods, this male. For most of my life I felt fractured in one way or another. But Tiernan's love fills me up so completely that I'm able to see myself through his eyes—a woman who is perfect just the way she is. Just as our future halfling children will also be perfect.

Remembering our conversation in the closet the night of the Ivy Moon Celebration Ball last year, I smile up at him. "So, to clarify, you're saying 'playboy Rebel Prince' *bad* but 'mated Rebel King' *good*."

"Being 'mated Rebel King' *very* fucking good." Laughing, he lifts me up against his body so our faces line up. "I love you, Little Red."

"I love you, too...Your Majesty."

Then he kisses the breath from me under the magic of the New Moon, and I know deep in my soul, that this is where I will always belong. He's my husband, true mate, and my king. He is my home.

EPILOGUE II

FINNIAN

As soon as I'm done with my morning training session with the Night Watch guys, I shower, throw on some clothes, and swing by Blood Sport to pick up Dmitri. We're following up on a lead about his sister tonight, but first we're making a pit stop at the ToR, where we're keeping Edevane for the rest of his supernatural-born life. Since we can't kill him and we can't hire anyone else to kill him, the only thing we can do is imprison him.

From the passenger seat, Dmitri slips his sunglasses on when the sun peeks out from behind the clouds. Daylight usually fries vampires on contact, but not the Romanov clan. Somehow, they're able to tolerate it. Glancing over at my new friend, I say, "You gonna tell me your secret of how you and all your comrades can stand to be in the sun yet?"

"What is the popular human saying? I could tell you, but then I would have to rip your throat out and drink you dry."

I make a face. "That's not what they say."

He shrugs. "Close enough. Tell me what you hope to accomplish by seeing the Light King."

My hands tighten their grip on the steering wheel. Everyone

has been on cloud nine since we outmaneuvered Edevane and beat him at his own game. But something about it doesn't sit right with me. I can't explain my unease, so I've kept it to myself. And with Tiernan's coronation and the Remembrance Ceremony, I've had plenty to distract me the past few weeks. But I can't ignore this gut feeling I have anymore.

The thing about Edevane is that he's always been one step ahead of us, and I can't get his parting words to us from that night out of my head.

Remember this moment...because you're going to regret it.

At the time, it seemed like your average sore loser speech. The thing every bad guy ever says when he said it, like he knew something we didn't.

And since his capture, he's been the model prisoner. No yelling, complaining, or ranting about revenge. He's not throwing food, fashioning shivs out of plasticware, or demanding to be set free.

So the question is, how does a guy go from being a king and murderous madman to a well-behaved prisoner in the blink of an eye?

Answer: he doesn't.

Flipping my blinker on, I answer Dmitri. "My brothers are busy with their mates and responsibilities. I'm taking it upon myself to make sure everything's copacetic over there, that's all."

"Hm," he says. "Perhaps one day we will trust each other with our secrets."

Others are naturally cagey and stingy when it comes to sharing personal things about us. In a world run by humans, to trust the wrong person is to hand them knowledge that can put you and yours in danger.

There's plenty I know he's not telling me—things that might even help me in my search for his sister, Taryn—but I haven't pressed him. He'll tell me if he thinks I should know.

"Perhaps," I say, turning onto the dirt road that will take us to the ToR.

It seems to lead to only more miles of empty desert. But ten minutes later, we pass through the cloaking spell hiding our greatest treasure, and the Temple of Rhiannon suddenly becomes visible. Even Dmitri sits forward and slides his sunglasses up to stare with appreciation.

"Impressive," he says, a slight tone of awe in his voice. Which, for the stoic Russian, says a lot.

"Yeah, it is." The ToR is my favorite thing about our court. Not because I'm particularly pious when it comes to the gods, but because my father designed it to identically match the temple back in our homeland that I will never get to see.

From the time I was young, I was obsessed with knowledge about Faerie. I've always felt this sense of loss that I would never know our true home. That my rights to even visit were stripped away centuries before I was born.

So, when I see the Temple, instead of the barren open space of the desert in shades of brown and gray, I picture its gleaming obsidian spires within a backdrop of lush greens and the purple hues in the sky.

I park around the back and use my access code to get into the private entrance used by the royal family. "You can wait in the main worship area. It's through those doors there. I won't be long."

Once he's in the other room, I walk over to the left wall and depress a specific tile. A hidden door pops open, and I take the stairs down to the underground level where my father built three cells strong enough to hold fae in case something happened to the treaty with the Day Court. I'm not sure if he was merely cautious, clairvoyant, or just plain insightful, but three hundred and some odd years later, his design paid off.

Murphy, the Watcher on duty, opens the heavy steel door.

Once it slams shut behind me, I regard the male in the center cell through the thick iron bars. He's sitting on the cot-like bed along the back wall, which is the only one that isn't made of iron, making it safe for him to lean against. To see the pompous ass wearing only a pair of sweatpants and plain T-shirt that he likely finds undignified is more than satisfying. And knowing that every time he takes a shit he has to wallow in his own stench makes me chuckle.

"Edevane. I trust you're hating the accommodations?"

He grins back at me. "Not at all. I didn't realize how much I needed a vacation. The solitude and no one asking me incessant questions about what they should be doing..." Edevane drops his head back to the wall and sighs. "It's been rather lovely."

"You'll rot away over hundreds of years with nothing more than these iron walls, a cot, and a shitter. I give you fifty years before you go mad."

He stares at me for a long time, and the amusement in his bright green eyes sets my fangs on edge. Propping the heel of one foot on the bed, he casually rests his forearm on his knee. "I've been patiently waiting for a visit from the House of Verran. How long have I been in here now, about a month?"

I don't bother answering. I have no doubt he knows how long, down to the hour. Crossing my arms, I wait for him to make his point.

"I'll admit, I didn't expect it would be you," he says, studying me. "But you'll do as well as the others. I want to have a chat."

"About?"

"The Spear of Assal."

My brows arch in surprise. Of everything he could bring up, the sun god's magical artifact wasn't on my Bingo card. I've come across writings about it before but not much. It was said to be a bloodthirsty, fiery lance that Lugh would unleash on his enemies, and after it cut them all down, it returned to his hand. When the sun god died, so did his spear's magic. His son Cú Chulainn gifted it to his father's worshippers, the Light Fae.

"What about it?" I ask him.

"Moira Verran stole it from us before the exile. I want it back."

The absurdity of that statement makes me laugh. "You expect me to believe that my sweet grandmother—the most benevolent queen in Night Court history—stole an important Light artifact? Even if she *was* capable of such a thing, the magic was gone, there'd be no reason to take it."

"I found my grandfather's journal; it's been a wealth of knowledge. So much of how our courts came to be exiled is a slew of half-truths carefully constructed to hide our ancestors' shame. And here's the real kicker—your sweet, benevolent grandmother is the villain of the whole story. I think she discovered how to activate the spear's magic, and she planned to use it to assassinate Aine.

"According to Cormac's journal, Moira admitted to him that she broke it in two, hiding the wooden shaft somewhere in Faerie and keeping the spearhead with her so she was the only one who could rejoin the pieces. Of course, then they were banished from Faerie, so the artifact truly was powerless then. And still, she refused to return it to the Lights. You've had it all this time. But I'm here to right a wrong and take it back."

I shift my weight and rub the stubble on my jaw as I consider his claim. "Out of curiosity, where do you think the spearhead is now?"

"It's in the one place a Light Fae could never access it." His gaze drifts to the ceiling.

Snorting, I shake my head. "This is getting more far-fetched by the second. There's nothing like that in the Temple."

He takes a few steps forward, stopping a foot from the

dangerous iron bars. "That's because it's glamoured to look like a smooth obsidian *triangle*."

I freeze. He's describing the Tri-Stone, a gift from Rhiannon representing the connection between her, the moon, and the Dark Fae. It's been in a glass case behind the altar since the ToR was built approximately three hundred years ago. But I never considered how it would have gotten here with us if it had been in a similar display back in the Tír na nÓg temple.

"Now he's starting to piece it all together. Excellent," Edevane says with a smug grin. "Perhaps I shouldn't have dismissed you as the throwaway Verran."

My hands curl into fists at my sides. Voice low and threatening, I glare at him through the bars. "Underestimating me will be the last mistake you ever make."

He smiles. "This is going to be fun."

"Fun isn't in your vocabulary anymore, and I'm bored with this conversation. Have a miserable fucking life, asshole." I spin on my heel, ready to get the hell out of here and go take a closer look at the Tri-Stone. If it really is a glamour, it should fall away as soon as I touch it.

"Do you remember what I said after you captured me?"

Stopping dead, I turn back slowly, my original unease returning like a two-ton weight on my chest. *Remember this moment...because you're going to regret it.*

"Ah, you *do* remember," he says, chuckling. "It's been bothering you, hasn't it?" Silence is the only answer I can give without admitting he's right. "I see now why it's a mistake to underestimate you, Finnian. Your brothers have intelligence and charm, but you...you have instinct and tenacity. I believe I'll enjoy our game the most."

"Your days of doing anything other than rotting inside this cell are over, Edevane."

He *tsks* with a shake of his head. "Come now, don't

disappoint me so soon. I'll tell you a secret about my conjurer. She's a Mystic."

My brows knit together. "What's a Mystic?"

"They're the most powerful of any specialty bloodline—conjurers, shifters, seers, healers, what have you. Ask your new vampire friend, he knows all about them. Now, a regular conjurer wouldn't be any help to me in my current situation. But a *Mystic*...well, that's a different story entirely."

I narrow my eyes and snarl, sick of his fucking games. "I don't give a good godsdamn who your friends are. Only Darks can get through the cloaking spell, so I wouldn't hold your breath waiting for a rescue party."

"Oh, don't worry about that. I don't need anyone's help. And it's true about the spell," he says, nodding in mock agreement. "You can't imagine how irritating it was to know the spear was in your Temple, yet not know the location or how to get in. But then I realized something. If I couldn't get through the security system, the way to get in is to simply be invited."

"What do you mean invi—" My eyes flare wide. *Remember this moment...because you're going to regret it.*

He *wanted* to get captured. It was his plan all along, and we walked him right through the front fucking door.

"Murphy!" I call out.

Edevane's lips peel back from his fangs in an evil grin that sends shivers down my spine. Green fire appears to spark from his irises as his fingernails lengthen and sharpen. The air around us vibrates, making every hair on my body stand on end.

Godsdamn it, we need to get Edevane in iron shackles and get him the hell out of here. Pressure builds in my temples, and my skull feels like it's about to implode. I turn around to bang a fist on the steel door, but my shins run into the metal frame of the bed.

What the fuck?

Whipping around, I find myself staring at the iron bars again, but from *the inside*. Somehow, I've switched places with Edevane, and he's nowhere to be seen.

"Murphy! Murphy, get in here!" I keep shouting for the guard until he bursts through the first door and stops dead in his tracks, his jaw on his chest. "Get me out of here right fucking now! Come on, *let's go!*"

He jams the key in the lock, turns it, slides it open with his gloved hand, and I'm out of there like a rocket. It takes less than two seconds for me to race up the stairs and burst through the hidden door. Dmitri, who's speaking in Russian on his cell, hangs up and tenses with alarm.

"What has happened?"

"Edevane." It's all I get out before running through the double doors of the worship area and up to the Obsidian altar.

The glass case on the wall that held the Tri-Stone is shattered, the artifact missing with a necklace hanging in its place. A long silver chain with a rectangular metal pendant engraved with the symbol of an Armas I recognize from my research.

Armas are like a coat of arms. They represent the different fae family lines and can sometimes be imbued with powers. I can't tell if this one has any special properties, but the Armas itself holds power simply because of who it represents: the Emory line.

As in Aine Emory, the One True Queen of Faerie and ruler of the Summer Court. This necklace either belonged to her or someone in her family. How the hell did Edevane end up with it and why did he leave it here for me? Those are the million-dollar questions.

I remove the necklace from the case and trace my thumb over the symbol. Tingles travel up my arm, and I have an overwhelming sense that I'm somehow connected to its owner.

Whether in a good or bad way, I can't tell. Only that my future is tied with theirs in some way.

Dmitri speaks to me from the other side of the altar. "The guard says Edevane escaped. How is this possible?"

I clench the pendant in my fist and turn to face him, a cocktail of anger and foreboding roiling inside me. "Had to be with powers he got from his conjurer. Which means he could've gotten out whenever he wanted to, but he specifically waited for one of us to come so he could continue his fucking mind games. *Godsdamn it!*"

As I walk around the altar, his gaze fixes onto the chain dangling from my closed hand. "What is that?"

His ominous tone makes me leery, and red is spilling into the ice blue of his irises. "Edevane left it behind as some sort of clue." I hold it out on my upturned palm. When he doesn't take it for a closer inspection, I realize it's because it's silver. "Do you recognize it?"

Barely contained rage emanates from the normally stoic vampire. "It is Taryn's. She never took it off."

I pin him with a dubious look. "This necklace belongs to someone related to the One True Queen of Faerie, Dmitri. So that begs the questions how did a vampire get her hands on it, and how did she wear it if it's made of silver?"

Bloodred eyes lift to meet my golden ones. "Because my sister is not a vampire. She is Taryn Emory—Aine's estranged daughter, heir to the Summer Court throne...and Mystic conjurer."

"She's a fucking *Mystic*?" I drag my free hand over my face and try to process this barrage of new information. The vampire I've been looking for isn't a vampire at all, she's fae. I knew Dmitri's sister wasn't his by blood, but I didn't know she was a different supernatural race altogether—*my* race.

That would be surprising enough as it is, but to find out she's the OTQ's estranged daughter who left Faerie to live her own life in the human realm is blowing my godsdamned mind. I can't even comprehend the fact that she's a Mystic conjurer— something I didn't know existed until five minutes ago but explains the Romanov clan's daylight walking capabilities—on top of everything else. My brain feels like it's about to blow a gasket.

Another flash of tingling ripples up my arm as though the chain is trying to tell me something. Like Taryn is reaching out to me through the metal, and the foreboding feeling in my gut gets even stronger.

No more fucking around. If Edevane has her plus half of the Spear of Assal, there's no telling what kind of destruction he's capable of if he manages to get his hands on the other half.

More than that, my mission to find Dmitri's sister just became exponentially more important to me. I can't explain it, but I'm certain my future is somehow entangled with hers. I can feel it. I can feel *her.*

Dropping the necklace over my head, I tuck the pendant inside my shirt. My skin warms where it touches, and I swear it gives off a feeling of contentment from where it now lies.

As though it's the most natural thing in the world, I caress it once through my Henley before dropping my hand at my side. Then I level a no-bullshit look at Dmitri "D'yavol" Romanov, Lord of the Vampires.

"I think it's about time you start sharing those secrets with me now, *comrade*."

ACKNOWLEDGMENTS

An eternity of thanks to Alyssa Rose who is my everything: daughter, best friend, astrology expert, #1 fan, amazing signing assistant, and dating advice giver (and sometimes lecturer). And to Austin James, even though he'll never read this, who is the absolute light of my life and never fails to make me laugh or turn my gray skies to an endless blue. I love you both to the moon and back times infinity.

To my work wifeys and soul sisters, Cindi Madsen and Rebecca Yarros, for everything and anything: plotting, reading, sprinting, blurb-shaping, whip-cracking, encouraging, supporting, laughing, and a thousand other things I could never list even if I tried. My life is immeasurably better with you in it, and I seriously don't know what I'd do without our daily conversations and weekly video chats. As a tearful Jerry Maguire once said, you complete me. #UnholyTrinity

To my incredible agent, Nicole Resciniti of the Seymour Agency, for her never-ending advice and support. To Jessica Turner for believing in this series and giving it the royal treatment in every aspect possible.

To Stacy Abrams for her amazing editing skills and taking the rock I gave her and guiding me how to polish it into the diamond it is today. To Heather Riccio, Riki Cleveland, Curtis Svehlak, and everyone else at Entangled who had a hand in getting this book baby out into the world, thank you so much for all your hard work.

To Elizabeth Turner Stokes, who created my favorite cover ever! You gave me a stunning cover with a chess board, so I rose to the challenge and incorporated the chess theme into the story and I love how it all came together.

To Erin McRae, my bestie and number one cheerleader. I never want to write a book without you in my corner. You went above and beyond during the writing process on this one and I can't thank you enough. To Miranda Grissom, without whom I couldn't function as an author and my good friend. To Paige Jenkins, my newsletter guru and her hubby for both doing awesome jobs promoting me, virtually and in stores to random strangers.

To Kristy Jewel, aka Caffeinated Fae in the book blogging world, whose vast knowledge about faeries was key to me creating this world. To Michael Madsen, my chess expert who had all the answers and gave me the coolest term to use that fit perfectly. *Zwischenzug!*

To Ella Sheridan, one of my oldest and best friends who gave me the tough love talk when I needed it and convinced me to give dictation a try. This book may never have been finished otherwise.

To everyone in the Maxwell Mob: thank you for sticking with me all these years and getting excited about my new projects in my ever-shifting publishing schedule. Your constant support, enthusiasm, and posts about Jason Momoa are what keep me going. Every. Single. Day.

A very special thank-you to all the bloggers, Bookstagrammers, and BookTokers who work tirelessly and *for free* to shout out about my books, make graphics, invite me for takeovers, offer advice, take time to read and review my ARCs, and are just in general super-amazing people whose passion is to lift up authors and their stories. You are the foundation of this book community we all love, and we couldn't reach nearly as many readers without you. I'm forever grateful for your help and humbled by your generous spirits.

As always, a thousand thanks to you, the reader, for giving my book a spot on your shelf and a place in your heart.

With literary love & kitten kisses... ~ G ~

The Rebel King is a sexy fantasy romance with a happy ending. However, the story includes elements that might not be suitable for some readers. Scenes with mentions of murder of loved ones, kidnapping, violent attacks, and unknown parentage/adoption are included in the novel. Additionally, there are dominance/submissive scenes including consensual acts of whipping, exhibitionism, and immobility. Readers who may be sensitive to these, please take note.

ENTANGLED
BRINGS THE
Heat

BLUSH

They might be best friends. But what he wants from her will make her... Blush.

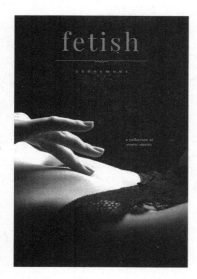
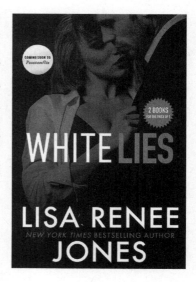

ENTANGLED
BRINGS THE
Feels

THE THINGS WE LEAVE UNFINISHED

This TikTok sensation examines the risks we take for love, the scars too deep to heal, and the endings we can't bring ourselves to see coming.

HIGHLAND BEAST

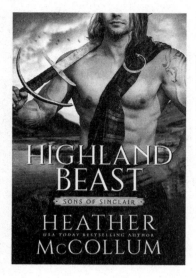

He has one destiny: to bring fear into the hearts of guilty men. But once he knows love, nothing will stop him from keeping it safe.

I AM AYAH: THE WAY HOME

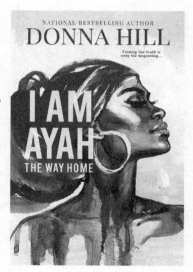

Set amid Sag Harbor's vibrant African American history, comes a stunningly rich story about finding the way home...no matter how long the journey takes.

ENTANGLED
BRINGS THE
Laughs

PLANES TRAINS AND ALL THE FEELS

Fans of Christina Lauren and Tessa Bailey will adore this witty and unforgettable rom-com about skyways, highways, and all the perfectly wrong ways to fall in love.

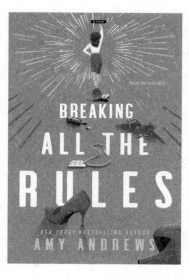

Breaking All the Rules

Sometimes you gotta toss your whole life into a burning dumpster to find what's most important...

You've Been Served

One woman puts love—and law school—into the hands of fate. Perfect for fans of *Legally Blonde* and *The Hating Game*.

ENTANGLED
BRINGS THE
Heart

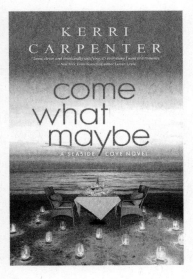

COME WHAT MAYBE

Returning home to Seaside Cove was supposed to be temporary. Now there's a baby on the way, and all her plans have gone right out the window.

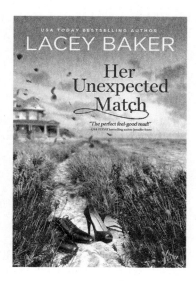

HER UNEXPECTED MATCH

The local matchmaker of the charming and quirky small town of Crescent Island has their work cut out for them this time.

THE SWEETHEART FIX

Return to Blossom Glen, where two opposites must put their differences aside to help the small town they both love.

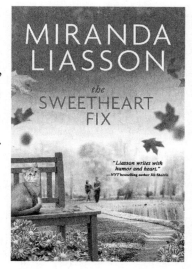

*Don't miss the exciting new books
Entangled has to offer.*

Follow us!

f @EntangledPublishing

◎ @Entangled_Publishing

◯ @EntangledPub

♪ @EntangledPub

an imprint of Entangled Publishing LLC